Geoffrey de Montbrai

Bishop in Arms

A Historical Novel

by
Berwick Coates

Published by Berwick Coates

Publishing partner: Paragon Publishing, Rothersthorpe

© Berwick Coates 2025

ISBN 978-1-78792-094-1

Cover design Stephen Goodwin
sgssdesign.co.uk

Book design, layout and production management by Into Print
www.intoprint.net
+44 (0)1604 832149

Contents

Dedication

To all those who seek, and hopefully find, interest, information, enjoyment, enlightenment, inspiration, solace, or therapy in History.

Speaking as one who has spent his life in association with it, in one form or another, may I assure them that whatever time they spend in the company of History will not be wasted.

List of Characters

Principal characters
Geoffrey de Montbrai, Bishop of Coutances
Mauger, lord of Montbrai, his elder brother
Father Gregory ('Gori'), priest and confessor at Montbrai, tutor of Geoffrey
Ivo, guardian and mentor to Geoffrey
Thierry, squire, courier, and servant at Montbrai
Sir Tancred of Hauteville, a knight of the Cotentin, close to Montbrai
Lady Fressenda, second wife of Sir Tancred
Robert, nicknamed 'the Guiscard', eldest son of Sir Tancred and Fressenda, Count (later Duke) of Apulia in Italy
Sybil, youngest daughter of Sir Tancred and Fressenda
William II, nicknamed 'the Bastard', Duke of Normandy, 1035-87
Matilda of Flanders, wife to the Duke
Sir William Fitzosbern
Sir Walter Giffard
Sir Roger of Montgomery
Sir Baldwin of Clair   All vassals and advisers of the Duke.
Lanfranc of Pavia, Prior at the monastery of Bec
Fulk the Angevin, a captain of mercenaries
Aimery, a mercenary soldier.
Ralph of Gisors, a scout
Goscelin, a master-mason and cathedral-builder

Torf of Malbec, an adventurer

Supporting characters
Bertha, servant at Montbrai
Gaimar, cook at Montbrai
Lambert, blacksmith at Montbrai
Boso, a Bellême labourer at Montbrai

Humbert, 11th son of Sir Tancred
Roger, 12th, and youngest, son of Sir Tancred
Constance, second daughter of Sir Tancred
Canon Thorold, servant of the old cathedral of Coutances
Mabel of Bellême, wife of Sir Roger of Montgomery
Hugh, Abbot of the monastery of Cluny in Burgundy, 1049-1109

Ranulf of Dreux, a military engineer
Lanfranc`s father

Occasional characters, or simply mentioned
Nigel de Montbrai, Geoffrey`s father
Helena, Geoffrey`s mother
William 'of the Iron Arm'
Drogo
Humphrey { all five sons of Sir Tancred of Hauteville by his first wife
Geoffrey
Serlo

Mauger
Aubrey
William { other sons of Sir Tancred by his second wife Fressenda
Tancred

Papia
Muriella { daughters of Sir Tancred and Fressenda

Peter
Walter { sons of Canon Thorold of Coutances, and canons of Coutances cathedral

Richard
John { sons of canon Peter, canons of Coutances cathedral

Robert, Count of Mortain, half-brother to the Duke
Odo, half-brother to the Duke, created Bishop of Bayeux in 1049
Hugh, cousin to the Duke, created Bishop of Lisieux in 1049
Mauger, uncle to the Duke, Archbishop of Rouen, deposed in 1054
Maurilius, created Arcbishop of Rouen in 1055
Yves de Bellême, created Bishop of Sées in 1035
Hugh, created Bishop of Avranches in 1028
Pope Leo IX, 1049-54
Hildebrand, sub-deacon at the Vatican
Count Guy of Burgundy, rival claimant to William`s duchy
William of Arques, another rival claimant
Enguerrand, Count of Ponthieu
Geoffrey, Count of Anjou

Henry I, King of France, 1031-60 – all plotters against the Duke
Henry III, Holy Roman Emperor, 1039-56
Felix, gardener at the convent of St. Amand, Rouen

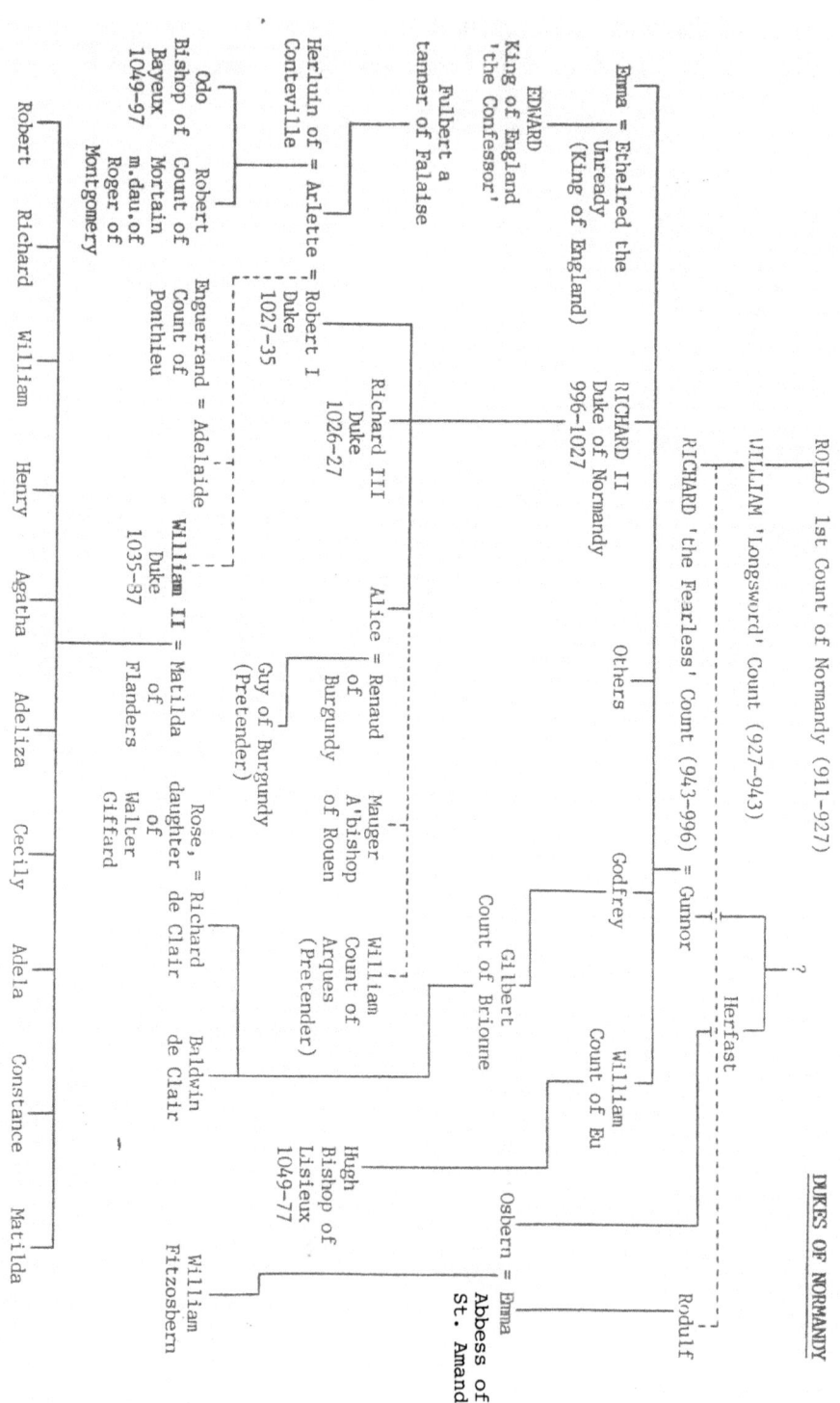

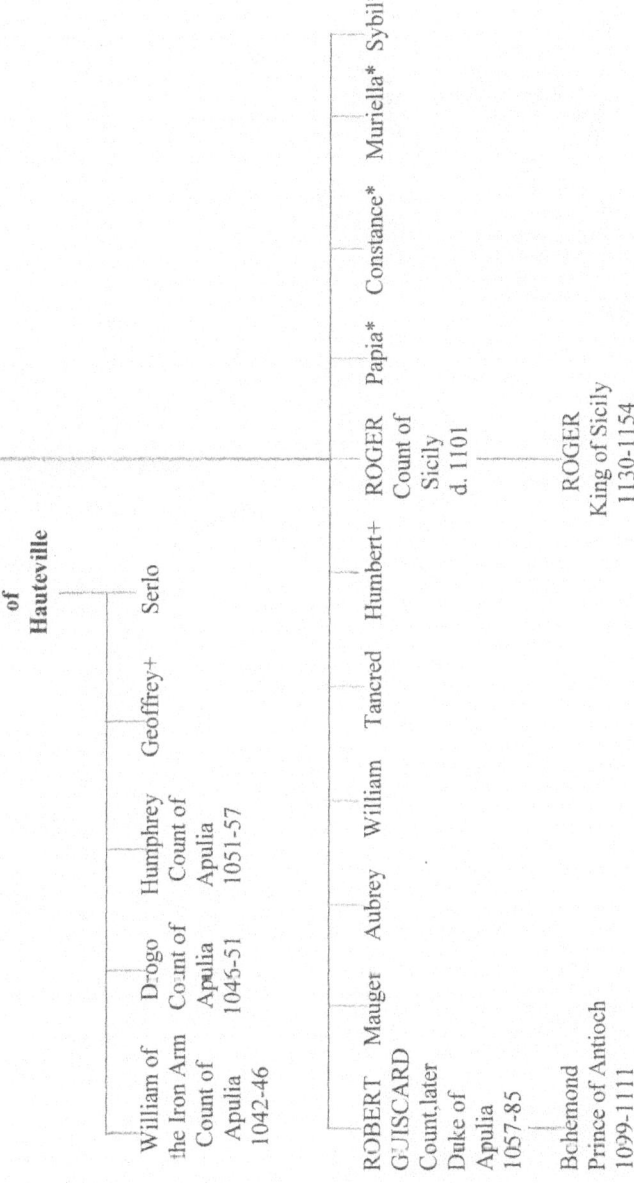

THE HOUSE OF HAUTEVILLE

Muriella(1) = **Tancred** = (2)Fressenda
of
Hauteville

William of the Iron Arm Count of Apulia 1042-46 · Drogo Count of Apulia 1045-51 · Humphrey Count of Apulia 1051-57 · Geoffrey+ · Serlo

ROBERT GUISCARD Count, later Duke of Apulia 1057-85 · Mauger · Aubrey · William · Tancred · Humbert+ · ROGER Count of Sicily d. 1101 · Papia* · Constance* · Muriella* · Sybil*

Bohemond Prince of Antioch 1099-1111

ROGER King of Sicily 1130-1154

* Sources known to me indicate that there were 3, maybe 4, daughters, to whom I have allocated likely names. One was really called Fressenda after her mother, but I have changed this in order to avoid confusion.

+ It was Geoffrey who really remained at Hauteville, not Humbert, but I have transposed them in order to avoid confusion with Geoffrey de Montbrai.

The Hautevilles were even more fertile than this chart indicates, and many of Tancred's children had large families. For example, one great-granddaughter married Robert, the Conqueror's eldest son. It would be impossible to include them all.

NORMANDY IN THE 1050'S

ENGLISH CHANNEL

JERSEY

BRITTANY

ANJOU

KEY:
- ○ Towns
- ✗ Battles

COTENTIN

Valognes
Carentan
Malbec
Isigny
Bayeux
Hauteville
Coutances
Lessay
St.Lô
Cérisy
Montbrai
St. Sever
Avranches
Mortain
Domfront
Vire
Sourdeval
BOCAGE
BESSIN
Val-ès-Dunes
Caen
Falaise
Argentan
Alençon
Sées
Bellême
Le Mans
Lisieux
PAYS D'AUGE
Jumièges
Bec
Brionne
Evreux
EVRECIN
Breteuil
Tillières
Dreux
Chartres
ROUMOIS
Rouen
VEXIN
R. Epte
Gisors
R. Seine
Paris
BEAUVAIS
CHAMPAGNE
PAYS DE CAUX
Fécamp
St. Aubin
Longueville
Mortemer
Dieppe
Arques
Eu
VERMANDOIS
PONTHIEU
FLANDERS

MAINE

BLOIS

10

Chapter One

'Diex aie!'

The bullish bellow soared above the thudding of the hastening hooves. Its tone wavered in time with the jolting of the torso in the heavy wooden saddle. The sword arm, gauntleted almost to the elbow, rested the weapon across the saddle horn.

Geoffrey steadied his horse, drew his sword, and did the same.

'Never raise a weapon until just before you are going to use it . . . Never tire your arm without cause . . . You must always keep enough strength to strike one blow more than the enemy . . .' Ivo's endless advice, dinned into his head since he could bestride a saddle, hummed again in the back of his brain.

'Diex aie!'

Geoffrey could see the wide-open mouth of his assailant; it was like a furnace door. The metal nasal of the helmet came down almost to the upper lip. Huge muscles surged and rippled on the destrier; the hooves greedily gathered in the ground as if tugging the enemy towards him on a green carpet.

Geoffrey shook his left shoulder to settle the shield straps on his arm, but even as he did so he knew it was unnecessary. He flexed his toes and braced his feet against the stirrups, but he knew Ivo would disapprove of that too.

'If you are prepared, you are prepared . . . fidget your arse and you end on the grass . . . still, and kill . . .'

Ivo demanded impossible standards; he was never satisfied.

'Diex aie!'

Geoffrey now heard the slap of leather and the jingle of mail. Puffs of misty breath flew from the destrier's iron-bound mouth. Beneath the helmet eyes blazed; beard stubble poked out on either side of the chinstrap.

Now!

Geoffrey raised his sword and swung. At the very last minute the man veered away out of reach. Whether it was a cowardly move or not, it showed that he had superb control over his mount. Nor had it been done violently; the horse's mouth did not suffer.

Geoffrey swung his own destrier's head round to face where the man had gone. If this attacker was hoping to wear him down by false charges and goad him into a careless thrust, Ivo had prepared him for that too.

'His is the horse that tires, not yours . . . The more often he does it, the more likely he is to make a mistake . . .'

Geoffrey waited smugly for the next false charge. The man struck instead; Geoffrey had the parry ready only just in time.

As he veered off to the original end of the clearing, he jeered.

'Ha!'

Geoffrey's dark cheeks glowed with anger. His fingers clenched on the hilt. He was already forgetting: 'Never grip tight until you strike . . . rest, rest, always rest . . . what do you think the thong is for? A bracelet?'

On the third charge the man went past on the left. Geoffrey swung hugely and uselessly, and shuddered as his weapon echoed on the raised shield.

'Ha!'

Geoffrey turned his horse again. The man cantered to the further end of the clearing, slewed round, and stopped.

For a while they watched each other in silence. Geoffrey began to fidget.

'Ha!'

To the Devil with him!

Geoffrey dug his heels. As his destrier responded, he took a fresh, and over-tight, grip on his sword, and inhaled deeply.

'Diex aie!'

God help us! He was committed. As he came nearer, he heard no jeers; he saw no furnace door of a mouth – nothing. Absolute stillness. Even the breath seemed to have vanished from the horse's mouth and nostrils. Eyes like chisels watched him. God help us!

He chose to thrust instead of to swing. His move was parried with insolent ease; the man's shoulder barely moved.

Instead of retiring to charge again, Geoffrey turned his mount in a tight circle, and returned to strike. Blade to blade they leaned and swung, till an uncontrolled movement from Geoffrey's horse took them out of each other's reach. Again Geoffrey wheeled and returned. Again they clashed. Geoffrey tried every variation of thrust, sweep, and swing that he knew – to no avail. He called up all that Ivo had ever taught him, sweating and grimacing as the pain of fatigue crept along his arm. This slit-eyed barrel of a man saw through all his ruses and scotched all his tricks.

Too late now to try and relax his grip on the hilt in between bouts of action – they were too closely engaged to allow respite. No resting of the blade, no blessed relief from a weightless arm. Worse, Geoffrey sensed that the man was only waiting his chance. So far he had been content to parry; and he had done that so casually that Geoffrey knew his problems were only beginning.

He broke away once more, and retired thirty paces or so. Turning and looking at his opponent, he marvelled again at his stillness and control. The man must have limbs like iron, and he was not young. The grey had shown in the beard stubble. His technique was brilliant too. Not a flicker of energy that was unnecessary, and never a jot of haste.

Nothing else for it. Geoffrey returned his sword to its scabbard, and tugged at the mace that hung from a sling beside his horse's shoulder. Not a refined weapon, the mace. Ivo did not approve of it: 'A villein's club. Too chancy – a gambler's weapon. Strike, and you win, but missing is too easy. The odds are too long.' Then Ivo was biased.

When he saw Geoffrey turn to his new weapon, the man sheathed his sword and did the same. His silent confidence was infuriating. Then he moved his horse slightly forward and sideways.

Geoffrey turned his own mount slowly as the man moved across in front of him. The only things that seemed in motion were his destrier's legs. His stillness was unnerving. Geoffrey felt as if he were being stalked.

With a roar of rage, Geoffrey urged his mount into a sharp canter. The man turned quickly away, and the ground seemed suddenly to give way under his animal's feet. He had been waiting rather close to the boundary bank of the woodland, and had almost certainly run foul of some over-used and untended warren that had poached on the meadow.

The man's leg was pinned under his horse's body. He fought to free himself, cursing as the thong of the mace tied his hand. The weapon that was to defend him was now his shackle.

Geoffrey dismounted and ran across the grass, shedding his own mace on the way and drawing his knife. With another curse of effort, the man managed to draw his own dagger and cut the leather of the thong, looking up quickly as Geoffrey closed the distance between them.

'Ivo! Are you all right?'

Geoffrey came and crouched beside him.

A rampart of curses broke and cascaded upon his head.

'Of course I am, Master Geoffrey. Get this animal off me. You just wait till I get my hands on that boy Nicholas. If I have told him once, I have told him a hundred times – especially at this time of year.'

'Ivo, you can not expect him to spend every hour of every day on patrol against renegade rabbits digging unauthorised burrows.'

Geoffrey tugged the horse to its feet, turned to Ivo, and grinned.

'So who won this time then?'

He sheathed his dagger and put out his hand. Ivo took it, and heaved himself to his feet, growling ill-humouredly.

'It only proves what I said, Master Geoffrey. Use a mace, and you need luck. Or a slice of the Grace of God. You seem to have been blessed with both.'

Geoffrey grinned again.

'I see. I suppose God intervened in time to turn your eyes away from those holes? A man of your experience too; must have taken a pretty large slice of grace. I wonder He could spare the time.'

Ivo adjusted his helmet, which had slipped forward over his eyes.

'A minor miracle,' he agreed imperturbably. 'Which is why I say the mace is a gambler's weapon. Or a saint's. But then a saint should have no need of one.'

Geoffrey handed his wooden drill sword to one stable boy, and the bridle of his destrier to another.

'Ivo, you are biased.'

Ivo grunted.

'Once a swordsman . . .'

They began tramping back to the castle mound. Ivo paused to stoop and recover the mace that Geoffrey had dropped. He handed it to one of the boys now following them. The child's face lit up with pleasure. He began swishing it back and forth in dramatic fashion and making battle noises under his breath.

'Perhaps the mace is the weapon for you though, Master Geoffrey. You are not the swordsman your father was.'

Geoffrey had heard the remark too often to be upset about it. Ivo tended to become more repetitive as he grew older.

'Ivo, you say the same about Mauger.'

'Because it is true. Your brother is not the swordsman your father was either. Better than you, but not as good as your father.'

Geoffrey did wince a little this time, because Ivo rarely differentiated between the two brothers. Everyone at Montbrai was used to Ivo going on about the old days. Father was this, Father was that. It was harmless enough. But Father was dead.

Ivo knew that Geoffrey did not take entirely seriously his remarks about his father. That did not matter unduly. The past was the past. But it was important that the boy should know the truth about himself. He must know his weaknesses as well as his strengths. That way he would have a better chance of surviving. He told Master Geoffrey the truth for his own good. Geoffrey knew that, and Ivo knew that Geoffrey knew.

One of the boys ran on ahead and held open the gate of the outer bailey for them. Geoffrey nodded his thanks.

'Tell me this then, Ivo. If Father was so good, and Father trained you, and you have trained me, what has gone missing?'

'I am not the teacher your father was either.'

It was an answer. Mauger had put it more sharply, if more cruelly, when he once whispered in Ivo's ear after watching Geoffrey at training: 'You can not put in what God left out.'

Maybe. It was certainly looking that way. Master Geoffrey would be competent, but he would never have the ease and suppleness of the natural talent. Sir Nigel must have been born with a sword in his hand; he could fight, yawn, and laugh all at the same time.

They paused at a trough and scooped some water into their faces to clean away the sweat. Geoffrey took off his helmet and tossed it to the smith's boy.

'Tell Lambert he is a splendid fellow, and it is a much better fit. Do it on the run, and you may borrow my drill sword.'

The boy's face glowed.

'Yes, sir.' He was off like the wind.

As they walked across the stable yard, Geoffrey put his arm round Ivo's shoulders.

'Tell me, Ivo, how do you do it? How do you stay so still? You must have mason's mortar in the saddle.'

'Laziness, Master Geoffrey. As you get older, you get lazier. You are always looking for ways of doing the same things with less effort.'

He looked sidelong at his companion. The reply seemed to satisfy.

Ivo disengaged himself from Geoffrey's arm.

'You must excuse me, Master Geoffrey. A call of nature. There is no way of doing that with less effort.'

Geoffrey laughed, and Ivo made his way towards the latrines behind the stables.

What an intelligent young man Master Geoffrey was. He would never be anything more than a competent warrior, but he was shrewd and observant enough to perceive the finer points of technique, and to understand and relish them for their own sake. Give him a few more years, and some battle experience, and he would make a fine trainer of men. People responded to him. Look at those boys, for example. And Lambert would do almost anything for him. Some of his father's charm there.

Ivo shook himself and adjusted his breeches.

A trainer of soldiers. Would he be content with that? As a younger son, would he have much choice? Lord Mauger had said something about plans for his 'baby brother', but Mauger talked a lot, and so many of his schemes came to nothing. Like Sir Nigel . . .

Geoffrey picked his way past sprawling piles of masonry that had lain so long that they sprouted weed and nettles. The steps up the mound to the hall and tower were full of traps for the unwary; it was lucky he knew them blindfold. The scrappiness of them annoyed him. At the top he paused and looked back

15

into the bailey. There was life, yes. Activity. Purpose. Yet there was so much that was untidy, incomplete, only half effective.

It was only partly Father's fault. He had been so eager, so romantic, so captivated by novelty. And of course so rarely there. It would appear that he never finished anything. Mauger had inherited a mess, but he too carried his share of the blame. He was too much of a bumbler to put any kind of order into it. Like Father, he was good at ideas, but useless at carrying them out. A poor administrator, and a capricious judge and lord to his tenants and servants.

Geoffrey felt a sudden surge of rage at both his father and his brother – at the one for his gullibility and weakness, at the other for his lack of system and plain incompetence. He renewed his private promise to himself that whatever else he did in life, he would not leave things unfinished; he would not leave loose ends all over the place. They made him so cross. All this – all this disarray. And all for the want of so little effort, such a modicum of elementary organisation, the merest dash of common sense.

'Master Geoffrey!'

Stung by the urgency of the whisper, Geoffrey whirled round. Thierry was leaning out of the guardroom door. He had a large pot in one hand, and was wiping his mouth with the back of the other.

Geoffrey beckoned to him to follow. Thierry looked regretfully at the pot in his hand. Geoffrey read his thoughts.

'Bring the damned thing with you.'

Thierry licked his lips.

'And perhaps my stew as well?'

'Bring anything you like.'

Thierry plunged back into the guardroom, and reappeared with his arms full of steaming bowls and hunks of bread and apples and cheese. Cider from the pot slurped on to his sleeve.

'On the road since dawn, Master Geoffrey. Not a morsel of warm food since midday yesterday.'

Thierry was always eloquent on the terrible deprivations constantly suffered by his stomach. Whenever he returned from a trip his first port of call was usually the kitchen, where he armed himself with an obese ladle to dip into the great iron pot that Gaimar kept suspended over the hearth night and day. Gaimar merely added to it when its level began to drop below a third full. At least that was how it seemed. Nobody could recall it being empty, and nobody outside the kitchen could remember seeing Gaimar cleaning it out.

'I daresay you have been making up for your hardships ever since you arrived back,' said Geoffrey drily. 'Does Lord Mauger know you are here?'

'Of course, Master Geoffrey. I know my duty. I reported to him at once.'

'You mean he grabbed you before you could find Gaimar and his precious pot.'

It was better to catch Thierry with an empty stomach; he spilled all his news quickly and succinctly as the only means of getting himself nearer his next meal. Question him on a full one, and his digressions and irrelevancies could be infuriating.

Thierry followed Geoffrey across the near-empty hall, furtively stuffing himself with dollops of stew. As he expected, Master Geoffrey began climbing the ladder to the solar. By performing prodigies of balance Thierry managed the ascent as well without spilling too much.

Geoffrey looked back down the hall. Nobody had spoken to them, but it had been noted that Master Geoffrey wanted some private conversation. Neither Master Geoffrey nor Lord Mauger went up into the solar without very good reason, ever since our lady Mother had died. Her clothes had been given away to the serving girls, but most of her other possessions were preserved in a great elm chest behind the bed curtains. Lambert had fashioned a new lock specially. Her embroidery frame stood in a corner covered with dust. In the awful winter of '44 Lord Mauger had thrashed a kitchen boy whom he caught in the act of putting it on the fire.

Geoffrey sat on a stool and motioned Thierry to another.

'Well? How is she?'

Thierry arranged his cups and bowls strategically around his feet.

'The lady Sybil is well,' he replied. 'And she thinks it is a good time for you to present your suit.'

Geoffrey frowned. It was unlike Thierry to be so formal in his reporting when they were alone.

'There is something else, Thierry. What is it? Is she ill?'

Thierry shook his head vigorously, as if relieved that he could give a completely truthful answer.

'By no means, Master Geoffrey.'

He bent and scooped up some bread and cheese.

'I must ask you, Master Geoffrey, to remember that I only *bring* news; not always rejoice at it.'

Geoffrey fidgeted.

'Holy Virgin, man, get to the point.'

Thierry took out his knife and carefully sliced the cheese. He offered it to Geoffrey, who waved it away impatiently. Thierry began eating slowly.

'It is rumoured – only rumoured, mind – that there is another suitor.'

'What?'

'Please, Master Geoffrey. I repeat – it is only gossip, tittle-tattle of kitchen girls and ploughboys. A wink here, a giggle there. My lord Tancred has not let a word fall from his lips on the subject. At least he said nothing when I spoke to him of you. I believe he likes you. He said to me – '

'Who?'

'Master Geoffrey?'

'Who is it?'

'And I may have got it wrong. There are other sisters, remember, and all older than the lady Sybil. My lord Tancred will probably want to marry them off first, and – '

Geoffrey leapt to his feet.

'Who is it?'

Thierry swallowed.

'His name is Torf, Master Geoffrey. From Malbec.'

'Never heard of him.'

'Nor I, sir.'

Geoffrey began pacing up and down.

'Torf! Some adventurer or other. Sounds like the bastard offspring of a Viking raider.'

Thierry fumbled for his apple without taking his eyes off Geoffrey.

'I believe his lands are near the western coast.'

'What did I tell you?'

Thierry made an effort to soften the blow.

'My impression, Master Geoffrey, is that you are much preferred. Not only the lady Sybil of course, but my lord Tancred, and the lady Fressenda. This Torf is of interest only because of his land.'

'And I have none!'

Thierry tried hastily to cover his mistake.

'It is only that Malbec is near to Hauteville, or at any rate nearer than Montbrai. The lady Fressenda would have her daughter only a day's journey away. What mother would not want that?'

'I have nothing. Do you understand, Thierry? Nothing.'

'You have your portion. Lord Mauger is due to give it to you, surely?'

Geoffrey sneered.

'Money. Coins.'

And probably not much of that, thought Thierry, if the stories about the late Lord Nigel's management abilities were to be believed. He felt sorry for Master Geoffrey, but felt too that he would very much like to find a way of easing himself out of an embarrassing situation.

He cleared his throat.

'Um – you never know, Master Geoffrey. Your "coins", as you put it, may yet be of use to you. One daughter less to support.' He paused to give effect to his next remark. 'And one more son to equip.'

Geoffrey stopped pacing.

'What was that again?'

Thierry threw the apple core over the edge of the solar, down on to the rushes in the main body of the hall.

'Master Geoffrey, there is another one going.'

Geoffrey stared.

'Another?'

Thierry gulped in his eagerness to pass on some – as he thought – safe gossip. 'Serlo.'

'The stodgy one.'

Thierry nodded.

'I think Robert going three years ago has always troubled him. Robert being younger and all.'

'Took him long enough to make up his mind.'

Thierry disagreed.

'My impression is he would have gone earlier, Master Geoffrey. You know, when the news of William's death was confirmed. He wanted to take his place.'

Geoffrey grunted.

'Can you see a pudding like Serlo taking the place of William? What was it? William "of the Iron Arm"?'

'He is an Hauteville, Master Geoffrey. Four brothers in Italy, and two of them with titles. Can you blame him for wanting to attempt the same? As I said, I think he would have gone much earlier, but his mother has held him back.'

'Perhaps she thinks he is not up to it,' said Geoffrey unkindly.

The truth was that Geoffrey could not blame Serlo, any more than Thierry could. He himself found it intolerable with only one brother and no land; the wretched Serlo had eleven. Eleven! To say nothing of four sisters. No wonder they were slipping off to Italy one after the other. The surprise was that more had not gone earlier. Perhaps the news of William's death had shaken them. Though he doubted it. Nor could he really see the lady Fressenda standing for long in their way. They were adult, most of them, and the lord Tancred took pride in their achievements. He would encourage rather than obstruct. So, frankly, would the Lady herself, from what Geoffrey knew of her. Anyone who mastered a brood of five stepsons, and another seven of her own – not to mention four

19

daughters – was no clinging cradle-rocker. When Geoffrey had first paid court to Sybil, he had been almost frightened of her.

'Brother Serlo is an Hauteville,' repeated Thierry. 'Make no mistake about that, Master Geoffrey. He does not have brother William's knightly skills, nor does he have the cunning of Robert. But he has the Hauteville energy and lust for adventure.'

Damn him, thought Geoffrey. And he has the support. And the opportunity.

'Perhaps it was the rebellion that held him back,' suggested Thierry, frowning over the problem like some mitred councillor. 'You know, waiting to see if there were any easy pickings. Now he sees that the Duke is still master, he is off.'

Geoffrey swore to himself. If his stupid brother had been able to make up his mind in time – either to join the rebellion or to help crush it, he might now have been in line for some reward from one party or the other. As it was, all Mauger's wonderful schemes had come to nothing – lost, faded, evaporated in a mist of loud intentions, false starts, and blind avenues.

Thierry's voice poked through his thoughts.

'I was saying, Master Geoffrey. If Serlo is about to depart for Italy, he will need money for equipment and escort. Money is the one thing you have – or will have. You wish to wed the lady Sybil, and I am sure my lord Tancred would be grateful to get a daughter off his hands without the burden of a large dowry. Likely a bargain waiting to be struck somewhere?'

Perhaps there was.

'Where is my brother now?'

Thierry drained the last of his cider.

'After I had given him my news, he went to the chapel.'

Geoffrey gazed in incredulity.

'The chapel?'

'Yes, Master Geoffrey.'

'What did you tell him, for God's sake?'

Thierry shrugged.

'What you would expect. What he sent me to find out. How things are settling down. A few fines and confiscations, but no hangings or mutilations. An exile or two. The Duke wants allies, not embittered enemies plotting revenge.'

Geoffrey nodded absently. He was trying to think what news Thierry could possibly have brought that would have sent his brother off to pray.

'Where have you been since you left?'

'Pretty well everywhere, sir – Avranches, Valognes, St. Lô, Vire, Bayeux. Most places in between. Even that new one – Caen.'

'Where?'

'Caen.'

'Where the Devil is that?'

'Near Val-ès-Dunes. Two rivers meet there, and it is near the sea. The Duke is very taken with it. It is not far from where they proclaimed the Truce of God a while back.'

'What is so special about it?'

'From what I can gather, the Duke plans to use it as a base for holding down the Bessin and the West. At any rate he is building there fast, and at Bayeux. He wants to make the Truce of God effective out this way too – as far as the great western sea.'

Geoffrey laughed ironically.

'The Truce of God? Half the knights out here will barely have heard of the Truce of God, and the other half will not understand it. How can they observe the Truce when they hardly know which day of the week it is?'

It crossed Thierry's mind to ask Master Geoffrey which half he thought his brother fell into, but he thought better of it.

Geoffrey began pacing again. Would his brother resort to his knees simply because the Duke was running up a few fortifications at an unknown river-junction? Would he be shivering in that dark, draughty little nave because the Duke had announced yet again that he intended to forbid private war between sunset on Wednesdays and sunrise on Mondays – to say nothing of the seasons of Advent, Lent, Easter, and Pentecost? It did not make sense. Men fought because they had little chance to pray; they did not pray because they had little chance to fight.

Geoffrey stopped in front of Thierry.

'Was that all the news? Was there nothing else?'

Thierry scratched his head.

'All the leaders of the rebellion have been taken and dealt with – '

Geoffrey waved impatiently.

'Yes, yes, you said that.'

' – except Guy of Burgundy. He has bolted to Brionne. The Duke has him besieged. It is only a matter of time.'

Geoffrey grimaced in annoyance.

'There is no cause there. Think, Thierry. Was there nothing else?'

Thierry spread his hands.

'No, Master Geoffrey. I swear.' He cudgelled his brains. 'The Duke had a bout of crouching flux at Isigny. His brother Odo attended a feast at Bayeux.'

'The one with the spots?'

'Yes. One of the Duke's distant kinsmen – Sir Baldwin de Clair – has returned from exile in Flanders. Two or three bishops have died.'

Mauger certainly would not waste any time mourning over members of the clergy. He had none of Father's respect for the tonsure.

'A funny thing about Sir Nigel,' Ivo would say. 'He always wanted so badly to be thought well of by the Church. All those pilgrimages – they really meant something to him, you know.'

Geoffrey sat down the better to think. Thierry coughed respectfully.

'Er – Master Geoffrey.'

Geoffrey looked up.

Thierry glanced furtively down the hall.

'When you ask my lord Mauger about my news – '

'What makes you so sure that I shall?'

'Because that is the only way you are going to find out what you want to know,' said Thierry. 'Please, Master Geoffrey, when you ask him, do not tell him that I visited Hauteville for you. You know what he will do.'

Geoffrey nodded solemnly.

'He shall not hear it from my lips, Thierry.'

For the very simple reason that he had probably heard already, indirectly, from Thierry's. If Thierry had been gorging and gossiping in the kitchen, and flexing tongue and drinking elbow in the guardroom, there would be hardly anyone at Montbrai who had not heard about the next Hauteville brother who was preparing to carve himself a fortune out of the lands in the southern sun. Mauger would probably beat him sooner or later. And if it came to light that he had made uncalled-for remarks about the lady Sybil, Geoffrey himself would beat him again.

Thierry began to collect his cups and bowls.

'If I might be excused, Master Geoffrey. It has been a long ride; my legs and back are stiff.'

Geoffrey nodded.

'And Gaimar's pies are ready to be taken out. Get on with you.'

In his eagerness Thierry nearly fell down the ladder.

*   *   *   *   *   *

Geoffrey pushed open the door of the chapel. It crunched on unswept grit at the threshold. Geoffrey, prepared to squint into the shadows, was surprised to see two candles alight on the altar. It was unlike Gori to allow such prodigality in the middle of a working day. The odd candle-end during vigils at Advent or Easter, maybe, but this was princely show.

There was a sudden scuffle from behind the altar, and Mauger scrambled to his feet. He looked flustered and embarrassed.

'What are you doing here? I thought you were out with Ivo.'

'I was. He had a fall.'

'Is Bracken safe?'

Geoffrey nodded, and stepped forward cautiously.

'Rabbits. No ankles broken. What are you doing?'

'That spreading warren again.'

Mauger brushed dust from his knees and came round to the front of the altar. Somewhat over-fussily he straightened an altar cloth.

'I am surprised Ivo did not remember. Somebody of his experience.'

'I fancy young Nicholas will remember for a while,' said Geoffrey. 'He will not be able to sit down for a week, and we shall have stewed rabbit for a fortnight.'

He came right up to his brother.

'Well?'

'Well what?'

'What are you doing?'

'Nothing.'

Mauger stretched over to the back of the altar, picked up one of the sticks and blew out the candle. He concentrated ferociously on the simple process.

Geoffrey laughed.

'Mauger, you are a dreadful liar. What have you been doing?'

Mauger whirled on him.

'Private! It is private. Nothing to do with you. Nothing at all.'

He busied himself with the second candlestick, taking great pains to set it exactly in the centre.

'Nothing whatever.'

Geoffrey put up both hands.

'So be it, so be it. I am sorry I spoke.'

Gaining confidence, Mauger frowned and peered at him.

'If it comes to that, what are you doing here?'

'Looking for you. I have just been talking with Thierry.'

'Is that a fact? Dear Sybil in eager health, is she?'

Geoffrey flushed.

'How should I know?'

It was Mauger's turn to laugh.

'You are a far worse liar than I, brother. Which reminds me – I must give Thierry a good thumping.'

Mauger did not beat his underlings; he 'thumped' them.

'You know about Serlo then?' said Geoffrey.

Mauger shrugged dismissively.

23

'That? Oh yes. Good riddance.'

'Is that the reason?'

'What?'

'Is that why you are here?'

For an instant it looked as if Mauger's returning confidence was about to evaporate again. He opened his mouth to bluster, then thought better of it.

'Sharp as ever, Geoffrey.'

Geoffrey frowned.

'Well, are you going to tell me any more?'

'No.'

Mauger walked up the short aisle, turned, and genuflected in perfunctory fashion.

'If you wish to talk to me,' he said, crossing himself, 'come to me in the solar in about an hour. I have some things I wish to say to you as well.'

As Geoffrey left the chapel, he caught a glimpse of grey skirts over ample hips skipping away with surprising nimbleness. Gaimar's mother had not picked up much gossip at the crack in the wall this time.

*   *   *   *   *   *

Chapter Two

'Father Gregory, what the Devil is going on?'

Gori smiled to himself as he turned away to put his book in the chest. He wrapped the separate leather covers over each other with fond care.

The restless young man in front of him had called him 'Gori' since he could talk, at a time when everybody else was trying with great persistence and deliberation to get him to say 'Fa–ther Greg–gory'. Because his unformed tongue had insisted on 'Gori', every pair of female hands at Montbrai had clapped in doting delight and promptly repeated it as if it were the funniest thing since Sir Nigel had got the hounds drunk. Everybody took up the nickname. By the time Geoffrey had reached adult stature, it was universal habit. It was at that moment that Master Geoffrey took it upon himself to show that he was now rid of childish weaknesses and began calling him, with stern formality, 'Father Gregory'. When he remembered.

'Lord Mauger has not confided in me.'

Gori too could be just as formal.

'I had a look behind the altar,' said Geoffrey.

'And found nothing.'

Geoffrey stared.

'How do you know that?'

The door of Gori's little wooden cell creaked open, and Bertha squeezed in. Because her hands were full, she swung her hefty hips to close the door and keep out the draughts. She placed a bowl of steaming broth on the cluttered shelf that served as store, desk, and dining table. She wiped her hands on a cloth that hung from the belt of her grey skirt, and proceeded to tie a napkin round Gori's neck.

'Now eat that while it is hot,' she fussed. 'It will ease the cough.'

Looking from Bertha to Gori, and back again, Geoffrey understood.

'So what was he doing there, Bertha?'

Bertha folded her hands over her stomach and raised her eyebrows.

'I am sure I have no idea, Master Geoffrey.'

'Well, you saw me; you must have seen him.'

Bertha assumed her most righteous pose.

'I am sure I have better things to do than peer through cracks in walls, Master Geoffrey.'

Yes, but not many.

Gori came to her rescue.

'Leave Bertha alone. If we upset her, she will not make a fuss of me, will she?'

He looked up at Bertha, and smiled devilishly.

25

Bertha broke the bread for him, and set the spoon beside the bowl. Gori looked at the contents of it, and grimaced behind his hand to Geoffrey. When Bertha caught him at it, he flashed a charming smile and said, 'Please thank Gaimar for his trouble. Tell him I am enjoying it enormously.'

'I made it myself,' said Bertha.

'In that case, I shall look forward to it all the more.'

She looked suspiciously at him, then dropped a small curtsey to Geoffrey. Gori patted her rump with absent fondness as she left.

Geoffrey leaned forward, rested his elbows on his knees, and looked intently at his old teacher.

'Now – tell me. What was Mauger hiding under the back of the altar?'

Gori stirred his broth with his fingers right at the end of the spoon.

'Hiding?'

'Father Gregory, do not treat me like a child. Cavities. Loose stones. Cracks without dust in them. The conclusion is obvious.'

Gori laid down his spoon.

'Geoffrey, one thing I have never done is to treat you like a child. Nor is it my practice to betray a confidence. And I do not refer only to the secrets of the confessional.'

'Is it to do with me?' persisted Geoffrey. 'At least you can tell me that.'

'All I can say to you is to suggest that you ask the one person who is in a position to explain.'

'So it is to do with me.'

'Ask Mauger. I have an idea he will tell you. You are now of an age.'

'It was my portion. My money was there. My share. Is that not so?'

'I am a guardian of secrets, not an owner. It is for Mauger to decide when to share them with you.'

'How much is there?'

Gori smiled.

'You will have to do better than that, Geoffrey.'

'Is it also to do with Sybil?'

Gori professed surprise.

'Sybil?'

Geoffrey sat back.

'Do not play the innocent. Everybody else here knows that Thierry has been to Hauteville and seen the lady Sybil. You know too, I am sure, that Serlo is about to leave for Italy. Bertha flaps her ears in kitchens as well as outside chapels.'

'What of it?'

Gori took a cautious sip of broth, and made a face. Geoffrey ran his hand

26

through his dark hair.

'What am I to do, Gori? If I stay here much longer, I shall go mad. If I leave without my portion I have nothing but what I stand up in. If I wait to receive it, the only thing I can do with it is to go to Hauteville and bargain with my lord Tancred for Sybil's hand. He needs the money for Serlo. Then, when Mauger finds out, even if he is too late to stop our marriage, he will forbid us to live here, and the last place Lord Tancred wants us to live is Hauteville. If I tell Mauger in advance that I plan to seek Sybil's hand, he will refuse to give me the money, and I am faced with either fighting my own brother for my rights, or staying on here as a poor relation. If I go to Italy with Serlo, Mauger will still not give me my money; I shall have to leave Sybil, and what will this Torf do in my absence?'

He stood up in his agitation, found no room to pace in, waved his arms in impotence, and sat down again.

'In the name of God, what has Mauger got against Sybil?'

Gori stirred the broth, hoping to improve the taste.

'Against the young lady – nothing. Her family? Ah, that is another thing.'

Geoffrey cursed.

'It has been the same as long as I can remember. The Hautevilles can never do anything right. Yet look at what those brothers are achieving, and look at us. Father constantly absent on pilgrimages while the estate went to rack and ruin, and Mauger with no capacity for rule and even less for decision.'

'You are being unfair,' said Gori.

'Am I? And Mauger is not, I suppose. The truth is as plain as the nose on your face; he is eaten up with jealousy. So was Father, for all I know.'

'That is not true. Your father had his faults, but I can swear that jealousy was not one of them.'

'Deny Mauger's jealousy then. I have told him to his face many times.'

A great help that was too, to domestic harmony.

Gori laid down his spoon, not without a certain relief. He went to the chest and opened it. He took out various leather packages. Geoffrey knew them so well that he could tell instantly which book was inside each one. Other familiar treasures followed – souvenirs of travels, carvings, a crucifix set with pearls, a pewter cup. At last Gori found what he was looking for.

He brought it up from the depths, carefully unwrapped its cloth cover, and unrolled it on his shelf desk. He motioned Geoffrey to come and look.

Geoffrey gasped. He recognised his own handwriting – spidery, blotched, crossed out, wavering all over the place. Childlike earnestness and determination shone from every line.

'Gori! I had no idea. You have kept it all these years?'

27

Gori nodded.

'Plenty more too. Look well. And while you are looking, remember a small boy in tears of frustration because he could not get the lines to go straight. He could not construe the irregular Latin verbs. He could not translate that difficult parable. And each time I told him that he must grapple with it, that if only he had the will to struggle, he would give his wit the chance to prevail. That I should not be teaching him if I did not think he had the skill to learn, or the grace to benefit from the learning.'

Geoffrey felt the slightest of lumps in his throat. Gori leaned past him and began to roll up the parchment.

'It is the same now, Geoffrey. I can not tell you what you have to do in order to achieve your heart's desire. I can only assure you that you must exert wit and energy in order to do so, and God in His Wisdom has given you a generous share of both. Nothing worthwhile comes without something of a struggle. And because you are what you are, I have an idea that you will be doing your share of struggling in the years to come. Never let your wit and your energy be clouded or misled by your anger or your frustrations. You have it in you to do big things.'

Geoffrey felt slightly uncomfortable, but excited as well.

'What suddenly made you say all that, Gori?'

Gori rubbed a palm over his tonsure and shook his head.

'For the life of me I do not know. I had been planning to say something of the sort for quite a while, because you will very probably leave home in the near future. I had wanted it to be rather special, but it came out with a rush.' He shrugged. 'Still, I daresay it would all have come down to the same thing in the end.'

*　　*　　*　　*　　*　　*

'Mauger?'

'Up here.'

Geoffrey climbed the ladder. He noticed that Mauger had cleared the hall. He had noticed too on the way in that his brother had stationed guards on every outside wall, and two on the main door. Not that that would be any great improvement; their ears were just as long as Bertha's or anybody else's. Assuming of course that voices were going to be raised. Sadly, they usually were, particularly in the last two or three years.

Mauger was standing in the far corner, running his fingers along Mother's embroidery frame, and blowing the dust off the tips. Geoffrey looked at once at the opposite corner, where Mother's great elm chest was visible through the partly-drawn curtains. It was as if Mauger was trying to put as much distance as possible between himself and the chest, which told Geoffrey immediately that

Mauger had been delving into it. His brother was an even worse conspirator than he was liar.

The key was still in Lambert's new lock, and two large saddlebags were propped against each other nearby. There was a pile of assorted travel equipment on the trestle.

Mauger came forward, rubbing his hands. It was a sure sign that he was nervous or excited.

'Ah, there you are,' he said unnecessarily.

'Yes, Mauger, here I am,' replied Geoffrey, sitting on the stool recently occupied by the ample rear quarters of Thierry.

Mauger missed the irony, and sat down opposite. With an effort he stopped rubbing his hands.

'I – er – I have to go away. I have to make a journey.'

'Oh?'

'Yes. A journey.'

Mauger rubbed his palms on the tops of his thighs. Geoffrey continued his deliberate silence, taking contemptuous pleasure in his brother's awkwardness.

Mauger raised his eyebrows.

'Are you not curious to know where?'

'I presume that is what you have summoned me here to impart.'

Mauger glared.

'Yes. Well. I am going to see the Duke.'

He waited to watch the effect. As Geoffrey said nothing, he added some more.

'I am taking most of the garrison with me.'

'Have you not heard? The rebellion is over.'

Mauger refused to take offence.

'I go to make peace, not war.'

'With a full military escort?'

'Breaking a rebellion does not eliminate rebels, brother; it only disperses them. It will be years before there is real peace in these parts. If at all. I intend to be safe when I travel a long distance. Do you care to sneer at the sense in that?'

'If you had declared your loyalty in the first place, before Val-ès-Dunes, you could now be the likely recipient of some fiefs taken from the confiscations of those punished.'

Mauger assumed an important air.

'As a matter of fact, I am to be involved in certain negotiations of some moment. Who knows what may come out of them?'

'You were content to let Thierry roam the countryside on his own.'

'Thierry did not ride in full military order, and he was under instructions not to move unless he was with some group of other travellers. I am going on a formal mission, and I intend to arrive in some style.'

Poor Mauger! He was torn between enjoying the sensation he could create by a full account of his plans, and savouring the secret of total discretion about them.

'How long will you be away?' asked Geoffrey. 'How long will these, er, "negotiations" last?'

'Two, maybe three weeks. Depending on how long it takes me to catch up with his Grace. I hear he will soon be laying down a siege at Brionne.'

Geoffrey smiled. So it was 'his Grace' now, was it? Up to now it had always been 'the Bastard'. At best 'the boy'.

'The Duke will have his hands full with Guy of Burgundy. Why should he take any notice of the likes of you?'

Mauger looked smug.

'He will when he hears what I have to offer.'

The cat was not out of the bag, but Mauger was clearly very pleased by the size of the cat he had in it.

A thought occurred to Geoffrey.

'You are surely not going to offer him military support at the siege?'

Mauger was not prepared.

'What? Well – no. Not exactly. I am sure his Grace would not have begun the siege unless he had adequate forces to sustain it. No, no. My negotiations are altogether of a much more delicate nature.'

'Nothing so drastic as a decision.'

'You can sneer,' said Mauger. 'You do precious little else these days. You can afford to; you have no responsibility. You are not the lord of a fief. You do not understand power politics.'

Geoffrey gazed in amazement.

'Power politics? Lord of a fief? You sound like the Duke of Anjou or the Count of Brittany. Mauger, for once face facts. Ours is a petty knight's fee of trivial importance in a damp corner of Normandy so deprived that even our own Duke is only just beginning to take an interest in it.'

Mauger hawked and spat over the edge of the solar.

'That is just the sort of remark I should expect you to make. You have not borne the burden. Whatever this place has become in the last fourteen years is because of me.'

'You can say that again.'

Mauger thumped the table.

'How dare you!'

One of the soldiers on guard outside the main door pricked up his ears.

Mauger leapt to his feet and began pacing.

'Do you know how old I was when Father died? Seventeen.' He stopped pacing in order to lean down and repeat the number in Geoffrey's face. 'Seventeen.'

Geoffrey raised his eyes to Heaven. Mauger nodded vehemently.

'Yes, you can raise your eyes. You have no idea what it was like. I had to hold this place together: protect Mother – who was for ever pining to go back to Italy; look after you, who clung to her lap till Ivo put some fight into you; keep an eye on Gori, who was either shoving a lot of useless knowledge into your head or putting his hand up skirts; and try and stay alive in a part of Normandy that was little more than a wilderness. You think it is desolate now. I tell you – when Duke Robert died and left that eight-year-old brat, the duchy was swarming with groups of rebels competing for the pleasure of cutting his throat.'

Outside the hall, two soldiers crouched. One had his ear to a crack.

'Now he is on to Duke Robert and the swarming rebels.'

Mauger began pacing again.

'I could have been swatted like a fly. Just like a fly.'

'We were not that important. Nobody took the slightest notice of us.'

'Now you come along – safe, adult, educated, full of long words and clever ideas, and tell me what I should have done. How dare you!'

Geoffrey put up his hands in a placatory gesture.

'So be it. I concede that you saved the family skin. Thank you very much. But that was then. I am talking about now. Look at the place – untidy, ramshackle, dues half collected. Unproductive, inefficient – a mill half-built, bridges falling down, a manor court months behind with its cases.'

'There is nothing to stop you lending a hand,' said Mauger. 'You prefer to go whoring at Hauteville.'

Geoffrey, also stung, got to his feet.

'Because everything here is yours. Nothing is mine. Nothing.'

'Nothing at Hauteville is yours either.'

The soldier pressed his eye to the crack.

'Going well, this one; they are both pacing now.'

'Yes,' said Geoffrey. 'And there is another mystery. Why can you never resist an insult to the Hautevilles? Wherein lies the threat? They are the only family of our class with less land than us.'

Mauger, now at the far end of the solar, turned and pointed.

'Let me remind you, brother, they are most definitely not of our class. Ours is a very ancient family with a most distinguished record. We go back to Roman times.'

31

'Pigs' ears! The only thing Roman about us was the name – "braies" – and it meant "breeches" in Latin. Gori told me only recently.'

'A lie! A scholar's lie. What proof has he?'

Geoffrey raised his eyebrows and sighed.

'I am afraid it would involve a knowledge of reading and writing, so it is pointless to try. But be assured that our family name that you think is so illustrious was bestowed upon some nameless ancestor as an insult because he was a barbarian bumpkin who wore trousers like the Gauls.'

Mauger frowned.

'Gauls?'

'Oh, never mind. All Father did was to knock the last letter off the end and stick a mound on the beginning – and behold! we have a distinguished family name.'

'I care not,' said Mauger, going back to what he felt was safe ground. 'The Hautevilles are not of us.'

'Then why the jealousy?' said Geoffrey, pouncing.

Mauger came up close and glowered into Geoffrey's face.

'If you were not my brother, I should thump you for that.'

'If it is not jealousy, why do you oppose my marriage to Sybil? What can you possibly have against her?'

Mauger hesitated.

'It – it is not her.'

'Then give your consent to our marriage.'

'No.'

Mauger turned away, muttering half to himself, 'A whole family of black sheep.'

Geoffrey followed him across the solar.

'Mauger, I at least have the right to know the reason. Is it something to do with Mother?'

Mauger turned and gave him a very sharp look.

'Why do you say that?'

Geoffrey shrugged.

'I am searching for reasons. If you say it is not jealousy, it must be something else. You were talking of family honour. Several Hautevilles have been to Italy; Mother came from Italy – though exactly where nobody seems to know. Gori's stories get taller every year; if you believe half what he says, she has blood connections with every noble family from the Empress of Constantinople to the Queen of Sheba. I wondered if there was some link between Mother and the Hautevilles.'

'Great saints, no.'

Mauger's reaction looked totally genuine, though he could have hardly been surprised at Geoffrey's next question.

'Is it to do with Father?'

Even before Mauger came out with the stout denial, Geoffrey could see from the look on his brother's face that he had struck the truth.

'Mauger, would you rather I got it from Gori or Ivo?'

Mauger waved him back to the trestle, and sat down once again opposite. He spoke in a low voice, motioning to the outside wall with his thumb.

'This,' he said, 'is in the strictest confidence.'

Geoffrey nodded. It always was.

'No, this time I mean it,' said Mauger. 'Not even Gori knows everything. How much Mother knew I was never sure.'

Geoffrey wondered what on earth was coming.

Mauger leaned forward, and looked at the palms of his hands, as if seeking inspiration.

'When Father left – '

Geoffrey interrupted.

'Which journey are we talking about?'

'The last one – the one with Duke Robert. The roads must have been pulsating with pilgrims just after '33; everyone was so grateful that God had not brought the world to an end a thousand years after the Crucifixion.'

Not for the first time, Geoffrey wondered what sort of God it was who was so indecisive that He should wait a thousand years before even addressing the problem of whether or not He should destroy His own handiwork. Or what sort of Church it was that should attribute such indecisiveness to an all-powerful God.

Mauger continued.

'You have heard stories about Duke Robert like everyone else. Have you ever noticed how similar he was to Father? Swaggering, generous, open-handed, good company?'

'So they tell me. I was only eight, remember.'

Mauger made a gesture of impatience.

'But you know. Well, it appears that Father and Duke Robert took to each other like ducks to water. They became inseparable.'

'What has all this to do with the Hautevilles?'

'Because it was about the same time that the first three Hauteville brothers set out for Italy – William, Drogo, and Humphrey. Nasty bit of work, Humphrey. There was something small about Humphrey . . .'

33

'I still do not see,' said Geoffrey. 'Duke Robert went to Jerusalem. He died in Bithynia. If Father was with him, presumably he did the same – or somewhere near. The Hautevilles went to Italy.'

'The Hautevilles went wherever there was money or treasure to be had. Duke Robert set out with a baggage train bursting with riches, and he made no secret of it. He scattered largesse wherever he went. They say he dazzled even the Greeks with it. It takes many months to make the journey to Jerusalem; the Hautevilles would have been drawn to that baggage train like flies to honey.'

'But Duke Robert reached Jerusalem. We know that. You just said he dazzled everybody at Constantinople with his ostentation.'

'True. He did. And when he was dying in Bithynia, it was on his mind how he was going to get the remainder of his treasure home so that it could be of benefit to the bastard infant he had left behind. Who better to entrust with the safe delivery of it than the boon companion who had been with him all the way from western Normandy?'

'Father?'

'Yes. Father loved oaths of loyalty and honour and sworn companions.'

'I always understood that money slipped through his fingers like water.'

'It did. But this was an oath to his Duke, and it was made at a death-bed, and it was made on a sacred pilgrimage to the Holy Sepulchre, no less. If there was one thing Father did take seriously, it was a pilgrimage.'

'And you are suggesting that the Hautevilles ambushed Father on his way back through Italy, killed him, and stole the remains of the ducal treasure?'

'Yes.'

'What evidence have you?'

'Members of the Duke's party who returned much later said that Father left them in Bithynia suddenly and secretly. The treasure disappeared at the same time.'

Geoffrey laughed.

'Well, you know what that could mean!'

Mauger shook his head.

'You and I know both know that Father could not do that. He was feckless, unreliable, romantic, and many other things, but he was not a common thief.'

'Not enough, Mauger. It does not brand Sybil the sister of a murderer.'

'We also know that the Hautevilles struck sudden riches in 1035, at about the very time that Duke Robert and Father died.'

'It could have been the loot of any one of a hundred Byzantine or Lombard churches.'

'That is not the end of it,' said Mauger. 'I have the word of a man who accompanied Father through Italy on his return journey. He says they were ambushed in Apulia by William of Hauteville and a dozen of his curs. Father was killed outright, the man was left for dead, and the treasure was stolen. He says that when he was well enough he had Father's body taken to the shrine of Monte Gargano, where he had made his first pilgrimage.'

'Very loyal of him,' observed Geoffrey.

'You do not believe it.'

'I think it most unlikely. Did Mother believe it?'

'I am not sure how much of this Mother ever knew. She would not talk of Father's death; only of her much-desired return to Italy. But that had little to do with Father. I did not bring the matter up because I thought it might distress her.'

'What became of this loyal servant?'

'Not servant – companion.'

'Companion then.'

'He came to me. He brought me one or two of Father's possessions that I recognised.'

'Where are they?'

'Perished. Save for one pewter cup. Gori keeps it in his chest.'

'Still not good enough.'

Mauger leaned forward.

'If I told you that he offered to go back to Italy and take vengeance on the Hautevilles, would that change your mind?'

'Take vengeance?'

'Yes. He said that Father had been his friend, and that he shared our desire for revenge. He said he understood that, as Father's heir, I could not leave Montbrai; I had too many responsibilities here. But we could come to some arrangement whereby he could go back to Italy.'

'You mean he wanted you to pay him to murder William of Hauteville?'

Mauger blushed.

'I told him I would have none of it. He persisted. He said that if I did not give him money he would spread the story that I *had* paid him to go and murder William of Hauteville.'

'What did you do?'

Mauger shrugged.

'In the end I gave him money to go away.'

'Mauger!'

'Ssssh! What else was I to do?'

Mauger got up and started his familiar pacing.

'At least he went. Geoffrey, I was a boy, struggling with a new inheritance.

How could I have had the experience to handle a situation like that?'

'So this was years ago.'

'Yes. I had long hoped that this creature had met the death he deserved somewhere in Italy. But I now know that he has returned to Normandy to claim an inheritance of his own. And we also have confirmation that William is definitely dead, probably a year or two ago, and almost certainly violently. It is too close to be a coincidence.'

Mauger stopped, and looked almost pleadingly at Geoffrey.

'And you choose this time to get yourself involved with Sybil. Can you now understand why I want no dealings with the Hautevilles? Gossip and questions, rumour and conjecture, which can lead only to trouble. The Hautevilles are not men of honour; they stop at nothing. Let us cut ourselves off from them. They are no loss.'

So Mauger was still biased, for all his doubts and cares. Geoffrey however resisted the temptation.

'Why have you never told me this before?'

'You have never been twenty-one before.'

'Does Ivo know? Surely he was Father's companion too.'

Mauger shook his head.

'For his last journey, Father gave instructions that Ivo was to remain at home to watch over you in case anything should happen. He did.'

Geoffrey nodded. Ivo loved Father, but he loved Geoffrey too. His only regret was that he had not been able to be in two places at once.

'I hope you are now answered,' said Mauger.

'Answered, but not satisfied,' said Geoffrey.

'You will get no more.'

'I expect only my due.'

'What do you mean by that?'

'My portion. When do I get that?'

A sudden thought struck Geoffrey.

'Holy Virgin! You did not pay this – this animal with my money, did you?'

Mauger swallowed.

'You will receive the value of everything that Father left for you.'

Geoffrey rose in wrath.

'So you *did* give it to him!'

'What choice did I have!' roared Mauger. And in a whisper, 'What choice?'

Geoffrey stared in incredulity.

'And all these years I have been waiting for something that did not exist.'

'I have made it up. All that neglect you have been accusing me of – the mill, the bridges, the river banks, the palisades – I have used the money to make up your precious inheritance. Do you think it has been easy?'

Geoffrey was also too far gone in anger to retreat.

'So it now exists – again.'

'Yes!' bawled Mauger.

'Then when do I get it? I am adult. It is due. This is the custom. Before you give it away again to some other plausible beggar.'

Mauger struggled to keep his temper, and his voice down.

'I am aware of custom. Believe me, I have been maturing plans for you over a long period. They are shortly to come to fruition. Give me only a little longer, and I promise that you will receive everything that is your due, and quite possibly a little more. Certainly more than you deserve after a remark like that.'

'What am I supposed to deduce from that?'

'Whatever your clever scholar's mind pleases. In the meantime, brother, you wait. After twenty-one years, another two or three weeks will not make a great deal of difference.'

Another smug reference to that secret journey to the Duke, to that large cat jostling inside the bag. Mauger was recovering himself.

So was Geoffrey. If his brother was going to be absent for three weeks, he would not know about every movement made in or around Montbrai. If Geoffrey bound Ivo to secrecy, there was no reason why he could not spend some time travelling . . . to Hauteville, for instance.

'Now go,' said Mauger, moving towards the saddle bags. 'I have preparations to make.'

As Geoffrey began to climb down the ladder, a thought struck him. He poked his head back over the floor of the solar again.

'This virtuous and loyal friend you spoke of, the one who wants payment for both his activity and his non-activity. What is his name? Do I know him?'

'I think not. He is not from these parts. He is from the north-west. From a place called Malbec. His name is Torf.'

*　　*　　*　　*　　*　　*

Mauger tightened the straps on the saddle bags. For the fifth time he checked the lock on Mother's chest, the new lock that he had discussed with such urgency with Lambert. He patted the waist wallet where he had placed the key.

He knew he could bind Geoffrey to a promise. If Geoffrey gave his word not to open the chest before his brother's return, he could be relied upon to keep it. No word had ever yet been broken within the family. After all, was it not agreed that he would receive his portion immediately afterwards?

It would not matter what he did then. For that matter, it would not matter what Geoffrey did while Mauger was away. He could go and court Sybil to his heart's content, bed her till he ached. He could fraternise with the Hauteville brothers, make plans with Serlo, and talk about details of the route to Italy until the last candle guttered.

From now on, there would be no more sarcastic remarks about poor management, and half-built mills, and collapsing bridges. No more scorn about surrender to threats and demands. After all that time of living in constant worry, all those years of scrimping and scheming, he was nearing the end. How satisfying it was going to be to prove that he too, Mauger of Montbrai, could conceive and bring to fruition long-term plans.

What a blow to the pride of the Hautevilles it would be. And what a masterstroke of politics too. What an investment for the future.

Mauger clapped his hands in sheer delight. For once, he was about to be brilliant – absolutely brilliant.

*   *   *   *   *   *

Chapter Three

Geoffrey lay back, put his hands behind his head, took a huge breath, and heaved a sigh of utter contentment. The sky was dazzling blue, the sun was warm, the breeze was enough only to stir the fern around them. He felt absolutely marvellous.

'Do I excite you?'

He knew the question was outright vanity, but he was so bursting with confidence and self-satisfaction that he could not contain it.

Sybil nestled against him and smoothed her dress.

'Put your arm round me.'

Geoffrey did so. He screwed his head sideways and downwards, so that he gave himself three chins.

'Well? Do I?'

Sybil did not move; she knew that all Geoffrey could see was the hair-parting on the top of her head.

'Do you what?'

'Excite you?'

Sybil stretched an arm across his chest.

'I find it very exciting that I excite you. To be so desired. And by one such as you, Geoffrey. It is an excitement and a thrill such that I could never fully describe it to you.'

Geoffrey frowned.

'No – but what I mean is – '

Sybil lifted her head, and gazed into his eyes.

'You have no idea, my love, how much you mean to me.'

The broad, open forehead, the steady blue eyes that always looked straight into his own, the rich resonant voice, the deep and obvious sincerity – it was a combination that Geoffrey could never resist. It melted any twinges of uncertainty into tears of fondness.

He slipped down beside her, gathered her into his arms, and gave her a kiss of surpassing tenderness . . .

Together they leaned over the parapet of the bridge and watched the women beating clothes on stones at the stream's edge. One of the women caught sight of them. She nudged a companion, who stood up and stretched her back. Some unheard words passed between them, and whoops of ribald laughter floated up to the bridge.

Geoffrey felt a twinge of embarrassment, but Sybil smiled amiably. She even waved back to the women.

'You should remonstrate with them,' said Geoffrey.

Sybil turned to him in surprise.

'About what?'

Geoffrey gestured vaguely.

'About – about what they are doing.'

'They are only teasing.'

'Well then.'

Sybil laughed – not a girlish giggle, but a full-jawed, broad laugh.

'Great saints, no. Geoffrey, I have twelve brothers and three sisters. There is nothing you can tell me about teasing. I was raised on it.'

Geoffrey frowned in concern.

'But they were disrespectful. And they are not your family. They are only villeins' wives and daughters.'

'Geoffrey, half the women down there have dandled me on their knee. I know them all, and there is nothing about me that they do not know. Why should I mind?'

Geoffrey grimaced awkwardly.

'This is different.'

Sybil shook her head.

'No. You do not understand, my darling. They are laughing and waving because they love me, not because they are being rude. Remember, they have watched me from the cradle.'

'I still do not see.'

Sybil prised a piece of loose mortar from the top of the parapet and tossed it into the water.

'Have you any idea what it is like to be brought up with twelve brothers to protect your honour? Wherever you turn, there is a brother somewhere to see that you come to no harm.'

'What is wrong with that?'

'That, my love, is a man's question. Geoffrey, I might as well have been raised in a convent.'

'I should have thought you would be flattered, to have so much care for your welfare.'

'There you go again, thinking like a man. Did it occur to you that they were not guarding a sister but protecting an investment? A marriageable daughter is a potential means of profit if the right alliance can be negotiated. If the goods are soiled it is harder to dispose of them.'

Geoffrey looked glum.

'I had no idea you were so eager to become – what you said.' He could say the

40

words easily about other women, but they stuck in his throat when it came to using them about Sybil.

'Silly. I was not. What I resented was the natural assumption that I did. I was hurt by the lack of trust.'

Sybil gestured down towards the washing women, who had returned to their work, with only the occasional glance over their shoulders.

'They knew. They understood. They saw me grow up. They saw that I was not like my sisters. Now Muriella and Constance – they did dream of escape, and still do. But their idea of escape is a stolen thrill behind a corn rick, flushed cheeks and a sudden tremble in a darkened solar.'

'Not yours?' Geoffrey was searching for reassurance rather than information.

'No. I too dreamed – but of a much greater escape. Of a flight to where someone trusted me, where someone actually had thoughts beyond stomach and loins and swords and baubles. A place where someone was not always looking. I think I have found it with you.'

Geoffrey pointed.

'They are looking. You do not seem to mind that.'

'True. They are looking, but they are not prying. They understand what I have found in you. And they are happy for me.'

'Then why so rude?'

'Because they are also human, Geoffrey. And they know that we are too. Is that so very wrong?'

'That means, then, that everybody – ' Geoffrey swallowed ' – everybody knows.'

Sybil laughed again.

'Well, of course they do. Geoffrey, I have never shown such fondness for anyone before. You are a handsome young man come from a neighbouring knight's fee on a formal visit to my father. What are they supposed to think? That you are come to hear my confession or to sell me a bolt of Flanders weave?'

Geoffrey turned away in bafflement. Sybil put a hand on his arm.

'Geoffrey, they like you. Everyone likes you. Father likes you.'

'And your mother?'

Sybil smiled.

'Mother is – well, Mother is Mother. Mother always waits and sees. Can you blame her?'

Geoffrey frankly had no idea what to make of the lady Fressenda ...

*   *   *   *   *   *

My lord Tancred of Hauteville glanced along the table at my lady Fressenda, and raised his eyebrows in a question. My lady nodded imperceptibly. Lord

41

Tancred clapped his hands.

'Ha! Good. Now jump to it. And bring the men.'

Geoffrey had been staying at Hauteville only five days, but the routine of the evenings had settled speedily into a pattern of seemingly immovable rigidity.

Servants cleared the table and brought fresh cider. Two small boys placed bowls of water and laid clean napkins. While the company washed and wiped their hands, Sir Tancred chivvied and barked grumpily.

'Lively now . . . careful with those blades, you numbskull . . . well, put it there, girl, put it there . . . Gah! Not like that!'

Nobody hastened his pace one jot.

'Yes, my lord.'

'Very good, my lord.'

'At once, my lord.'

Two girls helped my lady to her feet, two more carried her chair to its regular place in front of the hearth, and another tucked a large blanket round her knees. Her stitching frame was already in place before her, and there was a stool beside her for her needles and threads. At a gesture from her imperious hand, it was edged minutely nearer until she pronounced herself satisfied.

Right on cue, a boy appeared with a box and a folded cloth. Sir Tancred clapped his hands again, this time in pleasure.

'Ah! Splendid! The men.'

No matter how carefully or how quickly the poor boy laid them on the table, Sir Tancred would always say, 'Steady, steady. Well, get them out, lad, get them out.'

He would then follow every movement of the boy's slender white wrist as each of the pieces was placed on the chequered cloth. When the process was complete, he would lift his chin and look down over the whole display. His lips would tighten in a fierce grimace, and he would frown deeply, as if he were challenging any of the pieces to move before he was ready to begin. A final beckoning gesture with his left hand to make the boy with the candlestick move it a trifle nearer, and a last fussy little adjustment of its position, as if to point out that no servant could ever be trusted to place anything exactly where you wanted it.

Whatever sons who were in attendance rose, paid their respects to their mother, and withdrew. Except two.

'Serlo? You will remain.'

'Is it really necessary, Father? I have many matters pressing.'

'So you always say. But not as pressing as this. On this occasion we discuss your expedition. You want some money, do you not?'

Serlo sat down sullenly on a stool before the fire, and began whittling a stick.

Roger, the youngest brother, did not need telling. He knelt near Serlo and gave his attention to cleaning and greasing some harness.

Alone of all the sons and daughters, Roger showed hardly any rebellion against his father. Geoffrey had been struck not only by his good looks, but by his patience.

'He looks like someone who will wait a very long time for what he wants to happen,' said Geoffrey to Sybil.

Sybil smiled.

'Ah, Roger,' she said more than once. 'Roger is special.'

'You say that because you are closest to him in age.'

Sybil readily agreed.

'True. But there is more than that. Roger has a very deep mind. He watches us all, and he thinks mightily.'

'Will he go to Italy?'

'It is hard to tell, for Roger does not readily share his thoughts and ambitions, not even with me. Moreover, he is only seventeen. But if he takes it into his head to do so, he will surely go, and he will go in his own good time and in his own way.'

Sir Tancred clapped his hands again, and summoned Sybil to sit beside him.

'I shall need your help, against this young man of yours. Come, Geoffrey.'

Sir Tancred motioned Geoffrey into a chair opposite, while he himself leaned eagerly forward on his elbows, anxious to begin.

Geoffrey found the whole routine harmless and amusing, but he had been staying only a few days. He could readily understand how the constant repetition of it over many years could become unspeakably boring.

What with that, and my lord's blusterings and repeated jokes and endless fussing, to say nothing of my lady's fearsome discipline throughout the whole domain, it was no wonder that so many of the sons itched to be away. Daughters too, if they had half a chance. Sybil was the only one who regularly stayed behind after meals.

Sir Tancred nodded.

'Well, my boy – you start.'

Thus, day after day, they played.

My lord Tancred was too rash and impulsive to be a good player. He was a noisy one too. His own musings were punctuated with growls and grunts and hisses between his teeth, and the moves of his opponent were greeted by shouts of surprise and oaths of mortification and disbelief. He enjoyed himself enormously.

When Sybil offered suggestions, it was an occasion for great argument, but Geoffrey noticed that whenever he took her advice, it improved his game. Indeed, her good sense and caution made Geoffrey look the impulsive one.

All the while, Tancred talked about Sybil's dowry, and Serlo's projected journey, and Geoffrey's expectations. Every other statement was accompanied by a glance in my lady's direction. 'Is that not so, m'dame?'

Geoffrey had to follow the game, outwit Sybil's sharp moves, answer my lord's questions without allowing any annoyance to creep into his voice at the many repetitions, and glance furtively over his shoulder to try and see what sort of expression had formed on the forbidding features of my lady.

The conversation wound its way round the same topics every time.

'Well, it seems to me you are a lusty young fellow, to be sure.'

'If you say so, Sir Tancred.'

'And my Sybil is worth a chase, is she not?'

'That she is, Sir Tancred.'

'Probably caught her once or twice already, eh?'

Geoffrey glanced at Sybil, whose high colour glowed in the candlelight. They grinned at each other.

'I wish to marry her, Sir Tancred,' said Geoffrey, sidestepping.

'Hah! Hmm! Yes indeed. There are many things to be talked about before a couple go to the altar. Is that not so, m'dame?'

'I have good expectations,' said Geoffrey. 'My money is now due to me.'

'But no land.' My lady timed her interjection perfectly.

'My brother has given his word that he will render to me my full due the moment he returns.'

'But no land.' Delicate needle and gentle voice, both of iron.

'My brother at this moment is in negotiation with the Duke,' said Geoffrey, hoping to blur the issue.

'The Duke, eh? Well, I hope you are luckier than my boys were. Never got a thing. No, Syb. The rook, the rook.'

'I trust your arrangements for your son Serlo are proceeding satisfactorily,' said Geoffrey, blurring it even further.

'What? Serlo? Yes, yes. Going to cost me a fortune. Seems to get more expensive each time. Eh, Serlo? Going to cost me a fortune. Just so that you can go and make one yourself. Will you remember your dear old father then, eh? Eh?'

Serlo raised his eyes to the roof. Roger looked at Sybil and smiled.

Geoffrey tried to take advantage of the opening.

'It is possible, Sir Tancred, that my funds could well run to a certain amount of assistance for Serlo.'

My lady's needle poised in mid-air.

'You are negotiating for Sybil's welfare, not Serlo's.'

'Yes, yes, to be sure. Not that, Syb. Why move that? It will let him in . . . Ah, I see what you mean . . . clever girl . . . Yes, yes, to be sure, young man. Sybil must be our first concern. We must keep her safe here.'

'I am not going to try and steal her, my lord,' said Geoffrey.

'You do not steal that which you love; only that which you covet.'

'Mother!' Sybil allowed a trace of annoyance to creep into her voice.

Sir Tancred cleared his throat.

'Yes. And there is also the question of – um – other offers. Now I am not saying that you are not a fine young fellow, and this Torf of Malbec is a trifle older than Sybil, but the fact remains that he has land. Is that not so, m'dame?'

'Nearby.' From the stitching frame.

'How does he come to have land?' asked Geoffrey, probing. 'I understand he has spent most of the last fifteen years travelling in Italy.' 'Travelling' sounded more respectable than 'selling his sword', which was what the older brothers had been doing as well.

'A brother died, leaving no issue. No – legitimate issue,' explained my lady, with a meaning look. 'My lord Torf has returned to claim his inheritance.'

And enjoy his spoils, thought Geoffrey.

My lady raised her eyebrows in interrogation.

'And when can you reasonably expect to claim yours?'

'My brother will return to Montbrai within the week, or so he assures me.'

The needle was carefully inserted.

'Let us hope that your brother's estimate of time, and yours of money, prove to be equally accurate.'

'There you are, young fellow. Checkmate. If I may say so, you handle your knights quite well, but you do not have enough appreciation of the potential of bishops . . .'

*   *   *   *   *   *

Mauger replaced the last stone, stood up, and scooped dust into the cracks with his toe. He came round to the front of the altar, and replaced the candlesticks in their normal position.

Instead of the usual brief genuflection, he remained for a while on his knees . . .

Mother, he hoped, would be gratified. If her most ardent desire had always been to return to the sun of Italy, her second most heartfelt ambition had been to see her beloved Geoffrey set on a course in life that would be in keeping with his abilities and potential. Well, he, Mauger de Montbrai, had done his best; he could do no more. From now on, it was up to the boy himself.

As for Father . . . it seemed peculiarly fitting, all things considered. Perhaps his restless soul could lie in peace at last. The Lord had taken away, and the Lord had given back, as you might say. Mauger tried to picture the lonely grave at the shrine of the Archangel at Monte Gargano. Assuming that devil Torf had been telling the truth.

Although his pride told him that it was probably the cleverest thing he had done in his life, his brain reassured him that, given the opportunity and the circumstances, it was probably the only reasonable thing too. It really did seem to make the most tremendous sense. And would God have arranged for all these things to come together if it had not been sense? If he were God, he would certainly not feel like helping those fools who did not help themselves when the occasion was so obviously offered.

Mauger muttered a prayer or two, crossed himself, and got to his feet. He went forward to the back of the altar again, and had one last look to reassure himself. Fine. It would be quite safe. Geoffrey would be so occupied with his annoyance that it would never occur to him that his brother had been able to drive a harder bargain than he had dared to expect. The rest of the money would come in useful later at Rouen. After all, the house of Montbrai was a noble one; it would not do to appear as paupers before two kinsmen of the Bastard.

Mauger paused at the door of the chapel and looked back. One way and another, it had been a good fortnight's work. He would give anything to see the look on the faces of the Hautevilles when they found out.

*   *   *   *   *   *

'What do I do, Gori? For God's sake, what do I do?'

The shock was past. The rage. The search for a scapegoat. 'This was all your doing, Father Gregory.'

Gori stifled a smile. Master Geoffrey was a bewildered boy again, struggling with his Latin translation. No. He must be fair; it was more than that. It was a young man struggling with a new destiny. A young man who did not know his own way, did not comprehend his own powers. He was reeling from the total collapse of his plans, his ambitions. Furious at the readiness with which everyone else accepted a situation that found him speechless with rage and impotence and bafflement.

Already they were calling him 'my lord' and 'your Grace'. Eyes bursting with pride and pleasure followed him everywhere. Doors were held open, curtseys were ducked in the most unlikely places. Gaimar dropped a ladle into his stew when Geoffrey came unannounced into the kitchen. Lambert very nearly shoed the same horse twice while Geoffrey waited. The atmosphere of ease and familiarity had been replaced by a wall of sudden awe and awkward respect.

Geoffrey felt cut off, alone in a sudden limbo that was not of his making. It was all so unfair. And how on earth was he to break the news to Sybil? Or if she already knew, and she probably did by now, how was she going to receive him? Small wonder he dropped the formal 'Father Gregory'.

'What do I do, Gori?'

Gori coughed wheezily.

'First of all, Geoffrey, you must make up your mind about one thing: do you regard what has happened as the Will of God or not?'

'Of course not. It is Mauger's stupidity. He fancies he is playing the great statesman. He is bewitched by what he thinks is his own sharp wit. He can not see beyond his own nose.'

Gori held up a hand.

'All right, all right. I follow your general idea. So you do not accept it?'

'I most certainly do not.'

'Then you must do something about it. Do you agree?'

'Of course, of course. But what? What? I have seen Mauger do some stupid things in the past, but never anything remotely approaching this insanity. Quite apart from what he has bought, he has bought it blind. He has not the shadow of an idea what the Duke has taken his money for. Or rather my money. My money!'

'Patience, patience. You agree that what has been done has been done without any agency of yours. Yes, yes. Very well. It follows then that it has been done by the agency of others.'

'Gori, this is no time for philosophy. Reach a conclusion. Say something.'

'If you follow me, Geoffrey, you will reach it for yourself.'

'Well?'

'Take me. Even if I did offer some advice and comment to your brother, it was beyond my powers to force him into a decision, and it is now beyond my powers to undo what has been done. You agree?'

'Yes, damn you. If you had only had the sense to – '

'Follow me, Geoffrey. Only two other people were agents in this transaction – the Duke, and Mauger. Therefore only they can do anything to unmake this situation. Yes?'

'I suppose so.'

Geoffrey could already see where Gori was going.

'Mauger is too consumed by the cleverness of his plan to dream of undoing it, and the Duke is too poverty-stricken to return a penny.'

'I said you would come to your own conclusion.'

'So what use is philosophy? I can do nothing. Nothing.'

Gori poured out two cups of cider.

47

'Nothing – now. It is a wise man who does nothing when there is nothing that can be done – at the time.'

'The longer I leave it the worse it becomes.'

'Not necessarily. You are not yet consecrated.'

Geoffrey stared.

'You do not suggest I go through with that?'

'What choice do you have at the present? Disobedience to your overlord the Duke? Hardly a good start for a promising career, whether as cleric or as layman. The Duke is your avenue to promotion, whatever your chosen status.'

'So I give in?'

'No. You go along, albeit unwillingly. But go slowly, keep your eyes and ears open, and keep your wits sharp.'

Geoffrey screwed up his eyes in suspicion.

'You know something.'

'No.' Gori raised his eyebrows innocently. 'Only that there is soon to be a great Church Council at Rheims, presided over by His Holiness himself. It will investigate matters of irregularity in Church administration. Among them simony. If you could by chance actually prove that your bishopric was bought for you, and moreover bought without your knowledge or consent, you might – you just might – find a way out of this difficulty without danger of disobedience to your Duke. Indeed you would emerge as a most assiduous supporter of Pope Leo's reforms, and the Duke is a good son of the Church.'

Geoffrey snorted.

'With my luck, they would probably make me a cardinal instead.'

Gori laughed.

'Is it a greater risk than the one you run now – of being stuck with a bishopric?'

Geoffrey made a face.

'Well, it is an idea, certainly. It is worth thinking about.'

'And it gives time, Geoffrey. All sorts of things can happen in the interval. You never know; you might get used to *being* a bishop.'

Geoffrey shook his head.

'Remember? I said that I did not think this was the Will of God. I still do not think so. I am still tempted to break away from the whole thing and go with Serlo to Italy. Take Sybil with me.'

'No. Bad counsel. Never make more enemies than you have to, and certainly not without good reason. That is a last resort. The last cast of the desperate fugitive. You are a long way from that yet. If you can not see God's Will in being made a prince of the Church, you would have to look very hard to find God's Will in stealing a knight's daughter, deserting a brother, and defaulting on your pledged word to your overlord – albeit pledged for you. Pledged nonetheless.'

Geoffrey sighed.

'So I do nothing. Just sit and let it all happen.'

'Not quite. You now have a bishopric, a province, a cathedral. Go and see them.'

'Why? They are no use to me.'

Gori put down his cup.

'A short while ago you bitterly criticised your brother for accepting merchandise without examining it. You are now *rejecting* merchandise without examining it. Are the two errors not parallel? And that is not philosophy; that is plain truth.'

'Mmmm.'

'Go, Geoffrey. At least look. Find out for yourself. If you know what you do not want, you will see more clearly what you *do* want – freedom. And that is what you most desire, is it not?'

'That. And Sybil.'

Gori smiled.

'If Sybil loves you, and you love her, the two of you will find a way. Remember what I said: do not give in. Struggle. Give your wit a chance to seek the solution.'

Geoffrey wiped his mouth with the back of his hand.

'So – it is to Sybil, is it? And then Coutances.'

'No. Coutances. And *then* to Sybil. Your lady will not be able to show the way at Coutances, but what you find at Coutances may well suggest a way ahead for you at Hauteville.'

Geoffrey scratched his cheek with a fingernail.

'Hmmm.'

'God go with you, my son.'

Gori looked at the closed door after Geoffrey had left.

Had he really talked such common sense, or had he been trying to steer the boy? Had he tried to show him the true Will of God, or had he been hiding it from him? For the life of him, he did not know. He had done his best for him, and tried to show him how he could do the best for himself.

He smiled wryly. Perhaps that was the real Will of God.

*   *   *   *   *   *

Chapter Four

The wind blew straight into Geoffrey's face from the edge of the world. As he pulled his hood more tightly round his head and squinted westwards, he fancied he could taste salt in the drizzle that stung his cheeks with its spite.

He allowed his horse to pick its own way across the swollen stream called, he believed, the Soulles. It was years since he had been this far west. After all, who went into the Cotentin if it were not necessary? The joke was that folk round here tied granite slabs on their roofs to stop the thatch blowing away, and then tied more thatch on top to stop the slabs blowing away.

A short distance behind, in between gusts which magically silenced all sound, Ivo hacked at his cough. Geoffrey waited for him to catch up, along with Thierry, the grooms and the pack-donkeys. When they all drew level he pointed to the top of the hill.

'Up there.'

Ivo nodded, and wiped his nose with the back of a chapped hand.

'Behold!' said Geoffrey with heavy irony. 'Behold the city of Coutances.'

'Yes, master Geoffrey,' said Ivo patiently, and hastily corrected himself. 'Yes, my lord.'

Geoffrey muttered something in ill temper, and dug his horse forward. The heavy destrier's hooves thudded like falling rocks on the sodden track.

Geoffrey tried to arch his back to ease the stiffness, and cursed as the animal nearly stumbled beside a hole.

This was madness. Even in the cold, he burned at the stupidity of it all.

'My lord!' 'My lord bishop!'

Geoffrey sneered at the eagerness and regularity with which Ivo and the other servants used the new words. It was pathetic that they should take such childlike delight in them, as if, by the mere repetition of them, they could infuse them with greater significance, like a penitent chanting a *Paternoster*. It was like – it was like a grown man who thinks that if he waves his toy sword in the air enough times he can rush safely into battle and kill the enemy.

Madness, madness . . .

'I refuse to believe it. This is impossible.' Geoffrey ran a hand through his thick, dark hair. 'You are my brother; you could not do this to me.'

Mauger continued peeling an apple.

'I concede that it may take a little getting used to.'

Geoffrey nearly burst.

'Getting used to! Treachery. Theft. Blasphemy. Simony. Obtaining property by false pretences – '

'I think you are rather overstating the case, but that is understandable, under the circumstances. Believe me, I can sympathise; it must come as something of a shock.'

'Would you not feel shocked to discover that you had been robbed of your inheritance by your own brother?' Geoffrey shook his head in stunned amazement. 'I can still not take it in.'

Mauger carefully cut out the core.

'My guess is that you are furious because you think I deceived you into thinking your money was in Mother's chest.'

'You did.'

'I was merely taking a safety precaution.'

'You deceived me. You went through all that pompous pretence of swearing me to such secrecy and such security. "Give me your word, Geoffrey. Swear that you will not open the chest until I return. On our Mother's soul, Geoffrey." And I, like an idiot, swore.'

'As I fully expected you to; you are a dutiful son and brother.'

Geoffrey could have struck him.

'There was I, loyal and noble. " Only a matter of time," you said. "Give me just three weeks." And all the while there was nothing there. Empty as the Holy Sepulchre.'

'Exactly.'

'Tell me, tell me. What would you have done if I had refused to promise?'

'Threatened to take it with me. Would you have wanted to live with the worry of that? Of me riding half across Normandy with your precious inheritance in my baggage?'

'But you did!'

'Ah,' said Mauger with infuriating calm. 'You did not know that I was. Big difference. Your mind was settled all the time I was away, sure that your money was safe. I did take most of the garrison to guard it, remember.'

'You deceived me.'

'I did nothing of the sort. I asked you to make a promise – to keep Mother's chest locked until my return. I did not swear that your money was inside it.'

Geoffrey was enraged by so many things that he scarcely knew what to do with himself.

'Do you honestly think that this will stop me marrying Sybil?'

Mauger sliced off a piece of apple and carried it to his mouth on the blade. 'Yes.'

'Then you underestimate me.'

'On the contrary. It is because I have a very high estimate of you that I have done this. I know you, Geoffrey. You do things completely, right through. You always accept the implications of what you do.'

'And I am now the master of what I do. What is to stop me going straight to the Hautevilles now?'

'Nothing at all. But there is nothing to be achieved there either. You have nothing to offer.'

'Myself.'

'That will not impress my lord Tancred without something to back it up. He may be a bit of an old buffer, and you may let him beat you at chess, but he still loves his children; he wants something proper for them, especially the girls. And you will certainly not cut much ice with my lady Fressenda, if what you tell me about her is true.'

'What is to stop me taking Sybil away with me?'

'Honour. She is an honourable young woman. At least that is what you have been at pains to tell me – even allowing for pardonable lover's exaggeration.'

'I could explain the situation. I could persuade her.'

Mauger cut into his apple again.

'And what about her vast brood of brothers? You would not get further than Lambert's boy could throw an anvil.'

'Then I shall go to Italy with Serlo and make twice what you should have given me.'

'You would have to fight me before I let you go – after what happened to Father.'

'And if I still went? With an Hauteville? That would be one in the eye for you, eh?'

Mauger chewed stolidly.

'It will be one in the eye for you to come back and find her married to friend Torf – the neighbour. The neighbour with the land.'

Geoffrey tried to calm himself and think more purposefully.

'I could arrange for us to be married in secret.'

'Oh? And where would you find a cleric to administer this – interesting sacrament?'

'Gori.'

Mauger almost choked on his apple in his amusement.

'Gori!'

'He would understand my situation. He is in it himself.'

'Brother, Gori is most certainly not married.'

Geoffrey stared.

'But Bertha – they still – '

Mauger raised his eyebrows.

'That is something you must ask Bertha. But I assure you that they have never been married. And for your information, Gori is not a priest either.'

Geoffrey stared again.

'But – this is ridiculous. All my life – ' Geoffrey spread his hands. ' – Mass. Confession. The dying.'

'Exactly. All your life. That is all you know. And Gori has brought great comfort to many. What should we have done without him? But the fact of the matter is that he is a monk. Father found him in the same baggage train as he found Mother.'

The shocks were coming too fast for Geoffrey to absorb fully.

'Then why – '

'My dear boy, there was nobody else. In the pit of sinners, the half-shorn monk is priest. He has given the sacraments for so many years that I am sure he no longer thinks about it. But if you are looking for a legal marriage, you will not find it here.'

Geoffrey swallowed.

'Then I shall go to Bayeux. There is a married priest there – in the Duke's very household. You told me yourself.'

'He would not dare. Not under the Duke's nose. Father Arnulf has kept very quiet about his own marriage. He would never dare to parade another. Besides, why do you suppose the Duke has given you this charge?'

'I can not imagine. It surely can not be in order to keep an obscure younger son in western Normandy away from women.'

Mauger put down his knife and the remainder of his apple.

'Of course not, you idiot. It is the marriage, not the women, that concerns him. Nobody is so stupid as to say that you may not have women. All they are saying is that you may not marry them. Your loyalty must be in only one quarter – all the time.'

Geoffrey flushed in anger.

'So I can keep Sybil as – as Gori keeps Bertha.'

Mauger picked up his apple again.

'Of course – if you can get her.'

Geoffrey slammed his palm on the table.

'Damn you and damn you! That is the real reason. It is the Hautevilles again. All this talk of "providing for me", giving me a – what was it? – "splendid start", bringing dignity to the family. It is all your craven jealousy. You will even involve the Duke himself – anything to keep me away from the Hautevilles.'

Geoffrey leapt to his feet and began pacing. Suddenly he stopped as a thought struck him. He wheeled round and looked at Mauger.

'Very well. Two can play at that game. You involved the Duke. So shall I. Bayeux, you said. I shall go to the Duke myself.'

Mauger popped in another slice.

'And ask for your money back?' ...

As they came near the crest of the hill, they passed the first dwellings. Pitiful clusters of leaning shacks, perched on ill-laid masonry foundations. Between them scuttled furtive, hunchbacked figures, hooded and bowed beneath the weather. There was a square – at any rate a bare space, rutted and pitted and pooled. Dogs ran with lowered tails between piles of ordure. Now that they were away from the shelter of the lee slope, the wind tore at their clothes again, and whipped away the smoke from domestic fires like an idle shepherd boy cutting off the heads of nettles with a stick.

Geoffrey looked to his right, and frowned. Odd! Where was it? He urged his horse forward, between more lop-sided buildings, past dripping eaves, sagging beams, brimming butts, and murky yards. The whole place looked so feeble that it seemed to be ashamed of its own existence.

Faces vanished behind shutters and door-cracks. Dogs backed away, snarls rippling along bared gums. A gate slammed shut. The entire town was withdrawing like a snail into its shell.

Geoffrey came out on the western side, stopped, and gazed all round him. Nothing but neglect and loneliness – untended coppice, a bramble-clogged River Bulsard, a looted ruin of an aqueduct.

He felt another prickle of unease on his cheeks and neck. This town – ha! this 'city' – was holding him to scorn. It had hidden its fires, its people, its animals. Now the insult was complete – it had hidden its cathedral.

He wrenched his horse's head round and went back the way he had come, pretending not to notice the question on Ivo's face. He reached the vacant central square again. One side was almost bare, except for two gloomy, barn-like buildings, which looked more substantial than most. They had stone foundations and even a few irregular courses of masonry. Behind them clumps of gorse and heather stretched to the edge of the hillcrest before falling away to the River Soulles below.

Geoffrey bit his lip. This was where Bishop Robert should have begun his new cathedral. It was certainly the obvious place. Gossip in St. Lô, in Vire, in Mortain had spoken of it. It would have been foolish to expect gleaming roofs or soaring towers, but, surely . . . something! It was ghostly. Geoffrey's flush of embarrassment was replaced by a chill of dread. Bushes swayed like spectres in the wind-spun drizzle.

Ivo and the grooms waited silently a short distance behind him. The donkeys stood like statues, their hooves barely rippling the puddles.

Geoffrey grimaced in bafflement. This was impossible. He would have to do something. He kicked his mount forward, and began peering down, not quite sure what he was looking for.

After only a few paces, he heard a horseshoe ring on stone. Afraid of a stumble – or rather afraid of the loss of dignity in a fall – he dismounted, tied the reins to a bare, tremulous sapling, and proceeded on foot.

He soon found a regular line of half-buried masonry, then an angle, then another – and another. The minute he knew what he was looking for, he began to see – discolourations, lines, patterns, repetitions. Within minutes he had located the base of the two western towers and the main doorway. Then came the nave. Geoffrey hastened from side to side, peering, checking, and pacing, his awe deepening with each traverse. It was vast.

Was there a transept? Yes – there were the jagged remains of granite blocks, set in the tussocks of wild grass like broken teeth in a dotard's gum. Geoffrey could sense the great arms of the transept cross stretched out as would the arms of a priest at ordination.

There was one surprise – a well. Not covered with any great care either. A less cautious explorer could have fallen in. Then, on reflection, perhaps not such a surprise. Geoffrey had seen more than one church built over a pagan well or a sacred grove. It made things easier in a way. The spot was already hallowed ground; God did not have to work so hard to keep Satan away, and people felt safe and familiar in its precincts.

What was harder to decide was whether this 'cathedral' could be described as in any way 'built'. Geoffrey returned to the western doorway and looked down the nave. Now that he had seen the vestiges of it at close quarters, he could stand back, as it were, and see the whole building; the gaps, the tufts of grass, the variations of colour, the lumps and clusters – all now meant something. But what? Was he gazing on the past or on the future? Was this a cathedral in the grave or in the womb?

He remembered his predecessor, Bishop Robert. There had been talk for years of a new cathedral church. Surely it could not have been all lies. Geoffrey had seen the quarries busy near Montjoie, the wagons straining under the loads of granite as the drivers goaded the stumbling oxen towards the setting sun.

So where had it all gone?

Suddenly Geoffrey tensed, flung back his head, and turned round so quickly that Ivo leaned forward in his saddle expecting an order.

Geoffrey strode back to the town square to confirm what he now already knew. Peering through the flapping blankets of drizzle, he saw them again – the sills, the cornerstones, the gate-blocks, the troughs, the paving at thresholds. The town – the 'city', so called – had devoured its own cathedral . . .

'But why me? And at my age.'

'Because the Duke is running out of kinsmen. Lisieux goes to his second cousin Hugh – and he is barely older than yourself. Bayeux goes to his brother. Odo, incidentally, is thirteen. So much for considerations of age. The very fact that you protest your age means that you know it is not important. Never has been.'

'The Duke knows nothing about me.'

'He does now. I must hand it to Gori; I never thought all that Latin and law and reading and writing would be much use to you. Frankly I only allowed it in deference to Mother's dying wishes. Gori may be a half-tonsured lecher with a devilish tongue, but he is a scholar, and he has taught you well. It seems he has been proved right. All I had to do was tell the truth about you. The Duke was most impressed.'

'So Gori was in on this too?'

'The understanding and the advice were his; the decision was mine.'

Geoffrey fumed – not only with present rage, but with sudden pent-up fury at the memory: of all those bouts of frustration, all those wonderings at the point of it all; those struggles between his instinctive love of learning and his growing mannish spirit that whispered in his ear that it was soft and maidenly; all the fights he had had with bailey louts who had teased him with 'little priest' jibes. It was some time before he realised that Mauger was talking to him again.

'Geoffrey . . . Geoffrey! Listen to me. The Duke does not want saints; he wants good vassals. After this rebellion he wants men he can trust and rely on. He wants men who can govern. Yes, and fight if need be. Believe me, you will find scope for every one of your many gifts.'

Geoffrey sneered.

'Good vassals? It took you long enough to make up your mind.'

Mauger was not put out.

'In politics it is more often a matter of timing. That is something you will come to appreciate.'

'What you mean by timing is waiting to see which way the cat has jumped.'

Mauger refused to be annoyed.

'If you want to put it like that, so be it. But the realities are still there. What Thierry found out has been confirmed by my own travels and enquiries. The Duke is established. Maybe not secure yet, but established. He feels at any rate safe enough to start reaching out from Upper Normandy into Lower. Cousin

Hugh comes into Lisieux. Brother Odo in Bayeux. Now this building at Caen. Is it surprising that he seeks good men in the west?'

'He accepted your offer because nobody else was willing to take on a wilderness. You paid good money for something nobody else wanted.'

'It is true – the figure was tempting. The Duke could not afford to price himself out of the market. But then I did not have unlimited funds. Your portion was generous, but it was not princely. Our requirements fitted exactly. The Duke needs a good, vigorous man in the Cotentin; I have a worthy brother who badly needs a position. I know a bargain when I see one. Who cares what it is that is being sold?'

'A ruin, that is what is being sold. At least the Duke is building at Caen. What is there at Coutances? Nothing.'

'How do you know?'

'How do *you* know? Have you been there?'

'Not for several years, no.'

'There you are then. The stupidest villein in a market examines the merchandise before he parts with a sou.'

The last of the apple disappeared off the blade.

'I have not seen Coutances recently, no. I have not seen Rome either – ever. But if someone offered it at a price I could afford, I should buy it. As a sound investment. I regard Coutances as a sound investment. And, strange as it may seem, I regard you as a sound investment. So too, apparently, does the Duke.'

'I am sure his Grace is most grateful.'

'So too am I.'

'How very touching. Did anybody in this exchange of compliments and civilities stop to ask if the supposed beneficiary was likely to be grateful?'

'You will be, you will be – in time.'

'You are not grateful,' said Geoffrey. 'You are relieved. Brother Geoffrey is off your hands, and brave Sir Mauger of Montbrai has become boon companion to the Duke as his father Sir Nigel was an alleged boon companion of the late Duke Robert. Off together on a pilgrimage soon, are we?'

Mauger flushed. He hurled the apple core savagely on to the rushes below.

'I have suffered your sullenness and sarcasm for the last time. Yes, I have made my peace with the Duke. What is so very wrong with that? Would you prefer me to be a rootless failed conspirator like Guy of Burgundy? Or a wandering adventurer like Torf? Or a breeder of soulless mercenaries like my lord Tancred? And what if I do despise the Hautevilles? You seem to despise enough people, including me.' He wiped the blade of his dagger. 'My conscience is clear. I have held my inheritance and made the most of it. I have been faithful to Mother's memory in your upbringing, and now I have provided for you in a way that could well exceed your wildest expectations . . . Oh, come on, Geoffrey. I am your brother.' He made a vague, twirling gesture with the knife. 'All it needs is a little – a little flexibility of mind . . . '

Ivo hammered on the door with the hilt of his dagger.

'In the Duke's name!'

After various scuffles and whispers, a reedy voice quavered through a crack in the timbers.

'This is a house of God. If you swear that you come in peace, you will be welcome.'

Ivo lost his temper.

'Of course we do, you old fool. Look at us. Look at the weather. Do we look like an invading army?'

'That is no pilgrim's staff in your hand,' came the high-pitched answer. There was not much wrong with his eyesight.

'Sheathe your weapon, my son. I must remind you that it is Thursday, and the Truce of God prevails – as decreed by the holy Council of Caen in the year of Our Lord, 1047 – on pain of your immortal soul.'

'God's Teeth, open the door!' roared Ivo. 'Before I send the donkeys to bring up the siege train.'

The irony was lost on those inside. More whisperings ensued.

Geoffrey pushed Ivo aside.

'If you will not open in the name of your Duke, then open in the name of – of your Bishop.'

The problem now was simply one of shelter and food, not unfamiliar episcopal authority. They had to get indoors.

The whisperings stopped. Finally a younger voice said, 'Who are you?'

Geoffrey swallowed, but drew himself up to his full height. He took no notice of the rain falling on his dark face.

'I am Geoffrey de Montbrai, Lord Bishop of Coutances.'

He swallowed again. There. Now it was out.

A frenzy of activity took place behind the door. When it was finally swung open, a small forest of craning necks greeted them. Candle flames guttered in the draught. A smell of woodsmoke and stale straw hit their nostrils.

Five figures in clerical habits stood in a row. Behind and around clustered and squatted a small congregation of servants and domestic animals, eyes and ears sharp in anticipation.

The central figure of the five tottered forward. Wisps of wayward white hairs blew round his dome of a tonsure. His mouth hung open, revealing two or three lonely black teeth. The skin on his shaky hands glowed white and blue. His habit, stained with a hundred spilt drinks, hung from his shoulders like skins in a tanner's yard.

One would have been tempted to laugh had it not been for the look on the old man's face. So intense was the fire of hope in his eyes that Geoffrey felt a twinge of sadness that there was nothing he had brought, to his knowledge, which could possibly assuage such a desire.

The old man singled out Geoffrey as the tallest and most impressive, and shuffled to a halt in front of him, swaying slightly.

'You would not deceive an old man, my lord?'

Geoffrey shook his head.

'I am indeed Geoffrey de Montbrai, as I said.' He cleared his throat. 'Bishop of Coutances.'

The old man shut his eyes in ecstasy, and swayed so much that Geoffrey thought for a moment that he was going to collapse.

At last the eyes opened again, and looked at him. Geoffrey was not sure what to do next.

He felt a nudge from Ivo. Looking down, he saw Ivo gesture towards his hand. Ah!

He pushed out his hand, on one finger of which sat a small ring which Mauger had given him from their mother's jewels. Hardly the opulence of a prince of the Church, but the old man seized it as if it had been a relic from the tomb of St. Peter himself.

Not only did he clasp it in both hands; he was down on his knees and kissing it before Geoffrey could pull it away. Then followed an embarrassing scuffle while the other four figures in clerical dress rushed forward, helped the old man to his feet, and performed their own obeisances.

Nor was that the end of it. Under the old man's excited, wheezy instructions, every other human creature there did the same. Geoffrey felt violated; never before had his body been subjected to such varied intimate human contact in such a short time. Furtively he wiped the saliva of a score of eager lips on the inside of his cloak.

Holy Mother! Was this the shape of things to come . . .?'

?

'You should see it. You should just see it!'

Geoffrey ran his hand through his hair.

'There is no cathedral, no official residence. There is no altar, no crozier, no money. No property, no income.'

'They must live on something,' said Mauger with his mouth full.

Geoffrey gestured impatiently.

'Oh, a few acres, to provide food. They huddle together in one great barn like chickens cowering from the fox. There are supposed to be tolls at the bridge, but nobody collects them, because there is no bridge, and nobody ever goes there.'

'I am sure you exaggerate,' said Mauger, pulling out a piece of rind, and scraping off the fat with his front teeth.

'I have not told you the half of it. There are no books, no vestments, no ornaments, no relics. There is not even an episcopal ring. Robert took his ring with him to the grave, and I have nothing but Mother's little garnet. It barely fits on my little finger.'

Without taking his eyes off Geoffrey, Mauger held the rind under the table for the dog to gulp. He felt the familiar wetness of its tongue in his palm.

'Are you ashamed of it?'

'No,' said Geoffrey. 'I should rather die than part with it. But it does not befit a bishop. It is like a new king wearing his chamberlain's cast-off boots. Look at the great stone the Bishop Yves wears at Sées.'

'Yves de Bellême is a wealthy man and head of a powerful family. I have done the best I can for you. You are a bishop too.'

'Bishop of nothing! Those creatures have pulled down the whole cathedral that Robert had started. Nothing remains above ground. They scrape mud off their feet on the edge of stones that came from a tower, an apse, an altar. There is not a priest for miles. I have seen charms over doors and signs carved on trees that come straight out of Viking folk tales. The old gods are returning from the sea just as the Vikings raided in the old days. You can sense it like a chill on the back of your neck. They mutter spells and incantations under their breath.'

'So do all peasants.'

'Yes. But these do not care who hears them. There are no priests to apologise to.'

'There are five canons there; you told me so yourself.'

Geoffrey sneered.

'One trembling dotard, Thorold, who calls himself the archdeacon. His two sons – sons, mark you – Peter and Walter. There are two grandsons as well. So much for clerical celibacy.'

'You sound like the new Pope. Since when did the sins of the flesh shock you?'

Geoffrey leaned his hands on the trestle table in front of his brother.

'Mauger, please, I beg you – do not force me into this.'

Mauger wiped his fingers on the tops of his thighs and looked up.

'Let this cup pass from you, as you might say?' He drank some wine. 'I must say it is flattering to be in the same position as the Almighty.'

He drank again, swallowed noisily, and ran his tongue across the front of his teeth.

'However – if He will pardon the blasphemy – God knew what was best for His Son, and I know what is best for my brother.'

'I am the rightful judge of that. My best chance is now with Serlo.'

'That shows only what a bad judge you are. Geoffrey, they are wild, all of them, bandits and robbers to a man. How a respectable knight like Tancred could have fathered such a brood is beyond me. The Devil must have got between them under the blanket.'

'They are making their fortunes in Italy.'

'Do not believe all the stories. And whether they are true or not,' said Mauger, beginning to enjoy his self-righteous role, 'the Montbrais will not descend to brigandage.'

No, but they would have condoned rebellion if William had lost at Val-ès-Dunes, and his successors had been bidding for support with fresh lands.

Poor Mauger! He was so transparent. The success of the Hautevilles had eaten away at him for years, and now he was able to get one back at them. They might boast of vulgar riches gathered in armfuls from Byzantine altars and Saracen mosques in Apulia and Calabria, but they would never have a bishop among them. Denied the riches, Mauger could sneer at them from the vantage point of the new status conferred upon his younger brother. Geoffrey found himself smiling.

'Besides,' continued Mauger, 'Italy is far more wild than Western Normandy. At least in Coutances you will have no rivals.'

'I am not surprised,' said Geoffrey. 'The Vikings created a wilderness. No bishop has lived there since the last century.'

'How did Robert build his cathedral?'

'He only started it. And he lived at St.Lô, not Coutances.'

'Perhaps if he had, he would have finished it.'

Geoffrey held up both his palms towards his brother. He forced his voice down to a quiet, steady level.

'Mauger, listen. Forget the Hautevilles for a moment, and please try to understand. It is a void. It is nothing. You can not steal a march on people with nothing. It is a pagan emptiness. Nobody with any choice would dream of living there.'

'Those five canons do.'

Geoffrey pictured Thorold in his mind, as the old man devoutly recited the names of the previous incumbents.

'. . . Bishop Robert chose, alas! to live at St. Lô. Perhaps he found the regular travelling difficult. Before him was Bishop Herbert the Second, who was not

61

spared long by the Almighty. And before him came my lord Bishop Hugh, but God did not see fit to give him the occasion to make the trip from Rouen. It seems he was a bad traveller, as he used to inform us in his pastoral letter. Very few pastoral letters reached us, sadly, owing to the unsettled nature of the times . . .'

And so it had gone on. Thorold's memory seemed inexhaustible. Through his wearisome chronicle, there shone a touching innocence and devotion. Helpless to prevent the looting of the cathedral masonry; powerless to oppose neighbouring knights who nibbled away at outlying episcopal estates until there was almost nothing left; cowering before the fumes of paganism that rose from the surrounding swamp of desolation and neglect; huddled in their lonely refuge, they had tended the last candle-flame of Christianity with a sincerity that was totally un-self-conscious.

Geoffrey found himself voicing the thought he had had then.

'It is a miracle they have survived.'

'Ah!' said Mauger. 'So God is there.'

'God may be, Mauger, but He needs saints for company, not me.'

'It is what the Duke needs that matters. Order. God will go along with that for the time being. First things first. God understands things like that.'

Mauger leaned over the table.

'Think, Geoffrey, think. Forget your own anger for a moment. Never mind whether I despise the Hautevilles or not. Consider this Duke of ours. A young man who has shown us his mettle at Val-ès-Dunes and put down his first serious rebellion. He must now show the world that he can hold as well as win. He must watch the devil in Anjou, have an eye to the mischief in Brittany, secure the south around Domfront and Alençon, control the house of Bellême, guard against the King in the Vexin, hold the line of the Epte, keep order in Rouen, cock a glance at Ponthieu and Flanders – and he can not be everywhere. He needs good men. Not saints, but rulers, fighters if need be. Serve him well, and he will lead you well. I have met him, remember. Believe me, he is exceptional.'

When Geoffrey said nothing, Mauger pressed home his argument.

'You said you wanted a cause, something to work for. Well, now you have it.'

'I meant Sybil and Italy.'

Mauger spoke quietly.

'Perhaps God in His wisdom has come up with something else. I feel that He has. So does Gori.'

Geoffrey looked up.

'I am the one who has been made a bishop. Why is it that God is speaking to everyone else except me?'

'Geoffrey, it is the Duke who has placed his trust in you.'

'Because he needs the money.'

'Nevertheless, he has done it. Do you realise that you are now a prince of the Holy Church? I have often thought that you had it in you to rise higher than I. Now, the possibilities are limitless.'

Geoffrey was still unmoved.

'Tell me this. If you can descend from this heaven of ecstasy about the brilliance of your achievement, can you answer me this question? So far as I can gather from your breathless advocacy, Mother Church does not mind about its bishops being warriors, knights, rulers, administrators, lechers, sycophants, rulers' relatives, or beardless boys. But I seem to remember hearing something somewhere about its setting a little store by their being priests.'

Mauger laughed.

'You left one off the list. Bastards. The Duke's uncle. If my lord the Archbishop of Rouen is prepared to consecrate you as bishop, I should think having you ordained priest beforehand will be child's play. Besides, you are better educated than half the priests we have already.'

Geoffrey wiped his brow, and spoke half to himself.

'To buy a bishopric – like a – like a fine fur in a fair. I feel like a sort of clerical harlot.'

'The Duke is the one who has done the selling, not you. And I can assure you that he expects a good return on the transaction. Do not be so damned right-eous. Anyone would think you were the first one to have a bishop's mitre bought for him. Do not play the innocent; men have tried to buy the Papacy before now.'

Geoffrey tossed his head in exasperation.

'But we have not examined the merchandise.'

'Neither has the Duke.'

'So nobody knows what he is getting.'

'Absolutely true. Just like marriage. You are no worse off than you would have been with Sybil.'

A thought struck Geoffrey.

'What proof do you have of all this? How do I know that you have not pledged my money elsewhere?'

Mauger patted a saddlebag.

'I have the seals. You can examine them any time you like. Take it from me, brother, you are now his Grace the Bishop of Coutances.'

Geoffrey looked directly at his brother.

'And how do I face a dying man and try to save his soul?'

'Learn. Just as you learned to read and write and fight.'

'I will not do it.'

Mauger stood up, and frugally pinched out one of the candles.

'You will obey. You may in your error have thought it was your fortune to go looting churches in Apulia with the Hautevilles, or scavenging in Germany with Flemish mercenaries, or cutting Moorish throats in Navarre, but it is clearly not, and the sooner you understand that the better. You will obey me, and you will obey the dying wishes of your Mother, to whom I swore a sacred oath that I would provide in the best way I knew how. Moreover you will obey your Duke, and most important of all you will obey what is unmistakably the Will of God.'

And, did you but know it, you will ease the torment of the soul of your father.

Geoffrey spread his hands in a wide gesture of futility.

'I can only say I hope God knows what He is letting Himself in for. It is a wilderness. There is nothing there. On top of that hill, the wind blows in from the great western sea that stretches for ever. Mauger, it is the end of all the world.'

Mauger hitched up his belt.

'Then, brother, the end of all the world is what you have, by God's Grace, and it is all you have. I suggest you make the most of it.'

*   *   *   *   *   *

Chapter Five

'No, Geoffrey, not again. Not now.'

Sybil pushed herself away from him, and turned over.

Geoffrey leaned after her.

'Nobody will find us here. Not even your precious washing women know where we are. And as for your brothers – '

'No, Geoffrey. It is not that.'

Geoffrey put a hand on her shoulder.

'I did not – I did not hurt you, did I?'

Sybil shook her head.

'Not in the way you are thinking, no.'

'Well then, what is it?'

'We must talk.'

Sybil turned back and looked directly at him. The intense blue eyes commanded attention. Geoffrey saw that she would have her mother's authority when she grew older. He swallowed.

'Talk?'

'Yes. About what you are going to do.'

'Oh, that.'

'Yes, that.'

Geoffrey swallowed again.

'I told you. After Rouen, I shall go – '

'So you are going through with it?'

'What choice do I have? My money is gone. I am pledged to the Duke. If I go back on it, your father and mother will never let you go to a renegade.'

'You want them to let me go to a penniless bishop.'

'Not for long. Rheims, Sybil. All I ask is that you wait until the Council of Rheims. There I shall make my case, and Mauger will not be able to stop me.'

'It is not Mauger I am worrying about.'

'Sybil, an oath under duress is not valid. Neither is a consecration. The Duke knows that as well anyone else. Not even he can stop the law taking its course.'

'Nor is it the Duke that I am fearful for.'

Geoffrey frowned.

'Well then?'

Sybil shook him gently by the shoulders.

'It is you and I. We are the ones I worry about. Geoffrey, have you any idea what a Church Council is like?'

'No. Have you?'

'I have heard. If only half the stories are true . . . Geoffrey, you will have to meet the Pope himself. You will have to face Father Hildebrand; they say he can make men soil themselves by merely looking at them. These men are not castle priests like Father Gregory, correcting your Latin verbs and holding your hand through kitchen passages in the dark. These are men of power; they can hurl anathema and excommunication as a prince scatters silver coins to beggars.'

'I am offering them the very thing they want – to return a bishopric that was procured for money, and, what is more, procured without the knowledge, or the consent, of its holder. Are they not publicly dedicated to the rooting out of simony?'

Sybil put a hand on his cheek.

'You say that now, my love. But can you say it to Hildebrand's face?'

Geoffrey took her hand and kissed it.

'Yes, I can. And I shall tell you why. Because anger shall come to my aid. When I think of how I was deceived, I could face the Devil himself.'

'That is also what makes me afraid. I think that Hildebrand will notice the difference.'

Geoffrey frowned.

'I do not follow.'

'My love, are you sure about your motives? Is it the bishopric that enrages you, or the mere manner in which you came by it? Are you truly humbled by this new position, or just put out?'

'I was deceived, and any man has a right to be enraged by deceit. My money was due to me, and it has been taken away, for some idiotic scheme of my brother's. I have been simply tidied up and pushed aside; I have been seen to, provided for, just – just like a – '

' – just like a woman?'

'That is different.'

'Not at all. Women are being provided for all the time. The affront is just as great to our dignity.'

Geoffrey sidestepped.

'Well, I intend to do something about it.'

'You are lucky to be in a position to. Most women are not.'

'I must take what opportunities there are. I should be a fool if I let this go.'

'Very well. Suppose you do. Suppose you go to Rheims. Suppose you outface Hildebrand and Pope Leo. And suppose the Council decides against you after all. What then? You will not be the first simoniac bishop in Christendom. I am told men have bought the Papacy itself before now.'

Geoffrey shook his head.

'That is all speculation.'

'But suppose,' insisted Sybil.

'Very well. If I am to remain a bishop, then I am to be known as a bishop. There is nothing to force me to perform the duties of one. You can lead a horse to water . . . I shall still marry you. That is what we both want – in the end.'

'And if the Pope excommunicates you for marrying?'

Geoffrey laughed.

'Sybil, you have been listening to your washing women again. It is one thing for Hildebrand to mount a campaign against simony. It is common enough, but I suppose, with the co-operation of lay princes, he might make some progress in that direction. But to try and stop clerical marriage – it is ridiculous. You might as well try and ban spitting or making water.'

Sybil focused her steady eyes on him again.

'Would you face excommunication for me?'

'Why are you trying to drive me into a corner? You know I love you. You know that I would do anything, go anywhere for you. Only say the word, and we could find a way of going to Italy with Serlo, and face the wrath of your mother and father when we came back. Whatever happens at Rouen or Rheims, you must know that you are my first concern. No matter what comes out of this, I give you my solemn word that you will be provided for.'

Geoffrey could have bitten off his tongue.

*　　*　　*　　*　　*　　*

It was all over. Geoffrey heaved a huge sigh of relief. The episcopal robes seemed to weigh more than three coats of mail. His hand sweated where it had been clasping the crozier too tightly for too long. The mitre – saints be praised – remained in position, but his knees still trembled.

On his right, the new Bishop of Lisieux blew out his cheeks and raised his eyes in silent prayer of gratitude. He could not be much older than Geoffrey. He had a fresh, open-air, cheerful face that would have been more at home in a mail coif on patrol, or calling up the beaters on a boar-chase. He looked at Geoffrey and grinned. Hugh, son of William Count of Eu, and second cousin to the Duke, carried his nobility easily.

On Geoffrey's left, young Odo of Conteville, the new Bishop of Bayeux, and half-brother to the Duke, had no gift whatever for any kind of grace. Thin, spotty, with a ridiculously small head, he stuck out of his specially-tailored robes like a scarecrow.

What a contrast to the compact, dynamic Duke William.

However, Geoffrey was spared the further ordeal of meeting his Duke. Just as the time was drawing nearer for the feudal oath of homage, a young knight of about his own age pushed his way towards William and whispered in his ear.

Sir Baldwin de Clair, another ducal kinsman. Mauger had pointed him out. After his recent trip to the ducal court, Mauger enjoyed posing as the knowledgeable expert on matters of high state.

'Baldwin's father was one of the Duke's guardians when the Duke was a boy. When he was murdered by rebels, young Baldwin was smuggled out to Flanders. Now he has returned. He will give hands soon for a fief, so they say.'

Geoffrey liked the look of him.

The Duke, having heard Baldwin's news, hastily left the cathedral, pausing only to exchange a few words with Sir William Fitzosbern.

Fitzosbern called for attention.

'Urgent news has come. The siege of the rebel Guy of Burgundy has undergone a sudden change, and there is a distinct likelihood that it is about to be resolved. The Duke leaves at once for Brionne. Arrangements will be made for the new bishops to give hands after the siege is over. Meantime, the presentation and the consecration feast are to continue as planned. These are my lord Duke's instructions. If my lord archbishop would be pleased to continue . . . Sir Roger? Sir Walter?'

Sir Roger of Montgomery and Sir Walter Giffard followed Fitzosbern.

The Archbishop of Rouen, the Duke's bastard uncle, resumed his leadership of the procession, and together the three newly-consecrated bishops of Lisieux, Coutances, and Bayeux made their way through the great western doors. Together they stood on the steps outside, beneath the half-built towers, as the Archbishop presented them one by one to the populace. They bowed self-consciously to the applause.

Geoffrey's thoughts tugged away to what Sybil would be thinking. If he had been recounting this to someone as a dream, he would have sworn that he saw Sybil standing a short distance away, holding her arms out to him as a sudden chasm gaped in the earth between them.

He glanced at the expensive robes on either side of him – clear evidence that the Duke's treasury had been, for once, generous. But Mauger had not let him down. Although he had grumbled fearfully, he had come up with a set of robes that Geoffrey could wear with pride.

'It would not do,' said Mauger grimly, 'for the noble and ancient House of Montbrai to be shown up as paupers.'

Geoffrey straightened his shoulders. Coutances could take its place easily with Bayeux and Lisieux.

'You put the fear of God into me,' said Ivo later at the consecration feast. 'From where I stood at the foot of the steps, you looked enormous. And so solemn!'

Ivo held out a pitcher.

'Here, sir – have another. Sorry – my lord.'

They looked at each other and laughed.

'We shall both have to get used to it,' said Ivo.

'We shall see about that.'

Geoffrey drank and wiped his mouth.

'Seriously, Ivo, did I look like a bishop?'

Ivo drew himself up.

'Master Geoffrey, you looked magnificent. Better than the other two put together. We were all very proud of you. So would your father have been if he had been here to see you – God rest his soul.'

'Amen,' said Mauger.

*   *   *   *   *   *

'What do you think of him?'

'Mother, that is an impossible question, and you know it.'

'He deserves some kind of an answer.'

'The only answer he will get is a formal one, and therefore a meaningless one.'

The lady Fressenda gave her needle to one of the girls for a new thread to be inserted.

'You must have some opinion, if only for my ears. I saw you blush in his company. At least you reacted.'

'I did nothing of the kind. The fire was high, that was all.'

The lady Fressenda took back the needle without looking at the girl. It was unlike Sybil to fall back on weak excuses. It was also unlike her not to be complete mistress of the situation.

'He pronounced himself very taken with you. Your father and I were overwhelmed with his compliments.'

'That hardly surprises me. He has a tongue like a sorcerer.'

Then if she saw through him, why was she so disturbed?

'He said nothing derogatory towards Geoffrey; that surely shows great magnanimity.'

'That is one way of looking at it. Did it occur to you that his timing is faultless in coming here the moment he knows Geoffrey has gone and will not be back for several weeks?'

'There is no harm in a suitor being well-informed.'

'Too well-informed. Mother, he knows things he has no business to know. It makes you wonder how he came by his information.'

'He spoke no ill of anyone.'

'He did not need to. He left you to come to your own conclusion – and the

69

way he told you things there was only one conclusion to come to.'

'Explain yourself.'

'Mother, think back. He never said anything ill, I grant you. No detail that you could positively identify and remember. But consider not the sound of his words, but the taste, or rather the smell. Ask yourself in all honesty, since talking to him, do you think better or worse of Geoffrey and his brother?'

The lady Fressenda paused to think, but she would admit nothing.

'Be that as it may, Torf has a lot to offer, and Geoffrey has nothing.'

'Except a bishopric.'

'Which is worse than useless to you. A mitre will not put a roof over your head. A crozier will not feed you regularly. A mass a day will convey no status on you.'

'I love him. I do not love Torf.'

'Love has nothing to do with it. Land has. I am talking about status, legal position, security. What else do women have in life if they do not have that?'

'Geoffrey loves me. He will marry me. Mother, I know.'

The lady Fressenda came very near to a fond smile.

'I believe you, child. But such a decision may not be within his power.'

'Then he will provide for me.' Sybil lowered her head. 'Provide for me.'

'Sybil, try to understand me. I do not doubt you or Geoffrey. I know only about the world. Whatever your love, whatever your loyalty to each other, there can be no bond without a marriage, and no security. If anything should happen to Geoffrey, or if he should change – and people can – you are in a hopeless position. A widowed mistress or a cast-off mistress has no more rights when her man dies than a cast-off leaf when a summer dies.'

Sybil looked up again.

'What are you asking me to do – reject him before he has a chance to prove his promises?'

'No. I ask only that you keep an open mind. Remember that life is a long business. Father and I will not always be here. And I am sure that you would not wish to become an attached aunt in the household of one of your brothers.'

Sybil glared, and her mother knew that the shaft had gone home. Wisely, she immediately softened her voice.

'Sybil, I know what it is to be young. The call of the body is very strong.'

Sybil leaned forward intently.

'Mother, it is more than that with Geoffrey. For the first time in my life, I do not feel un-private with somebody. I can talk to him about anything. He is the first young man I have met who assumes that I have a mind.'

'Is it your mind that he makes love to?' asked the lady Fressenda drily.

'That is different.'

'Nonsense. It is the same as it has always been. I do not doubt Geoffrey's sincerity, and I do not doubt yours. But life's decisions get made by more things than sincerity; they get made by circumstances. And the more we can put ourselves in harmony with circumstances, the more secure we are likely to be. Give this Torf a chance. He can court you just as well as Geoffrey if you will only let him. He is moreover unusual. There is something about him that is attractive to women. Even at my age, I have noticed it, and he is not courting me.'

Oh, yes he is. Torf of Malbec bore two organs of seduction around with him – one between his thighs and one in his mouth. In spite of her dislike of him, Sybil could feel both attracted to him, and at the same time annoyed by him. Annoyed by his insidious confidence in his own ability to charm. She had no wish to be caught like the rabbit by the snake.

The lady Fressenda bit off a thread.

'A woman may not have as many options as a man, but she has options nevertheless, and she must exercise them wisely. God may be responsible for our entry into the Kingdom of Heaven, but we are responsible for our journey through this earthly life, and there are times when we must take conscious decisions to ensure that our journey is as comfortable as possible.'

'I hear you, Mother.'

'Never pass up possible advantages. I tell you, this Torf is unusual. Most men are dead from the ankles up.'

'My reasons exactly for loving Geoffrey.'

'Wait and see – that is all I ask. Keep an open mind. There is nothing to bind you to Geoffrey yet.'

Oh, but there was. Only a suspicion at present. She did not dare to hope; it was too dangerous. But another month and she would know.

*   *   *   *   *   *

Geoffrey waited while Thorold scraped away the encrusted dirt. He shivered. Was it always so windy? Was there never any respite?

The old man peered at the surface of the stone for a moment, then stepped back and held out an open hand.

'Read for yourself, my lord.'

Geoffrey leaned over and read.

' "This stone was laid by . . . " It is too faint.'

Thorold stepped up beside him and traced the lettering with a black-grained finger.

' " . . . laid by the Duchess Gunnor, wife of Duke Richard the Fearless of immortal memory." '

'That must be over fifty years ago,' said Geoffrey.

'No, my lord. It was some considerable time after the death of the late Duke. The lady Gunnor outlived him by many years.'

'Still a long time.'

Thorold inclined his head by way of agreement. White hairs waved violently in the wind.

'Indeed, my lord.'

'Tell me,' said Geoffrey, 'why is the stone engraved on its top surface? Surely other courses would have been laid to cover it?'

'They would, my lord. Alas! I have to report that in the many years of depredation, the stone was turned over on its side.'

Geoffrey stared.

'You mean someone tried to steal a consecrated foundation stone?'

'They did, my lord. And a ghastly sacrilege it was to be sure. But God, ever watchful for such behaviour, exacted a fitting punishment for the crime.'

'How do you know?'

Thorold bent down to where the stone's bottom edge was masked by grass. He pulled out one or two tussocks, and stood up again, wheezing gently.

'If my lord will be pleased to bend and look.'

Geoffrey stooped.

It looked like a bone, a human bone, sticking out from underneath.

Thorold answered the question in his eyes.

'It is as you suspect, my lord. The thief was trapped by the object of his own greed. A careless knot, a broken lever, who knows? God punished the evil-doer. So perish all those who oppose Divine Will.'

Thorold pushed his hands into his sleeves and settled his wrinkled features into a grimace of tight-lipped righteousness. So rarely did God appear to take vengeance on sin in his world that he could be forgiven a little satisfaction when it did.

'What happened to the rest of him?' asked Geoffrey.

'My lord?'

'The bone – it has been severed. He does not lie completely under there, does he?'

'No, my lord. It was during the night that he tried to steal it. So when it fell, nobody heard his cries. The wind, you understand. By morning, there was no life in him. We could not leave him like that – the smell, for one thing. There was no point in lifting the stone, merely to scrape . . .'

Thorold shrugged.

'We gave the half of him a Christian burial, which was more than he deserved.'

Geoffrey walked away with his hands on his hips.

The passivity, the hopelessness, the total lack of resources! The bridges were down. The mill wheel had seized up; wives made do with tedious hand querns. There were only two smiths, and one aged wheelwright. No copper was worked. The last tanner had just died. The quarries were closed. There was total absence of spirit among the townsfolk. They avoided his eye. They evaded questions. They hardly spoke even to one another. Like Thorold and his sons and grandsons, they were merely clinging to the wreckage. One more storm, one more raid, one more bad winter – and everything would be swept away.

The cheers and the applause at Rouen now seemed a mocking dream. This – this was the reality. A city of ghouls, a cathedral of rubble. A dying diocese in a pagan wasteland, whose last heartbeat was being nurtured by five lonely clerks, four of whom owed their very existence to the breaking of the clerical vows of devotional chastity.

Thorold had spread his hands.

'I have lived here, my lord, for over seventy years. All that time ago I saw Vikings jump from longships by the shore. While they pillaged and burnt, and since they have ceased to pillage and burn, I have waited for a bishop to come again and rebuild in God's name. This city has had no aid, no comfort, no shepherd. No inspiration, no protection, no rule. No preaching, no sacraments. Would it have been your wish to deny us every consolation?'

'I can not be your only hope,' said Geoffrey. 'Surely there are other lords, other knights, who hope for peace in the next world.'

Thorold shook his head.

'They no longer endow churches; they plunder them. They do not encourage trade; they bleed it. Fields to them are for trampling, not for ploughing. What they need they steal. Poor men are ground to dust between the hammer of bitter greed and the rock of bitter need. You are our only hope.'

Geoffrey sighed. Sybil had been right . . .

'Why are you returning to Coutances, if you do not intend to retain it?'

'Because I owe it to the old man to tell him face to face. I am not the person he has been hoping for.'

'You will tell him that?'

'I shall. And that will be an end of it.'

'I see . . .'

'Surely there must be somebody,' said Geoffrey to Thorold.

Thorold considered.

'We did indeed hope for a short while, when a newcomer came. He spoke softly and often, and honey dripped from his promises. He would protect, and he would rebuild –oh, yes. The cathedral, the town, the bridge, the aqueduct.'

'What happened?'

'Nothing. We paid him what little we had left. After all, he said, it could not be done without money. He said he knew the best masons. Alas!'

Thorold lifted his whole scrawny body in a shrug.

'Who is this seller of lies?'

'His name is Torf. From Malbec, to the north.'

*　　*　　*　　*　　*　　*

'Geoffrey de Montbrai, who is styled Bishop of Coutances. You will please rise.'

The voice was weak, barely audible in that vast concourse of prelates. The thick Italian accent made the words even harder to understand.

Geoffrey stood up.

The dark, squat figure came and stood before him, bunched in its black habit. A document was held impressively at arm's length. The face was covered in the blue shadow of a bad shave almost up to the eyes. Black hair sprouted from nostrils. Thick hair grew on the wrists that protruded from the wide black sleeves.

He made a show of reading carefully from the document, but he was clearly familiar with the words.

'You, Geoffrey de Montbrai, are summoned to and required by this Apostolic Council of Rheims, assembled on the express authority of our Holy Father Pope Leo IX here present, to give a full explanation and justification why you purport to hold the diocese of Coutances, of the archdiocese of Rouen, not by free canonical election but by simoniacal purchase, which is contrary to the ordinances and decrees of our Holy Catholic Church. How do you reply to the charge of simony?'

The head lifted. Geoffrey had heard men speak of sub-deacon Hildebrand's eyes, but he was still not prepared for the flame that burned there. What consuming desire, he wondered, lit a blaze like that?

In the silence that followed the statement of the charge, Hildebrand dropped his arm, turned, and tossed the paper he had been holding on to the table. He turned back to Geoffrey, stared, and said one word.

'Simony!'

In the deep-roofed space of the silent hall, it penetrated to the furthest corner. Its sibilant passion gave to the offence a dimension of unimaginable evil.

Geoffrey returned Hildebrand's gaze, showing more confidence than he felt. Then he looked at Pope Leo, also an impressive figure in his own right. Trust a malign Fate to have him called before the most effective pontiff in years.

The Papacy had in living memory been at the mercy of German Emperors and corrupt Roman nobles. There had been weak popes, sick popes, time-serving popes, juvenile popes, evil popes, libertine popes, antipopes, even simultaneous popes. Now at last there was an honest pope – a German maybe, but a sincere reformer, dedicated by his own public pronouncements to the rooting out of simony, corruption, and clerical marriage, and to establishing the purity of free canonical election of bishops. A much-travelled, energetic pope too, as his presence in Rheims proved. It was rumoured that the King of France was already regretting having allowed this saintly aristocrat to hold his great Council at the mystical seat of French royal power. King Henry had tried bringing pressure to bear on some of his bishops not to attend. Leo had opened proceedings by excommunicating them.

How much of what Leo did was his own idea, and how much of it was Hildebrand's, was a hotly-debated point. Either way their combination of authority, purity, and passion was an awesome prospect.

Geoffrey kept his head. He was not going to get another opportunity like this.

'Holiness, eminences, graces, holy fathers, highnesses, my lords. You must forgive the language of a plain young knight of Normandy. I do not have the skill of the lawyer, nor the subtlety of the theologian – '

But you have the wit and education of a highly personable young man, thought the Prior of Bec, sitting among the assembled abbots.

' – I do not command the correct forms and practices, but my words are, I hope, simple and direct. Firstly, then, I acknowledge freely and completely that the bishopric of Coutances was obtained by the process known as simony. Second, this was not at first known to me. Third, as soon as I found out, I used all my power to try and ensure that my consecration should not go forward. However, since it did, I have endeavoured to fulfil my episcopal duties to the best of my humble ability. I have obeyed your summons to attend this Holy Council, and, if you now, in your wisdom, should direct that my elevation to the rank of bishop is invalid, then I happily lay down the ring and staff of my office. Indeed, I welcome the release.'

He paused. Should he say more?

No. Enough was enough. He sat down. The first thought that filled his mind, though he tried to expel it, was that his mother would have been disappointed in him. But she did not know, he reminded himself. She had not seen.

A rumble of comment ensued. One or two cardinals, stiff from long sitting, crossed the floor, ostensibly for learned consultation, their expensive silk robes billowing and whistling. Clerks peered at long case lists. Hildebrand put his chin on his hand and looked searchingly at Geoffrey.

He was interrupted by the sudden sense of someone standing beside him.

'Father Lanfranc, Prior of Bec.'

'Father Hildebrand, sub-deacon to the Holy See.'

Each inclined the head the smallest degree consonant with courtesy.

Lanfranc came straight to the point.

'I should be grateful for a few private words, which I suggest to you could be to our mutual benefit. Shall we talk in Italian, or shall we go somewhere alone?'

Lanfranc deliberately stressed the Lombard accent, and saw the gleam of recognition in the swarthy deacon's eyes.

Hildebrand gathered up some papers.

'Too many cardinals here with long ears,' he said. With his quiet voice, it was hard to tell whether he meant to be whispering or not. 'Come with me.'

He paused to say something in His Holiness's ear. Leo nodded.

'Hear what he has to say. Lanfranc never makes idle statements. It is near midday. Tell them to adjourn for an hour.'

*　　*　　*　　*　　*　　*

Geoffrey handed to reins to Ivo. While the horses were being watered, he walked up and down to ease his muscles.

'Drink, you stupid beasts, now that you have the chance . . . Have a care! I am not here for a bath . . . Enough,enough; do you wish to swamp your great fat stomachs . . . '

Ivo's never-ending, amiable abuse blew across the ears like a breeze sighing in tall trees; you would notice it only if it stopped.

Geoffrey looked upstream at the small town of Gisors, then up at the weather. Neither looked particularly promising. Clouds were gathering to the west. At best they would have only two more hours of dry riding. They could push on down the road, and the River Epte, to St. Clair, but it was a mean place, for all that it lay on the main road between Paris and Rouen. Geoffrey had made the mistake of stopping there on his way out to Rheims. Its inhabitants paved their yards with stones from the road, and tried to put a surcharge on their prices to pay for what they called 'necessary road improvements'. A group of Flemings on leave from siege duty at Brionne had shown their disapproval by getting drunk and burning down a stable.

Gisors was not much bigger, but prices ought to be lower, as it was off the main road. There was no monastic house, but there should be some knight's holding near the town which could accommodate Geoffrey's party. He was prepared, in extremis, to use his new rank to hasten a favourable decision in the mind of a reluctant host.

He was still a bishop, despite all his efforts. He had not been able to argue with Mauger, and he certainly did not intend to argue with the Pope. And when sub-deacon Hildebrand had stood up after that adjournment and pronounced the Council's verdict, he had found no means of arguing with him either. Was it also the truth that he was glad that he had not had to argue with his mother?

Instead he had sworn at Ivo and the grooms and the horses.

'God's Bread! Why is there this universal conspiracy to set a mitre on my head?'

'Perhaps God thinks it is a good idea,' suggested Ivo, who usually regarded the will of the Almighty as the random decisions of a gruff, demanding, and inscrutable parent.

The welcome from the knight's household was far more fulsome than Geoffrey could have dared hope, but not for any reason that he could have imagined.

'God be praised! A miracle!'

Geoffrey glanced in alarm at Ivo, who shrugged.

Hands tugged at Geoffrey's sleeve.

'Hurry. Please hurry, my lord. There is little time.'

Through the smoke-filled hall. The straw on the floor rustled with dozens of rapid feet. There must have been a score of kneelers round the open curtain of the solar at the end.

Geoffrey hesitated. He had seen crowds like that before. One of his earliest memories was the murmurings of babbled, jostling prayers, the ranks of bowed shoulders, stifling incense, and the stench of soiled bedding. The moanings, the mysterious errands, the unseen mystery within a forest of legs, and not one word of explanation. At the end of it all, a lonely angular shape outlined by a blanket, and a priest with a wart on his cheek who patted him heavily on the head and said, 'My son, your grandfather has departed to the realms of bliss.'

One of the kneelers turned, saw him, and nudged the potboy beside him. A ripple of nudges spread from end to end, and an avenue opened up towards the bed. The gap behind him was sealed off by more of the household, and he was led forward by scores of expectant eyes.

Two braziers glowed at the foot of the bed. Over one hung a small pot of some nameless bubbling mixture. Candles dripped. A mother kneaded one of the invalid's hands; two sisters clawed at the coverlet on the other side. Bird-droppings from the roof stained the blankets. In the shadows stood two pale brothers. One appeared to be on the verge of vomiting; the other let silent tears stream over his cheeks.

Geoffrey felt a nudge at his elbow.

'Please, my lord,' said the knight, 'before it is too late.'

'Yes, of course. Yes. Er – what is the name?'

The face, bound and swathed, was sexless.

'Michael, my lord.'

Geoffrey nodded several times.

'Michael. Yes. Very good.'

He licked his lips.

Holy Virgin!

Ivo coughed.

'Perhaps, my lord, if we were to clear the chamber.'

'What? Oh. Yes. Er – clear the chamber. Yes.'

Father pulled away the wailing sisters. The elder brother leapt at the chance of release, and fled up the hall to the main door. The younger brother, his cheeks gleaming in the candlelight, tenderly lifted his mother to her feet and took her out.

Ivo had the stifling braziers moved back. When the solar was clear, he pulled the curtain. He turned back to Geoffrey and nodded.

Geoffrey looked at the frightened eyes staring up at him from the bed.

He heard his own voice saying to Ivo, 'Get out! Leave us!'

After one short surprised glance, Ivo obeyed. There was a vague communal sigh as he appeared to those out in the hall and turned to draw the curtain again.

Geoffrey came and stood beside the bed.

It was a boy, racked and wasted. He could not have been more than fourteen or fifteen. He was so weak that when he coughed, it seemed as if some spirit gripped him from inside and shook him like a jester's dummy. He was soaked in sweat. He had long since ceased to fight whatever fever it was; it was just a question now of when the fever should choose to come out of him into the air and leave him in the peace of death.

Geoffrey remembered when his sister had fallen out of a tree and broken her ankle. She had stopped crying when he held her hand.

He knelt now, and took one of the boy's hands in his own. It felt so hot that he almost dropped it in shock. He fought down his fear of illness.

'Do not be afraid,' he whispered. 'I am – I am a bishop.'

Hope, second thoughts, incredulity, wariness, fear, followed each other across the boy's face in rapid succession. Geoffrey translated each one.

'No. It is true. I really am a bishop. Confirmed by His Holiness the Pope only last week. On my own soul, I could not lie to you at a time like this.'

Honesty at least. It was all he could think of.

'Shall I – shall stay with you for a while?'

The eyes glowed. A flicker of pressure from the burning hand.

Geoffrey licked his lips.

'Perhaps, if we prayed a little. I could say the "*Ave Maria*" for you. I am sure Our Lady will forgive us our sins.'

*　　*　　*　　*　　*　　*

Chapter Six

At Vernon, on the Seine, they came out of the forest at last, and caught up with a party of monks. Each group, tired of travel and bored with familiar company, was glad to rest and mingle for a while with the other. Each, however, posted a sentry to watch for unwelcome arrivals, whether from Paris or from the Duke's capital at Rouen. There was also the small matter of the siege at Brionne, where the last of the rebels were still holding out. Although it was nearly forty miles distant, deserters or fugitives could easily pass this way.

Geoffrey, remembering his manners, went to pay his respects to the monk who appeared to be in charge. As they advanced to meet, Geoffrey frowned. Where had he seen him before?

'Ah! My lord bishop! A happy meeting. Perhaps we can share part of your return journey to Coutances.'

In answer to Geoffrey's look of surprise, he smiled.

'I apologise. An unfair advantage, but a situation which my legal training and sense of the dramatic made it hard for me to resist. I am Lanfranc, Prior of Bec. You last saw me in the great hall at Rheims.'

Geoffrey remembered. It was difficult for a prior in a black habit to be conspicuous in two whole rows of priors and abbots in black habits, but Lanfranc had managed it. His presence was commanding even in the company of men used to authority.

'Where did you lie last night?' asked Geoffrey. 'We did not see you at Gisors.'

'We were at Gisors two nights ago,' replied Lanfranc. 'I am afraid we can not travel as fast as yourselves.'

He indicated the motley of ponies, mules, and donkeys who nuzzled and munched at undergrowth at the edge of the Vernon Forest through which they had just passed.

'Did you rest well?' asked Lanfranc politely.

Geoffrey thought of the fetid air in the solar, the hours of vigil – mercifully, for both of them, not many – the embarrassing gratitude of the family – for what? – the pathetic attempt afterwards at cheerful hospitality, the brave farewells.

'It was good enough.'

No wonder they had ridden twenty miles that day; anything to get away. He allowed a sigh to escape him.

'There was trouble?' asked Lanfranc.

Geoffrey winced slightly.

'Illness,' he said. 'A boy was ill.'

'Dying?'

'Yes, dying.'

Geoffrey suddenly felt tired.

'And I could do nothing. I knew nothing.'

'You were not there as a doctor,' said Lanfranc.

'No. It was what they expected me to do for his soul. There! There lay the shame.'

'Did you not try?'

Geoffrey grunted in disgust.

'It was pitiful. I had no oil, no missal, nothing. And I should not have known what to do if I had.'

'But you did something.'

'I held his hand, yes. And we said some prayers. Or rather I did, and he watched me.'

'Did he understand?'

'Oh, yes. I think he liked the "*Aves*" and "*Paternosters*". We said enough of them. I did not know any others.'

'So he died at peace?'

'Yes,' admitted Geoffrey, as he recalled the scene with a twinge of surprise. 'Yes. I think he did. There was no more fear on his face. There was a smile there when – afterwards.'

'Then you did well.'

'I did nothing of the sort. It was a travesty. I blush at my own inadequacy. I am no bishop.'

'On the contrary. You held a sick boy's hand and calmed his fears and took him happily to meet his God. Many a trained and experienced prince of the Church would have done less. Yet you did it from natural wit and charity. You have no cause for shame.'

Geoffrey cursed.

'Devil take the Council of Rheims.'

Lanfranc allowed a smile to enter his eyes.

'Spend the night with us. I have lodging arranged just beyond Vernon.'

'So that you can preach to me?' said Geoffrey, who instantly regretted his own childish response.

No trace of annoyance showed on Lanfranc's steady face.

'No,' he said. 'So that I may get to know you better. I find you an interesting person. I wish to ascertain whether my interest in you is well placed.'

The answer caught Geoffrey off balance.

'Um – '

'You must be tired after – after all that has befallen, and I do have lodging arranged, as I said. At least be practical.'

Geoffrey smiled a trifle sheepishly.

'Then, to be practical, are you sure they can accommodate all of us?'

He waved a hand towards Ivo, Thierry, and the rest.

It was Lanfranc who now smiled.

'If they can make room for a prior, they will certainly make room for a bishop. So long as you fulfil the duties of a bishop – and you appear to me to have made a most promising start – God, I am sure, will see no harm in your enjoying the privileges of one.'

* * * * * *

Ivo went out to have a last look at the horses, and no doubt to swear at them a little. Thierry collected spurs and weapons, rolled them in a blanket, and stowed them in his sleeping space for safe keeping. Then he returned to the kitchen in the hope of second helpings.

Lanfranc wiped his mouth, laid down his napkin, and put out his hands to the blaze.

'Do you know these parts?'

Geoffrey shook his head.

'No.'

'You came through St. Clair today. Does the name mean anything?'

'No.'

'Does the name Rollo mean anything?'

'Of course. Our first duke.'

'Ah. Then we have a starting point.'

Lanfranc began talking. About the days of the Viking raids, and the misery they caused. About longships far up the Seine. About Paris itself under siege. About the failure of the old kings – the last weak scions of the decaying house of Charlemagne – to drive the Northmen back, or even to contain them. About the huge Rolf, or Rollo as he became known in France, who, they said, was too large – or too fat – for any horse of the time, and so went on foot and was called Rolf the Ganger. Then King Charles the Simple – who was clearly not so simple – had the idea of buying them off, not with money, but with land. At a meeting in St. Clair on the River Epte, Charles invested Rollo with the lands around Rouen, and with estates along the Seine in the bishoprics of Evreux and Lisieux. Rollo swore homage in return, and so became technically the King's vassal.

Geoffrey had learned a little disjointed history from Father Gregory. Ivo and the others had told him tall stories round the winter hearth. Once or twice a minstrel had stayed the night on his way from Brittany, and had bewitched one and all with the great legends.

Lanfranc was different. His account shed light on a hundred dark corners. It was clear, it was straightforward, it was consistent, and complete. It pulled so many pieces together into a coherent pattern.

It was stimulating too. Geoffrey had to give his full attention, but relished Lanfranc's compliment to his intelligence. This impressive Italian, who spoke good French, with barely a trace of accent, made few concessions to simplicity for its own sake. Nobody had talked to Geoffrey before about matters like the administration of an empire, the conception of northern France as a whole, the problems in the collection of a whole country's taxes. Charlemagne began to emerge from the misty past as a human figure, no longer the omnipotent Christian Roman Emperor of legend, the all-seeing demi-god.

Prompted by Lanfranc's account, Geoffrey found himself asking questions, which produced yet more interesting answers. There were no evasions, no circumlocutions, no platitudinous pieties. Lanfranc's learning had something fresh and spring-like about it, as if it had been drawn straight from the fountain-head of revealed Truth.

Lanfranc in short was a born teacher, and a brilliant one. He also appreciated the value of a good joke as a means of fastening down facts.

He chose an anecdote from the chronicler, Dudo of St. Quentin. Dudo had solemnly recorded that Rollo, while willing to perform the ceremony of homage to the extent of placing his hands between those of his new overlord, King Charles, had been taken aback by the further demand of feudal convention that he kneel to place a token kiss of submission on the King's foot.

He turned to one of his retinue and jabbed a thumb in the direction of the throne. After a brief glance of surprise and bafflement, the man shrugged, stepped forward, grabbed the King's foot, and, without further bending, lifted it to his mouth. King and throne went over backwards, and a hundred Vikings rolled on the ground whooping and roaring.

Geoffrey laughed too.

'A most reluctant vassal,' he agreed.

Lanfranc refreshed himself with a drink and motioned to a boy to replenish the fire.

'As you are a most reluctant bishop.'

Geoffrey stopped laughing. Lanfranc put down his cup.

'I think it both timely and fitting that I explain something to you, and I would ask you to grant me the favour of hearing me to the end.'

Geoffrey looked puzzled, but nodded.

'You may remember,' said Lanfranc, 'that there was an adjournment immediately after your few words of explanation and mitigation.'

'Yes.'

'Would that all speeches for the defence were as succinct and relevant, and I speak, remember, as a lawyer.

'However, I had listened to you and I had watched you. I also made some enquiries about you. It was I, assisted by the sub-deacon Hildebrand, who initiated the adjournment, during which time I was received by His Holiness.

'I pointed out to him that, despite the irregular manner of your appointment, you showed every sign of having the energy, intelligence, and dignity that would befit the type of reforming bishop that the Church needs.'

Geoffrey opened his mouth, but Lanfranc put up a hand.

'No, no. Hear me through. You gave your word. I also reminded the Holy Father that he was about to issue a statement proclaiming invalid the Duke's proposed marriage with the lady Matilda of Flanders.'

'The blood ties are too close,' said Geoffrey.

Lanfranc pursed his lips.

'The exact closeness of the degree of consanguinity has not yet been established by full legal inquiry, and I pointed out that a spirited defence by the Duke's legal representatives could result in a tiresome prolongation of the proceedings. Whereas a tacit acceptance of the position for the present moment could hasten the closure of the Council, and enable His Holiness to proceed to Mainz in good time for the opening of his other council according to plan.

'Furthermore, I suggested that if the results of a full investigation into the matter of consanguinity were to be placed before a committee of Roman cardinal-bishops, they would have ample opportunity to examine them before making a final pronouncement at the Council of Rome next year.'

'Another council?'

'Indeed. Pope Leo is a tireless traveller, and his sub-deacon Hildebrand a passionate reformer. Believe me, they will leave their mark on the Church.'

'So they agreed?'

'Not at first. Hildebrand did not like the idea. To him simony is simony, and he is dedicated to eradicating it completely, regardless of cost. He is an idealist, not a lawyer. His Holiness, however, is a pragmatist, having been both bishop and soldier. He is moreover German and an aristocrat, and does not have Hildebrand's fire and peasant obstinacy.'

Lanfranc allowed himself a private smile.

'And His Holiness enjoys bargaining. In the end, I had to promise my assistance at the Council of Rome in the defeat of this new heresy of Berengar of Tours.'

'Heresy?'

Geoffrey felt a quiver of shock at merely using the word.

'Perhaps that is putting it strongly,' said Lanfranc. 'But it is a wayward idea concerning the nature of the Holy Bread and Wine, which, if allowed to develop without control, could cause confusion in the minds of the Faithful. Prohibition leads only to its spread. What we need is refutation, by Scriptural chapter and verse, and that takes time and scholarship. I have offered both, and the Holy Father has accepted. I do not like leaving Bec again, but needs must when the Devil, in the shape of Berengar, drives.'

Geoffrey scratched his cheek with a fingernail.

'If I have understood you correctly, you are responsible for my being confirmed as a bishop.'

Lanfranc hedged.

'His Holiness decided that a speedy closure, and assistance in the silencing of Berengar, were more important than one irregularly elected bishop in a distant diocese.'

At the end of all the world, said Geoffrey to himself. And to Lanfranc. 'Then let me put it this this way: if you had not spoken that morning to Hildebrand, I should not now be a bishop.'

'You see?' said Lanfranc. 'Already you argue like a canon lawyer. My confidence was not misplaced.'

Geoffrey swore, but Lanfranc laughed.

'Young man, do not be surprised if I do not tremble at your wrath. Your reaction is a pale reflection of what the Duke will say when we meet.'

Geoffrey frowned.

'Why?'

'Because he was relying upon me to get His Holiness to approve of his marriage. I shall have to tell him when we meet that I have been unsuccessful, if he has not found out already, and his only consolation will be you.'

'You said it will be approved in Rome next year.'

'I said that it *could* be approved. And next year is next year – a long time when a young duke wishes to marry. Put yourself in William's position. What would you rather have – an eager bride or a reluctant bishop?'

Geoffrey was so angry that he got to his feet and started walking up and down. Lanfranc called after him.

'Compose yourself. It is I who will bear the brunt of his wrath, not you.'

Geoffrey whirled round.

'Damn you, I am not afraid!'

'Good,' said Lanfranc. 'Then come with me to see him. I believe you have never met?'

'No. Not face to face. He was called away from Rouen to the siege.'

'It is time you did. I travel home now to Bec, and the Duke lies still at Brionne, where the siege nears its end. Neither is far out of your way. I take it you have no objection to meeting the Duke?'

Devil take Lanfranc! One minute Geoffrey was willing to sit at his feet, and the next he wanted to wring his neck.

'No objection whatever.'

What else could he say?

*   *   *   *   *   *

They were within sight of the abbey church at Bec when a mounted party came upon them from the direction of Brionne.

Ivo and Thierry half drew their swords and looked to Geoffrey for a lead. The other soldiers closed up from the rear.

'There is no cause for alarm,' said Lanfranc, shading his eyes. 'It is the Duke.'

Lanfranc hated having to travel with armed guards, but was realist enough to know that they were necessary. The Duke's authority was becoming respected, but it was by no means ubiquitous. Count Guy had endowed his abbey of Bec with enough land to support a handful of men-at-arms.

Geoffrey motioned to Ivo to relax, and put his horse alongside Lanfranc's donkey.

'Then let us face his Grace together.'

Lanfranc smiled.

'Yes. Let us do that.'

They told their respective parties to remain a pace or two behind, and set out side by side.

'One thing though,' said Lanfranc. 'William is young like yourself, and easy to anger. But you must remember why; he carries a great burden. Whatever he possesses he has fought for since he was a child, and he continues to fight for it. He needs to know whom he can trust. There can be no double answers or half-truths. Say what you think, and say it clearly.'

Geoffrey's mind went back to the day when Ivo had mounted him on a destrier for the first time. There had been no preparation or warning. One blazing early morning, with the sun tugging the dew off the grass, Ivo had snuffed the air and said suddenly, 'Put the saddle on Whitestar. I think Master Geoffrey is ready.' Geoffrey would remember to his dying day both the fear of the great pawing hooves, and the fierce pride because Ivo had shown such confidence in him at such an early age.

For some reason which he could not understand, Lanfranc was showing similar confidence in him.

86

William reined in his horse with much snorting and slapping of leather. He was bigger than Geoffrey had remembered from brief glimpses at Rouen, though it was hard to be sure when a man was mounted. A helmet hung from his saddle horn, and his mail coif had been slipped back from his head. He looked older than twenty-two.

'My messengers bring me bad news,' he said to Lanfranc without preamble or formal courtesy.

The voice was deeper and harsher than might have been expected from a man of his age.

Lanfranc rested his hands on the donkey's back.

'It is indeed true that there has been some delay in the matter of your Grace's marriage receiving the blessing of His Holiness – '

'You mean you failed?'

'I should not exactly say that, my lord – '

'I should. It is my marriage; I should know.'

'There were other matters of great complexity to be considered alongside with and in relation to your Grace's marriage. If I might explain – '

'Did you speak for me or not?'

William tugged at the reins of his restive mount.

Lanfranc patted his donkey's neck.

'No, my lord. Not at that time.'

'Then you can get out. I want no twisting legal tongues in my duchy. You are either with me or against me.'

'The matter will be fully reviewed at a Council in Rome next year,' said Lanfranc imperturbably.

'Then the sooner you start for Rome the better. Go and tie your lawyers' knots there.'

'Give me a proper horse, my lord, and I shall get there that much faster.'

The monks round Lanfranc gasped. Geoffrey felt a twinge of unease.

William glared down at Lanfranc. The prior, still and impassive, his feet poking out from under his black habit either side of the scruffy donkey, looked an odd mixture of dignity and comedy. Like a pope on a privy. William burst out laughing. He slapped his thigh and turned to one of his companions.

'A fine picture – eh, Fitz?'

William Fitzosbern joined the laughter. The humble men-at-arms showed their loyalty with furtive sniggers. Laughing at priors to their face was a practice they considered inadvisable if one's share of Divine Grace was to be forthcoming when most needed.

The Duke wiped an eye with a gloved hand.

'You shall get your horse, my lord prior. Now – who are you?'

He turned to look at Geoffrey.

'My lord duke, I am Geoffrey de Montbrai, your new Bishop of Coutances.'

'I remember now,' said William. 'Rouen. So – you got what you wanted.'

'My lord?'

'The Council gave you what you wanted.'

Geoffrey looked at Lanfranc.

'There was an – arrangement,' said Lanfranc.

He gave a brief account of the bargain he had struck with Pope Leo, leaving out the scholarly theology concerning Berengar.

'Ah!' said William.

He turned back to Geoffrey. Though he concentrated on the conversation, his eyes were not still. The pupils moved restlessly from side to side, watching everywhere.

'So your bishopric has cost me my marriage.'

'Believe my, my lord,' said Geoffrey, 'it is the very last outcome I should have wished.'

'Do not concern yourself. These lawyers will unearth some legalistic process; they always do. It is not your fault.'

'I spoke the truth at Rheims, my lord,' said Geoffrey. 'I did not ask to be a bishop.'

'I did not ask to be a duke.'

'I am not sure I have made myself clear, my lord. There is nothing to be bishop of. There is nothing there.'

William shrugged.

'I too started with nothing.'

'Nothing,' repeated Fitzosbern grimly.

William leaned across from his saddle.

'Think yourself lucky you are alive, adult, and not hunted. As for your precious diocese, you are not there to complain; you are there to build. Build!'

He tugged at his gloves.

'Come, Fitz.'

'I trust, my lord, that the siege of Brionne proceeds towards a satisfactory conclusion.'

William seemed to be in such good spirits that Lanfranc felt safe in asking the question.

'It is done,' said William. 'Over. The castle is ours. The rebels are dispersed. Count Guy has fled. We can now proceed in safety to Rouen.'

'May I congratulate your Grace on the fact that God has showered his blessings on your arms.'

'You may,' said William, not sure about the precise depth of irony in the Prior's remarks. 'And you can save your respects for the new overlord I shall find for you at Bec now that Guy is gone.'

'I shall await your Grace's will with interest,' said Lanfranc.

'Who is that?' said William suddenly, pointing towards a man at the back of the group.

Without turning, Lanfranc answered.

'Your Grace is as observant as ever, to remark on a new aspiring member of our community. May I present Brother Alessandro, who comes from Lombardy to study with us and to share with us the fruits of his learning.'

William was not fooled by the measured formality of Lanfranc's reply. Scholars came to Lanfranc like flies to honey. Distance simply did not matter. He would have been foolish indeed to enforce his idle threat uttered in temper, and to let this brilliant man go. Fitz would have stopped him, thank God.

Fitzosbern, he was sure, had seen, like himself, that this clever Italian was also an honest man, who spoke his mind without fear or favour.

Worth remembering.

*   *   *   *   *   *

It was a soft autumn afternoon, with the sun disguised as midsummer. Ivo dozed in the saddle, his regular cursings for once silent.

They had rested for three days at Montbrai. Now, their stomachs full of Gaimar's pies, and their heads replenished with castle gossip, they jogged quietly towards Avranches, where lodging was arranged in advance with Bishop Hugh.

'Hugh will tell you what to do,' said Lanfranc. 'He has been there for twenty years.'

'Why can you not help me?' said Geoffrey, who had quickly slipped into the habit of asking Lanfranc what he thought.

'I have done enough for the present time,' said Lanfranc. 'I have negotiated to obtain for you an opportunity, and I have placed before you a challenge. Hugh is a practitioner; I am a theorist. Hugh will give you sound advice. I know him well. I kept a school there for three years.'

Lanfranc, as usual, understated. Geoffrey had found out, during his stay at Bec, that Lanfranc on the contrary was a very good administrator. The abbot, Herluin, had told him moreover that Lanfranc had started his school at Avranches from nothing.

There was another striking man – Herluin. Even Lanfranc took his advice. Geoffrey had not wanted to leave this place, which surprised him. Quite apart from its peace and serenity, Geoffrey was held by curiosity; what force was it, what pull, that had made an ex-soldier like Herluin withdraw to the back of beyond with only fifteen like-minded followers and his own mother to do the washing? Geoffrey wanted to stay behind and find out more, but somehow it seemed assumed that he would journey on to Coutances, and he had not been able to formulate either proper acceptance or outright refusal.

His head was too full of all the things he had seen in the last few months, and of all the remarkable men he had met. Pope Leo, Hildebrand, Lanfranc, William, Abbot Herluin – they were all men of such purpose. They were men who could shake the world. It was intoxicating to be in their company.

'I envy them their certainty,' he said to Lanfranc. 'And I envy you.'

Lanfranc shook his head.

'It is not certainty which drives them on; it is the willingness to search. We have so little light to show us the way.'

Well, that may or may not have been true, but these men certainly made Christendom come alive. Geoffrey had had no idea that there was such a lot going on in the world. There was so much – well, so much pressure.

The household had been pleased to see him and to listen to his gossip. Ivo and Thierry had enjoyed being the centre of attraction among the swineherds and stable boys. But he had caught himself looking forward to the trip to Avranches. Montbrai was becoming a bore. He had tasted the cup of travel and wanted more. Even if Mauger had shown the resolve and intuition that Geoffrey so often said he should have; even if he had joined the Duke before Val-ès-Dunes; even if he had won enough land to be able to endow a younger brother – Geoffrey was not sure that he would be entirely content with a knight's fee on the edge of the Cotentin. Not now.

And the alternative? Italy with the Hautevilles? Annoyingly, that was no longer so bewitching either. Now that he had dined with the brothers at Bec, and survived a first meeting with Duke William, and knelt at a Mass said by His Holiness the Pope, and listened to Lanfranc expounding theology, somehow the prospect of sitting round endless camp fires in Apulia, gnawing bones with the Hautevilles, did not seem so attractive. And yet, and yet . . . What was there at Coutances but an awful nothingness that yawned before him?

And Sybil. What about Sybil? What would Bishop Hugh say about her? Was there any help to be had in Avranches? Geoffrey had not mentioned Sybil to Lanfranc. Such was Lanfranc's natural air of virtue – without a trace of self-right-eousness – that Geoffrey had not been able to bring himself to broach the subject.

Then there was Torf. What had Torf of Malbec been up to while his back was turned? Sir Tancred may think him a 'fine, lusty fellow' while he was winning at chess, but my lady Fressenda bargained more shrewdly for her daughter's future.

Geoffrey swore mindlessly. It was all so damned unfair. All he had wanted was to get his hands on his money and marry Sybil. And now, all this.

He heard Ivo wake up with a grunt and begin swearing gently at his horse. Avranches came into view.

He might as well see Bishop Hugh, having come this far. Though he could see no way in which his lordship could be of any help.

*　　*　　*　　*　　*　　*

'It is all very well for you,' said Geoffrey. 'You are a monk. You at least have a vocation.'

He really did. Geoffrey had seen no women close to the bishop. So much for advice in that quarter.

Bishop Hugh clambered under a scaffolding pole.

'The house of Fécamp does not produce builders and fighters. Look at this.'

He gestured at the confusion of broken slabs, frayed ropes, and rusting pulleys.

'You say you have no cathedral. Look around you. Twenty years' work. And a child could still jump over the walls. If only I were a man of action, a soldier, like you.'

'I am not a soldier,' said Geoffrey, who resented being identified with mercenary riff-raff from Brabant or Hainault.

Hugh dusted his hands.

'Do you deny your skill with the knightly weapons? The time may well come when your diocese will need it, and you will have cause to be grateful.'

'Granted, you have only half a cathedral, but what about your school? It is famous throughout Normandy.'

'The school of Avranches owes its fame to one man,' said Hugh. 'Lanfranc. He left to go to Bec seven years ago, and we are still thriving on his reputation. You have met him; you must know.'

'I should like to know him better.'

'Then accept his invitation and go to Rome with him.'

'Hmmmm.'

Geoffrey scratched a cheek.

Hugh watched him as they walked back to the episcopal hall, which he had prudently ordered to be built first.

He was beginning to understand why Lanfranc had shown such interest in this tall young man. There were huge gaps in his resources, but already great promise was discernible. He could be the making of Coutances; and Coutances could be the making of him. He did not know it, but he badly needed something to get his teeth into.

91

Geoffrey picked up a chip of rock and tossed it listlessly to one side.

Hugh paused at his door.

'May I make another suggestion?'

Geoffrey nodded.

'That is what I am come to hear.'

'Forget your decisions and your problems – even your woman – and simply make the journey.'

Now how the devil had he known?

'What journey?'

'Any journey. It matters not. Why do pilgrims travel? For ease of mind on the road as well as peace of mind at the end of it. A long journey means a leaving behind as well as a going towards. It is a great feast of forgetting. Accept the journey with Lanfranc. It will occupy mind and body. There is nothing to surpass a daily purpose of miles for controlling worries and doubts.

'You will have the constant company of the clearest mind in Normandy, which – whatever you finally decide – can not but be for the good. You will see the Council of Rome, which will be even greater than the Council of Rheims.'

Geoffrey looked doubtful.

'The end is to Lanfranc's purpose. What is there to mine?'

'Make something. Think. What do you need most at Coutances?'

Geoffrey blinked.

'Everything – you know that. There is no cathedral, no – '

'Yes, yes. But what must come first?'

Geoffrey still looked blank.

'Money,' said Hugh. 'You need funds. And you are luckier than I.'

'Why?'

'Because Hauteville is in your diocese, not mine. Go to the Hautevilles. Put it to them. What better way can they ensure the happy immortality of their souls than by endowing their own cathedral? Piled beside their camp fires must be the plunder of a hundred Greek and infidel shrines. It can not warm the body in this life, but they could use it to prevent the fires of Hell from warming it in the next. Rogues and bandits they may be, but they too must aspire to enter the Kingdom of Heaven sooner or later, and I am sure, given the choice, they would prefer the former, especially with their record.'

Geoffrey did not know what to say. For weeks he had been searching for a good reason to leave Coutances behind and go at least to have a look at the Hautevilles. Now he was being offered a glittering vindication of just such a quest. He could moreover think of two or three excellent uses for ready money above and beyond ruinous cathedrals.

So why was he hesitating?

Hugh smiled.

'If she is anything like you, she will be there when you return.'

Asking Sybil's brothers for charity! What would Mauger say? At least it would have the virtue of infuriating him.

*   *   *   *   *   *

'Why did you not tell me before?'

'I was not sure.'

'You are sure now?'

Sybil nodded.

'You are not angry?'

Geoffrey had begun his familiar pacing. This, surely, was added reason. Even though it took him away for several months, it was now imperative that he travel to Italy. Sybil, he knew, would be well cared for during his absence. A sudden thought struck him.

'Does your mother know?'

'No. But she will soon divine the truth. Mother divines everything. However, I think I shall tell her anyway.'

Geoffrey stopped pacing.

'Is that wise – so early?'

Sybil laughed.

'Geoffrey, you should see your face. You look like the small boy caught with his spoon in the honey pot.'

'You do not see,' said Geoffrey. 'If we can keep this a secret until I return from Italy, I shall have the means of caring for you.'

Sybil smiled wickedly.

'Of providing for me? My love, it is you who do not see. The sooner I tell Mother that I am with child, the sooner she will send Torf packing. If all else fails, she can use the fact in our favour. No suitor can sustain his ardour for a bride who carries another man's child.'

'What about your Father – your brothers? The dishonour?'

Sybil smiled confidently.

'Mother can handle Father. Indeed, there are times when I think he is a little frightened of her. And she is more than a match for any three of my brothers. As for the dishonour, it is only a dishonour if anyone outside the family knows. We tell Torf only if it becomes absolutely necessary.'

'How do you keep a secret like that?'

'Geoffrey, do you remember telling me that your cook – what was his name, Gaimar? – was the bastard of your Father Gregory? Now tell me – how old were you before you found out? And you *lived* there!'

'How do you prevent your brothers in Italy from hearing this news? Surely Serlo will tell them when he gets there. If they find out that the bishop who is asking them for funds is the man who has dishonoured their sister . . .'

Sybil shook her head firmly.

'Serlo is a pudding. It has taken him six months to make up his mind whether it is worth going. He is still nowhere near ready. If he set out tomorrow, he is so slow that you could travel to Italy and back three times before he reached Burgundy. You will have plenty of time – assuming you still want to . . .'

She could not bring herself to use the word 'marry'. Partly because she did not want to embarrass Geoffrey into making fulsome promises that he might not be able to keep, partly because her own doubt was beginning to grow.

Geoffrey took her in his arms.

'I love you. You surely know that.'

Sybil looked down at the small crucifix on her breast.

'Yes. I know that.'

Geoffrey squeezed her.

'And believe me when I say I shall find a way. I can not find it here, or at Coutances, or at Montbrai. But I shall find it in Italy. And I shall return.'

'To me or to your cathedral?'

Geoffrey swallowed.

'If my diocese provides me with the means of securing our future, I should be ill-advised to abandon it – do you not agree?'

Sybil lifted a hand to Geoffrey's chest.

'Why do you wear this crucifix?'

Geoffrey partially released her and looked down at it.

'This? Oh. It was a gift from Lanfranc. And it reminded me of yours.'

Sybil sat back and spoke with certainty.

'You admire Lanfranc; it shines out of you.'

'I have told you often – yes. He is a great man.'

'And Hildebrand? And the Pope?'

'Yes. And Abbot Herluin. And Duke William. And a lot of others whom I have met. What difference does that make?'

'None to me. But it has made a difference to you.'

'I do not see it. I still love you. I am still the same person.'

Sybil shook her head.

'You think you are, my love. But you are not. Or you are the same person, and I did not know you before.'

'What is that supposed to mean?'

'I can not say for sure.' She stood up. 'Give my greetings and my love to my brothers. And hurry back to me. I should like you to be near when my time comes, whatever you – whatever the outcome of your quest.'

Geoffrey was overcome with tenderness and admiration. He rose too, and took her once more into his arms.

'I love you, and I love the fruit of our love that you carry. And I shall return – God willing – to take you from here and care for you both. Believe me, I intend to find a way.'

Sybil noticed that no mention was made of that way leading to the altar. Perhaps a miracle really did take place when they made a man a priest. Who was to know?

As the last of his hoofbeats died away, Sir Tancred put an arm round his daughter's shoulder.

'A fine, lusty young fellow, eh, Syb? May God bring him back to you in health and grace.'

Sybil revelled in the comfort of her father's arm.

'Yes, Father. May God bring him back – all of him.'

'That is what I say, my treasure, every time one of them goes. And it hurts just the same every time.'

Sybil looked up, and saw a tear on her father's leathery cheek.

'Oh, Father!'

She stretched up and kissed him.

Sir Tancred sniffed.

'Yes. Ah – hum. How about a game this evening? This time I shall have to have you against me.'

Sybil snuggled against him again.

'I think that will be a lovely idea.'

'But let me win just now and then, eh?'

*   *   *   *   *   *

Thorold laid his thin hand on Geoffrey's arm.

'My son in Christ – if my lord will forgive the familiarity – I can now rest at ease, for I know that the feeble flame which I have tended so unworthily all these years will now pass to you. Held aloft in your strong hands, it will become a great torch that will shine as a beacon to all of Normandy.'

Geoffrey shook his head.

'I can make no promises.'

'You do not need to,' said Thorold. 'As a man of my years moves nearer his Maker, a few tiny shafts of the Divine Light of Heaven shine towards me, and I am given grace to see what is hidden from others. You will return, though I shall no longer be here to welcome you.'

Geoffrey opened his mouth to interrupt. Thorold stopped him.

'I ask only that you make my grandson Richard the archdeacon. You will need a young man, and his father Peter is better left as dean. My other son Walter is a good boy, but, sadly, of cloddish disposition, fit only for copying and repetition. But my other grandson, John, has promise.'

'I assure you that none of them shall want,' said Geoffrey.

'I pray too that you will remove the threat that hangs over us even as we speak.'

'Threat?'

'Do you remember? I told you of this knight Torf of Malbec.'

'Who cheated you of money?'

'Just so.'

Damn the man, and damn him!

'Surely you have not been deceived again.'

'You can not take coins from an empty purse. But you can take eggs from a fertile hutch. Since you were last here, his men have now set up a toll on the road out to Lessay, and they demand produce from all men who would pass. Men go there regularly for the pasture and the kindling and the peat. He knows that.'

'And if they refuse?'

Thorold shrugged.

'The biggest clod can fire a house or two. It serves also as a beacon of warning to others.'

Geoffrey swore. Was he never to stop running across this creature's handiwork?

Thorold affected not to notice Geoffrey's wrath.

'And finally – '

He fumbled in the threadbare folds of his habit.

' –I beg you to accept this.'

He produced a gold ring, set with a huge ruby. The workmanship was breathtaking.

'It belonged to the late Bishop Gilbert, who died at the hands of the Vikings.'

The 'late' Bishop Gilbert! It must be all of seventy years ago.

'Before he was carried off to eternal bliss, he gave it to me to keep it for the next bishop who would give himself to the blessed church of Our Lady. It was an easy promise to make, but – '

Thorold's face puckered in grief.

'Alas! I could do so little. I have been such a disappointment to him.'

Geoffrey remembered Thorold's sons and grandsons, and suddenly realised the cause of the old man's sadness. He gripped Thorold's arm.

'My lord,' said Geoffrey, 'you were not blessed with a bishop's mitre, but you

96

truly carried the burden. Your father would have been proud of you.'

Tears streamed down Thorold's furrowed face.

'Surely God would not deny us every consolation? Surely you are the sign of His forgiveness?'

He placed the ring on Geoffrey's finger, and knelt to kiss it. Geoffrey could feel tears on his hand.

He helped the old man to his feet, and held him round the shoulders till his sobbing had passed.

When Thorold had wiped his nose and sniffed a few times, Geoffrey said, 'Tell me, how did you hide the ring safely all those years?'

Thorold sniffed once more.

'There were indeed many who would have liked to possess it,' he said. 'And not only Vikings,' he added significantly.

He began to totter away.

'There were frequent dangers, but I was not always as you see me now.'

'Well?'

He paused and turned. A suspicion of a twinkle came into his eye. He gave a final sniff.

'Let us only recall that when I was younger I had a strong digestion.'

*   *   *   *   *   *

Chapter Seven

Geoffrey wiped the sweat out of his eyes for the hundredth time. God's Bread, what a country! Fog, rain, mud, feverish mists, swamps, floods, snows, wind, pitiless sun and blinding white rock – in three months he had seen it all. Had it not been for the roads, he would have been tempted to wonder why the Almighty had seen fit to place here the Head of His Holy Catholic Church. The roads, he suspected, had survived from ancient times only because the Romans had built so many other things that lazy masons had chosen to loot ruins above the ground rather than prise out stones set so firmly into it.

What an amazing land Italy was! He would never be able to describe it when he returned home, because he would never know where to start. With the wonders of the past?

The aqueducts, the walls, the palaces, temples, colonnades; the pictures, sculptures, mosaics, carvings, friezes; the craftsmanship, the technical brilliance, worldliness, sophistication – which even in ruin took the breath away. What genius had conceived these wonders? With what soaring confidence had men approached their execution? What race of demi-gods had actually lived among them and taken them for granted? Geoffrey was not the first, or the last, to feel dwarfed, cowed, overwhelmed. It was as if the world had since passed from a great sun into a great shadow. What was it Lanfranc had said? 'We have so little light to show us the way.' Small wonder.

Small wonder, too, that Geoffrey's mother had so often told stories of the prodigies of her country. As a child he had sat on her knee in fascinated awe, absorbing not only the content but some of the language in which they were related. For Helena of Montbrai had been in the habit of sprinkling Italian words and phrases all over her lilting French. As a growing boy he had begun to suspect that there was a fondness for exaggeration, and the exaggeration sprang from that fondness, but now that he saw for himself he realised that Mother had not told him the half of it.

'*Magnifico! Stupendo!*'

He could see his mother's expansive gesture with both hands.

It surprised him to discover how much Italian he had remembered. It enabled him to avoid a lot of swindling by traders in markets and guest-masters in monasteries.

Geoffrey took to Italy. He could not say in truth that he found himself at home, but he was surprised to discover how un-strange he felt.

That did not mean that he lost the capacity for wonder. It was not only the heights of ancient aspiration that kept his mouth almost permanently open; it was also the depths of contemporary decay. There was grandeur still, but it was a corroded, flimsy sort of grandeur; the gilt veneer barely concealed the fungus-like rottenness underneath. No longer did a single noble race stand proudly on their achievement; grasping tribes of lesser mortals – Lombard petty princes, greedy Milanese merchants, German mercenaries in the pay of the Emperor; corrupt aristocrats in a half-wooden Rome that reeked in summer heat astride a turgid Tiber; subtle Greeks who still dreamed of regaining the old conquests of Justinian for their remote Emperor in Constantinople; infidel Saracen adventurers, half pirate and half zealot, who built slave-markets with one hand and mosques with the other – all these, and many others, prowled and pounced on the scraps of empire, each convinced that the morsel they shook free and held aloft in tawdry triumph contained the seeds of a new harvest of glory.

And what would Geoffrey's hearers say if he told them in all truth that Italy was also a land of great natural riches – vineyards, fields of corn, endless groves of exotic fruits of a fullness beyond the palate of ordinary men accustomed only to the stodgy apples of Normandy? Small wonder yet again that his mother looked out at the slanting chill rain of Montbrai and yearned for the Italian sun.

What about the craftsmen he had seen, the stalls, the markets in Milan, Florence, Pisa, Bologna? Geoffrey himself did not believe all he was told of the prodigies of Venice – and he had passed within a hundred miles of it. However, he had seen clanking, galley-blocked harbours in Genoa, Amalfi, Salerno, Bari, and Brindisi, thronged with men from lands that were barely known even in legend.

Could he describe the teeming business in a city like Pavia, where it was easy to understand at a glance why Lanfranc had been able to build such a thriving legal practice. It was Lanfranc's home, and Geoffrey was intrigued to see a human side to his constantly prodigious companion, as Lanfranc took him to the churches, and the libraries where he had studied, and the courts where he had practised, and finally to his family house. His aged father provided touching hospitality, and listened graciously to Geoffrey's stumbling thanks, before plunging into eager gossip with his son, of whom he was both intensely proud and slightly in awe.

The humanity and comfort of it all made Geoffrey wonder, more forcefully than before – and he had thought about it enough times – why Lanfranc should have given it up to go, so far as he could see, on a sort of aimless quest in France. For what?

'For knowledge, for truth, for enlightenment,' said Lanfranc. 'What else?' As host, he spoke in Geoffrey's northern French. Geoffrey did not dare to try his Italian in a household such as this.

'Could you not have continued your work here in Pavia as well?' said Geoffrey. 'Here you have success, love, power, esteem.'

Lanfranc made a wry face.

'You would think that ought to be enough, I agree. Yet – I was restless. And, worse, I was restless *because* I was restless. Perhaps it was the fact that it had all come so easily.'

He waved a hand round the room – the mellow furniture, the bright curtains and hangings, the bowls of bursting fruit, the clear glassware and Sicilian wine, the well-scrubbed serving girls, his beaming father who could not understand his son's French but simply loved listening to the sound of his voice.

'Love, comfort, security. A chance to use my head instead of my hands. I was born to it. I deserve no credit for that.'

'But your brilliance at the law,' said Geoffrey. 'You worked, you studied.'

'It was like breathing,' said Lanfranc. 'As peasants reap and sow, or Jews buy and sell, so I pleaded and negotiated. For doing nothing but follow my instincts, I achieved success, fame, and wealth. For what? For praise and jealousy.

'My family, my friends, my clients heaped upon me enough compliments and admiration to turn the head of a saint; my rivals and defeated litigants waited in the gallery with sharp eyes and drawn fangs, eager to pounce if I made one slip. The more I won, the more my supporters thought I was infallible, and the more certainly I knew that the time for my defeat must come that much nearer.'

Lanfranc poured some wine for them both.

'You may as well make the most of this; you will notice the difference in Rome. I swear the cellarmen in the Vatican were trained in a brewery.'

Geoffrey savoured not only the wine, but the texture of the glass, the gorgeous leatherwork on the chair, the maturity of the massive carved table, which must have been polished by those serving-girls' grandmothers.

'It was like living in swaddling clothes,' said Lanfranc. 'I knew I could come to no harm, but I could not move.' He shook his head in annoyance. 'No – not exactly that. I was not doing enough. God had showered his blessings upon me, but what had I done to deserve them? It was as if I was expected to celebrate the arrival at a destination without having experienced the hardship of a journey. There was no strain, no uncertainty, no element of chance.'

'Surely it is certainty that we all crave in this shaking world,' said Geoffrey. 'You were born with it, and yet you wanted to cast it away?'

'It bothered me,' said Lanfranc. 'It bothered me that I had not worked it out for myself, or, if you like, that God had not rewarded me with it. I might as well have been grateful for being born with a nose and two ears.

'Some well-meaning friends said I was not using my talents to the full and that I should go into politics. Foolishly accepting the flattery, I entered the heaving sea of faction and strife that prevails in any Italian city – as you will discover also in Rome. I was not equipped. Like many clever young men, who owed their initial success to cleverness, I thought that cleverness was enough for success anywhere else.'

'What happened?'

'It was pitiful. I was like a bear in a pit with hounds. They never stood still long enough for me to crush them with the heavy paw of my well-rehearsed arguments. Before long I had not only lost my name and my fortune; for the sake of my family's safety, I had to leave. The pursuit of justice had left me an aimless advocate; the pursuit of power had left me a bitter refugee.

'After months of wandering and charity and self-sympathy, I at last faced the truth: that I had nobody to blame but myself, and that if I wished to know what was God's will for me, it would make sense to study again, this time more closely, what He had said in the Scriptures. So I went to school once more. I devoured Holy Writ like a greedy penitent gorging himself after Lent. When I had exhausted a monastery's library, I moved on. The Prophets, the Judges, the Chronicles, the Apostles – I wolfed everything indiscriminately. When that failed to satisfy, I turned to the Ancients, where I found much insight and wisdom. I do not share the view of Abbot Hugh at Cluny that all pagan learning is a potential corruption of spiritual purity.'

Lanfranc sipped some wine.

'It was not enough. Oh, I gained much knowledge, but it was all of man's imperfections, man's mistakes. I wanted to know how to put them right. It was not enough to know where we had been; what is important is where we are going. All that study, all that poring and pondering, had not revealed to me God's purpose. And yet I felt it was there somewhere, if only I had the wit to see it. After all, if we are too stupid to see His Will in His Word, and we have already crucified His Son for trying to tell us face to face, what hope is there?'

Geoffrey was not sure he understood, but he had caught enough drift of Lanfranc's argument to feel a chill of unease. He reassured himself with a swig of wine, and tried to steer Lanfranc back to the thrilling story of his pilgrimage of the soul.

'What did you do then?'

'I opened a school – at Avranches, with your neighbour, Bishop Hugh. I owed him hospitality, and it was a breathing-space. I could not go on beating my head against books and altars in the search for Truth; I should go insane. I had noticed, moreover, that wherever I went, I was asked to give lessons. I had done it in Pavia, trying to hammer Canon Law into the heads of spoilt sons of rich parents. In France I had always taught to pay for my keep, so, to oblige Bishop Hugh, I did it again. As soon as I had paid off my debts, I intended to move on.

'To my horror, the school grew like a mushroom in an autumn night. Within three years – and I say this in pain, not conceit – I was famous. I was trapped once more by success. I was in the ridiculous situation of expounding Scriptures that made little sense to me. I was teaching subjects the usefulness of which I had spent nearly a decade questioning. I felt I was only perpetuating the doubt from which I was trying to extricate myself.'

'The blind leading the blind.'

'Exactly. Once more I knew I had to escape. This time, however, an escape not into the outside world, but away from it.'

Geoffrey felt a thrill of excitement.

'You were called at last – called to the monastic life.'

Lanfranc shook his head.

'Nothing of the sort. There is nothing exciting about what happened to me. Those who get blinded on the road to Damascus are, in my experience, very rare. I simply drew up a small list of last resorts to save my sanity, and, with great misgivings, adopted the one which seemed the least unpromising. You must remember too that I was only thirty-four then; I am only forty-two now.'

He beat his fist on his heart.

'I am Italian, born in the sun. I feel things!'

'Why did you choose Bec?' said Geoffrey.

'Because it was small, and obscure, and young. I thought I could find there the simplicity I yearned for. All my life I had been taken up with learning, scholarship, subtlety, complexity. How could I hear the still small voice with all that buzzing inside my head like a swarm of bees? I had tried to argue myself into understanding and acceptance, and it had not worked. I know now that there is not enough knowledge in the world to do that.'

'And you had heard of Herluin?' said Geoffrey, who, like most Normans, had heard of him too.

'Yes. He had wanted escape from a different world – from saddle and sword.'

'What did you have in common?'

'As I said, it matters not so much where we have been as where we are going. It struck me that Herluin and I might be after the same thing. If he had found it, or even if he had approached it more nearly than I, then Bec was the place to go.'

'Herluin welcomed you, I am sure.'

'Not at all. He thought I was entirely unsuitable – much too highly-charged, too intense. It took all my persuading.'

'But you won him over.'

'No. He agreed to give it a try. If I could prove that I might fit in, then there was a chance.' Lanfranc smiled wryly. 'I was to be brother number thirty-five. Very good for me too.'

'And there you found peace,' prompted Geoffrey, anticipating with pleasure the happy ending.

'No,' said Lanfranc. 'Even Bec did not satisfy me. I was not alone enough, not close enough to God to hear the small voice. I told Abbot Herluin that I would have to go on to the ultimate.'

'To the hermit's life?'

'Yes.'

When Geoffrey was a boy, there was reputed to live, in the forest near Montbrai, a solitary holy man. Folk referred to him with a mixture of tolerant wry humour, ridicule, and a dash of fear. Small boys boasted of chance sightings. Having a sort of live saint – if only invisible – nearby was a pleasant change from the many demons and devils who most certainly did inhabit other forests.

Now, to meet one face to face – and to know what a towering intellect he had – at once invested the hermit existence with magic, if not romance.

Something of Geoffrey's admiration must have shown in his face, because Lanfranc shook his head firmly.

'Do not be misled, my friend. No hermit loves the wilderness. He is human, and he does not go there from free choice. He goes there because he can honestly see nowhere else to go, because he does not *have* a choice.'

'What –'

Geoffrey stopped. It felt silly to ask 'what was it like?' Yet he wanted to continue the conversation.

However, Lanfranc drained his glass, and brushed some invisible crumbs from his lap. He seemed slightly embarrassed, as if he had already said too much.

'We must not leave my father out of the conversation too long.'

Geoffrey looked disappointed. Lanfranc laughed.

'Do not worry. It is a long way yet to Rome. I trust you still wish to attend the Council with me. After all,' he added with a smile, 'it is because of you that I am going.'

*　　*　　*　　*　　*　　*

Ralph shook his brother's hand.

'Thank you for your good wishes.'

He knew Aubrey was not sincere. Ever since he had announced his intention of leaving home, Aubrey, while professing regret, had constantly pressed small gifts on him, suggesting that they would be 'useful' or 'good for the road' or 'a happy reminder of home'.

So long as Michael had lived, Aubrey had kept his selfishness in check. Michael was so good and so well loved by everybody that any attempt by his eldest brother to secure any more than an equal third would have put him at once in the wrong. Michael never argued, never fought for his 'rights', never gossiped, and never lied. He was open, friendly, happy, and strong – everything Aubrey was not. Aubrey hated him. Worse, had to contain his hate, because any jealousy shown of Michael at once reflected back on the one who was jealous. Michael's total lack of artifice shone a pitiless light on the artifice of others.

Michael's illness was doubly difficult for Aubrey. He was of a sensitive stomach, and was revolted by the sights and smells of bodily weakness; and it was a constant effort to simulate even a fraction of the genuine distress felt by the whole household. When that bishop had arrived out of nowhere and cleared the solar, his relief knew no bounds. Outside in the night, he sucked in great lungfuls of air as if both body and spirit depended on it for survival.

Michael's funeral preparations imposed strain once more. Aubrey dug his nails into his palms to prevent himself shrieking at the ceaseless tears of his mother and sisters, and his brother Ralph's silence drove him to distraction. For Ralph knew.

Once the period of mourning was over, Aubrey's temper burst, and the mortification which had festered over the years poured instead on to the head of his second brother. Ralph and he seemed always to be fighting.

Ralph was no better and no worse than most middle sons, so Aubrey had less fear of being permanently in the wrong. Their mother did not help matters by wringing her hands and saying, 'If only Michael were alive; you would not fight if Michael were alive.' It brought a flush to Aubrey's cheeks and a lump to Ralph's throat.

There seemed only one solution.

'Where will you go?' said his father.

'To the King. To the Duke. To anyone who needs soldiers.'

'I can not provide you with mail. And as for a destrier – do you know what Walter Giffard charges with all that new Spanish stock? I could not get near those prices. I should think they are even dearer in Chartres or Paris.'

'I shall manage, Father. I have my health and strength and my wits. If I fail to become a knight, I shall be an archer, an engineer, a courier, a scout – anything. But I must get away. Surely you understand.'

His father nodded sadly.

'Your mother will weep.'

'She will weep even more if Aubrey and I come to serious blows. It is only a matter of time.'

His father sighed.

'Ah – Aubrey.'

But he was thinking of Michael.

'It will be better when I have gone,' said Ralph. 'Aubrey will know then that everything will come to him.'

'What about your sisters?'

Ralph smiled.

'Rest assured, Father, Aubrey will become a most devoted brother, dedicated to the search for suitable husbands for them. If they prefer the secluded life, I should hate to be the abbess he bargains with for their presentation price.'

Ralph's father dug into a pile of old chippings from recent coppice work. He tossed a handful or two on to the fire, and rested his elbows on his knees, his hands dangling.

'Why do all these things happen, Ralph? Why are people what they are? Does the fault lie with us? Am I being punished for something?'

Ralph looked at his father's bent, defeated shoulders. He could think of no comfort.

At last he stood and stretched. His father looked up.

'When will you go?'

'As soon as possible.'

'Come back to see us, eh? Now and then.'

'As often as I can, I promise.'

Aubrey stood waving longer than anybody else.

*   *   *   *   *   *

If Geoffrey was going to find it difficult to describe Italy, he was going to find it impossible to describe Rome. The riches, the ruin, the intrigue, the corruption, the wonder, the miracles, the misery – all that he had seen in Italy he saw again, in a sort of distillation, in Rome. Men thought that Italy, for all its shortcomings, was somehow worthwhile; Rome, however, was indispensable. Everybody, from the mightiest emperor to the lowliest pilgrim, was drawn to it like looters to an unguarded treasure – in many cases for similar reasons.

However, if men had thought the magic of Rome's spell could not be improved upon, God had shown otherwise by adding, not simply another ingredient, but a totally fresh dimension. To the glory of empire had been added the mystery of the Holy Catholic Church. True, in a thousand years the fortunes of the Holy See had fluctuated, and there had been times, many of them quite recent, when men began to wonder whether God had had second thoughts. The election of 1049 settled their minds.

The new Pope, Leo IX, was breathing life again into the Vatican. The cracked gilt that Geoffrey saw, the veneer that allowed glimpses of rottenness underneath, was about to be removed. Pope Leo and his deacon Hildebrand were beginning to show that there was life beneath even the rottenness under the veneer, that God had not allowed the body of His Holy Catholic Church to die. He was present in his Church at Rome, just as His Son was present, in the flesh, in the Holy Bread consecrated at Mass by His priests.

Pope Leo had provided the confidence, the initiative, to summon to Rome the heretic Berengar of Tours for daring to suggest otherwise. Geoffrey sat and listened while the Papal advocate, Prior Lanfranc of Bec, marshalled the arguments to prove that Berengar's theories were a heresy inspired by the Devil to divide the Church and distress the Faithful.

As Lanfranc cited his authorities and piled his precedents, Geoffrey gazed in admiration at his clarity, his conciseness, his total command. Where other lawyers displayed language to mask the truth, Lanfranc harnessed language to illuminate it. Geoffrey thought of his conversation in the house at Pavia. To listen to Lanfranc, at the height of his powers, and in full brilliant spate, it seemed inconceivable that he should experience any doubt about his calling.

Berengar was duly declared in gross error and heretic. Sub-deacon Hildebrand read the decree of excommunication, his soft voice trembling with passion, his eye flashing fire.

When he had finished, it chanced that he glanced in Geoffrey's direction. He frowned absently in the effort of recall. A sudden stabbing glare showed that he had probably remembered. He shuffled some papers in his hands, clearly changing some prearranged order. What he next read out proved that he had most certainly remembered.

'It is another decision of this Holy Council of God's Catholic Church – whose Bishop has the primacy – that the proposed marriage between Duke William of Normandy and Matilda daughter of Count Baldwin of Flanders, is against God's Law on the grounds of consanguinity, in that the lady Matilda's mother was formerly married to Duke Richard III of Normandy, the uncle of Duke William. This Holy Council, therefore, confirms, reinforces, and reiterates its ban on the aforesaid wedding, as first promulgated at the Holy Council of Rheims, in the year of Our Lord, 1049, declaring it to be abhorrent and anathema.'

After a final gleam of challenge towards Geoffrey, Hildebrand turned to other business.

'He is a cheat and a liar!' said Geoffrey to Lanfranc later.

Lanfranc shook his head.

'No. He is a single-minded zealot, and that is much more dangerous. Hildebrand, I am afraid, recognises no virtue in compromise.'

Geoffrey suddenly saw a ray of hope.

'Does this mean he will relieve me of my bishopric?'

'No.'

'But the arrangement was that I stayed in Coutances if the ban on the Duke's marriage was to be lifted at a later date. Surely if the ban remains, my diocese goes. Or Hildebrand is not a man of his word.'

Lanfranc shook his wryly.

'On the contrary. Hildebrand is much more a man of his word than you give him credit for. He promised that you would remain in possession of the mitre of Coutances, and this promise he has kept, though believe me he would dearly like you removed. Secondly, he promised, with regard to the Duke, only to have the case re-examined. This too he has done. He gave no guarantee as to the outcome. He has therefore fulfilled every undertaking he gave at Rheims, to the letter.'

Lanfranc's measured lawyer's sentences and bland acceptance of the situation made Geoffrey only the more angry.

'Traitor!'

'No,' said Lanfranc firmly. 'Hildebrand may be many things, but he is no traitor to his cause. His only serious fault is an excessive devotion to it. You know already what he thinks of simony and clerical marriage. In that he has the full support of His Holiness. But it is my belief that, given the chance, he will go further. Did you hear that phrase – "Rome has the primacy"?'

'Yes.'

'Now what do you think that means?'

Geoffrey thought.

'I suppose he means that the Bishop of Rome comes before all others.'

Lanfranc nodded.

'Good. Now, think again. Suppose Hildebrand were to invest it with another meaning – that the Bishop of Rome comes not only before but above all others.'

'All other bishops?'

'Yes. Not only in France or Italy or Germany, but in the east – above Alexandria, Antioch, above Jerusalem, above Constantinople itself – above all the patriarchs of the Eastern Church.'

Geoffrey stared.

'Impossible.'

'You think so? Come now, Geoffrey. You have been listening to lawyers for two weeks. Surely you can see how that phrase – "Rome has the primacy" – is open to different interpretations with a mere stroke of the pen, or a change in the tone of voice. A harmless, formal generality, accepted for centuries, can, in the hands of a zealot, become overnight a clarion call to the Faithful. Every bishop's throne could rock under the blast of it.'

'Do you really think Hildebrand is aiming at that?'

'I say only that he could be,' said Lanfranc. 'He is not a lawyer, nor is he, frankly, much of a theologian, or why did he ask for me to come and destroy poor Berengar? He does not stop to think out where his crusading zealotry will lead him. However, I tell you that there is no end to the desires and ambitions of the single-minded man. And, mark, it is not for himself that he does this. Hildebrand is totally selfless and totally pure. No human corruption could live in a man in whom such a passionate fire burns. His will and the Will of God are as one to him. Others, being of lesser purpose, will give way before him.'

'Surely he can go no further than – than what you have suggested,' said Geoffrey.

Lanfranc thought.

'I am only guessing now, you understand, and it is only an academic exercise. But take that phrase again: "Rome has the primacy". You agree that, on previous assumptions, it means simply an accepted first place in precedence?'

'Yes.'

'Second, if we start to play with the word "primacy", we can induce it to mean not "precedence before" but "rule over" all others.'

'Yes, we agreed that too.'

'Now consider. We are working on the assumption that "all others" means "all other bishops, archbishops, and patriarchs".'

'Yes, of course.'

'But suppose it were taken to mean "all others", that is "all those in authority, whether spiritual or temporal".'

Geoffrey gasped. Lanfranc nodded.

'I see you have it. That powerful phrase could – I say only "could" – be stretched to justify the Papal primacy not only over all bishops and patriarchs in Christendom, but over all princes, kings, and emperors in the world.'

Geoffrey shook his head.

'I can not take in all this.'

Lanfranc laughed.

'Do not fear, my friend. It was, as I said, only an academic exercise. And Hildebrand is only a sub-deacon, not a cardinal, much less a Pope. Still, you have seen him. Remember him.'

'I shall,' promised Geoffrey fervently. 'I am sure he remembers me.'

'Ah, yes,' said Lanfranc. 'I saw him shuffle those papers. That decree was timed especially for you.'

'Why? Surely I can not be that important?'

'Probably not. But you are Norman. And Normans are important to the Holy See at the moment.'

'In what way?'

'That,' said Lanfranc with a puzzling smile, 'you will discover when you meet the Hautevilles and ask for their money.'

*　　*　　*　　*　　*　　*

'Constance! Muriella!'

'Mother?'

'Up here – immediately.'

Both sisters sighed.

'Yes, Mother.'

Wearily they climbed the ladder to the solar. Beside their mother's bed stood a terrified serving girl, clutching a wooden bowl to her skimpy bosom.

Lady Fressenda wasted no time on apologies.

'Muriella? You will go at once, show them the – the mess that they have given her to bring up to me – a sick, old woman – and you will tell them to prepare something better at once. I have tasted warmer onions in a winter pig trough. You will tell them also that if it is not to my satisfaction, then, ill though I am, and infirm though my bones may be, I shall have the litter brought to the kitchen. And for every twinge of pain that it causes to my back there will be a stroke of the broomstick to theirs from Humbert. Tell them.'

'Yes, Mother.'

The lady Fressenda flapped an impatient wrist at the cringing girl.

'Well, go with her, child. You are no use to me here. No, not you, Constance. I want you to get some men here for the sling.'

'It is early yet, Mother. You do not usually come down until – '

Fressenda rapped the end of her stick on the boards of the solar.

'Do as I say. I come down when I wish, not when stable clods feel they have the time. I wish to talk with Sybil.'

'Then why not get her to come up to you?'

'Mind your own business.'

Constance smirked.

'We must not strain Sybil, must we?'

Constance should have known better.

'My dear, your jealousy is surpassed only by your stupidity and your lack of discrimination. You throw yourself against everything, and catch nothing. If you had more glow between your ears and less itch between your thighs, you might get somewhere.'

Constance flushed right up to her forehead.

'At least I did not get caught.'

'Because nobody is after you,' said her mother, deliberately missing the point. 'Sybil has two very eligible suitors. As things stand at present, your father and I will have to exercise our inventive powers to the uttermost to produce convincing arguments on behalf of you and Muriella. Now go and do as I say.'

Choking back tears of rage and mortification, Constance climbed down the ladder. She flounced across the hall and almost bumped into Sybil coming in from outside.

'Hussy!' she spat.

'Do not distress yourself,' called the lady Fressenda from the solar. 'Constance and I have been talking.'

Sybil smiled. Talking!

Half an hour later, the lady Fressenda pronounced herself satisfied with the position of her chair, her stool, her cup of hot broth within arm's length, her spare shawl, and her foot-muff. She dismissed the panting crowd of bailey hands and house girls with a regal wave of the arm, and looked intently at Sybil.

'Now. Tell me – how are you feeling?'

Sybil gave a slight toss of the head.

'Mother, I am very well. I am more disturbed in the mind than in the body.'

'We can remove some of that worry, you know.'

'You can not bring him back.'

'I did not mean that, and you know it.'

Sybil tightened her lips.

'Has Torf been here again?'

Her mother sipped carefully at her broth.

'He has – communicated with us.'

'Mother, if you think you can talk me into a rapid marriage with him, so that I can pass off the child as his, I tell you it is out of the question. It is too far advanced; he would guess at once.'

'What if he did? It would be too late by then. There is also the question of honour.'

'Torf? Honour?'

Fressenda conceded the point with a brief smile.

'Very well. Expediency. By that time he would have your dowry, and he would have the Hauteville connection. He would not lightly surrender either. And, most important, you would have security.'

'And what about the child?'

'Cared for. If he kept you, he would have to keep the child. It would be the perfect solution.'

'Mother, I sometimes I wonder if you know me at all.'

'I know you very well. And I know the world. The world deceives; it promises much, and fulfils little. Geoffrey for you is the world's promise. But he is all vow and passion, and he is not here. And we do not know what will happen if and when he returns. Torf is here, and has something definite to offer. A timber roof in a knight's domain is hard, unyielding, and deadly dull, I grant you, but it is protection, and it is solid. It is all there is.'

'I do not want it.'

'But you do, child,' insisted Fressenda. 'You would rule it. You would be safe and secure, and you would rule. I know you; you are like me. Before long, you would rule. And like me, you would come to enjoy it. Power! That is what matters.'

'I would have more power as the consort of a bishop.'

'If such an outcome were possible, that may be true. But it is so uncertain. Geoffrey may mean what he says, but it may turn out to be impossible for him to fulfil what he promises. We both know it is within Torf's power.'

Sybil grimaced in frustration.

'Mother, I do not even like him. Try to understand: I am carrying Geoffrey's child. The thought of Torf touching me . . . '

Fressenda shook her head.

'I will not have that. I saw you when he visited you for the first time. I have never seen you so disturbed. You are putting up this front now not because you recoil from the thought of his touching you, but because you are afraid of what might happen if he did. Believe me, I can understand; he is a man who can convey great excitement.'

Sybil began to lose her composure.

'I love Geoffrey. And I enjoy his embraces.'

'Embraces! Torf or Geoffrey – what does it matter? If it comes to that – liking or loathing. A man is a man. Any man's demands become tiresome after enough time. It is what happens in between their demands which is important. It is what you build there that determines your life. God knows, women have few enough options, but we do have a huge option there; it is up to us. Establish a pattern, and a man will fall into it. He will not be able to help himself. As for his – demands, even they disappear in time. Habit again, you see? Habit brings disinterest; disinterest brings peace.'

Sybil found herself smiling.

'Mother?'

'Yes?'

Sybil looked meaningly.

The lady Fressenda put her nose into her steaming cup again.

'Your father was a more – dutiful man than most, that is all.'

*   *   *   *   *   *

The further south Geoffrey went in Apulia, the more he saw of smoking villages, blocked streams, slashed vines, burned cornfields. Every time he asked after Count Drogo of Hauteville, or Sir Humphrey, or any other brother, fear or hatred appeared on peasant faces. Either way he gained little news. Ivo, at the rear of the column, heard men spit as they left.

Normans were not the only culprits; terrified townsfolk barred their splintered, paint-stripped gates just as frantically, and often as vainly, against German mercenaries, Saracen raiding parties, Lombard levies, or Byzantine regular army detachments. However, the general impression gained – from maimed swineherds, weeping children, or bloodstained pilgrims – was that the Normans were the most efficient and the most dreaded.

Their camps, when Geoffrey found them, were wolf lairs, lurking in scrubby groves on mountainsides, or festering in fever-ridden valleys, or perched on open hilltops with more sentries than snakes hidden between sun-blinded rocks.

Nothing, it appeared, was sacred, from pilgrims' pockets to Papal estates. Every village, every farm, every town, and every traveller, was robbed with total impartiality towards wealth, status, race, age, sex, or religion. The only exception was the shrine of the Archangel Michael at Monte Gargano. Some shred of decency, some clinging vestige of awe, perhaps a twinge of fear, remained from childhood and the brooding reputation of the Mount of St. Michael in Brittany. In fact, the Archangel's shrine was being regularly adorned with the Hautevilles' brusque, if somewhat inverted, generosity.

Geoffrey's father Sir Nigel must have been truly devoted to this seat of holiness to be prepared to tolerate such stern, unforgiving surroundings, and such unholy behaviour on the part of his fellow-countrymen. Geoffrey remembered his father as a laughing man; he could not see him as a wanton looter and killer.

The other inhabitants were not impressive. Like many northerners everywhere who travelled south, Geoffrey found the locals corrupt, devious, effete, lacking in character, or too clever by half. But he was forced to admit that the reputation which the Norman adventurers – Hautevilles and many others – had carved for themselves was unique and deserved. His fellow-countrymen were quite clearly a plague, a scourge, and a menace.

If Papal estates had suffered as much as others from them, Geoffrey could well understand why His Holiness, much less Hildebrand, was not prepared to bend any rules of consanguinity in order to do Duke William a favour and

112

facilitate his marriage to Matilda. The way the Papacy felt about Normans at the moment, they could, and almost certainly would – if there was any Divine justice – all go to Hell.

Geoffrey finally ran one of the Hautevilles to earth in Calabria, on a remote hilltop called San Marco Argentano. He expected a leering, furtive, bullying bandit; he found instead a prodigy.

Robert of Hauteville was enormous. He had breathtaking health, inordinately good looks, and boundless confidence. His eye was of a piercing blue, and reminded Geoffrey of Sybil with its intentness. He had a booming voice, and a shattering laugh. Everything about him was larger than life. Any other leader in those frankly sordid surroundings would have been circumscribed by them. Robert looked as if he was merely tolerating them, until he moved into the larger arena which inevitably awaited his colossal personality. Or, as Ivo put it, 'When he speaks of small plans today, he is thinking of big plans tomorrow.'

When he sat and talked with him, Geoffrey felt rather as he thought Moses must have done beside the burning bush. One had to keep distance in order to avoid being consumed, but one also had to stand ground if one was going to be noticed.

For Robert enjoyed testing people. Bishop or no bishop, fellow-Norman or no fellow-Norman, Geoffrey knew he was being tested.

When Robert let loose a searching question or deliberately threw out a challenging statement, or delivered a consciously controversial opinion, he had the trick of lowering his head and of looking out of the corner of his eye. Duke William had a similar habit of moving his eyes to right and left without much turning of the head, but in his case it was from watchfulness. Robert did it from mischief, slyness, cunning. William did it to detect and thereby avoid a suspect; Robert did it to entrap one.

Geoffrey decided that attack was the best form of defence. If he allowed Robert to keep the initiative, this crafty brigand would run rings round him and he would never get a penny. He recalled something Lanfranc had told him.

'You are now a prince of the Church. You have power, whether you like it or not. And power not only in this world but the next. Like the servant with the talent, you must become accustomed to using it when necessary. If you do not, you are guilty not only of fear but of negligence and disloyalty.'

Robert spread his huge hands and grinned.

'You see our circumstances, my lord bishop. Why come to us?'

Geoffrey cleared his throat.

'Because your family estates lie within my diocese. You are part of my flock. I am concerned for your eternal soul. I am offering you a chance to save it.'

Robert roared with laughter.

'You hear that, lads? His Grace comes all the way from Normandy to tell us that we are sinners. Ha!'

His booming laugh caused puffs of vapour on the chill night air.

'Did you not know, my lord, that sinners are poor? Or have you not yet read that far in your Bible?'

Geoffrey felt the sharpness of the barb, but held his ground.

'It is only the penitent sinners who are poor. Satisfy me that you are penitent, and you convince me that you are poor.'

Robert made a grimace of appreciation.

'Good! Good! I see they make better bishops now than they did in my father's day. How is my father, by the way?'

'Sir Tancred is well. And the lady Fressenda too. Your sister Sybil sends her love.'

'Ah!'

For a moment the bantering smile left Robert's face, to be replaced by an absent look of genuine fondness. He raised his head again.

'You know her then?'

Geoffrey swallowed.

'We – are acquainted, yes.'

'And my other dear sisters?'

The playful smile had returned.

'All well. Your brothers too send their greetings – '

' – and hope soon to join me in the profits. Yes, I am sure.'

'So you do have profits?' said Geoffrey innocently.

'Legitimate spoil,' said Robert, pretending to sound virtuous.

'Others might describe it as loot,' said Geoffrey.

'Normans and other Christian knights fight a holy war against the infidel in Spain, and you priests bless their arms and call them crusaders. We fight the infidel Saracens here in Italy and you call us looters. Why?'

'Because you fight the Papacy too.'

Robert waved airily.

'Only because they get in the way. If they came down off their righteous mountaintop and asked for our help, we should be only too pleased to provide it.'

Robert lowered his head, and shot a sly glance at him.

'Yes,' agreed Geoffrey. 'For a price.'

Robert opened his arms wide to take in the support of the whole gathering.

'Naturally. Who fights for nothing? Every man has his price.'

'Even St. Peter?' suggested Geoffrey. 'Will you take your "legitimate spoil" in great sackfuls to the Gates of Heaven and negotiate the price of salvation?'

Robert picked up a huge silver cup that had stood between his feet. Its jewels glittered in the light of the camp fire. He caressed it gently, the big square finger-nails black-edged with dirt. He drank a great draught from it, wiped his mouth, and thoughtfully stirred the ashes round the fire with his toe. He picked up a couple of chicken bones and threw them on the embers.

At last he sat up straight, tossed out the dregs of the wine, and let out a great guffaw of laughter.

'By Saint Michael, we can not deceive you, my lord bishop, can we?' He shrugged massively. 'So be it. Let us therefore to business.' He threw the cup at Geoffrey.

Geoffrey felt his stomach relax. It was a good thing he had not been dealing with Lanfranc. That sharp legal mind would have found the weak spots in his argument.

$$*\qquad*\qquad*\qquad*\qquad*\qquad*$$

The lady Fressenda looked up wearily.

'How is he?'

'Sleeping,' said Sybil. 'And some colour has returned.'

Fressenda sighed.

'You go to bed now. You need the rest.'

'What about you?' said Sybil.

'I can sleep just as easily sitting up these days. I wake up so many times that it does not matter what position I am in. Go on – off you go. Humbert will tell me if there is any change. Where is Roger?'

'Still there. He has hardly left Father's side since dawn.'

Fressenda nodded.

'He is young; he will sleep at the bedside, no doubt.'

But she smiled too.

When Sybil had gone, she motioned to one of the yawning girls to put some more logs on the fire.

It was now in God's hands. The bathing, the bleeding, the purging, the praying. All that was left was the waiting. He would either get better or he would not. It struck her suddenly that the positions were reversed. How many times had Tancred sat down here in lonely vigil while she and the waiting women struggled in her many labours, none of them ever knowing if either she or the child would see the light of the next day. She found herself growing a new type of respect for him.

Odd how you continued to find out new things about those close to you after

115

such a long time. Tancred was not to know how things were going to turn out. Eleven healthy children and only three miscarriages and one stillborn in all those years – God had been kind to them, all things considered. Tancred had never been one to make much fuss.

'Oh, madam, if my lord is to be taken from us!'

'Hold your tongue, you silly girl. He is as likely to live as to die. Use your energy for prayers, not tears.'

The girl sniffed.

The lady Fressenda blinked and sat up straighter. Her reaction to the girl's wailing had been instinctive, but it had helped her to pull herself together.

My lord Tancred was going to live or he was going to die. If it pleased God to ordain the latter, it behoved her to think of what to do. Humbert and the other three would share the property, if they could manage that without quarrelling. Roger would probably go south to Robert, to Apulia. None of them would want to be bothered with portions for sisters. Constance and Muriella would almost certainly throw themselves at the first jingling saddlebag that passed through. Sybil was the worry.

Something had to be done about Sybil. If the worst happened, and the boys took over the property, they would have less time for their mother. Lady Fressenda fidgeted. She would soon lose some of her authority. She was getting older every day. If her status was gone, she could not do it all on sheer personality for much longer.

And Torf had gone south. Humbert had told her only a few days before.

Why? Why? Just when she might have been in a position to carry the argument with Sybil.

'See that Sybil does not know.'

Even a clod like Humbert could see that Sybil might worry about Geoffrey if she knew that Torf was abroad on the roads up from Burgundy. And worry was the last thing she wanted at a time like this.

The lady Fressenda frowned.

So she had information. How could she best use it? What a good thing it was that Humbert was in the habit of coming to her with any news. It was a practice she had encouraged and fostered in all the boys ever since they had left the cradle.

'Now, still and silent, boys – and we shall all hear our news. `Robert first; Robert is the eldest...'

The five elder stepsons were a little old to be thoroughly drilled, but she made her influence felt even with them. She made a great point of listening to them whenever they came home from Italy on their midsummer visits to the June feast.

It was Drogo who brought the most useful news of all. And sadly the most painful too – that the eldest stepson, William of the Iron Arm, was dead. But the titbit that followed was stored carefully away. It concerned a certain knight called Sir Nigel of Montbrai and a certain soldier of fortune by the name of Torf of Malbec.

News was knowledge, and knowledge was power. If Torf was to come into the family, she needed the means of controlling him. Blood was not there; knowledge would have to serve. She admired Torf in a perverse way. He knew exactly what he wanted, and he made the very greatest possible use of his limited gifts in order to get it. The very fertility of his lies showed his resource and his determination to attain his ends. She did not like him, but she was beginning to find him a worthy adversary. She was fond of Geoffrey, but did that young man have a clear enough idea of his own real desires to be a fitting protector for her Sybil?

If Geoffrey was not prepared to fight for her, then he was not the man that Sybil thought he was, and she would be better off with Torf.

The lady Fressenda pulled up the blanket to her chin, and sniffed at it. It was fresh from recent washing, and smelled of lavender. How many days would it be before it again gave off the familiar odour of stale smoke?

*   *   *   *   *   *

'It must be big – big, you understand.'

Robert wanted to know all about it – size, materials, ornamentation, endowments.

'Bigger than Avranches. And beautiful. We must have beauty. And class.'

Robert was most insistent about the 'class'.

Since nothing existed above ground, Geoffrey was obliged to give his imagination full rein, allowing himself dispensation from punishment for falsehood on the grounds that it was in God's own cause. If he was expected to fight for the Church, then surely he could also be pardoned for lying for it. Would God, he wondered, be as broad-minded if He saw that much of this fighting and bargaining was for Sybil too? A double cause at least produced a double fertility of thought.

One particularly felicitous figment of Geoffrey's imagination that seemed to catch Robert's fancy was the project for statues in the aisle – of Sir Tancred, the lady Fressenda, and all twelve of the Hauteville sons. There was much talk of engravings and inscriptions, and Geoffrey added further attractive possibilities in the shape of specially planned graves for every member of the family, right against the church wall so as to secure the greatest possible share of Divine Grace by their proximity to the holy relics beneath the altar (Geoffrey delicately omitted to tell Robert that the holy relics were not exactly in place yet, deciding that it was the spirit of the intention that really mattered).

117

If any of the brothers should be so unfortunate – as William of the Iron Arm, regrettably, had already been – as to die outside Normandy, Geoffrey felt sure that some arrangement could be made to have the bones transported from Apulia to Coutances at some future date mutually convenient to both parties. And talking of bones, if Robert happened to know of any holy relics – say, from the vast repository of St. Michael the Archangel at Monte Gargano – that could be added to those already at rest under the altar at Coutances, thereby enhancing Robert's share of Divine Grace at the Ultimate Hour, then he, Bishop Geoffrey, would be only too happy to arrange for their immediate transferral, promising that Robert's generosity and piety in such an endowment would be enshrined for all to see and admire in a most impressively carved and inscribed reliquary.

Robert, though touched by such a delicate sentiment, suggested that it was only fitting that Geoffrey should respond in like manner by agreeing to officiate at the wedding that had been recently arranged between himself and the lady Aubreda of Buonalbergo, a nearby lordship in Apulia.

Geoffrey, who, thanks to Lanfranc's tuition and some tentative practice in churches on the journey through France and Burgundy, had become reasonably familiar with the conduct of the Mass, was not, however, conversant as yet with the order of service for marriage. He pointed out, therefore, that, in order to receive the sacrament of marriage, especially from a prince of the Church, Robert would have to be in a State of Grace, which would mean in turn that Bishop Geoffrey would have to hear his confession and impose suitable penance before granting absolution. Since there appeared, from his recent journey through Apulia, to be ample evidence that a great measure of sin might lay upon Robert's soul, Bishop Geoffrey suggested that the most fitting way of removing the weight of this sin would be by an appreciable additional contribution to the coffers of the cathedral restoration fund. Faced with such dazzling proof of Robert's true and sincere penitence, Geoffrey would have no choice but to grant full absolution, thus allowing Sir Robert to come pure and unspotted to the altar of holy matrimony.

Robert replied that, on reflection, perhaps it would be more fitting, and no doubt more pleasing to the lady Aubreda, to have the wedding service celebrated by a local priest of her acquaintance. Geoffrey solemnly agreed that on balance it was a wise decision worthy of Solomon himself.

When the time came for Geoffrey to begin the homeward journey, Robert draped a huge arm round his shoulders.

'Build well and build big, my bishop.' He pointed at Ivo. 'And do you guard our treasure with your life.'

'As if it were my own, Sir Robert,' said Ivo with a grin.

'How can you be sure we shall not treat it as our own?' said Geoffrey, sharing the joke.

'Because,' said Robert, turning his glittering blue eyes upon him, 'nobody travels a thousand miles to a wolf's lair for a lie. I have not survived this far without being able to judge men well.'

He let out a great blast of laughter.

'Besides, I still have some brothers at home. They will keep an eye on you. Sooner or later, I should know whatever you do in this world.'

'True,' said Geoffrey evenly.

He made the sign of the cross.

'And I can say with authority what will happen to all of you in the next. My thanks and farewell.'

Ivo flatly refused to carry, or in any way be responsible for, the holy relics. So did Thierry. So it fell to Geoffrey. It was difficult to feel constant reverence for a constant burden.

The treasure they decided to share between them and to carry in donkey packs. A bishop with a lumbering cart would be too conspicuous and too vulnerable. They wore mail whenever possible to deter likely assailants, which accounted for Geoffrey's frequent complaints about the heat.

Ivo agreed.

'Italy moreover breeds the most stupid donkeys I have ever encountered.'

'Perhaps you do not swear at them in the right language,' suggested Thierry.

'Perhaps,' agreed Ivo. 'My lord,' he went on, breaking into Geoffrey's thoughts, 'do you know what they call Robert of Hauteville?'

'No.'

'The Guiscard.'

'Guiscard?'

'Yes. It means many things – the fox, the weasel, the wily one, the know-all, the one who is not caught napping, who has a plan for everything.'

Geoffrey thought of that sly, sidelong glance. Not a bad name.

He thought too of the men who followed the Guiscard, and of the life they led. The dirt, the squalor, the lash of the elements, the caves and the camp fires, steamy breath on cold air, lonely sentries behind rocks. Of terrified victims on their knees, the crackle of thatch afire, the petty squabbles over looted trinkets. Of raid, skirmish, ambush. Of ruse and trick and treachery. Of elation and misery, gloating and grovelling, roaring lust of juicy life and gagging fear of sudden death.

It was a world away from the picture he had made for himself in his daydreams at Montbrai: battles, adventures, fine clothes, adoring people waving beside his stirrups. In one respect, though, the reality had exceeded expectation.

Being near Robert Guiscard was like resting beside a tensioned trap; you never knew when it was about to snap shut.

What Robert had said, when Ivo and Thierry had set out with the pack animals and the two of them were alone, had been the biggest shock of all.

'Take good care of Sybil.'

Geoffrey was thrown off balance. He stared at Robert, fighting to gain time.

For once Robert looked deadly serious, even earnest.

'Brother Serlo arrived from Normandy last night. He tells me you and Sybil have – plans.'

Even though it might cost him the treasure in his saddlebags, Geoffrey saw no point in lying.

'Yes.'

To his surprise, Robert nodded his approval.

'Good. I thought you might be an honest man. Now I know. My sister will be in good hands.'

'You do not mind that I am – a – '

Robert snapped his fingers.

'A mitre more or less. A man makes his way by using whatever drops into his lap. If I had been made a bishop at your age, I should be a cardinal by now and half way towards the Papal Chair. Ha!' He hawked and spat. 'And as for Sybil – why should a man be denied other pleasures because he has wit and enterprise? We are told that the early fathers of the Jews had numerous wives. And Holy St. Michael, look at Solomon! All you are asking for is one. Besides – ' He shrugged and looked sidelong ' – popes have done it; why not you? However – '

'Yes?'

'I suggest you hurry home. Serlo says you have a rival pressing his suit harder than ever.'

'Torf? Impossible. Not now that – '

He stopped himself, but too late.

'The child? Do not be so sure. You do not know my mother. Her resource is infinite, believe me.'

'Do you know this Torf?'

'I know *of* him. My brothers have told me. He tricked them of many a bauble when he was here.'

Geoffrey remembered his talk in the solar with Mauger . . .

'No, this really is in confidence . . .'

He looked again at Robert.

'Are you sure that is all he did?'

'All?'

'Do you know how your brother William died?'

It was Robert's turn to look taken aback.

'You mean Torf? Torf?'

He put his hands on his hips and leaned back in gusts of laughter.

'That grubby cheat? That sweaty coward?'

'Do you know how your brother died?' persisted Geoffrey.

Robert stopped laughing.

'Yes. He slipped on an icy rock in an ambush, fell into a gully and broke his neck. Served him right for being careless. Now hurry back to Normandy, slit that ferret's throat, and look after Sybil.'

Father! Father! Ask about Father. And William. Was Torf lying about that too? Ask now. When will there be a better chance?

Geoffrey looked at Robert, at the broad face brimming with confidence and goodwill. At the ice-blue eyes, Sybil's eyes . . .

Geoffrey mounted.

On impulse he held out his hand. To his amazement, Robert took it in his fingers, not his fist, bent, and kissed the ring. Then he slapped the destrier on the rump.

'Build, my bishop, build! Big, beautiful. And give it class – plenty of class!'

*   *   *   *   *   *

121

Chapter Eight

Ralph limped late into Alençon, and scavenged for scraps behind a tavern stable. He waited behind a water butt in the yard for the grooms to fall asleep, then crept into an unused loft and buried himself in the straw as much for warmth as for concealment.

His long cloak, the one which his mother had stitched with such tearful fondness for his travels, had been wrenched off his back by three large troopers from Brabant in the pay of the Count of Beauvais, who had refused him employment. At Troyes, neither the Count of Champagne nor his constable had deigned to speak to him. At Paris, loungers at the King's court had laughed at him before throwing him into the Seine, and the garrison at Chartres had stolen his horse after pretending that they were going to take him to see the Count of Blois. He could not even find the Duke of Normandy. Now that the siege of Brionne was over, the surrounding camp was a ghostly shambles; a scattering of furtive looters, freed at last from their long imprisonment, picked like crows at gutted wagons and tumbled tents. Where was the Duke? Gone to England, they said. Ralph had no way of knowing whether they were teasing him or not.

He knew his skin was grey with dirt, his clothes stiff with it, and he smelt offensive even to himself. He could not remember when he had had his last hot meal.

He shivered under the straw, curled up as tightly as he could, and crossed his arms around himself. Not the dirt, not the cold, not the hunger – none was as great as the fatigue, nor as compelling. If he was found and whipped, if the stable burned down, if he died from cold in his sleep – nothing mattered but rest. Rest. He had no recall of shutting his eyes.

Sunlight was flooding the loft when he opened them. At once he knew it was the voices below which had wakened him. One voice in particular stood out as being in command. Not from its loudness or fierceness either. Nor from its profanity. On the contrary, it was remarkably measured and level, yet it managed to convey total confidence in being obeyed. Ralph noticed an Angevin accent too.

He levered himself quietly on to his hands and knees, and began to crawl towards the open shutter giving on to the stable yard. Suddenly a board gave way under him, one leg went clean through, and he was clawing with remaining limbs to prevent himself from falling. No wonder this loft had been empty!

'Well, well, what have we here? An angel from on high.'

A grip of iron closed round his dangling ankle.

'It seems as if his wings are continuing to keep him up in the air. Shall we see what the rest of him looks like, lads?'

A sharp tug almost dislocated his hip, drove a broomful of splinters into his clinging hands, and brought him down through the hole like a crumbling pile of autumn apples.

Just as he braced himself for the shock of hitting the ground, two powerful arms broke his fall, swung him away, and set him on his feet all in one movement.

'A very grubby angel, to be sure.'

The men in leather jerkins round him sniggered. The speaker, in full-length mail, was rubbing his blue jowl and pretending to examine him like a buyer in a slave-market. Dark, thick-set, with the shoulders of an ox, he had surprisingly young features, which would have looked almost handsome were it not for a fleshiness about the cheeks and neck. The smile which hovered about the lips was not reflected in the pale grey eyes.

Ralph wiped his palms on the back of his thighs. This bear of a man could not be all that many years older than himself, but the face showed every sign of a deep acquaintance with the bad things of the world from an early age. There was something cat-like – merciless and capricious – about the way he prowled right around Ralph, savouring the initiative and milking the moment for all it was worth. The soldiers glanced at each other and grinned.

'How about looking for the colour of his wings, Fulk?'

'Or seeing if he can fly.'

'Perhaps he has a message for us from the Almighty.'

Fulk wagged a finger infinitesimally, without looking at any man to see if he was going to be obeyed. Having completed a full circle, he came to a halt right in front of Ralph. He put out a hand and touched the dark patch under each of Ralph's cheekbones. No dirt came off.

'A hungry angel too. Eh, boy?'

Before Ralph could react, fingers gripped his upper arm and squeezed. Fulk raised his thick eyebrows appreciatively.

'But no beggar. From a good home, I should say, and not all that long ago, from his clothes.'

A hand lingered on the collar of his jerkin.

'Speak, fellow. Find your voice, or these lads here will find your wings.'

Ralph took a deep breath.

'I am the son of a free-born knight of Normandy, from Gisors. I am on my way to – to seek my fortune in my profession.'

'A very long way, by the look of it. It is always a long way for second sons, is it not? Tell me, were there no vacancies in Blois or Champagne?'

'It – it did not appeal to me.'

123

'Ah!' Again that humourless smile. 'Was even the King's service in Paris not up to your – fastidious requirements?'

The soldiers were chuckling openly. One thing about Fulk: he was a bastard, but he did provide entertainment.

Ralph flushed with anger.

'I chose to seek the lord of Bellême. Or, failing that, maybe the Duke of Anjou.' He mimicked Fulk's Angevin accent. 'If he is willing to employ you, I should think there is hope even for me.'

If he was going to be beaten up, or worse, he might as well have the satisfaction of saying what he thought.

The soldiers stopped laughing.

'Give him to us, Fulk. We can teach him some manners.'

Again that miniscule wave of the finger.

'No, no. This angel has his share of spirit, for all that it may not be very holy. Tell me, my thin-cheeked angel – ' fingers took a pinch of flesh around his jaw ' – what do you do?'

Ralph looked blank.

Fulk stepped back and waved impatiently.

'You talk airily about the profession of arms. Very well. What do you do? Where is your destrier?'

'My horse was stolen.'

'And your spear, shield, mace, and so on, and your ponies and squires sold off – yes, yes, too bad, I am sure.'

Ralph flushed again.

'Would you be an officer without that hauberk and without your grovelling audience?'

One of the outraged audience took out his knife and began to advance on Ralph. Fulk knocked him down with the flat of his hand, and turned back to Ralph almost before he hit the ground.

'Yes,' he said simply. 'Because I have my pride and I have my wits. And so, I see, do you. How are you with horses?'

Ralph lifted his head proudly.

'Name it.'

'I want someone to guard them, feed them, lead them. I want someone to break the trail and be the first into ambush, and someone to ride behind and be the first to fall to the pursuit – we are no angels either.'

'I did not think that the Duke of Anjou was interested in angels.'

Fulk's voice became even quieter.

'You have made your gesture and your point. I now know you have spirit.

124

There is no need to continue proving it. And, for your information, the Duke of Anjou has been laying off many of his troops now that Touraine has fallen to him. Why do you think we are so far north? We are now free agents. If you join us, we are currently contracted to travel far, far – Burgundy, maybe Provence and Savoy. You will receive no pay while we are on the road, but you will be fed and clothed. If we complete the contract, there will be good pickings for all. I can offer nothing else.'

Burgundy, Provence, Savoy – they were only names to Ralph; they might be behind the moon.

'I accept.'

Fulk smiled.

'Good. Just one more thing – rules. Quite simple. There is only one.'

'Yes?'

Fulk turned to where the fallen soldier was struggling on to his hands and knees, and launched a mighty kick into his buttocks which sent him sprawling into a clatter of buckets and pitchforks. The rest laughed just as heartily as they had laughed at Ralph.

Fulk jerked his head.

'Pick him up. His name is Aimery. Tell him to feed you.'

* * * * * *

When Geoffrey called at the house in Pavia on his return journey, Lanfranc's father was delighted to see him. Geoffrey was grateful to accept his pressing invitation to stay a while; they had been on the road from Apulia for over two weeks.

'Ah!' said Thierry. 'Lombard cooking!' And proceeded to get off again with one of the highly-polished serving girls.

Ivo called constantly for hot water, and soaked his feet by the hour.

Geoffrey soon found that the physical fatigue of the road was replaced by the mental exhaustion of trying to keep up a constant flow of conversation with the eager old man; his meagre Italian creaked under the strain. It was the more embarrassing because his host had so much to say and was so obviously excited by the visit.

Much of his talk, naturally, was about his son; his pride in Lanfranc's achievements and reputation shone through every sentence.

'And do you know, *mio padrone*, there are greater things to come.'

Geoffrey smiled.

The old man raised his eyebrows.

'You think it is the talk of a foolish old man crazed with pride? No, my friend. I do not understand matters of high politics, or deep scholarship, or complex spirituality. Fortunately the lord God has, in His wisdom, given my son brains far beyond the capacity of mine to grasp them. God has also given him a character with which to handle them and interpret them. Now character I do understand. And I understand Lanfranc better than he understands himself. Because he has tried many paths and not succeeded according to his own exacting demands, he feels that he has failed and therefore made a mistake in attempting them. He equates failure with error. Because he is at bottom a humble man, he blames what he thinks is his pride for leading him into this error. He equates natural intelligence, imagination and energy with pride. The result is that he now suspects his own gifts as vessels of unholiness. He fancies that true peace lies with avoidance of the occasions of using them again.'

'Impossible,' said Geoffrey. 'Things will come to him. Situations will develop around him. Nothing he did could dim the light he carries within him.'

'Exactly. Only he can not yet see that. Or, if he did, he would at once put it down as pride. So you see? The time must come when those gifts are to be fully employed. And he will have to come to terms with the conflict inside himself.'

The old man leaned forward and refilled the wine cups.

'Talking of which, my lord bishop – ' he stressed the formal title just enough to make his point ' – how are we proceeding with our own destiny?'

What was it – the wine? The care and comfort after the fatigue of the journey? The burden of guarding the treasure and the holy relics? The worry about Sybil and the child? The physical deprivation of her embraces? The endless searching in his mind for a solution? Recollection of the unbearable pain of hope on the face of Thorold? Dark rage at the scheming of Torf? The still lingering anger at Mauger for placing him in this impossible situation? Fury at the remoteness, almost the silliness of a bishopric like Coutances?

Whatever the reason, it all came pouring out. Some of the sentences became entangled in Geoffrey's poor Italian, but Lanfranc's father had only to catch the passion in his voice and see the look on his face to grasp the general drift. The old man was a good listener.

Geoffrey at last talked himself to a standstill, and sat somewhat sheepishly twiddling the stem of his cup. Lanfranc's father coughed gently.

'I should imagine that advice is the last thing you would want at a time like this, but may I venture to make one observation?'

Taking Geoffrey's offhand shrug as agreement, he continued.

'It seems to me that, rather like my son, you are equating two things as one when they are in fact quite different. You seek purpose and you seek peace of mind, and you assume that the one will lead *ipso facto* to the other, almost that they are both part and parcel of the same desirable destiny. This is not so. Pursuit of purpose means energy, struggle, conflict; peace means that the conflict is over. Such peace, alas! we can hope for only in Heaven. Our time here is therefore, perforce, one of conflict. It is a natural condition. You can no more spend your time bewailing it than you can complain of constantly breathing.'

'But conflict to what purpose, sir? How can I be sure that I am fighting the correct fight when I feel so – so beset with problems which demand an answer? Your son talks a lot of God's Will and of his search for it. If his is so fraught with difficulties and setbacks, how much the more will mine be? All this mental struggle only tells me that I am miles away from it. I become so exhausted with the fight that there are times when I do not care whether I am near or far.'

Lanfranc's father smiled.

'There, if I may say so, you go again – confusing things. You assume that conflict is disharmony. That is not necessarily so. To be out of tune with God – that, I agree is a serious matter. But the very fact that you search so hard for a way tells me that you are not out of tune with Him. However, search means also conflict, and you must not worry about that. So long as every step you take forward, however much conflict you may have suffered before taking it, is taken for the best reason that you can think of at the time, then you are going in the right direction – even though you may have no clear idea of what that direction is.'

Geoffrey remembered Gori's words about taking time and using 'wit and energy'. Wit and energy.

The old man must have read his mind.

'There is nothing in Holy Will which insists that you solve every problem at the same time. Even God gave Himself a rest on the seventh day.'

And so they talked.

Geoffrey in the end made the excuse that he was anxious to return for Sybil's welfare and in order to set afoot various schemes for rebuilding. What was troubling him still more was the fact that Thierry was becoming extremely friendly with the serving girl. It was not so much the liaison itself – though that could prove embarrassing under another man's roof – as the possibility that one fine evening Thierry, full of wine and confidence, would start talking about the contents of the saddlebags, and telling news in confidence to any sparkling serving girl was as good as shouting it from the housetops.

As they stood saying their farewells, Lanfranc's father laid a hand on Geoffrey's arm.

'Do not spend too much time chewing on scruples; they make a most disturbing diet. God gave you common sense as well as conscience. And one last thing – in all your doubts and speculations – about your brother, your enemy, your lady, your child, your inheritance, your broken cathedral – do not lose sight of one confirmed fact.'

'Yes?'

'You are a bishop of the Holy Catholic Church. By the miracle of God's Grace, therefore, you have powers. Remember. And now farewell.'

The old man took his hand and kissed the ring. He looked up into Geoffrey's confused face and smiled.

'Have no fear; you will acquit yourself well. My son is of the same opinion; he thinks highly of you. Oh – I nearly forgot. Lanfranc recommends that when you enter Burgundy on your return journey you stay a short while at Cluny. He has warned Abbot Hugh to expect you. God go with you.'

*   *   *   *   *   *

Aimery stood in the open doorway and shook the rain off his cloak.

'God's Breath! What a night! Surely nobody will travel in weather like this.'

Ralph shivered.

'While you are making up your mind, shut the door, damn you.'

Ralph had soon found out that Aimery took easily to obedience. He disliked alternatives, and, when faced with a couple, turned to anyone who would choose one for him. He teased Ralph about his knightly manners, but never seriously attempted to cross the social divide between them. If the truth were told, he went in awe and fear of Fulk, but then so did nearly every member of the party. Ralph felt fear too, but his breeding and dignity would not let him show it. Aimery respected and admired him for it.

The surprising quietness of Fulk's voice conveyed menace. So did the ever-present threat of sudden violence, as Ralph had seen on that first morning. Never overdone, rarely expected, always perfectly judged. Profanity was there too, but not the usual mindless swearing of the professional soldier. Fulk gave the uncomfortable impression to superstitious, low-born men-at-arms that he not only thought out his unholy oaths but meant every word of them. There was a touch of gentility about the diction too. Older members of the party told stories.

'They say his father was a bishop or a vicomte.'

'Wrong side of the blanket, of course.'

'He can read, you know. Seen him do it.'

'Had his mother locked up. Funny in the head. You can hear her in the night if you stay there in summer. I had a cousin worked there.'

They all obeyed Fulk at once and implicitly. He was a superb soldier, a born leader, and a thoroughly efficient mercenary. Ralph soon found that he expected similar efficiency in his underlings. In the long ride to the south from Alençon, he dismissed two men and took on three more, and one of those lasted only a few days.

'You can not let the numbers drop too far, Fulk. Provence and Savoy still have Saracen raids, they say.'

'Quality, not quantity. It is the will, not the wish, that matters,' said Fulk, in a rare foray into philosophy. 'Besides,' he added with his quiet smile, 'the fewer we are, the greater each share of the loot.'

He seemed satisfied with Ralph's work with the horses, and offered few criticisms of Ralph's performance as scout ahead and rearguard behind. It involved little more fieldcraft than he had long since mastered in the vales and forests around Gisors, though he learned a lot about roads and inns and monasteries. As a middle son of a poor Norman knight, he was not without resource and powers of decision, and he possessed the natural confidence that went with consciousness of his position in society.

Fulk had provided him with a good horse, frankly better than the one of his father's which had been stolen in Chartres.

'You have to hand it to Fulk; he does look after you.'

Ralph, however, was content with his lowly duties, because they kept him out of Fulk's way. He had never got over his physical revulsion of the closeness of the man on the morning of their meeting. He also found that he enjoyed working alone. Ever since Michael had died, there had been nobody to whom he could open his heart. He was developing an absent, taciturn manner. It grated on Aimery's more gregarious nature.

'Why do you not say much?'

Ralph shrugged.

Aimery put out his hands to the blaze.

'Brrr! I shall be glad to get back. Talking to you is like talking to one of those mountain walls out there. Though at least they echo.'

Ralph looked up.

'So we are going back?'

'Mmm. Fulk said to give it five or six days. We have waited a week.'

They had been to every hospice and every hut for fifty miles either way. They knew about every party, every pilgrim, every goat that had crossed their path in the last six weeks. Not one creature remotely fitted the description of the man they were looking for.

A sudden thought struck Aimery. He looked anxiously at Ralph.

'You think the same – yes?'

Ralph nodded. Poor Aimery; he had nearly caught himself doing some independent thinking. And he was the one who had been entrusted with Fulk's orders.

'I agree,' said Ralph. 'They did not come this way.'

'So it is either the Cenis down to Vienne, or the Little Saint Bernard straight down to Lyons.'

'Or the coast.'

Aimery shook his head.

'Too risky – pirates, Moors, Saracens. You can never tell. Fulk says his party is not a large one.'

'All the same, it will pay us to keep our eyes open on the way back.'

'Oh, definitely, definitely.'

Aimery broke a loaf of bread in half across his knee.

'My money says Fulk has already located him. He has worked out the most likely route, and is sitting in some comfortable tavern with his feet up, waiting for the prey to walk into the trap. We are simply the nets to be hung over the other bolt-holes just in case. Cunning devil!'

'Who is this man anyway?' said Ralph. 'What is so special about him?'

Aimery munched stolidly.

'Fulk will tell you that when he is good and ready.'

Ralph smiled. No danger of Aimery taking the initiative and providing the information himself. If indeed he knew.

'Did you meet the man who hired us?' asked Ralph.

'No. Fulk never says.'

'And you accept that?'

'Not much choice. But do what Fulk says, and he will see you are all right.'

Aimery hoicked a crumb from his whiskers with his tongue.

'He must be carrying something precious enough to make a man's head spin. Fulk did let slip that our – er – employer was so eager to get us that he was willing to pay with his wife's dowry. Imagine! Says he has great expectations.'

Ralph felt a twinge of unease, and not for the first time.

Why should a knight in Normandy or Anjou be paying a group of mercenaries – paying with his wife's expected dowry – to intercept a travelling nobleman who was supposed to be carrying something very valuable? The whole thing smelt worse the more he thought about it.

No wonder he was such poor company for Aimery.

Still, it was work. And he was hundreds of miles now from home.

*   *   *   *   *   *

'*Diex aie!*'

It was the first time that Geoffrey had heard Ivo's war-cry while looking at his back. How many hundreds of times had he winced with the thunder of it as he faced that jutting chinstrap and bristling whiskers! He felt a surge of confidence as he spurred to draw level with the tight, bunched, eager figure in front of him.

No more wooden drill swords now.

'*Diex aie!*'

Thierry and the others came in on either side of him.

'*Diex aie!*'

Already the vermin were running. Was it not typical? Creep up on a peaceful column of innocent travellers and loose a flight of furtive, hopeful arrows? And as soon as some of the column take off their cloaks and show signs of fight, scuttle for the trees.

Now they were splitting up and bolting for their separate holes. Ivo turned off to the right in pursuit of one, still roaring. Geoffrey singled out another immediately in front of him, while Thierry wheeled to the left to bring to bay two more.

Geoffrey plunged into bracken which came up to his spurs, still keeping his eyes on the bobbing head of his quarry. Suddenly the fern was alive with clutching hands and snarling faces. He heard Ivo swearing, and the clash of blades.

He got in one full swing with his own sword before he was dragged from the saddle. He heard a scream just before the breath was knocked out of him by the impact of the fall. A boot smashed into the side of his face . . .

'The sin of pride, my friend.'

A quiet, mocking voice. A composed, if slightly disdainful, expression.

'The cardinal error of the second-rate talent – underestimation of the opposition.'

'Who are you – ah!'

Geoffrey cried out with the pain of simply drawing breath. He was shocked to see blood in the area of the right ribs. His mail hauberk had been taken. He looked hastily about him. Ivo was bound too, and bleeding from the mouth, but seemed otherwise unhurt. He looked more furious than anything. One of their men-at-arms lay on his side, grotesquely twisted and obviously dead. The other was tied back to back with Thierry. One of their attackers was trying on Ivo's hauberk.

'My name is Fulk – not that it will mean anything to you. And your name, if I mistake not, is Geoffrey de Montbrai.'

Geoffrey stared. Fulk enjoyed the moment.

'And you are travelling to Normandy with something of great value.'

Geoffrey began hot denials, but Fulk held up a hand.

'Please. Spare me the performance. Most unbecoming to a man in your present – shall we say – terminal situation.'

'You have to attack the whole column, and they outnumber you, and now they will expect you. How can you identify our horses?'

Fulk smiled.

131

'Baggy merchants? I think not. A scare here, a buffet there, a bribe somewhere else. And *voila!*'

He stretched out an arm, and there was Aimery leading in the pack-horses. Geoffrey's and Ivo's saddlebags were already propped beside a tree.

Geoffrey glanced at Ivo, whose face had turned into stone. So . . .

To his surprise, it was Thorold who came into his mind; he could see clearly his blue-veined dome of a head, the wisps of white hair blown by the west wind, the eager hope in his eyes.

'What now?'

Fulk caught sight of a leather thong round Geoffrey's neck. He reached forward, casually cut it with his knife, and drew out from inside the bloodstained shirt the crucifix, the one Lanfranc had bestowed.

'What now? Oh, we kill you of course. I am sorry you are now awake to witness it. Had you not regained consciousness, we could have performed the task without causing you any distress. As it is, however – ' he spread his hands ' – fortunes of war.'

A gust of laughter burst from a knot of Fulk's men. The one with Ivo's hauberk was parading around, the mail drooping from him in voluminous folds, the sleeves hanging far below his fingers. Nobody looked at the man in the bracken – the one caught by Geoffrey's sword – the one sprawled out with his eyes staring and his neck cut half through.

Fulk stood up and slipped the crucifix into a wallet on his belt.

'Your executioner should be along any time now. I apologise for the delay.'

Geoffrey tried to sit more upright, wincing at the pain in his side. If he was going to die, it might as well be in the most dignified position possible.

'Do you intend to kill us all? If it is me you want, and my treasure, why not let the others go?'

To his surprise, Fulk agreed.

'A waste of manpower, especially as I have just lost two. I had thought of that, as a matter of fact. With you – er – no longer with us, these worthy fellows will be without a master, and I can always use good men. Especially as one of them was responsible for killing one of mine. I have seldom seen such swordsmanship. My compliments.'

He bowed in Ivo's direction.

'So what do you say?' said Fulk. 'Come with me and see the world. And you can still share the treasure.'

The soldiers stopped laughing at the baggy hauberk, and looked at Ivo. They had seen him fight. There was both praise and hope in their eyes.

Geoffrey felt the silence. He looked at the bad-tempered slits of Ivo's eyes . . .

There was a short silence . . .

Ivo spat.

Fulk dusted his hands.

'As you wish. A manly gesture, albeit an ill-judged one. However . . . Ah, here comes our executioner.'

'Are you afraid to do it yourself?' growled Ivo.

'Not in the least,' replied Fulk. 'In your own case, I can probably oblige. But I like to involve everybody of our company in what we do. It provides a bond between us. I plan the operation; my lads here carry it out, to the best of their limited ability – ' he gestured to the bodies of their fallen comrades – 'and there remains only our chief scout to make his own small contribution to the proceedings by giving the *coup de grâce*. He has recently joined us, and in the interests of mutual confidence, I think it only fitting that he provides us with a tangible token of his good intentions. Ralph?'

Geoffrey dropped his head and sighed. It all seemed such a pity.

He could hear Fulk's voice talking low to this scout. After a while, he heard footsteps rustling through the crushed bracken and couch grass.

They stopped in front of him. A dagger rasped against its sheath.

Geoffrey remembered that Ivo was watching. In a strange way, that meant that Father and Mauger were watching too. For their sake, he had to lift his head.

The face in front of him was pale and tight like a death mask. He was barely more than a boy. Their eyes met.

A flash of recognition lit the youth's face. The shock was so great that he dropped the dagger and fell back on to his buttocks. At once he scrambled to his feet and scurried away as if he had disturbed a trapped boar in a thicket. He tripped over a tussock of grass and fell again, this time into the knot of soldiers gathered to watch the sport . . .

Fulk frowned. He could not make out the urgent whispers. Geoffrey frowned too, in the effort of recall. Where had he seen that face before? He knew only that on the previous occasion also it had been pale and drawn. A glance at Ivo told him that Ivo too was baffled.

Fulk at length lost patience.

'By the vitals of all the saints, what is the matter with you?'

They turned to face him, clustered together for mutual support, like a group of small boys caught stealing fruit. Nobody said anything. Fulk glared.

'Well?'

At last a disembodied voice came from somewhere about the middle.

'You said nothing about murdering a bishop.'

'A what?'

'A bishop. The boy knows him.'

'He is the Bishop of Coutances,' said Ralph, still breathless with shock.

'Prove it,' said Fulk.

'He has to us,' said the voice. 'You deceived us.'

'I have done everything I promised. Brought you safely here, found the quarry, carried out a successful raid. The treasure lies there, ready to be shared.'

'You never said he was a bishop,' said the voice doggedly.

There was a murmur of agreement.

Geoffrey glanced at Ivo, who jerked his jaw Heavenwards, then made a silent snarling grimace.

Fulk put his hands on his hips and let his eyes wander over every one of them, his expression one of steadily deepening disgust.

'This is ridiculous. They are our prisoners. The treasure is ours. Nobody from the rest of the party will bother us. Kill the others and there will be no witnesses. What are you afraid of – the bogeymen in the forest?'

'You know what it is, Fulk. A bishop. There is only one worse crime; it is but one step removed from killing the Pope himself.'

'You will burn in Hellfire!'

Geoffrey had found his wits and found his voice.

That last look from Ivo had triggered a voice in his memory.

'Use your powers!'

As he lay in the grass, with the blood caked on his shirt and ribs, shivering with shock and the wind on his sweaty back, he could suddenly smell polished oak and Sicilian wine and the bloom on the flesh of serving girls as they leaned over him to take away the dish.

'Use your powers!'

Back came the words that Lanfranc had drummed into his head:

'I can forgive your sins or I can bind you to them. Whatsoever I bind on earth shall remain bound in Heaven.' He now found a few of his own. 'Touch me, touch my servants, and your immortal soul shall fry in torment in the furnace of Hellfire for all time to come. As a prince of the Holy Catholic Church, I tell you this for your own good.'

They shuffled closer together, their eyes pinpoints of concentration, their arms hanging impotently by their sides.

Geoffrey pressed his advantage.

'Murder is evil enough. Dishonour to your father is most heinous. Blasphemy and disrespect to God worse still. But violence to your father in God – for this God in His most righteous wrath has reserved his most dire punishment.'

They melted and shrank together like butter in the sun.

Geoffrey pursued them.

'And if any one of you should touch the relics that I carry – precious relics of God's consecrated saints . . . '

'Holy relics!'

'All it needs is a touch – the merest brushing of the fingertips, whether by accident or design it matters not.'

One or two of his mesmerised audience began to cross themselves.

'Pull yourselves together!' shouted Fulk.

'You kill him then.'

'Very well.'

Fulk bent and picked up the dagger that Ralph had dropped.

'If you allow it,' said Geoffrey, keeping his eyes on the soldiers with a huge effort, 'it is as bad as if you had done it with your own hands. Violence to a guardian of holy relics is as mortal a sin as disrespect to the holy relics themselves. Do you think God is to be deceived by stupid tricks of mere men to ease their conscience?'

Before Fulk could think of another answer, the knot of drooping men had broken up and re-formed in front of Geoffrey. The owner of the voice found himself face to face with his leader.

'We obey your orders, Fulk, but not even you can countermand God.'

Fulk's voice dropped to a whisper.

'Which one of you do I have to kill first?'

Every palm was wet.

'A man who dies trying to protect holy relics,' said Geoffrey, 'will go straight to the Holy Bliss of Heaven. I, your father in God, tell you this.'

The man in front of Fulk looked him straight in the eyes.

'You heard him. Whoever you kill goes to Heaven for guarding the holy relics. Whichever one of us kills a bishop, we all go to Hell. We can not have that. Let us take the treasure and go.'

Fulk's fingers fidgeted round the handle of the knife. Now Geoffrey did think of Sybil.

'Not even you could kill everybody and get it all back on your own,' growled Ivo.

Slowly, very slowly, Fulk's expression eased. The sardonic curl returned to the lips.

'Cut them loose.'

He bowed low before Geoffrey.

'I take it that God your accomplice has no objection to our removing the treasure as our price for sparing your life. I presume that as a reasonable being

He will not drive so hard a bargain as to make mere theft a corporate Hellfire matter as well.'

Geoffrey took the point.

'I am sure God sees the wisdom of a fair deal.'

Fulk nodded his approval.

'Good. Then we shall be on our way. You will forgive me if we leave the burials to you, since you have proved so conclusively that you have special insight into death and the hereafter.'

Fulk picked up the saddlebags and tossed them to Aimery, who` recoiled as if they were on fire. Nobody would touch them. Fulk himself was the only one who would take out the treasure, and the others watched in wary suspense.

'Careful!'

'They are double-wrapped at the bottom,' said Geoffrey.

Fulk glared at him, but Geoffrey noticed that he left the package carefully alone.

He mounted, and looked down at Geoffrey.

'I heard that you were a knight.'

'I am.'

'Then perhaps one day I shall meet you when you do not have your illustrious Ally at your side.'

'Perhaps. And since I have saved your soul, perhaps you could save my curiosity.'

Fulk inclined his head with an ironic smile.

'Favour for favour.'

'How did you hear of our journey and our errand?'

As Thierry did not rush to reassure Geoffrey about his total discretion throughout the whole ride from Apulia, it was clear that for once he had been totally discreet.

'From a quarter that you obviously did not expect,' said Fulk. 'And now that I have met you, I must confess that it baffles me.'

For a moment it crossed Geoffrey's mind that Robert Guiscard had had second thoughts about parting with so much hard-won loot and had sent some hired killers to get it back. However, Fulk's next remark removed such a thought.

'I had assumed that the whole enterprise was some kind of rivalry in love, but now that I see that you are a – well, I confess myself, as I said, baffled.'

Geoffrey frowned.

'I do not follow.'

'I was hired,' said Fulk, 'to ambush you and to steal your treasure.'

'Yes, yes. But by whom?'

'By someone who was prepared to pay me, or to promise to pay me, with his wife's dowry. I naturally concluded that you were a rival for the lady's hand.'

Geoffrey felt such rage rising within him that he stopped shivering.

'Would his name be Torf?'

'Truly a divinely-inspired guess.'

Geoffrey looked this way and that, dying to stand and start pacing, furious at his impotence, bursting with far too many emotions to speak.

Fulk looked at Ivo.

'You know this Torf?'

Ivo nodded.

'We do. And I should wager that you have been paid so far with sweet words and promises.'

'True. There has indeed been little so far in the form of hard coin. Still – ' Fulk gestured towards the treasure packs. ' – at the moment we have the better of the bargain. I should however like to return to meet him in order to see whether he intends to fulfil the whole of the agreement.'

'Do you?' asked Ivo.

Fulk smiled devilishly.

'My dear fellow, what a leading question.'

'I shall kill him. I shall kill him!'

Fulk looked back at Geoffrey.

'I begin to understand. It really was some kind of love quarrel. My lord bishop, you are a much more interesting man that I had first thought. My respect for you grows. What a good thing that I did not have you done away with. Truly God moves in a mysterious way.'

'Will you return to Normandy now?'

'Yes, if only to find our friend and wring some money out of him before you return to wring his neck. Who knows? He may have some more similarly profitable commissions for us. Tell me, tell me, do you intend to kill him in your capacity as a knight or as a bishop? And do you intend to excommunicate yourself afterwards for murder? Ah – I have it: you will execute him as a felon in your capacity as a knightly guardian of the peace, and you will give yourself absolution in your capacity as a bishop and a curer of souls.'

Fulk laughed.

'Does it not occur to you, my lord, that you have found the perfect pattern for living? Fare you well.'

'Will you take our horses as well?' said Ivo.

'Alas, yes. Business is business, I am afraid. But take courage, my friend. If God has saved you from me, I am sure it is not beyond His powers to save you from the Burgundian weather.'

Fulk gestured to Ralph.

'Here, boy.'

When Ralph stood close, Fulk spoke again to Geoffrey.

'I shall leave you one thing, though. My scout, Ralph. Too many tender feelings for my liking.'

The name Ralph . . . Gisors . . . tender feelings . . . tears . . . pale faces . . . a dying boy . . .

Geoffrey suddenly remembered.

Fulk leaned towards Geoffrey like a conspirator.

'He allows these tender feelings to get in the way of his loyalty. No iron – shall we say – in the belly. Perhaps we can remedy that.'

Before anyone could move, Fulk drove Ralph's own dagger into him. He looked down at the body writhing in stupefied agony.

'He never did fulfil his promise.'

*　　*　　*　　*　　*　　*

Chapter Nine

If it was good fortune that Geoffrey's wound did not prove serious, it was little short of miraculous that Ralph's did not prove mortal. The worst was on everyone's mind.

Ivo said so openly.

'Why slow us down and risk your own life? He will never survive.'

'I owe it to him,' said Geoffrey.

'What you owe him is a quiet place to lie down and make his peace with God. You can see it in his eyes. He is waiting for you to do the same as you did for his brother.'

Geoffrey did not need to be reminded. Every time they rested and set down the litter, he could see in Ralph's face the same look of appeal that he had seen in Michael's on that awful night at Gisors.

For a day and a half they struggled. Geoffrey hardly noticed the pain in his own wound, but he was impatient with Ivo's weak ankle, savage with any complaints from Thierry and the other soldier. Every time they stopped, Ivo looked at his side, and grunted. Then he looked at Ralph, glanced back at Geoffrey, and made no noise at all.

Ivo was right, but Geoffrey could not bring himself to do it.

'Cluny can not be far,' he kept on saying.

Was the boy hoping that he would perform miracles? Or was he merely waiting for Geoffrey to see him safely into Heaven? For the life of him Geoffrey did not know. Either way he felt that yet again someone was expecting more from him that he felt able to give.

And now Cluny. Abbot Hugh would be expecting him; Lanfranc had seen to that. So there would be more lectures and homilies. How often had they been putting their heads together about him? 'Talk to him,' Lanfranc would have said. 'He is a most promising young man. Put him on the right road. Give him some of your wisdom.' Ha! What about Lanfranc's father? Perhaps that was Lanfranc's work too; had he put the old man up to it? And the Guiscard in Apulia – sitting back and waiting blithely for some huge cathedral to go soaring up to Heaven at a word from the prodigious Bishop of Coutances.

He stumbled, clutched his side, and cursed. His thoughts overflowed into speech.

'I am sick and tired of people thinking well of me. Everywhere I go there is someone telling me that they have every confidence in me. Well, I don`t see it.'

'Just as well,' growled Ivo. 'You can be difficult enough as it is.'

*   *   *   *   *   *

'A man could drown in prayer here.'

Ivo voiced the thoughts of all of them. Long journeys gave a man a wide knowledge of monasteries, but no journey, be it to the outermost limits of Christendom, prepared him for Cluny. Its sheer size, its modernity, its riches, its unending ritual – all beggared description. They felt drained of personality, their minds taken away from them, their bodies carried along in a vast tide of holiness and seething, stifling, swamping worship. As a man forced to spend time in a leper colony feared inevitable, progressive, and fatal infection, so they felt that it was only a matter of time before they would lose the power of ordinary fallible human thought, that they would become an involuntary part of this all-devouring heavenly limbo on earth. The world was a thousand miles away, its worries and dangers unreal and difficult to conceive. The only reality was the endless, unstoppable *horarium*. Whatever time of day or night they rose to take food or drink, or to change dressings on wounds, or simply to see to the needs of nature, a bell was ringing, a column of black habits and drooping cowls was gliding across scuffed flagstones, chant and litany and hymn and anthem were rising on the incense-laden air. Devotion, obedience, corporate spirituality, seemed total.

'It is like being in a fish market,' said Thierry. 'Only instead of everything smelling of fish, everything smells of holiness.'

Yet it was not as if anybody bothered them, much less tried to preach to them. On the contrary, they were left almost to their own devices, beyond the obvious medical care which they were freely given. Good medical care too. It was not callousness either; it was simply that the business of prayer was so consuming that little time seemed left in the terrifyingly long day for anything so mundane as a group of recently-robbed travellers.

They received Christian charity, and that was about all.

'I will admit, though,' said Thierry, 'that they do feed you well.'

'With a regime like this, I should think they would need to,' said Ivo grimly. 'It is far tougher than being on campaign.'

Even though Geoffrey was a prince of the Church, Abbot Hugh gave him no more time than was consonant with bare courtesy.

'Do they not realise who I am?'

'Perhaps they realise only too well that you do not want the mitre,' said Ivo mischievously. 'They refrain from observing your rank out of deference to your tender feelings.'

The irony served only to annoy Geoffrey further.

Abbot Hugh, for all his obvious sanctity, had shown little interest in Geoffrey's problems. When Geoffrey, in his account of the robbery, threatened dire retribution, and talked of formal excommunication, Hugh was so lacking in sympathy as to disagree. Geoffrey felt piqued.

'But Lanfranc has never ceased to tell me that I have powers. "Remember," he says. "You are a prince of the Church. Accept your destiny. Use your powers." '

'Yes,' said Hugh. 'Use them; not abuse them. Any fool can become aware of his power and begin to swing it round his head like a madman's mace. Did not Lanfranc make mention of discretion too?'

Geoffrey threw up his hands.

'I give up. I shall never thread my way through it all. I am tied to a destiny for which I am not fitted; every effort I make in all sincerity to fulfil it as it is explained to me meets with bafflement, frustration, and failure. My most natural instincts are now held to be against the law of the Church as expounded by Hildebrand. My charitable desires to make provision for the woman I love have been thwarted by a cheat and a murderer. I have had foisted on to me a bishopric which must be a laughing-stock for any group of prelates in Christendom. My attempts, despite misgivings, to raise funds for it have met with complete disaster and total loss. I have no money, no status, no prospects, and no vocation.'

Hugh shrugged dismissively.

'Then give it up.'

Geoffrey stared.

'What?'

'Give it up. As you put it, there seems nothing to be gained by going forward. So retrace your steps, to the point of original departure, and strike out in a different direction.'

Geoffrey continued staring.

'Where?'

'Does it matter? It can not be worse than the direction you are taking now. If what you say is true, I can not in any conscience advise you to continue. I must admit that I find it difficult to imagine what it is like to have no vocation. I was born to nobility, and I soon realised that I was also born to the cloister. For me there was no struggle. My life would make no sense if I were not doing exactly what I am doing now. But I can well understand that if a man feels no vocation, then his life must indeed be empty and purposeless. I am sorry for you.'

Geoffrey blinked.

'We shall pray for you,' said Hugh.

'They will too,' said Ivo, when Geoffrey told him the story. 'There is one thing that makes the brothers here different. And Abbot Hugh.'

'What is that?'

'They really mean it.'

141

'Oh? You think so?'

Ivo smiled to himself. It would not do Master Geoffrey any harm to be pushed on one side now and again.

Ivo noticed, however, that Abbot Hugh went out of his way to come and see them off.

Ralph looked pale after his long time abed.

'They tell me from the infirmary that he has made a good recovery,' said Hugh. 'Youth is on his side.'

Geoffrey thanked him formally for the abbey's care and hospitality, and apologised that he had no means of showing tangible appreciation in the box at the main gate.

Hugh allowed himself a rare smile.

'You can thank me by giving a little thought to this: do not look for prodigies to show you the way. Should you want miracles, however, they are under your very nose, in the sacraments which it is your duty to administer so long as you wear the mitre. You are consecrated; there is another miracle. Whether you choose to run away or not, you can not escape the miraculousness of it. Until the day you die, you are the vessel of the sacraments – every occasion, every place, every time you consecrate the bread and wine, it changes. Every single time. It is the regularity and reliability of it that shows the Wonder of God. There – in the very ordinariness of it – lies the real miracle. It is not you who must feel miraculous, or uplifted, or transported with sanctity. You are not there to feel it at all, much less enjoy it. You are there to provide it, for sinners before God.'

'Amen,' said Ivo quietly.

'What did you say?' said Geoffrey sharply.

'Nothing, my lord.'

Ralph and Thierry looked at each other and grinned.

'One last thing,' said Hugh. 'When you have decided the direction your life is to take – and should it be in the direction of Coutances – I happen to know of a mason-architect who can build the sort of cathedral you or Robert of Hauteville may have in mind.' He waved a hand about him. 'Some of his work is here, so you can see he needs little recommendation.'

The party paused at the main gate and looked back. It had been a vast shock to the system to be enclosed in Cluny; it was just as big a relief to be free of it. And a regret at the same time.

'Like leaving the womb,' said Thierry.

Ivo coiled the reins in his gnarled fist.

'Well, my lord, where is it to be – Normandy, or Apulia?'

*   *   *   *   *   *

142

'For God's sake, Mother, let me alone!'

The lady Fressenda plied her needle.

'The time is past for self-pity.'

'I do not feel self-pity,' said Sybil, close again to tears.

Fressenda held the needlework at arm's length and cocked her head in comtemplation of it.

The poor child did not know at the moment what she did feel. It was ill-timed of Torf to bring his news on such an occasion. Then, on reflection, perhaps it was extremely shrewd timing indeed. Torf made it his business to be well-informed, and any man with a honey tongue took care to catch his prizes when they were at a disadvantage. It made his offer look that much more attractive.

'I do not want his treasure,' said Sybil, sniffing noisily.

'Not his treasure; Geoffrey's. It was sent home especially for you and the child. Why would Torf tell such a lie? Would it not have been easier for him to keep the treasure for himself?'

'Why did Geoffrey not send it direct?'

'There was nobody he could trust. By giving it to Torf, he was saying that he was giving place to him as well.'

'How do you know that?'

'Torf told me. He said that he had no wish to give you pain at this time, but that I was to tell you when I thought you had sufficiently recovered.'

Sybil set her jaw.

'My dear child,' said Fressenda, 'what more proof do you want?'

She pointed to the crucifix that lay in the cradle.

'Would Geoffrey have parted with that save for a special reason, and to convey a special message?'

Sybil's lips trembled again, but Fressenda fought against the urge to put her arm round her daughter's shoulders. The shock was hard, but it must be borne. Still in sore trouble from her own recent loss, she did not see why others should be spared the truth when it was clear that the truth was for their own ultimate good.

'Why Cluny?' muttered Sybil. 'And why did he not talk about it before he left? We have never kept secrets from each other. That was part of our strength.'

Fressenda stood up with difficulty, pressing her hands on her knees, and working them up her thighs until she could straighten her back. She took her stick and came to Sybil's bedside.

'Perhaps he did not know until he reached there. Perhaps he had a change of heart in Rome. Who knows? Perhaps it was Lanfranc.'

'Devil take Lanfranc! And Devil take his precious crucifix! He is the one who has eaten his way into Geoffrey's conscience.'

Fressenda, balancing herself with one hand on the top of the stick, fussed over the bedding with the other.

'It is true that Lanfranc knows Abbot Hugh and the house of Cluny. Small wonder that he should recommend it for retreat and meditation. Torf says it is a truly remarkable place.'

Sybil slapped her hands down into her lap as the tears returned.

'Why is it that Torf knows everything and I know nothing?'

While she waited for the tears to subside, the lady Fressenda looked into the swaddled doll in the cradle. Wisps of dark hair curled over the tiny scalp. The same colour as Geoffrey's. But he had his mother's blue eyes. The Hauteville eyes. Tancred would have been so proud of him.

'What are you going to call him?' said Fressenda.

Sybil wiped her nose.

' "Raoul." Geoffrey said he liked it.'

Fressenda patted her on the top of the head. Turning with difficulty, she edged her way towards the ladder.

'Muriella! Constance! Tell them to get the sling.'

'But Mother!' wailed Constance. 'It is not long since you were taken up. The pot is up there if that is what you want. They have only just begun their meal.'

'Then tell them to leave it. And I do not want the pot; I want to leave Sybil in peace. She needs rest. So stop weeping and wailing, mind your manners, and do as I say.'

The lady Fressenda gave no thought to the creaks and jerks of the sling and the rusting pulley-wheel, the dark looks of the kitchen staff, or their puffings and gruntings.

It was a good offer. And a generous one. What if he had borrowed the dowry in advance? He had made good his promise a dozen times over with the share of treasure that Geoffrey had sent. Most men would have taken it for themselves. And what if he had wheedled it out of Geoffrey? It was Hauteville treasure in the first place; Robert was always open-handed when once he had decided to give.

The touch with the crucifix had been a clever idea. Had he really persuaded Geoffrey to part with that? Or had the worst happened? If so, he was being even more clever to suggest that Geoffrey was still alive. Had he brought word of Geoffrey's death, Sybil would never have married him. At any rate not for a long time; it would have taken a great deal of work on her part. But by telling of Geoffrey's rejection, it aroused other emotions that could easily propel her in the opposite direction. If one desired the love of another's betrothed, better she be mad than sad.

Fressenda disentangled her stick from the meshes of the sling prior to coming to earth.

Either way, it was better for Sybil that she be married, and quickly. With my lord gone, and the remaining boys undecided about Italy, it was imperative that provision be made. And what other knight would have been prepared to accept the child? Sybil ought to be grateful.

Perhaps she was, behind all the tears and tempers. She must know her difficulty; she was not stupid. And, behind all the tears and tempers again, Fressenda was almost certain that Sybil found Torf attractive. Indeed, it could partly explain the tears and tempers. Torf certainly had a devilish persuasive way with him. Even at her age she could feel that.

The sling touched the ground with only the slightest of bumps. The sweating scullions wished they had a penny for every time they had done it. If my lady was not satisfied, she was quite capable of ordering them to take her back up and down again until she was. They thought of their dinner getting cold.

Fressenda frowned.

There was a third possibility, of course, but, should it ever materialise, it would resolve itself.

Geoffrey would either fight for her, or he would not. If he would not, she was better off with Torf. If he did, and won, then God's light would truly shine on everybody, and a good thing too. If he lost . . . But that was unlikely, because Geoffrey would be so stern in resolve.

Or he would be after she had had a talk with him.

A woman fought with the power that God in His inscrutable thrift had seen fit to give her. Knowledge was part of that power. Knowledge would keep too.

* * * * * *

Mabel of Bellême was not by nature hospitable, but she was a snob; a bishop under her roof suited her. She flashed rings, eyes, new inheritance, and border gossip before him.

Geoffrey did not like the idea of staying there, and he liked it even less after an hour in Mabel's company.

'Holy Virgin!' he muttered to Ivo when he escaped for a while to the stables. 'What a cat!'

'But what a catch!' replied Ivo. 'I am surprised the Duke himself did not think of her.'

'He would have strangled her,' said Geoffrey. 'From what I have seen of him. The man willing to marry her must have the patience of a saint and the will of an emperor.'

'Or the hunger of a young Norman knight. Have you watched him?'

145

'Montgomery?'

'Yes. Why else would he be staying here?'

Roger of Montgomery had a different story.

'I am glad we have met,' he said to Geoffrey. 'The Duke wants you to attend his council at Bayeux. I am sent to summon the bishops and senior knights of the south and west.'

Geoffrey was glad they had met too. He liked Roger of Montgomery. They were about the same age. After talking only a short while, they seemed to have the same outlook on life. There was something easy and uncomplicated about Roger. Comfortingly ordinary. It was such a relief after all the prodigious men Geoffrey had been meeting.

'Not a great thinker,' observed Ivo.

'No,' agreed Geoffrey. 'But not devious either.'

'His brothers were a dreadful crew.'

'I have not met his brothers. I know only him. And he seems all right to me.'

'Then you will enjoy the trip to Bayeux with him,' said Ivo imperturbably.

Geoffrey swore.

How many more delays would there be? It was as if God in a bad mood had sentenced him to exile from Normandy, an exile which was capriciously extended every time Geoffrey showed signs of a successful return.

The first lingerings had been enjoyable, certainly interesting – Lanfranc's house in Pavia, the other Italian cities. Later, stimulating – the Council at Rome. Then it had started to become tiresome – the search for the Hautevilles. After that, the weary journey back up through Italy, the endless checks and inquiries and bribings and detours through Lombardy and over the Alps.

After the robbery, Ralph's convalescence at Cluny. Now was added the rage at Torf – at the trickery, at the heinousness of the crime, at the awful prospect of what Torf could now be engaged upon in Normandy.

The greater rage still at the need to return to Apulia – to crawl like a knee-bound penitent to the Guiscard.

'So you are going back to him?' observed Ivo unnecessarily.

'What choice do I have?' roared Geoffrey. 'Whatever I do, I must have funds. Where else can I get them?'

For once Ivo did not growl into his whiskers.

'Yes, of course, my lord.'

Robert of Hauteville did not make matters any better by laughing with a hundred teeth. He made Geoffrey sweat for it too.

'Look about you, my lord bishop. There is not much relaxation for my lads these days. How would it be if we bargained over your request and provided

146

them with a little entertainment at the same time?'

Geoffrey's eye took in the smoke-stained marble of a half-ruined Byzantine palace. Wooden trestles stood on a leaf-strewn floor inlaid with porphyry. The familiar kite-shaped shields leaned against a wall half of which consisted of a huge mosaic of fishermen at their nets.

Robert clapped his huge, spade-like hands.

'We shall play for it. And I warn you; I am better than Father.'

And so, morning, noon, and night, while the winter rains poured down outside, and patrols tramped mud across the inlaid floor with their regular reports, Geoffrey and Robert Guiscard played – game after game after game.

The two piles of treasure and coins at their feet grew or shrank according to their changing fortunes or flagging concentration. Whatever the time of day or night, there was always a noisy audience of Robert's men.

Only food, wine, and pride kept them going. At last, when Geoffrey was ready to fall off the stool in stupor, Robert stood up noisily and flung his chair over.

'I concede.'

The pile at Geoffrey's feet was at its largest.

'Why?' asked Geoffrey when they parted.

'It was the only way they would accept such a loss. Oh, and something else. Your man Ivo has some more; I persuaded most of them to wager some of their own treasure on me. So you can build even bigger now, eh?'

Again that dip of the head and the sidelong glance.

'Tell that creature Torf that if any harm comes to Sybil I shall return to cut up or cut off anything that you have not already seen to. And use that scout of yours properly; he seems a good man. Should keep you out of trouble.'

'Thank you once again.'

Robert made a dismissive gesture.

'Ah – easy come, easy go. Plenty more where that came from. Remember now – plenty of class!'

Geoffrey burned the miles on the way back, pausing only, and then reluctantly, when Ralph's scar showed signs of giving him trouble. Thierry complained bitterly that he was being worn to a shadow. Ivo said so little that he stopped swearing at the animals.

They avoided cities, and deliberately took the longer route over the Great Saint Bernard to Geneva. In Burgundy, they used river transport whenever possible to lessen the danger of ambush. After the long sweep of the Loire to Orleans, they had come straight up the road to Bellême.

They had heard gossip about the Duke of Anjou pushing up through Maine to press against the frontiers of Normandy – 'not content with Le Mans, he wants Domfront and Alençon now' – but Geoffrey wanted no involvement whatever. Having come this far, and having been away for so many months, he could not wait to get back.

And not only for Sybil; he found himself yearning for the familiar sights of Montbrai. Home!

'You know, Ivo? I never thought the day would come when I would look forward to Gaimar's cooking and Bertha's gossip.'

'It all has its place,' said Ivo darkly.

And now – this. Devil take the Duke!

'You are also required to give hands for Coutances,' said Montgomery.

Geoffrey suddenly saw a shred of profit to be snatched from the tearing of his plans.

'Does that mean that I shall receive land at last? Where? How much?'

Roger put up a hand.

'Just – just a moment. My understanding is that you are to be formally invested with the bishopric. There was no mention of endowment with land.'

Geoffrey snorted.

'I should wager that Bishop Hugh of Lisieux and baby brother Odo of Bayeux will not go wanting.'

Roger nodded in agreement.

'Kinsmen. What would you expect? Another cousin, Baldwin, has also collected a fief or two.'

Geoffrey remembered the name.

'Baldwin de Clair?'

'Yes. Back from exile in Flanders. Guy of Burgundy has been ejected from his bolt-hole at Brionne, and Baldwin has picked up his castle and various other fiefs round about. Including Bec, I believe.'

'What, Lanfranc`s house?'

Roger corrected him.

'Lanfranc is only Prior; Herluin is still abbot.

'But Baldwin is now the overlord.'

'Yes.'

Geoffrey snorted again.

'It seems the only way to get on in Normandy is to be born into the Bastard`s family. God knows it is big enough .'

'I am not so sure; a lot of relatives can be a mixed blessing. I am still living down my own brothers' reputation. As for the Bastard's clan, look at Guy of Burgundy. Then there is William of Arques – shifty if you ask me. Ambitious too – far above his station. And have you met Archbishop Mauger?'

'He consecrated me.'

'Would you trust him?'

Geoffrey smiled at Roger of Montgomery's simplicity and directness.

'No.'

Roger smiled too. He liked this tall young bishop with the western accent.

'Look. I know it is none of my business, but may I offer a suggestion?'

Geoffrey nodded.

'Please do not take offence,' said Roger. 'But I understand that you obtained the bishopric of Coutances by purchase.'

With almost anybody else, that would have been the signal for Geoffrey to start pacing and waving his arms about; but Roger's manner was so mild and thoughtful that Geoffrey sat and listened.

'The situation as it appears to me is this: the Duke has little chance to grant more land in western Normandy. He has rewarded his chief tenants with the estates of the rebels, and there is very little left. He has lands of his own, of course, but he is not inclined to release any of them to anyone who has not proved himself.'

'Exactly my dilemma,' said Geoffrey, beginning to get excited. 'I can not get land until I have proved myself, and I can not prove myself until I can get land, resources, a base to start from.'

'Yes, yes. Just be patient. I was about to say that the Duke may not be inclined to grant land out of his grace to an untried tenant such as yourself, but he might well be persuaded to sell some. He sold the see, and he still needs money.'

Geoffrey caught the drift.

'And a purchase would be a sign of good intent.'

Roger nodded.

'In your case, virtually the only sign you could give. You are in no position to render knightly service without land to support men.'

Geoffrey was suddenly smitten with the family habit of thrift.

'I am not made of money, you know.'

And Ivo and Thierry were sleeping on saddlebags in the stables with enough treasure inside them to build three cathedrals.

'You must also have somewhere to live,' prompted Roger. 'A bishop has to keep some kind of state.'

A roof for Sybil.

'One thing,' said Geoffrey wryly. 'There will be few others in the market. Have you seen Coutances?'

'I should not be so sure of that,' said Roger. 'Which is why I take the liberty of suggesting that you move fairly quickly. I hear that there is at least one other bidder. Neighbour of yours, I believe. From Malbec.'

All the way from Bellême to Bayeux, not a word was uttered. Thierry looked at Ivo, and gestured towards Geoffrey's back. Ivo shrugged.

*   *   *   *   *   *

Geoffrey would not have admitted it to Ivo, but he enjoyed the Council of Bayeux. What young knight from the west would not? A chance to rub shoulders with nearly every senior prelate and tenant-in-chief in Normandy.

Bishop Hugh of Lisieux was pleased to see him; they had not met since their consecration at Rouen. Bishop Odo of Bayeux, still nursing his spots and sheltering behind his brother's ducal power, made condescending remarks about Geoffrey's western accent and poor appearance.

Bishop Hugh of Avranches asked after his trip to Apulia.

'Mixed fortunes, my lord,' said Geoffrey, 'but not without success.'

Roger of Montgomery introduced him to a lot of people. There was a feast after the ceremony of investiture for the three young bishops and the formalities of giving homage for new feudal tenants.

Geoffrey got his land in and around Coutances, and, thanks to Roger of Montgomery, at a reasonable price. Geoffrey was grateful that, as a relative newcomer, he could not have driven as a good a bargain. Roger was mild-tempered and quietly-spoken, and, as Ivo had noticed, not especially intelligent; but he understood his own circle through and through, and he knew how to talk to the members of it. He was not subtle, but he was not easily shifted.

'There you are then,' he said to Geoffrey. 'You now have a foot in the door.'

He changed cups from a tray that was being carried round by a pink-cheeked serving boy.

'My thanks,' said Geoffrey.

Roger took a swig and waved the cup in casual acknowledgment.

'Tell me,' said Geoffrey. 'Why were all the negotiations with Sir William Fitzosbern?'

Roger grinned.

'Fitz? They always are. He is the Duke's right hand. Never does a thing without asking Fitz.'

'You mean Fitzosbern takes the decisions?'

'Saints, no! The Duke is his own man. Fitz never leads, but he guides – all the time. And he supports.'

'A good man to have,' said Geoffrey politely.

'The sort of man the Duke is looking for all the time. Ideally, he would like the dukedom full of tenants-in-chief called Fitzosbern.' He took another draught. 'Which reminds me – '

Geoffrey smiled.

'You are about to give me some more advice.'

Roger laughed.

'As a matter of fact, yes. When you get back, get some knights settled on those estates of yours as soon as you can. Build yourself a base at Coutances. Get a proper military organisation going. The sooner the Duke sees that you have something to offer, the sooner he will use you, and the sooner therefore you can do something that he can reward.'

'Thank you. I will try and make a start.'

'And another thing,' said Roger. 'You will need military mounts, proper destriers. I shall introduce you to Walter Giffard; he breeds the best in Normandy. Has stallions sent up from Spain.'

Geoffrey smiled again.

'Anything else?'

'Yes. Think about an official episcopal residence; start setting up a bit of state. It all adds to the image. You will not find everybody taking kindly to what you want to do in Coutances, and the more impressions you can create the better. I assume you have plans afoot for a cathedral?'

'I have a builder with me, yes. Hugh of Cluny gave him to me when I passed through. He has quite a reputation, it seems.'

'Name?'

'Goscelin – from somewhere round Chartres, I believe.'

'I know of him. He has a lot to his credit already. Moody devil, they say. Artistic temperament, I suppose.'

Somebody nudged their elbows as he pushed past.

'Ah, my lord,' said Roger.

The hard-faced bishop with the beaky nose paused.

'Geoffrey, let me formally introduce you. My lord, may I present to you Geoffrey de Montbrai, Bishop of Coutances. Geoffrey, may I present to you Bishop Yves de Bellême, Bishop of Sées.'

They had seen each other, of course, but had never spoken.

Yves de Bellême exchanged the barest minimum of civilities before turning back to Roger.

'What is this I hear about you and Mabel?'

Roger bowed.

'I have had the honour of paying my respects to your niece. With the full approval of his Grace the Duke, may I add.'

Bishop Yves looked him up and down.

'What makes you think you have mine?'

A herald banged with his staff on the floor.

'Ah,' said Roger. 'The formal announcments. I wondered when we were going to get round to that.'

In answer to the question on Geoffrey's face, Roger explained.

'It was unlike the Bastard to summon the complete clerical and lay tenantry of Normandy simply to witness some investitures – with due respect to yourself. Now, it seems, we are to be told. Here, let me take your cup.'

Roger put Geoffrey's and his own on a boy's tray, and together they pressed forward towards the ducal throne that had been set up on the platform.

Duke William strode on in his usual impatient way, his restless eyes darting to every corner of the hall. Behind him came his uncle, the Archbishop of Rouen, and, inevitably, Sir William Fitzosbern. They sat on either side of him a little to the rear. Four mailed and helmeted bodyguards stood at the back.

'Any guesses?' whispered Geoffrey in Roger's ear.

'The England trip, I should say.'

'England?'

'I was forgetting; you have been out of things. When the Brionne siege was over, the Duke paid a visit to England. Officially to see his great-aunt, the lady Emma.'

'I thought she was dead.'

'She is, nearly.'

'But why make a formal report on a visit to his aunt?'

Roger held up his hand. The Duke was on his feet . . .

. . . Knots of men stood all round the hall, their heads together, their faces animated. The hubbub was deafening.

'The crown! . . . It is unbelievable! Do you think the Bastard got it wrong? . . . He is a blood relation. Edward will have no sons of his own; he has not laid a finger on his wife in years, they say . . . Silly old fool; probably did not know what he was saying . . . My information is that the King has no power to leave the throne in his will; only the Witan can decide . . . God's Teeth! One in the eye for Godwin and his brood, eh? . . . Godwin will never stand for it . . . The Bastard is hoping for the moon; he can barely hold the duchy . . . The Godwin clan is in disgrace, maybe even in exile by now . . . The Confessor has asked for Robert of Jumièges to be his new Archbishop of Canterbury; surely that is significant . . . Do not underestimate Godwin; look at the land he holds. Between them, he and his sons have nearly half England. They will bounce back, you will see. And then how safe will our precious archbishop be on his new throne? . . . And where will that leave the Bastard? Looking foolish . . . '

'Have you seen her? She barely comes up to his chest . . . I never thought the Bastard had it in him; I have never seen him look at a woman before – was beginning to wonder . . . What will the Pope do . . .? Leo? Nothing. He is a pragmatic man; the Duke is doing his work in other ways. Leo will not upset that . . . Popes have turned blind eyes before . . . Have you seen Hildebrand? No chance of blind eyes there . . . What can they do? We are the ones who keep the Bastard on his throne, not them . . . There will be no excommunication; there will be a deal. Lanfranc will go to Rome and he will negotiate a dispensation; you can get a dispensation for anything if the price is right . . . Do you think the Pope will listen after what the Hautevilles have been doing to Papal property in Italy? . . . Well, good luck to him, I say . . . She is a girl of spirit; she will stand up to him . . . Whatever else it does, it will put her father out of the reckoning; at least the Flanders frontier is safe now . . . So he could not wait; at least it shows he is human . . . Ha! When she drops the child it will not have far to fall . . .'

Roger shouldered his way back to Geoffrey.

'Well, what do you think?'

'Mmmm?'

'I said "What do you think?" Is he not a rising star, our Duke?'

'Maybe. Maybe.'

Roger chuckled.

'Did you see the look on the face of William of Arques?'

'The Duke's uncle?'

'Yes. Thoroughly sick, I should say. That marriage has put his plans for the succession right out of court. Trouble brewing there, or I am much mistaken. He had better hurry up, or there will be a legitimate heir as well as a bastard duke in his way.'

'Mmmm.'

Roger nudged him.

'You are great company, I must say.'

Geoffrey did not even hear him . . .

If Roger of Montgomery could contemplate marriage with Mabel in the face of the opposition – or at least the suspicion – of her uncle – a bishop, no less; and if the Duke had actually gone ahead with a marriage which had been expressly forbidden by His Holiness himself . . . He, Geoffrey de Montbrai, now had title, lands, funds, position, connections . . . There was nothing in the way.

*   *   *   *   *   *

Chapter Ten

'It is a good offer, Roger.'

Roger of Hauteville looked up. He was the only one of the sons to have his mother's eyes. Perhaps that was one of the reasons why she had a specially soft spot for him. That, and his excellent sense. He had a longer head than any of his elder brothers except Robert. Of the girls, only Sybil came near him in depth of character. It was a constant surprise, and joy, to the lady Fressenda that the baby son of the family should show such a concentration of the Hauteville qualities of initiative and resource, when one would normally expect the stock to be on the verge of thinning and weakening. Naturally, therefore, Roger was a source of great pride to her.

She respected Roger too. He was not as transparent as the others, yet she knew that he thought mightily. Moreover, he obeyed and honoured her out of love and pride, while most of the others did it out of inertia, habit, or defeat. He was not impatient like Humbert or Aubrey or young Tancred either. That was why she expected sound advice now. The others would be too bewitched by the attractiveness of the offer, and Sybil was still in no state to be capable of balanced judgment. As for Constance and Muriella . . .

Roger secured the bar of the hall door. He climbed the solar ladder and put his head over the upper floor to make sure that Sybil was asleep. No sound came from the cradle – a happy relief; the infant had the lungs of a cavalry drill instructor. He came down again, and checked that no kitchen boy was hiding behind the stack of trestles balanced tidily against the far wall. He pulled up a stool to the hearth, and carefully laid another log or two on the fire so as not to make a noise.

'It bristles with selfishness; you realise that.'

The lady Fressenda warmed her hands round her hot cup.

'I am not a fool, Roger. But nobody makes an offer which benefits only the recipient. Of course Torf gets Sybil.'

'He gets status too. We are a better family than his. In fact we know next to nothing about his family at all.'

'That may be true, but look at what you boys are getting. Tancred and Aubrey have been hardly able to sit still since they heard. Even Humbert is alive to the possibilities.'

'If he had left it at that, I might have been more impressed,' said Roger. 'It was when he offered to let you and Sybil go and stay for a season at Malbec that I began to be wary. What was it? – to let you "judge for yourselves"?'

'I thought it was generous of him. It was a way of getting round Sybil.'

Roger smiled.

'Mother, it was a way of getting round *you*. I am surprised at you.'

'What harm is there in seeing Malbec?'

'None, in itself. But the offer is unusual, you must admit. Did Father show you Hauteville first?'

'Then why do you not like it?'

Roger leaned down and ruffled the dog's head behind the ears.

'Because it is too good. A merchant offers his wares for a just price, or he overprices at first. If he offers something else to induce you to buy, there is something wrong with the wares themselves.'

'Do you not like him?'

'Not overmuch. But that is no reason for rejecting him. If a man refused every marriage offer for his sisters simply he did not feel fond of his prospective brother-in-law, there would be a large number of maiden aunts in knightly households.'

'Then you are for accepting?' said Fressenda, pouncing.

'No. I am for accepting that part of it which seems safe.' He dropped his voice a little lower. 'We agree that Sybil must be provided for. If he really will take the child, then I am of your mind too that it is a good offer.'

'He says he is building a lot at Malbec.'

Roger waved a hand.

'That may or may not be. However, he must have some kind of an establishment, if only for his own head. We have some knowledge of the extent of his land. So Sybil will have a position, and she will have security. I also incline to your view that she does not find him as unwelcome as she would have us believe.'

The lady Fressenda sipped her broth.

'Well then.'

'It is the rest of the offer that we must be wary of.'

'The money for your equipment?'

'No. Money is money. What worries me is that he has made it so attractive that he can be almost sure that we will accept.'

'There is no point in making any other kind of offer.'

'But do you not see? If we take him up on all of it, we put ourselves in a most vulnerable position. Sybil in Malbec. You in Malbec. "For as long you wish" – remember? And all of us on our way to Italy, rejoicing in our future adventures.'

'I should not stay long at Malbec. I have no wish to be in the way.'

Roger patted the dog, who stretched himself languorously.

'And who would bring you home? You can not travel by yourself now, and if every one of us were to be away . . . You see?'

'You think he is as untrustworthy as that?'

155

Roger shrugged.

'I have no way of knowing, but I do not intend to run the risk of finding out.'

'Are we risking Sybil then?'

'No. I think not. Torf is land-hungry like any other Norman knight, and land is hard to come by in this part of the world. Look at us . . . No. I almost respect him for it. As for Sybil herself, anyone who has tried as hard as he has to get her must want her as a wife. It may be that he even likes her. But we must not put ourselves completely at his questionable mercy.'

'A dubious attitude to a future member of your family,' observed his mother.

'Not at all,' said Roger. 'You are our mother. When have you ever put yourself completely at our mercy?'

The lady Fressenda was forced to smile.

'So what is your word?'

'My word,' said Roger, 'is to let Sybil be married. You stay here. And I shall stay also.'

'You are burning to go like the others.'

'That is exactly what Torf is hoping for. That we all want to go, that we all quarrel as to who stays behind, and that in order to resolve our dispute we agree to go together. And who better to ask to keep an eye on our lands while we are making our fortunes than our devoted brother-in-law Torf of Malbec? No, Mother. We grant his request for Sybil's hand, and we politely decline his offers. And thus we shall find out how anxious he is to have his request granted.'

'Do you not mind remaining?'

'I am the youngest. Another year or two – ' He shrugged.

The lady Fressenda found herself admiring once more her youngest son's resource and patience and utter confidence in himself.

'So that is settled?'

'Yes,' said Roger. 'Unless Geoffrey comes back.'

'Then he will be too late.'

'You are prepared to take that chance?'

'There is no "chance", as you put it. It will by then be out of our hands.'

It would not, but there were some things that the lady Fressenda did not confide even to her wisest son.

*   *   *   *   *   *

'How is our yokel bishop today?'

Geoffrey had not liked the look of Bishop Odo of Bayeux ever since they had stood together on the steps of Rouen cathedral on the day of their consecration. Gossip had not enhanced the picture. After several days at the Council of Bayeux, Geoffrey had seen nothing to induce him to revise his early impression.

156

To add to the stupidly small head and youthful spots, Geoffrey had come to notice a built-in sneer and a cruel, manic little laugh that was almost a girlish giggle. It was also clear that Odo, for all his tender years, was worldly enough to take ruthless advantage of his position as the Duke's half-brother. He had a sharp brain and a wicked tongue, and many a vassal writhed in fuming silence at his jibes, usually delivered in front of an audience, most of whom obligingly came in on cue with the required guffaws.

He further embarrassed those about him by making similar tasteless remarks about his own family. He enjoyed making references to the Duke's new wife, especially about her lack of inches. He would carelessly drop words like 'dwarf' and watch like a cat to see the reaction. He even ventured on to the dangerous ground of his brother's illegitimate birth, and horrified his hearers by throwing phrases like 'fresh hides' and 'the smell of the tanner's yard' into the conversation, and making random asides about 'the son of the tanner's daughter'. Having words with Odo was a strain, as much on the nerves as on the temper.

'How do you tolerate it?' said Geoffrey to Roger of Montgomery.

'Not much choice,' said Montgomery. 'He is there to stay, especially now that he has Bayeux, so you have to put up with him, like the weather.'

'We shall see about that,' said Geoffrey.

'Be warned,' said Montgomery. 'Answer back, by all means. It works in some cases. He never goes for Walter Giffard; Walter bites his head off, and Devil take who knows. Then Walter is old enough to be his father. Most others steer clear of him. He is clever, and he is also a tale-bearer.'

For three days Geoffrey stayed silent, through impertinent reminders about his western accent, and unfavourable comparisons between the dioceses of Coutances and Bayeux, and delicately-barbed questions about Geoffrey's 'noble neighbour' Torf of Malbec . . . 'a brave knight, to be sure. He asked me if I could help him to get that land around Coutances, but I told him that it was a wilderness, not worth having. To think that only the next day you should come along and buy it . . .'

Then Odo did it once too often.

'And how is our yokel bishop today?'

'As fit as the beardless one, my lord. But then, it is a mercy that no razor is necessary, with all those spots to negotiate. We must all be grateful for these little favours of the Almighty, do you not agree?'

Odo flounced away in a swish of oversized robes.

'You have made yourself one fine enemy there,' said Montgomery.

'It was worth it, just to see the look on his face.'

'I agree,' said Montgomery, 'but then I shall not have to pay the reckoning.'

Geoffrey glared after Odo.

'It will be worth building a cathedral better than his for the pleasure of seeing that look again.'

'Then you had better hurry, because Odo will tell his brother, and you need to have something to show when the Duke comes to see you.'

Geoffrey blinked.

'To see me?'

'Oh, yes. Do you think he has given you the diocese and the land just to while away the long winter evenings? You have no idea how much he travels – always where you least expect him. Part of his success. He will give you time to get started, but after that – well, watch out. Remember I warned you. He will speak to you here before you go.'

Geoffrey grunted.

'I shall believe that when I see it. I have been tapping my heels here for five days because Fitzosbern told me to wait.'

Montgomery chuckled.

'Well, who do you think you are? The Emperor? He has six other bishops to talk to besides you, to say nothing of a duchy-ful of tenants-in-chief. Do not forget, too, that he has a new wife, of whom he is surprisingly fond. Just be patient.'

Patience was a quality that Geoffrey found elusive at the best of times. Now – with his longing for the familiar sights of Montbrai; his new desire to begin building at Coutances if only to spite Odo; his yearning for Sybil; the worry about her and Torf which was causing him more disturbed nights than he cared to admit to Ivo; and the passion for revenge – he found his situation almost unendurable.

As a means of reassuring himself that he was not being totally inactive, he made arrangements for the treasure to be sent on ahead with Ivo and Thierry. Anywhere would be safer for it than the milling crowds of knights, squires, grooms, servants, and hangers-on at Bayeux. With all the extra cooking, feasting and drinking, it was a wonder that Thierry had kept his mouth shut this far.

Geoffrey also felt that Ivo needed a rest. He seemed to have acquired a permanent limp since his ankle injury in the ambush. His cough, which had always troubled him during wet or cold days, now seemed to take longer to clear up when the better weather came. Ivo protested at being sent away, but not very much, Geoffrey noticed.

'No. You go. I shall send two of my new knights with you as an escort. You can amuse yourself training them while you are waiting for me to return.'

'From what I have seen they could do with it,' said Ivo grumpily.

'There you are then. I shall do the same here. Sir Roger of Montgomery is going to help me to find some more. The Duke is collecting troops for the siege of Alençon.'

'You will not find decent knights at sieges,' said Ivo. 'No scope. You will get only riff-raff.'

'Nevertheless,' said Geoffrey, smiling. 'Stop grumbling, and do as I say.'

'Where do we take it?' asked Ivo. 'Montbrai?'

Geoffrey thought of Mauger and his little hole behind the altar. He saw his brother rubbing his hands in that manner that always betrayed excitement and embarrassment. If someone like Torf could talk him out of treasure once, he could do it again. The possibilities were too awful to contemplate.

Geoffrey found his thoughts spilling over into speech.

'Saints, no! I should find myself having to excommunicate him.'

'Where then?'

'Coutances.'

A year or two ago Geoffrey would never have thought it had any use at all, certainly not as a safe repository for a personal fortune. However, there really was nowhere else. He dared not trust Mauger. He could not possibly hope that Sybil could keep it out of the clutches of her needy brothers. If he left it with Bishop Hugh of Avranches, that was putting temptation in the man's way. Bishop Hugh was also trying to build a cathedral, and, for all that he was a monk, he was only human. The house of Fëcamp produced men sworn only to the triple vows; it did not guarantee to produce saints.

Geoffrey twiddled the ring on his finger. The huge ruby that Thorold had given him. That frail old man had guarded it successfully, kept it out of thieving clutches for seventy years. Hiding a treasure that had been secured for the rebuilding of his precious cathedral would concentrate his mind wonderfully well. If he was dead, his sons could be relied upon.

He found Ivo looking at him in a questioning manner, and decided to brazen it out.

'Well, it happens to be the place where we are expected – expecting – to spend it.'

Ivo nodded.

'Indeed it is, my lord. You will wish me, of course, to call at Hauteville to tell the lady Sybil all the news.'

Geoffrey raised his eyebrows.

'Of course. Tell her – tell her – ' What, for God's sake? How to put it all into one message. 'Say I shall come as soon as possible.'

He dared not say more, in case he said too much.

'It is not an answer to make a woman very happy,' observed Ivo.

'God's Bread!' snapped Geoffrey. 'What else can I say? I am tied hand and foot here. Do you think I want it?'

Ivo did not think that, but he had observed that his master derived great solace from training his new knights while he waited for his audience with the Duke.

'He may look busy,' said Ralph, 'but he is impatient – as if there is something driving him.'

'There is,' said Ivo. 'More than you think; more than he thinks. But those knights will keep him busy.'

'They are not very good,' said Thierry.

'Then they will keep him even busier. If his mind is occupied, it will give his imagination a rest.'

Poor Master Geoffrey! He did not even know yet if it was a boy or a girl.

Ralph asked particularly to be allowed to stay at Bayeux. Geoffrey was flattered, and frankly glad to have the continued company of somebody familiar. In the journeyings they had shared since the ambush, he had come to develop a regard for this young man. He was silent and undemonstrative, but he was thoughtful, he was attentive, and he was proving to be reliable. Ivo spoke well of him too.

'He thinks the world of you.'

Geoffrey made a dismissive gesture.

'Gratitude. And slightly misplaced gratitude at that.'

'If you say so, my lord.'

If Geoffrey was hoping for compliments from Ivo, he was going to be disappointed. Ivo knew that Geoffrey was perfectly capable of working it out for himself, and he had no intention of turning his master's head more than it had been turned already. All these travels and councils and meetings with celebrities – yes, and compliments – it was a lot for a green young knight from Montbrai, mitre or no mitre. It needed to be rationed.

Ralph really was grateful, but even if he had never met Geoffrey until the ambush, he would have enjoyed serving him much better than he had Fulk. Moreover, a young man like himself had his way to make, and scout service with a bishop promised much better than duty as horseboy and semi-slave with a sergeant of Angevin mercenaries. Being in close proximity to the Duke might throw up further opportunities, and Ralph willingly joined in the knightly training sessions which Geoffrey organised every morning on the flat meadowland around the outskirts of Bayeux, while surly peasants herded terrified pigs and sheep into cottage yards. Who could tell when his Grace might come along to watch?

160

It was a frustrating time for him, for all that. He was practically born on horseback, but he had little experience of the heavy destrier. His father, being a poor man, had rarely been able to afford the bloodstock needed to provide regular training. Ralph could throw spears with the best of any boar-hunters; he swung a competent sword – on foot; he was tough, agile, and resilient. But his middleweight frame found it hard to control the massive destrier for any length of time; he could not afford a full suit of mail, so gained no experience of fighting in it; he was not adept at handling the shield in mounted combat; and he had no knowledge whatever of the mace.

His eye was critical enough to see that Geoffrey's new aspiring recruits had a lot to learn, but a lot of the basic technique had been almost bred into them. Ralph could appreciate that they had enjoyed advantages denied to him. They seemed to have an instinctive balance and co-ordination which he was having to learn patiently muscle by muscle. Mere horsemanship was not enough; a man had to be master of a hundred items of equipment; he had to have instant access to a wide variety of weapons – sword, javelin, stabbing spear, dagger, mace – and he had to have such mastery over them that each became a mere extension of his arm. And all this while handling a heavy kite-shaped shield, and keeping control over a thoroughbred tempest of horseflesh while stirrupped into a throne-sized wooden saddle like a prisoner in a cage.

Ralph could also see, after quite a short time, that he was not going to close the gap between himself and these eager young men. He continued with the training, because he liked watching Geoffrey at work, and because he was still eager to learn whatever was available to be taught. However, he no longer hoped that the Duke would stroll by with his retinue just as he executed a particularly adept manoeuvre.

Life being what it was, the Duke chose just such a time to come along. Ralph was being anything but masterful at that moment, so the Duke blessedly did not notice him.

In any case, his Grace had come to see his new Bishop of Coutances.

'Fitz told me you were out here.'

Was there anything that Fitzosbern did not know?

Geoffrey bowed slightly.

'Do you wish me to stop, my lord?'

William shook his head.

'No. I am interested to see what you have taught them. Give them a few more turns.'

Geoffrey ordered some grooms to set up the straw-filled sacks again, and re-issued the throwing spears.

'Now, again. From the right. Keep the sun behind you. And the arm high – high. A straight action. Feel it brush your ear.'

The Duke had retired a short distance, and was talking to the group which had accompanied him. Geoffrey could not hear what he was saying, but he could sense the Duke's interest. As he shouted instructions to his new men, he could feel the skin tingling on the back of his neck.

'All the motion must be forward; no wasting of strength to the side. And plenty of follow-through. Ready? Now!'

God bless Ivo! Up to now, Geoffrey had had no idea that so much of Ivo's wisdom and training had sunk in.

When the throwing arms became tired, Geoffrey gave everyone a rest, and walked over to the Duke's party. He paid his respects to the Lady Matilda, who, he noticed, handled a horse well. Beside her sat Sir Baldwin de Clair. Rumour had it that it was he who had brought the lady Matilda and the Duke together. Roger of Montgomery was there, and an older knight, to whom he had been introduced by Roger – Sir Walter Giffard. Odo hovered on the edge.

'I see you believe in discipline and detail,' observed the Duke in his rough voice.

'And one other,' said Geoffrey. 'Drill. It is drill and detail that produces the discipline and the technique. No success is possible without them. No reliable success anyway.' He stopped himself, fearing that he had said too much. He was talking to a young man who had already commanded in battle.

Something of his awkwardness must have shown in his face, because the Duke made a deprecatory gesture.

'No, no. I agree. But you must accept that the mounted knight depends also on his shock value. He must be given his head. A knight has his pride.'

Geoffrey screwed up his eyes as he looked up at the Duke. Just what was he implying? Anybody who had any experience of training knights knew perfectly well that giving a knight his head was an invitation to him to lose it. William had fought at Val-ès-Dunes; he knew that.

The Duke was testing him. Just like the Guiscard! So be it.

'A man's pride can be his downfall, my lord. Pride leads to anger, and anger to carelessness.'

He could see Ivo and Thierry and himself chasing Fulk's men at the ambush, bellowing in righteous rage; failure, much less defeat, had never crossed their minds. If they had stayed together, the ambush would not have succeeded.

'Do you wish to train a man's pride out of him?' asked the Duke.

'Not at all, my lord. I should rather temper that pride with discipline, and turn it into purpose. The pride can come after the victory, not before.'

Geoffrey was surprised that such common sense seemed to make such an impression. He was stung by an interruption from Odo.

'My lord bishop has commanded in battle, of course, and speaks from experience.'

Geoffrey turned towards him.

'No, my lord bishop of Bayeux. But your brother the Duke has. I ask you, your Grace, to cast your mind back to Val-ès-Dunes. From what I have been told, it was a loose engagement of many widely-separated bodies of men. Surely your victory would have been more complete if you had had larger, more compact formations of knights?'

The Duke offered no answer, but he made no denial. Odo tried to retrieve the situation.

'I had no idea that my lord of Coutances was such an authority on military theory. Would he not be better employed on more sensible practice? Like building? Unless his ideas there are merely theoretical too.'

Odo may have been young, but he was clever, and he polished a sharp insult. Geoffrey made a mental note not to underestimate him in future. He was also more determined than ever to put this arrogant puppy in his place.

'Yes,' said the Duke, coming out a brief reverie. 'My brother tells me that you have made progress at Coutances.'

'Only theoretical, it seems,' said Odo.

'On the contrary, my lord,' said Geofffrey, ignoring him, but pointing his words at him. 'I have been to great trouble to raise funds for the rebuilding; unlike other new bishops, I am not in a position to rely on family charity. I have recruited a first class mason-architect from Cluny with a recommendation from Abbot Hugh himself. I have not as yet seen signs of activity on any site for a new cathedral at Bayeux. A case of funds without initiative, perhaps?'

'That will teach him,' whispered Sir Walter Giffard to his friend Roger of Montgomery.

'Where did you raise these – funds?' asked the Duke.

'From among my flock.'

'I understood that Coutances was a poor diocese?'

'Very poor, my lord. I had to travel far afield to members of the flock who had gone far to seek their fortune.'

'The Hautevilles?'

There seemed little harm in admitting it, now that the treasure was safely on its way.

'Sir Robert, to be precise.' Geoffrey did not know whether Robert had been officially knighted, especially as his father was still alive when he left, but it would do no harm to dignify his bandit benefactor with a worthy distinction.

'Ah, yes,' said the Duke. 'The Guiscard. He wins many conquests in a foreign land, does he not?'

He looked at the lady Matilda. Already, after only a short association, few words were necessary between them.

Roger of Montgomery and Walter Giffard exchanged significant glances. They knew the Bastard's mind quite well too.

'So,' resumed the Duke, 'you are ready to build?'

'Just as soon as I can return and draw up plans,' said Geoffrey.

'Hmm.'

The Duke walked his horse a short way off, stopped, waited, turned, and came back. He was humming tonelessly to himself.

He came to a halt in front of Geoffrey again.

'Come to Alençon with us.'

'My lord?'

Geoffrey was still pondering the hugeness of the commitment he had just made to his Duke about a cathedral; he was extremely wary about making another.

'Anjou,' said William. 'Their Duke has seized Domfront and Alençon. His greed extends beyond his conquests in Maine and he reaches out for Normandy. We go now to burn his fingers for him.'

Geoffrey fought for time.

'My lord, I – I am no expert in siege warfare.'

Montbrai, Coutances, Sybil – all were fading into the distance again.

'It is not you I want; it is your builder. We spent over a year at the siege of Brionne. His skill might shorten the time for us.'

Geoffrey found himself looking at Roger of Montgomery, who was making vigorous faces at him behind the Duke's back to accept.

'You would probably find some more knights looking for employment,' prompted the Duke. 'They would come cheap.'

'Very well, my lord. We are at your disposal.'

'Good.'

William began his unmusical humming again.

'Come!'

The lady Matilda, Sir Baldwin, and Odo prepared to leave with him. The Duke half turned to throw an invitation over his shoulder.

'There is a party out this afternoon. Boar. Join us.'

Roger of Montgomery dismounted and stood with Geoffrey.

'You did yourself a bit of good there.'

'Good! I am in up to my ears.'

'Nonsense. You impressed him. Keep your head at Alençon and you never know.'

'I know nothing about sieges.'

'Stop worrying. Just keep your head and use your wits. Something might turn up. There are renegade Norman knights helping Anjou; there always are. If the Bastard recaptures both towns and sends Anjou packing, there will be punishments for the renegades, and you know what that means.'

'Confiscations.'

'Exactly. Prove yourself – just by being there. A few choice plums could drop into your lap, or I am much mistaken. And keep your eyes open for suitable men for your own contingent.'

'Am I not running before I walk?' said Geoffrey. 'I already have half a dozen. I have little equipment for them yet. I must see my new land before I start to allocate it.'

'No time like the present,' said Montgomery. 'See you go to boar with the Duke this afternoon too. If you are going to be here, be close; favours do not get thrown long distances, but they can often be thrown on impulse. Walter? You remember my lord of Coutances. Geoffrey, this man breeds the best destriers in Normandy. Now I shall leave you two together. I must make a visit before going to Alençon.'

Sir Walter Giffard laughed.

'Stay clear of her claws.'

*   *   *   *   *   *

Goscelin soon gave the first example of the artistic temperament that Roger of Montgomery had referred to.

His leathery jowls quivered in revulsion:

'Siege towers at Domfront?'

'And Alençon,' said Geoffrey. 'The Duke wants the sieges laid down before the worst of the winter weather.'

Goscelin was a tallish man, but had a bowed back. His head did not so much sit on his shoulders as hang suspended from them on a long drooping neck, rather like a gloomy heron. He now drew himself as upright as his physical shortcomings would allow. The inner ends of his eyebrows soared upwards in a triangle of deep aesthetic anguish and disdain.

'My lord, I am an artist in stone and fine timber; I am not a camp carpenter.'

Geoffrey bridled a little.

'You are in my employ; you will carry out my instructions.'

Goscelin pursed his thin lips.

165

'My lord, I have agreed, as a favour to Abbot Hugh, to accompany you to inspect the site and assess the availability of materials. Whether I accept the commission or not is, with respect to your Grace, up to me. I can not be expected, like the Israelites, to make bricks without straw.'

Geoffrey remembered a laconic hint from Abbot Hugh – 'try flattery'.

'I am sure you appreciate that a builder with your experience and skill appears very rarely in Normandy; it is hardly surprising that his Grace the Duke would wish to avail himself of your valuable services.'

The triangular eyebrows lowered themselves the smallest trifle.

'My lord, I trained and worked in Italy. I have studied some of the finest work of the Romans and the Byzantine Greeks. My building will recall for you the wonders of the ancient past. And you wish me to nail together rough-hewn – ' he groped for a word that seemed suitably undignified ' – devices?'

'I am sure his Grace would not expect you to share in the physical work of actual construction,' said Geoffrey, shifting his ground craftily, 'but your advice and expert opinion would be much valued. It would not be for long. A week or two at most. Believe me, I am just as anxious as yourself to reach Coutances.'

And Hauteville.

Goscelin's eyebrows came down like a huge beam across the bridge of his nose, then rose in perfect symmetrical arches. He sighed like a dispirited saint.

'Very well, my lord. So long as it is clearly understood that I shall be present merely in a consultative capacity.'

*　　*　　*　　*　　*　　*

Chapter Eleven

'Pitiful! Pitiful!'

'Take care that you do not say that to the Duke's face.'

Geoffrey was beginning to wonder whether it had been a good idea persuading Goscelin to come.

Goscelin pointed towards the town of Domfront, then swung round with a sweep of his arm to take in the siege preparations. Lopsided catapult frames without ropes; a half-finished siege tower on its side, another in charred ruins; a scattering of abandoned tools already beginning to rust; piles of uncovered equipment dripping in autumn rain; lack of purpose, division of energy, and disarray. Frustration and failure hung over everything like a marsh mist.

It really was a most dispiriting sight. Geoffrey found himself in unwilling agreement. He felt it necessary, out of respect to the Duke, to make some kind of extenuating remark.

'He did drive off the Angevin army.'

'Army?'

Goscelin turned towards Geoffrey with his eyebrows in their familiar triangle of pain.

'God knows, my lord, military matters are no speciality of mine, but one does not have to be an expert to detect inefficiency and inconclusiveness.'

Once more, Geoffrey was forced to agree. The Duke had achieved tactical surprise, but had squandered his advantage in the scrappy series of petty skirmishes that had followed. No overall plan or conception, and virtually no direction once the battle had been joined. Little groups of knights had pleased themselves where they went forward or retired. Mercenary infantry had been wasted in unco-ordinated scrambles over open ground. Isolated bands of archers found targets for themselves on the ramparts of the castle, many of which they were too stupid to see were out of effective range until they had wasted most of their shafts. So far as Geoffrey could see, it was Val-ès-Dunes all over again.

Geoffrey was right to give credit to the Bastard for driving off the Duke of Anjou's force; Goscelin also was right for attributing his success to the even greater incompetence of the enemy. That, and perhaps William's undeniable energy and bravery. He did lead, and he did inspire, which was more than could be said for the Duke of Anjou.

The Duke of Anjou, however, was no fool. He had wisely recognised that his troops were not up to defeating the Normans, and had retired to let the coming winter do it for him. His fortress of Domfront was richly supplied and provisioned, and in the spring he could bring another force to attack the remaining soldiers of the Bastard who had survived a winter in the open without dying of fever or deserting.

'Anjou will not attack before the spring,' said Geoffrey. 'We have plenty of time to reduce the castle.'

'You are going to need it,' said Goscelin, gesturing again towards the debris of abandoned siege equipment. 'My lord, they have no idea of simple principles of construction. It is not a question of knocking together outsized frames and chests. One of those towers fell over before they had moved it a score of paces. Look at the gradient on the slopes up to the donjon. They are like babies: attempting the impossible with the inadequate.'

Geoffrey scratched his cheek with a fingernail.

Would the Bastard be honest enough to see this for himself, or did he need someone to tell him? It might be better if it came from Roger . . .

'Why me?' said Roger of Montgomery.

'He will take it from you. After the news you have brought him from Bellême, you can do no wrong at the moment . . .'

The Duke stopped pacing and stopped humming.

'So be it. Fitz – I shall leave every third man with you to keep their heads down. With the rest – we ride at dawn for Alençon.'

*　　*　　*　　*　　*　　*

It was thirty-five miles to Alençon, and the mercenary infantry had a different swearword for every one of them. Only one group enjoyed the comfort of wagons. From under the heavy, flapping covers came jeers and catcalls as they jolted along beside those condemned to trudge in the mud and slanting rain.

'Go to the Devil!'

'Certainly,' shouted Fulk. 'If the Devil has a wagon, it is the only sensible place. Eh, lads?'

One scowling archer looked about for a stone to throw, and became more bad-tempered when he could not find one. He spat instead.

'What a campaign! One third of the army left behind to pretend there is a siege. Half the infantry riding in carts like women. Knights who fight as if they are out for boar. Deserters falling out like corn from a broken sack. Have you heard the latest? Arques has gone now.'

'William of Arques?'

'Taken his men and gone.'

'He is a kinsman.'

'They are the most ambitious; look at Guy of Burgundy. The Duke is furious.'

'What will he do?'

'Punish him – as soon as he can untie himself from these sieges.' He jerked

168

a thumb over his shoulder. 'After that shambles, God knows how long it will take.' He hunched his shoulders, and gave a hitch to his dripping cloak, deriving a perverse satisfaction from the increasing gloom of his thoughts. 'Alençon will be just as prepared as Domfront. For all we know Arques has gone ahead and warned them. He is probably plotting with Anjou himself by now. And Anjou has probably retired to plot with the King.'

'Do you think we shall get paid?'

'How the Devil should I know?'

Fulk would – lucky bastard! He always got paid.

*   *   *   *   *   *

Whether William of Arques had warned the garrison of Alençon or not, they seemed ready for the Duke when he arrived. Walls and gates had been strengthened; ditches deepened, and lined with the usual sharpened stakes; surrounding estates had been stripped of food stores and livestock. Extra barns, byres, and stables had been built up against the town, and two fresh bailey walls had been hastily constructed in unseasoned timber from the nearby forest of Ecouves. The two enclosures projected westwards from the stone walls in insolent challenge; they were parading their vast food supply, and exhibiting with their extra stables their capacity to make cavalry forays against negligent guards of besieging camps. Fresh hides hung in profusion over the timber stakes, though with all the unseasoned wood and the wet weather, the chances of fire were slim.

When Duke William rode round on reconnaissance, a babel of jeers floated across to his party.

He was tight-lipped and impatient when he presided at the meeting of group commanders in his tent.

'All sappers and engineers to be engaged in making ladders, with immediate effect from this meeting. Ropes and slow torches to be carried by every assault party. Every infantry group to be re-organised into two echelons, one for each of those baileys. We go in together, and we go in at night.'

'At night!'

There was a murmur of discomfort. William glared.

'Can you think of a better way of surprising them?'

Nobody wished to make reference to the futile siege trappings in front of Domfront – eloquent proof of poor preparation and haste.

After a pause, Fulk's languid voice was heard.

'May I ask, my lord, what our gallant knights on horseback are going to be doing all this time?'

If William noted the jibe, he ignored it.

'We shall need them for the pursuit on the morrow. I wish this defeat to be complete. There must be no regrouping. Anjou will have nothing to come and rescue.'

An insolent smile blew across Fulk's face.

'I wish our mounted members a comfortable night abed.'

This time William did react.

'They will earn their keep when the time comes. As I expect you to. Your time simply comes earlier.'

'We earned our keep in front of Domfront, fighting off the Duke of Anjou. May I remind your Grace that we are professional swordsmen, not scaffolding monkeys with owlish eyes.'

William leaned forward slightly.

'And may I remind Fulk – the Angevin – ' William loaded the word with enough stress to point the irony of Fulk fighting against his own Duke ' – that he and his men are engaged for the season, not by the day. Now – ' he turned to his own senior vassals. ' – Giffard, Montgomery, you will allocate the various groups to the two assault parties. We will go in just before moonrise. I shall lead the one against the left bailey, and the right-hand command will go to our intrepid Angevin.'

He turned back to Fulk.

'Let him demonstrate his pride in his professionalism. And if his bailey is the first to be taken, I promise him double pay. Let us see if the light of gold opens his – owlish eyes for him.'

Geoffrey had said nothing throughout the whole proceedings; as a newcomer from the west, he felt it was hardly his place. He was surprised, however, that nobody else spoke. Two simultaneous night attacks, across unfamiliar ground, against a well-prepared position, with disparate groups of irregular infantry, half of whom seemed disaffected already – it did not exactly glitter with potential success. He looked across at Roger of Montgomery. Roger read his thoughts, and shrugged.

With the Duke in his present mood, and with no Fitzosbern at his elbow, who was going to tell him?

As they filed out of the tent, Geoffrey bumped into Fulk. He had known of his presence in the Duke's army, but this was the first time they had come face to face. The suddenness caught him off guard. Fulk seemed not in the least put out. He bowed.

'Ah, my lord bishop. A pleasant change to meet on equal terms. A happy fate, to be sure, that finds us on the same side.'

Geoffrey kept his temper with an effort.

'Ralph told me that you had only recently been in the service of the Duke of

Anjou, and here you are in the camp of Normandy against him. Who is to say when you will be on the opposite side again?'

Fulk smiled easily.

'Who indeed? But may I remind your Grace that you too, as vassal and bishop, can enjoy the luxury of similar choice; you can serve God and Mammon as your interests dictate. I at least do not add hypocrisy to the sin of inconstancy.'

'And I do not include attempted murder in the code of soldiering.'

Fulk brushed aside the answer.

'Ah – the boy! He was disloyal. I and my profession survive on loyalty.'

If he had overheard the remark passed to somebody else, Geoffrey would have laughed. The man's effrontery was breathtaking.

'Talking of murder,' continued Fulk, 'have you caught up yet with our mutual friend Torf?'

Geoffrey was beginning to realise that strong reins on the temper were vital to survival in any conversation with this man.

'God in His infinite wisdom has not yet seen fit to place him at my mercy.' Geoffrey assumed Fulk's air of innocent inquiry. 'I presume you have yourself renewed acquaintance with him, and discharged your part of the agreement.'

Fulk bowed.

'Professional etiquette, my lord. He paid, and I delivered.'

'You surprise me.'

'Because you assume that it was out of moral decency. You were not listening; I said "professional etiquette". Our friend Torf may have similar interesting and remunerative commissions for me in the future. Surely it would be ill-advised to lose such a potentially profitable source of income. Certain people, I have discovered, have a gift for generating wealth, just as our gallant Duke may have a gift for generating power, or as you and your party seem to have one for survival. You said "attempted murder", so I take it that he lives.'

And had better stay out of Fulk's way. Geoffrey would have to restrain Ralph.

'You mean you gave it all to him?'

Fulk smiled.

'Come now, my lord. Has the mitre fallen completely over your eyes? I have a satisfied customer; is that not enough?'

'I understood that only my death would bring satisfaction.'

Fulk, surprisingly, nodded in agreement.

'Yes, so did I. However, he was able to turn the slightly – incomplete situation to his advantage. He seemed to be of the opinion that, while news of your death would be a tragedy, news of your unwillingness to return would constitute rejection. The one would provoke grief, which would not be to his purpose; the other

171

would provoke fury, which most definitely would.'

Geoffrey could have struck him. With a great effort he turned away in the direction of his own tent. Could Ivo put it all right?

'Nothing personal, my lord,' called Fulk after him with a laugh. 'And remember – my terms are very reasonable.'

*　　*　　*　　*　　*　　*

The attack was a shambles.

The garrison had prior warning – probably some spy of William of Arques' left behind for just such a purpose. It was a pitch-dark night, which hampered the approach. The moon did not appear to light the assault once it had gone in, because of heavy cloud. When the rain began, the slow matches were either mostly extinguished or dropped into the ditches in the confusion. Hastily-constructed ladders broke under the weight of too many men on them.

The Duke's group scaled the walls of the left-hand bailey only because of his dynamic leadership and example. Those on the right, who were late, soaked, confused, and divided, never made a serious attempt. Fulk, furious at the incompetence, refused to commit his own men to such a mess, and no amount of abuse or threat on his part could restore unity of purpose or obedience. He threw up his hands and withdrew, and that settled the matter as far as the right-hand attack was concerned. The garrison commander, clearly a man of energy and resource, as soon as he saw that one assault had broken down, transferred most of the defenders from that bailey into the other.

Thirty more fresh men poured out of the gate in the stone wall into the left-hand bailey and threw themselves on the Duke's force, now all inside and fighting for their lives.

If there was one thing that the Duke had known and understood since his childhood, it was sudden threat and rapid reaction. His darting eye, his swift decision, his raucous voice, his urgent gestures, his prowess and his nerveless example rallied his faltering forces.

'*Diex aie!*'

Terrified horses burst from the stables, and reared and plunged and kicked. Wounded men writhed and screamed in the mud, arms over their head in futile protection against feet and hooves alike. Excited defenders on the stone ramparts of the main town hurled stones into the dark void below, regardless of the owners of the heads that they could barely see. Rain rattled on to metal helmets and chain mail, thudded on to leather jerkins. Somehow or other the thatched roof of a storehouse had caught alight; in the rain it belched smoke right across the bailey. Men roared and swore and swung and thrust; they blinked into the darkness; they coughed in the smoke; they spat raindrops off their lips.

'*Diex aie!*'

The Duke's will and energy began to prevail. The defenders were steadily reduced and driven back. The garrison commander showed now not only his resource but his ruthlessness. He ordered the main gate in the stone wall to be closed and barred, so that the remaining defenders in the outer wooden bailey could not escape back inside. Terrified men, thinking that an awful mistake had been made, pounded with fists and handles of weapons on the massive wooden planks and screamed, their faces turned up white into the rain in desperate entreaty to their comrades on the battlements.

Denied, they turned about to face the panting, coughing, streaming attackers. For the first time, men had the chance to think and to grasp the situation. Suddenly, the only noises were the crackling of thatch and the drumming of the rain.

One of the defenders threw down his sword . . .

*   *   *   *   *   *

The recriminations lasted until dawn. Feudal levies blamed unreliable mercenaries; front-line swordsmen cursed stupid planning and bad staff work; men of the Pays de Caux said that no good ever came from relying on tremblers from the Bessin; archers blamed wet bowstrings; wounded on litters, their limbs in makeshift splints patched together from broken ladders, condemned to Hell all camp engineers; the Duke spent two hours in red-faced, hoarse abuse with Fulk and other detachment commanders of the right-hand assault group; everybody blamed the weather. Only hunger, thirst, and exhaustion prevented half the besieging camp from coming to blows with the other half.

Deprived of vindication, denied comfort, furious at retreat, they cast about for something that could not retaliate . . . Thirty-four prisoners had surrendered in front of their town gates on the assumption that anything would be better than the death that had stared them in the face . . .

As the first shafts of dawn lit the eastern sky behind the defiant stone ramparts of Alençon, the Duke and his survivors collapsed on to any bedding that lay near.

Barely four hours later, William was up and out again, patrolling round the walls, studying, assessing, calculating. His temper seemed to have gone; on a fresh mount, and with a good breakfast inside him, he rode and circled and gazed and tried to plan afresh.

Two men-at-arms watched him as they relieved themselves into a boundary ditch.

'You have to hand it to him, you know. He never gives up.'

'Yes. He is the sort of man who is never satisfied unless he is making things happen.'

173

William turned to the group who were riding beside him.

'I am going closer.'

'Stay out of range, my lord,' warned Walter Giffard.

William grunted.

'Their archers are even worse than ours. Come.'

The rain had stopped at last. Indeed, a watery sun was trying to make its presence felt. Heads began to bob and move on the tops of the walls. Small clusters of them began to gather to watch the approach of the Duke's party.

Shouts floated in their direction. As they moved nearer, the tone of the voices became evident. Nearer still, and individual phrases leapt out of the general babel.

'Wet our leggings last night, did we, my lord?'

'Lose our way in the dark?'

William grunted, and continued his reconnaissance, examining the extent of the damage to the broken bailey. Already, men were swarming over the breaches, mending breaks, dragging away smouldering wreckage, hanging freshly-soaked skins to protect from fire.

William rode and stared and hummed to himself.

Somebody leaned over the wall and patted the new skins.

'Fresh hides, fresh hides! Plenty of work here, my lord. Work for the son of the tanner's daughter!'

William stopped humming, and reined in his horse with a savage jerk.

'Tanner's work for the tanner's boy!'

More and more men leaned over the walls and began to beat with sticks and the flat of swords on the hanging skins, falling into a steady rhythm.

'Tan-ner! Tan-ner! Tan-ner!'

William, his face blotched and swollen, rode past his men towards the camp, jostling them without noticing it. In muddled urgency, they wheeled to follow. William did not stop until he had reached the lines of Fulk's mercenaries. He bellowed for their commander.

Fulk languidly pulled aside the door of a tent.

'You called, my lord?'

William fidgeted unnecessarily with his reins. He could barely sit still.

'I want a score of your best swords. You have a chance to make up for last night.'

Fulk stroked a half-shaven chin.

'May I ask the nature of our errand, my lord?'

'No you may not. Get them out, and tell them to come to the prisoners' compound.'

'Right now, my lord? They have not yet breakfasted.'

For a moment it looked as if William was going to dismount and attack him.

'Splendour of God! Do as you are told – if you want any payment at all. Or I put you in the compound with them.'

Walter Giffard, who had now caught up, looked at Roger of Montgomery, who had come out to see what the fuss was all about. They exchanged surprised faces.

The bantering smile left Fulk's face.

'Very well, my lord.'

He tossed aside his napkin and stalked off. Giffard and Montgomery threw more glances of wonder at each other.

Half an hour later, thirty-four prisoners from the garrison of Alençon were kneeling in full view of the walls of their town. Round them stood Fulk's men, still only half dressed, with drawn swords.

Word had spread like fire in thatch, and curiosity had pulled from their collapse men who five hours before had resolved that nothing was going to get them up for at least a week. In the town, heads and shoulders clustered in murmuring anticipation on the battlements.

'What is he going to do?' said Geoffrey to Roger of Montgomery.

Roger shook his head.

'I have never seen him like this before. If it is what I think it is . . . '

A prayer flashed through Geoffrey's head: 'From sudden death, good Lord deliver us!'

William stood in full view of the walls, slightly in front of the prisoners, confident that he had an iron grip on the initiative. Not one shaft was loosed in his direction, though he was now well within range. The murmuring had stopped. Geoffrey noted, however, that – typically of the professional – the Duke was taking no chances; he was wearing full mail and had his helmet strapped under his chin.

The numbers from the besieging camp grew steadily, until most of William's army had gathered in whispering clumps in a huge half-circle round Fulk and the kneeling men, though at a wary distance, as if reluctant to be too closely associated with what they began to suspect was going to happen.

The Duke was clearly waiting for something. He leaned on a drawn sword and gazed at the top of the wooden walls of the bailey whence had come the chanted insults. Nobody was beating the skins now.

At last a small group of armourer's mates pushed through the rows of spectators, staggering under the weight of a huge slice of tree trunk, from which sawdust still dribbled. The Duke pointed with his sword; they set it down beside

175

him, and retired hastily, wiping their hands on their jerkins.

The besiegers shuffled closer together as if for reassurance. The murmur of curiosity fell to a rustle of foreboding.

'A tanner's block! Christ and Mary!'

Several men furtively crossed themselves.

William looked at Fulk.

'Do it.'

'Why us?' said Fulk.

'You let them down last night.' William waved towards the rest of the army. 'Now they must see that they can again trust you.'

Fulk recalled their furious altercation of the previous night. He sneered.

'More likely that you do not trust them to carry out your orders. That is why you need me.'

William took a step forward. His face was still mottled and oddly thick-featured. He jabbed with the point of his sword several times into the grass. His rough voice grated like the teeth of a saw.

'Do it! Earn your money. Since when have – mercenaries been in a position to choose?'

'But they have always been in a position to bargain, my lord. For this I want double pay – for all of us.'

'Treble. Only do it!'

William turned away, walked a few paces, and stopped, his eyes never leaving the top of the walls of Alençon. Without looking back, he said, more quietly, 'One by one. Take your time.'

Fulk shrugged, and beckoned to the haggard prisoners.

'Right, lads. You heard what his Grace said: one at a time . . .'

Some men cheered at first. Ribald remarks flew thick and fast, and drowned the screams. Insults and jeers were bawled at the forest of raised fists on the battlements. It was their way of getting back for all the mess and chaos of the previous night.

But there were thirty-four prisoners in all, and Fulk, as he had been told, took his time. It was one thing to vent their anger and frustration on a gang of bound captives who could swear back – to tease and kick and poke and leer. It was another to stand apart and watch – for over an hour – the repetitive butcher's work that now was being performed like some hideous parody in reverse of a Devil play.

Chained to the spot by morbid fascination and by chill dread of the man who had ordered it, they fell silent, their noses revolted by the drifting smell of sweat, sawdust, slaughter, and excrement, their ears raped by screams and groans and dull thuds. Many turned their eyes away from the growing forest in the grass of flailing stumps. Ralph and some of the younger men vomited where they stood.

All the while the Duke had not moved, nor turned to watch. His shoulders hunched and set into stone, he continued to gaze at the now frozen heads on the battlements of the town that had dared . . .

At last – God's mercy! – it stopped. Fulk's men stood up and stretched their backs. An audible sigh rose from the army.

The Duke still did not turn.

'Now the feet!'

An archer crossed himself, and this time did not care who saw.

'Holy St. Michael – he has been counting!'

*   *   *   *   *   *

All the time Geoffrey groped and staggered through the human wreckage, part of his mind was telling him that he would have nightmares about this. To be clutched at by fingers that were not there . . .

'Bless me, father, for I have sinned . . . '

Amazingly, it was the Duke himself who had ordered it.

'See them into Heaven. God knows it was not their fault.'

Geoffrey stared. He thought of the set shoulders and the blotched face.

'You do not mind?'

The Duke stared back.

'I have the town.' He gestured towards the waving stumps. 'You have their souls. Look to them. It is the least we can do.'

Older men in the Duke's army provided further charity in the shape of a sharp knife to the heart – to those who begged for it. And, truth to tell, to some of those who did not, if a glimpse had been caught of a valuable crucifix around a sweaty neck. Besides, it was a way of escape for everybody; how could they live with – with that nearby?

It had taken some time for the gates to open, for all that. Even after the Duke had ordered every hand and foot to be thrown over the walls. Or perhaps it was because the garrison commander, a veteran of many years of frontier warfare, did not believe that a young duke who offered to spare the remainder in return for surrender could hold back his own troops from further slaughter. If so, he was speedily overruled by the panic caused at the Duke's next move. Know-alls in the Norman army swore afterwards that it had been Fulk's idea.

'Evil swine. I tell you, he was enjoying it.'

At any rate it was the braziers and hot irons that settled the matter. When the Duke rode into Alençon, the population was on its knees, rigid with dread. Men and women alike put up their hands in involuntary protection of their own eyes.

Those close to the Duke found it very difficult to find something to say to him. The long silences did not seem to bother him.

'How is he going to live with it?' said Geoffrey to Montgomery.

Roger made a face.

'Hard,' he said. 'But he will. He grew up with worse than that.'

The Duke's orders came soon after.

'To Domfront on the morrow.'

'Very good, my lord.'

Not even the outspoken Sir Walter Giffard made a comment.

When the orders were conveyed to the men, the Duke made it his business to be on hand to watch faces. Horror was there, and shock. But nobody was slow to obey.

Well, let them murmur. Let them fear their nightmares. What did they know of nightmares? They had not woken to the sound of throats being cut in nearby shadows; they had not scuttled like rabbits while men tore aside furniture with wet knives in their hands; few of them had changed their place of rest every other day for months on end; fewer still had killed from the saddle at fifteen. How many of them heard an ambush in every rustle? How many of them, on entering a building, looked at once for another way out? Nightmares ... Matilda now knew, and she was already beginning to understand ...

Anyone who had survived such a childhood seized whatever weapon dropped into his lap. And he had just discovered one – by accident, maybe, and it would not always do to rely on temper for such fortunate chance inspiration. Nevertheless ... with any luck his men would not need to worry; they would not need the block and the braziers and the hot irons again. His new weapon would take Domfront for him.

*   *   *   *   *   *

Geoffrey took it as a great compliment that Sir William Fitzosbern came to the gates of Domfront to see him off. They shook hands.

'I fancy you will not be idle this winter,' said Fitzosbern.

He meant the cathedral plans and the new knights.

'Too true,' said Geoffrey. He meant plenty of other things besides.

Fitzosbern looked up at a bleak sky.

'I wonder what sort of winter it will be.'

'A quiet one, I trust. Now.'

Fitzosbern put on his glove.

'You mean Domfront? Maybe, for a while. But terror like that does not last through a winter. It is a weapon that cools quickly.'

'The Duke has gone to ground,' said Geoffrey.

Fitzosbern smiled.

'The Duke has a new wife. He knows too that rebellions do not flower in the snow. But they can germinate under it.'

'William of Arques?'

'Yes. Already he plots with Anjou.'

Geoffrey waved a hand at the frowning walls of Domfront.

'We now hold this, and Alençon. Thanks to Roger we have Bellême too. What danger is there?'

'None – here. For the moment,' he added in his cautious way. 'The frontier, unfortunately, is long. If it is secure at one end, you probe the other. Do you know where Arques is?'

Geoffrey hesitated.

'Not exactly – no.'

'Beyond Rouen, near the border with Ponthieu. Count Enguerrand of Ponthieu is no lover of Normandy because we squeeze him against Artois and Flanders. And who is married to the sister of Count Enguerrand?'

'William of Arques.'

'Exactly.'

'Surely the Duke is prepared; his sister Adelaide is married to Count Enguerrand himself.'

'So our security,' said Fitzosbern, 'could depend on which of two negotiated marriages proves to be the more – persuasive. Could you sleep easy in a situation like that?'

Geoffrey could not sleep easy, and Sybil had not yet declared her intention of marriage yet – to either suitor.

Fitzosbern leaned forward, and spoke quietly.

'Something else too. Keep this to yourself. The King has gone very quiet of late. My guess is that he is digesting the news about this.' Fitzosbern waved a hand to the walls behind them. 'He was willing to support us while we were the underdogs. So long as Anjou went from success to success in Maine, he supported us. Now the tide has turned. He can not afford to have a vassal on his frontier who is too powerful.'

'You think he will change sides?'

'More than likely.' He chuckled. 'But keep it from Walter Giffard; he will want to go marching along the Seine to attack Paris next week.'

Geoffrey smiled, but said, 'It is that bad?'

'Let us say,' said Fitzosbern, 'that next year could well prove rather more difficult than this one.'

It was typical of Fitzosbern to understate. As Geoffrey saw it – with a potential alliance of William of Arques and any more disaffected Norman vassals he could persuade into another adventure, of the Duke of Anjou, of Count Enguerrand of Ponthieu, and of the King of France himself – Duke William of Normandy could be fighting for the very survival of his duchy before another year was out. And all Fitz could say was that it might be 'rather more difficult'.

He saw Fitzosbern smiling, as if he had read his thoughts.

'You know what they say – "one damned thing after another." Fare you well. Be on time for the council in the spring.'

As he rode through Mortain and swung north for Vire and Montbrai, Geoffrey was not the best of company. No Ivo, and no Thierry. Ralph had asked for leave to go home to Gisors for the winter season.

'If I let you go, will you come back? Look at you now.'

Smart, trim, full-cheeked, with a confident, ambling stride that was on the edge of becoming a swagger. His jerkin was well oiled, his weapons worth stealing. He had picked up a silver buckle from one of the dead at Domfront.

Ralph kissed the ring.

'It is all thanks to you, my lord. I shall return – if you will have me.'

Geoffrey felt pleased.

'Come to Coutances in the spring.'

Coutances, noted Ralph. Not Montbrai or Hauteville.

Geoffrey now had only one man with him whom he knew well – the last survivor of the ambush. The rest who rode with him were virtual strangers. This soldier – a brother of Lambert, the blacksmith at Montbrai – took it upon himself to become the fount of information on their new master.

'A hard man to please, his Grace. He tolerates no negligence or shirking. I remember once, when we were in Italy . . . '

The new knights took it all in, adding varying pinches of salt according to disposition, character, and experience. After all, did anyone ever know what he was letting himself in for? What did it matter? – a knight's fee was a knight's fee . . .

Geoffrey jogged along broodingly, thinking, as people in discomfort often do, of the last time he had been comfortable – at the last evening's drinking in the great hall at Domfront.

'Come and see me in the spring,' said Walter Giffard. 'We will talk horses.'

'It is a long way,' said Geoffrey doubtfully, remembering also Fitzosbern's summons to the Duke's council.

'Come to Bellême,' said Roger of Montgomery. 'It is nearer.'

Giffard laughed.

'If she gives you permission.'

Roger turned towards him in his slow, patient way.

'Who not come yourself? Bring some horses with you. I shall want to buy some too – especially now.'

'Spreading the Bellême wings, are we? What does Mabel say?'

Roger refused to take offence.

'Unless of course you are afraid of her.'

Walter nudged Geoffrey.

'I should have thought that one stallion at Bellême was enough for the time being.'

They laughed and passed the jar.

Walter Giffard wiped his lips.

'These new manors of yours – '

'At Coutances?'

Walter waved impatiently.

'No, no. The ones the Duke gave you after – after Alençon. Where exactly are they?'

'North of Coutances,' said Geoffrey. 'Around a place called Lessay.'

'Do you know it?'

'Barely. But I know about some property quite near to it – Malbec.'

Roger of Montgomery patted him on the shoulder.

'Remember what I said? "Stay close." You see?' He took another swig, and burped. 'What did I tell you?'

Walter Giffard shook his head.

'Malbec. Never heard of it.'

'That is what I said once,' said Geoffrey.

*　　*　　*　　*　　*　　*

Chapter Twelve

It was heady stuff. Montbrai was in a ferment of delight and shared pride. Curtseys were dropped; heads were ducked; salutes were given. Amid the tide of deference, Geoffrey also noted little pieces of driftwood that indicated the currents of family affection – urgent calls through doorways, hasty beckonings, beaming smiles – 'Come quickly; Master Geoffrey is back!'

So many familiar faces – from barn and bailey, field and furrow, stable and stream, midden and meadow. Mauger's reeve was powerless to prevent everyone downing tools – Boso, with his fierce squint, stumping forward eagerly, using as a crutch the very scythe that had given him the limp; Gaimar, prised out of his kitchen, still with his ladle in his hand; Bertha, eyes creased with pleasure into veritable slits, arms folded into her apron, so that she could put her hands in her lap even when she was standing up; Neel the brown-faced, silent forester, with his three sons, two of whom now topped him; Lambert's boy, bright-eyed as ever, and still absently picking his nose.

Hands were raised in amazement at new trappings, or clapped in appreciation at some other piece of wondrous equipment. Many were the whisperings and pointings at the new knights in the train. Boys fought to find a grip on the bridle of my lord's horse; Thierry officiously pushed back the bulging crowd to make a way; women jostled to kiss the ring; men patted horseflesh and raised eyebrows to each other in know-all appreciation.

Beaming faces surged round his stirrups. To think – he had gone off partly in search of just such a welcome, so often lived in the adventures of his imagination, and God had made him wait to find it all unbidden in his own place of birth.

The glow carried Geoffrey and everyone else right through the evening. Mauger had been generous in providing a board groaning with solids and delicacies, which steamed, shimmered, bubbled, and shone until demolished by a hundred eager spoons and knives. Gaimar had excelled himself. Unbidden guests clustered un-punished in the sacred solar, wolfing looted scraps; a dozen unknown dogs availed themselves of a unique opportunity, gobbling greedily round tolerant ankles. Eyes shone and faces sweated. Family jokes were re-lived to the accompaniment of whoops and roars. Manners were forgotten as the consumption of drink rose, and the 'my lord's' and the 'your Grace's' replaced by the 'Master Geoffrey's' – and not too many of those. Two men fell off the solar ladder. Ivo had abuse heaped upon his unrepentant head a dozen times when he kept leaving the main door open to go and relieve himself. Gori insisted on arguing in wine-soaked Latin, and made a pass at three serving-girls, all unavailing.

'If I had said yes,' giggled one of them, 'I doubt he could have managed it.'

Thierry made up a speech of welcome, forgot his lines, and collapsed off the back of a bench with his heels in the air.

In the morning, everybody avoided Geoffrey's eye. At first he thought it was simply the bad heads from the night before. However, the day wore on, and he found it almost impossible to strike up any kind of conversation with anybody. He sought out Mauger in the stables.

'What are they all afraid I shall ask?'

'I should have thought that was obvious,' said Mauger, patting a line of noses. Geoffrey waited. Mauger stopped to murmur to his favourite.

'Well,' said Geoffrey at last, 'how is she?'

Mauger rubbed his hands, remembered, and stuck them firmly into his belt. 'Ask Ivo. He was the one you sent there.'

$$* \quad * \quad * \quad * \quad * \quad *$$

'She said that she would wait until the child was a year old. After that . . . '

'Did you argue? Did you say what had happened?'

Ivo winced.

'If your Grace will lower his voice just a trifle.'

Did you reason with her?'

Ivo put his rough palms against his throbbing temples. Reasoning with a rejected woman, by proxy! If this was the extent of Master Geoffrey's knowledge of the opposite sex, no wonder God thought it was a good idea to set a mitre on his head.

'My lord, she was not there. It was to the lady Fressenda that I spoke.'

Geoffrey swallowed.

'Where has she gone?'

Ivo paid him the compliment of looking straight at him.

'To Malbec. She is now the lady of Malbec. She has married Torf of Malbec.'

Ivo could have whipped himself for the pain on Geoffrey's face. The familiar pacing began, hands raised and lowered many times.

'But she said she would wait until the child was a year old.'

'She did,' said Ivo. 'I arrived two weeks after its first birthday.'

Geoffrey ran his hand through his dark hair.

'Surely the lady Fressenda tried to stop her. Lord Tancred liked me. He said so often . . . all that chess.'

Master Geoffrey was clutching at straws. For his own good, he must be made to see.

'My lord, the lady Fressenda was for accepting Torf's offer from the outset. So was Master Roger; he told me so. And I have to tell you that my lord Tancred is dead.'

183

Geoffrey collapsed on to a stool, his back turned. Ivo knew that further conversation was going to be impossible. The blow had been delivered. Now came the recoil and the pain, and in the first shock there were no words known to man that could be of any use.

Ivo stood patiently, waiting for one more question the answer to which he knew would also give anguish.

'Did you see Raoul? Did you see the child? Is he a fine boy?'

'Alas, my lord. The lady Sybil has taken him with her to Malbec. But the lady Fressenda says that he is indeed a bonny infant. Dark hair, like yourself. If your Grace will excuse me . . . '

*　　*　　*　　*　　*　　*

Mist hung like a death shroud. In the shivering darkness of a November early morning, with every bare twig dripping, Geoffrey left Montbrai. Only the most hardy and faithful of bailey staff were up to see them off. Both sides behaved awkwardly, as if each wished to get the departure over as soon as possible.

Mauger and Geoffrey shook hands perfunctorily. Mauger wished him a safe journey, and Geoffrey blessed the household and domain. He did not offer his ring, and Mauger did not seek it. Each was still smarting from the altercation of the night before. If it had not occurred, Geoffrey still would have found it difficult to remain much longer. He had said all there was to say to Gori. In fairness to the household, he could not stay at Montbrai for long with such a retinue, with his new knights and their servants eating Mauger out of house and home. The castle and manor staff could not loiter round the bailey doing nothing but beam at him. Already the awkwardness was returning, that wall of formality and awe that he had initially noticed when news of his mitre had first leaked out.

'You are what you are, my lord. There is no going back. It is not their fault.'

'I know, Ivo. I know.'

It did not ease the pain of separation, however. What with that, and with Sybil, it was a double loneliness.

'They enjoyed you saying Mass for them,' said Ivo, trying to soften the blow. That had been Gori's idea.

Geoffrey thought of all those bowed shoulders, all those gnarled hands knitted in prayer . . . So many of them had shown him how to fasten fishing lines, how to adjust bridles, how to select stones for dry walling, how to plait laths into hurdles. If the truth be told, many too had cuffed him for clumsiness or stealing or bad manners. Now they knelt before him as their father without the slightest trace of awkwardness or reluctance. Rather the opposite. His household, his estate, his family, had become his flock. It bound him and cut him off at one and the same time.

'It is not the same, Ivo.'

Ivo, as so often, read his thoughts.

'Family or flock, what does it matter? They are the same people.'

It was a weary plod. The new knights could not understand.

'He could not sit still at Bayeux and Alençon. Now he does not seem to care whether he gets there or not.'

As they moved further north-west, the fog cleared, to be replaced by a drizzle that sapped the spirits and gnawed the patience. My lord of Coutances offered no comment or encouragement, and my lord's shadow Ivo was his usual gruff self. Once again, the new men looked at each other and wondered what sort of furrow they were digging for themselves.

'At least sieges gave you a chance of profit. They say Coutances is a ruin.'

'On the edge of the world.'

'Jesus and Peter!'

Goscelin, not the best of horsemen, crossed himself and grimaced, his eyebrows raised in a towering triangle of anguish.

Geoffrey had his rage to keep his mind off the discomfort of travel.

How could Mauger be so stupid! Especially after what had happened before. Would he never learn? . . .

'He lied to you before, and then took your money under false pretences. Or rather my money.'

'How do you know?'

'Because Guiscard told me. Torf never killed William of Hauteville. Nor did he ever have any intention of doing so. All he wanted was to make some profit out of you.'

Mauger sneered.

'I suppose you would take an Hauteville's word for it.'

'I should take anybody's word against that of Torf of Malbec.'

'You can not think straight about this man, simply because he stole your woman.'

Geoffrey put both fists on the table.

'Mauger, may I remind you that this man paid scum to ambush and murder me. Sybil has nothing to do with it. And you expect me to stand by while he inveigles you into this mad scheme? We are talking now not of mere murder, or of a little private war, but of rebellion.'

Mauger leaned back and picked his teeth.

'I agree it looks a little inconsistent,' he conceded. 'But I do not have to like him, or trust him, if it comes to that. However, he has opened my eyes to some political realities in western Normandy.'

Geoffrey tossed his head in impatience.

'Mauger, you are pathetic. You have no idea of political realities. You are letting this creature spin a web of intrigue around you, with his talk of a "great alliance of western knights to preserve our liberties". The minute you commit yourself, he will rush to Bayeux and betray you to the Duke. Already he has the ear of brother Odo, another tell-tale. And then what will happen? You will be disendowed – at the very least – and our brave subject Torf of Malbec will receive Montbrai as reward for his loyalty. Montbrai – the home of our father and our grandfather and others before them.'

Mauger examined his toothpick.

'All this travel and meeting famous people has gone to your head, brother, and driven out what little good sense was ever in there.'

'Oh, come now, Mauger. I know you have always been jealous of the Hautevilles; I refuse to believe that you are also jealous of me.'

Mauger affected lofty disdain.

'I shall treat that with the contempt it deserves. It is time, my much-travelled but unobservant brother, to acquaint you with some "political realities", as you put it. Have you ever heard of William of Arques? Ah, I see. Well, you perhaps do not know that he is in process of building an alliance against the Duke that would make an emperor blink.'

Mauger ticked off the names on his fingers.

'Geoffrey Martel, Duke of Anjou. Enguerrand, Count of Ponthieu. His own bastard brother, Archbishop of Rouen. A host of border knights in the north-east towards Artois. And just to make up the numbers, the King himself, no less. Henry is now drooling over border fortresses in the Vexin. And if you think that is not enough, Godwin of Wessex, for all that he is in exile, is pouring funds into it – anything to put the Bastard further from the crown of England.' Mauger sat back. 'Brother, by the end of next year, there will be enough troops out against the Bastard to put him off the ducal throne six times over.'

Geoffrey sat stony-faced.

'Mauger, you are a fool. You are still living in the past. The days are gone when warrior knights waged war wherever they liked in Normandy. Or at least going. We now have a Duke who has a vision of the future, who has it in him to build a united duchy, a truly powerful realm. He is attracting around him men of similar vision, and of great loyalty.'

Mauger laughed.

'You sound as if you are under a spell – vision of the future! United duchy! Great loyalty! What is this – the "Song of Roland"?'

'Mauger I have met some of them. I know. Why else do you think the King is scheming to attack him? Not because he despises him for being weak, but because he fears him for being strong. In which other lands of France do you hear of the Truce of God being enforced so successfully? Believe me, this Duke is exceptional. Holy Virgin! You told me so yourself.'

'I truly thought so. But no man, however exceptional, can stand against such odds. Whether you think me a fool or not, I can count. Moreover, I said that before the madness descended upon him.'

'What madness?'

Mauger spread his hands.

'The crown. The crown of England. If that is not proof of lunacy, I do not know what is. A Norman usurper – even a Norman claimant – who can not yet control his own duchy? The Saxons will laugh at him. He will not even be worth brushing away. It is enough to make God chuckle.'

'God helps those who help themselves,' said Geoffrey.

'A bishop should be able to manage better than that. Do I have to tell you, a prince of the Church, that God is no man's accomplice.'

'He does not stop a man bettering himself.'

'He puts order into the world. God ordains a place for each and every one of us. I should have thought that "Duke" would have been rank enough for the orphan of a tanner's daughter. Further than that, and you push God too far. You talk to me of political reality. I put it to you – your precious William is a bastard adventurer with a few lucky successes at sieges, who now has delusions of grandeur.'

Geoffrey snorted.

'Meanwhile, you, naturally, are wise and prudent. My lord Mauger of Montbrai sees fit to enter, blind, an alliance of western knights dedicated to – what was it? – your "liberties", at the instigation of a liar, a cheat, an adulterer, and a murderer.'

Mauger raised his eyebrows.

'As I said, you are biased . . . '

Geoffrey reined in beside Goscelin, and pointed to the top of the hill above the River Soulles.

'Coutances. We shall build up there.'

The rain had at last stopped, and a late autumn sun was setting behind the crest. Goscelin held up his hand to shield his eyes.

'A weary way to drag stone, my lord.'

It looked a promising position, but it would not do to show enthusiasm too early. He would look first at the view from the top.

As they began the ascent, Geoffrey could hear Ivo hacking away at his cough, just as he had done on their first arrival. Holy Virgin! Was it really two years ago? Yes, and more.

He heard also the rumble of many hooves behind him. A change from the wretched knot of mules and drenched donkeys that Thierry had towed unwillingly on that first day. His new men would have to be speedily settled. There were a hundred tasks to be attended to, or they would lose patience and leave. Already, their silence was eloquent testimony to their lack of enthusiasm. New manors would have to be surveyed, sites arranged for new houses and fortifications; then the allocations, the swearings, the giving of hands; purchase of weapons and equipment, drawing up of schemes of training; provision of skilled labour for each new knight's fee – he would have to rely on Thorold's sons and grandsons for local information about any surviving wheelwrights, carpenters, millers, smiths. There would be no end to it.

There was the small matter of his own residence. Montbrai was now out of the question; as Ivo had said, there was no going back. He built here, or he had no roof at all.

And the cathedral. For the whole of the journey from distant Cluny, he had thought little beyond getting the long-suffering Goscelin to Coutances, assuming blithely that, once he was installed, a cathedral would mysteriously arise out of the ruins as if from magic and from a parchment or two in Goscelin's bony hands. Now that they were actually here, the enormity of the whole task struck him for the first time.

Even the cathedral was not the end of it. Thanks to Roger of Montgomery's shrewd bargaining, he now owned half the town as well. That too had to be made to pay, or the investment would be worthless. He cursed his own ignorance. Mauger had been right; he should have paid more attention to his brother's work on bridges and markets and tolls and fords and customary dues and seasonal payments and fees of justice.

Dear God! Where did he begin?

And how could he concentrate on anything, when his mind kept swinging away to Malbec and Torf and Sybil . . .

'I shall kill him!'

'Oh?' said Mauger. 'You think the way to your lady's heart is to make her a widow?'

He scanned the repairs in the banks of the mill pond, and nodded his approval to the miller. Geoffrey fidgeted impatiently.

'Then I shall ruin him. I shall tell the Duke of his treason. At the very least he will suffer confiscation of property. It will give me the greatest pleasure to be the bearer of the Duke's sentence.'

'I see,' said Mauger, peering into the mill leat and dropping in a twig to confirm the rate of flow. 'So if you do not make Sybil a widow, you will disinherit her and make her an outlaw. The law makes no provision for wives of traitors, you know.'

Geoffrey fumed.

'Then I shall challenge him, man to man. He will have to meet me.'

Mauger looked up at the huge, dripping wheel.

'I seem to remember you saying something about the Truce of God. Now you tell me that you propose to wage a little private war on your own account against a man who is the legal owner of his property and who has been legally married, in order to deprive him of both estates and wife. Going to give yourself a dispensation, are you? Is the Duke as good a son of the Church as all that, to tolerate your actions as a brilliant exception?'

'He is more likely to tolerate my actions than he is yours,' said Geoffrey, retreating to the more familiar ground of fraternal abuse.

Mauger motioned to the miller to go and get the money.

'Within a year, brother, the Duke will in no position to take a stand about anything. When that time comes, as come it will, it will behove all men of honour and birth in the west to be aware of their identity, of their common destiny.'

Geoffrey groaned.

'Oh, Mauger, spare me!'

'Sneer if you like,' said Mauger. 'It is what you have always done. You have never had the worry and the responsibilities – until now. We have yet to see whether you will live up to them.'

Geoffrey flushed.

'How dare you!'

Mauger pointed past the wheel to the west.

'Then get out there and prove it. And if you do, it will be because part of you wants to show them in the east that we in the west can be just as good as they think they are.'

Geoffrey thought of Odo's spots and tiny head and wicked little laugh; of his jibes about Coutances and about western accents. It showed on his face.

'You see?' said Mauger. 'You are a man of the west, like the rest of us. Torf is absolutely right, whatever you may think of him. We men of the west must hang together.'

He took the leather pouch proffered by the miller, and began to count out the total of milling fees collected since harvest time.

'Fine words,' said Geoffrey, 'straight out of Torf's own mouth. And you have fallen for them. What they really mean is that you want to "hang together" now and ruin the future for Normandy, just so that you can all have the chance to go back to the past and hang each other separately. And who will be the beneficiaries? Scavengers like Torf. Predators like the King.'

It was Mauger now who enjoyed the chance to sneer. He looked up from his counting.

'Saints, what sophistication! The King a predator. Do we have a snap verdict on His Holiness as well?'

Geoffrey sighed.

'Mauger, you are so simple. You are more like Father than I thought. Missing what is under your nose. Bewitched by wild schemes and adventures.'

Mauger beckoned the miller close again.

'You were the one who went to Italy, not I. You are the one who looks with favour on the Duke as the next King of England, not I. If you wish to prove to me that you have your feet on the ground, then get out to Coutances and start building. Make something that we men of the west can be proud of. God knows you have it in you.'

'By the same token,' said Geoffrey, 'show me that you are free from the honey tongue of this wretch. Do something to show your loyalty to the Duke. I know that you have it in *you*. I do not wish to return from Coutances and find you deep into treason. At least wait for me to deal with him.'

Mauger counted a few coins back into the miller's whitened palm.

'You? Deal with Torf? You have not the faintest idea how to go about it.'

He looked at the miller.

'There. That should cover it for now. Do a good job on the gearing and we shall see.'

The miller made a face of glum acceptance.

'Not a penny more,' said Mauger. 'Quite enough sticks to your thumb as it is. I wonder how you have the face to put a bag like that in my hand.'

Geoffrey turned away towards the stream.

'I shudder to think what I shall find here when I return. Who knows? Perhaps he will even have married you off – to one of the Hauteville girls.'

The miller smirked. Mauger swore at him, and whirled round to Geoffrey.

'If you were not my brother, I should thump you for that . . . '

Goscelin walked the length and breadth of the nave, his shoulders hunched, his cloak pulled tight around him. He picked his way painfully between the tussocks of couch grass which might conceal protruding stones, lifting his feet high like some wary, fastidious stork.

Geoffrey fidgeted. Thierry cleared his throat.

'If I might offer some advice, my lord,' he ventured.

Geoffrey growled something unintelligible; Thierry took it for agreement, however unwilling.

'We have talked much on the road from Cluny, Goz and I. He has explained to me a lot of his work.'

That was true. A friendship seemed to have sprung up between them, if anything so emotional could be credited to such a mournful and resigned character as Goscelin. They certainly had talked a great deal, for which Geoffrey had been grateful. Nobody else liked trying to make conversation with him, and Thierry seemed to have the trick of keeping him in a tolerably equable frame of mind. The fact that Thierry had a diminutive name for him indicated some kind of intimacy and affection. Geoffrey had enough experience to know that travel and hardship and lack of familiar surroundings resulted in the most unlikely relationships; he did not waste time trying to understand why.

Ivo had an explanation, expressed in his usual gruff way.

'They both like eating.'

If the feast at Montbrai was anything to go by, Ivo had a point. Goscelin had been seen actually to smile once or twice. Thierry had been pleased to see him after leaving him with Geoffrey at Bayeux, and had plied him with a never-ending succession of meats and pastries. They were later seen together, haunting Gaimar's kitchen.

On the weary road from Montbrai to Coutances, they had ridden side by side all the way. Now that the column contained Geoffrey's new knights, Thierry felt released from his usual vanguard duties. He had listened tolerantly to Goscelin's complaints of saddle discomfort.

Now he watched while his friend stepped cautiously across the open transept.

'He is an artist; he must be left alone to – to create.'

Thierry made an expansive gesture.

Geoffrey turned to gaze in amazement. It was the first vaguely cultural remark he had heard Thierry make in his life.

Ivo as usual put it more practically.

'Thierry is right, my lord. The man must be left alone. I am sure that designing a cathedral is not like choosing a camp site. It is not as if we have nothing else to do.'

Geoffrey knew they were right, which annoyed him. He knew that Goscelin was going to be difficult, which annoyed him more. He knew further that his own knowledge of building and design in stone went no further than some dry walling at Montbrai. He had witnessed no larger construction than the bulging, lopsided, lower wall of the family tower. He was going to be completely in the hands of this dismal, temperamental, triangular heron.

*　　*　　*　　*　　*　　*

White puffs of breath came from the nostrils of the ox-team, which stood still in the traces, grateful for the inactivity. The carter and his boy, their shoulders hunched under sacking against the chilling rain, stood beside one of the thick, solid wheels.

In front of them swaggered two men in mail hauberks. One had drawn a knife, and tapped the point of it into his other palm. His partner grabbed the boy by the scruff of the neck. The carter spread his hands. The boy's shrill cry carried across the intervening distance.

Geoffrey could not hear actual words, but he had a good idea of the spirit of what was being said.

'We go only to the heath, my lords, for a little peat. The winter will be hard this year, they say.'

'So hard that you can not afford an offering for the use of my lord of Malbec's road?'

Geoffrey glanced to left and right. The horses were fifty paces away, guarded by a third man, who was squatting in the doorway of a cottar's hovel and eating scraps of roast chicken looted from inside. The cottar's family cowered helpless in the rain.

Across the road, on a knoll half-covered by brown bracken, Ivo raised his sword. Geoffrey looked further away again to his right. Two of his new knights waited in readiness, their hands fisted over the reins. On the left, two more flexed their toes in the stirrups. The game must not be allowed to escape. The first encounter had to be a success, however modest. Geoffrey was determined that the first pawn to fall should fall to him.

Geoffrey lifted his sword and turned to Thierry and the men behind him.

'Ready? Now!'

He let his arm fall, and the four groups of horsemen converged on the cart in the rain-flecked puddles.

Both men turned at the same time when they heard the hooves. Both saw Geoffrey and swung round to go the other way, only to stop again when they saw Ivo and his companions. From cunning and experience, they split up and ran in opposite directions away from the road, but the mud slowed them down before they could reach the heathland on either side.

Geoffrey caught up with one as he was trying to clamber across the ditch. Killing was not his plan or his inclination – not yet. Geoffrey raised his drill mace and caught him fair and square between the shoulder blades. On the other side, Ivo leaned from the saddle, grabbed the other by the scruff of the neck, and lifted him bodily off his feet. In total control of both horse and prisoner, he swung round and deposited his load with a great splash in a deep puddle in front of the oxen.

Wrenching his horse's head round, Geoffrey bawled to his other men.

'Get those horses. And bring the other one here.'

They had anticipated him, and none too gently. The third man was practically ridden down, his mouth still full of unswallowed chicken. The cottar's family cowered away further, their eyes wide. It did not help when one of Geoffrey's knights waved his sword impatiently.

'Well, go on, you silly sheep. Get back inside. It is all over.'

Nevertheless, they waited until the knights had returned towards the wagon with their prisoner, who was stumbling along, half choking and half winded. Then they scurried inside like startled rabbits, leaving amulets and charms swaying on their strings over the threshold.

Ivo yanked all three captives into a close group, and cuffed them once or twice to ensure that they paid attention. Shivering without hauberk or leather jerkin, their leggings black with wet from falling and, now, kneeling, they gazed sullenly at Geoffrey. One of them was trying to clear something from the back of his throat.

'You will shortly return to your lord, Torf of Malbec,' said Geoffrey. 'You may consider yourselves lucky to be alive – for the time being. You will tell your lord that it was I who allowed you to live, and why. Your lord will know that he has done me many wrongs in the past; you will take to him the message that the time has now come to begin the reckoning.

'We are making a start here. From this moment, there will be no more levying of unlawful tolls along this stretch of road. Anyone who does so without my express permission will be breaking the peace and order of the lands of Geoffrey de Montbrai, lord Bishop of Coutances, and will pay the penalty.

'You will also tell your lord that there will be no more pressure of any kind brought to bear upon the canons or lay workers of my cathedral church, upon pain of both earthly and eternal heavenly punishment by virtue of the power vested in me as a prince of the Holy Catholic Church. Is that clear?'

One of the men muttered in surly fashion.

'Yes.'

One of Ivo's knees thumped him in the shoulders and sent him sprawling. With his hands tied behind his back, he was unable to save himself.

' "My lord," ' prompted Ivo.

The man spat mud.

'My lord.'

'You will tell your lord further that I have been invested with lands around Lessay, over towards Malbec, and that we are almost, in a manner of speaking, neighbours. If he inquires as to the provenance of these estates, you will inform him that the Duke recently confiscated the lands of those rebels captured before Alençon and Domfront. It is intended to serve as a warning to any future possible rebels. If, when I arrive, I find that any servant of my lord of Malbec has been seen on or near my lands, I shall treat it as felonious trespass, and will deal with any culprits that I catch far more firmly than I did with you. Now stand up.'

Ivo walloped them again just in case they had not heard.

'Up!'

Hunched, filthy, soaked, and shivering, they shuffled together, looking if anything more pathetic than the two peasants they had recently been bullying.

Ivo checked that the bonds round their wrists were not too tight, and nodded to Geoffrey.

Geoffrey beckoned with his head up the road towards Lessay and Malbec.

'Now go. And praise your God for His mercy – and mine.'

They gazed in horror.

'My lord,' one of them whined, 'it must be fifteen miles to Malbec.'

'Then the sooner you start the better,' said Ivo.

Another half-turned as if to offer his wrists.

'What about these?'

Ivo pointedly put his thumbs into his belt.

'You walk on your feet, not your hands. Now be off – before we hobble your ankles as well.'

As they trudged off, Ivo gathered up the jerkins, hauberks, and weapons.

'First blood, my lord.'

Geoffrey grunted.

'So far, so good. A satisfactory opening move. Now we wait to see how he will react.'

'If at all,' said Ivo.

'If at all,' agreed Geoffrey.

Ivo held up his bundle.

'What do we do with these, my lord?'

Geoffrey jerked a thumb towards his new men.

'They can draw lots for the hauberks and the horses. Weapons stay with me. Give them to Thierry and tell him to start a store in a safe place.'

'The jerkins?'

Out of the corner of his eye, Geoffrey noticed the two wretched peasants, who had scarcely moved from their original refuge against the great wheel of their cart. Baffled, shocked, and frightened, they did not know whether to run and risk a spear between their shoulders, or to stay put and risk being robbed further by an even more terrible set of strangers.

194

Geoffrey beckoned the man towards him.

Very reluctantly, very slowly, the man obeyed, like a stray wild dog lured by proffered food.

Geoffrey tugged his gloves firmly on to his hands.

'Do you know who I am?'

The man swallowed.

'My lord?'

'I said, "Do you know who I am?" '

'My lord.'

Geoffrey leaned forward and recited clearly and slowly, as if for a foreigner.

'Your lord. I am your lord. I am Geoffrey de Montbrai, Bishop of Coutances.'

The man nodded his head in time with the words, concentrating intently. When Geoffrey had finished, he swallowed his saliva and took a breath.

'Montbrai, lord bishop of Coutances.'

It was an outlandish accent, the offspring of local inbreeding and lack of contact with the outside world. Holy Virgin! How did one make a start with people like this?

'I shall protect you,' continued Geoffrey. 'From now on you need not fear men like that. Do you understand?'

The man frowned fiercely, as if turning over a great weight in his mind. He looked up hopefully.

'Does that mean we no longer pay?'

'Yes. Now go, and be grateful, and tell others whom you may meet. The days of terror are over.'

As the cart creaked away into the rain, the boy looked frequently over his shoulder. Ivo and Geoffrey led their mounts over to the cottar's hut, to where his knights were examining the captured horses and haggling over the drawing of lots.

Ivo made a noise that was half sigh and half grunt.

'What is it, Ivo?'

'My lord?'

'Out with it. I know you too well.'

'My lord, is it a good idea to let them think that there will never be anything to pay? Do you not intend to levy tolls yourself? They should not fall to thinking that you are a weak lord who wishes to be liked.'

'Have no fear, Ivo. I intend to make everything pay. But it must be made profitable first. You feed the bird before you pluck it.'

They stopped in front of the cottar's hut. The door was still firmly closed. The charms had stopped swinging on their strings – crudely-fashioned likenesses in bone. A falcon, a leering boar's head, a horse. A complete necklace hung separately. On the wall nearby was nailed the dried skin of a black cat.

Geoffrey flicked them with his gloved hand.

Holy Virgin! How did one make a start?

* * * * * *

Chapter Thirteen

'Steady, steady. Just a little more.'

Geoffrey watched while the sling creaked its way down to the ground. He saw the familiar imperious flapping of the wrist. Serving girls fussed and scurried with shawls and baskets and mufflers; the smith, summoned from his forge in the hasty search for muscle and sinew, along with two sweating grooms, puffed respectful obedience.

'Very good, m'lady.'

'Yes, m'lady. Arm round my shoulder now.'

'Nice and easy, m'lady. Have you there in no time.'

She looked older, but otherwise unchanged; the inner energy, the fire, the command – all were undiminished.

When she was finally settled, Geoffrey bowed formally. He would have sat down, but she beckoned him closer. To his surprise, she insisted on kissing his ring.

'You will forgive an old woman for not kneeling, I am sure.'

'I should have forgiven you for not getting up at all,' said Geoffrey. 'It is only a quick visit; I did not wish to cause any inconvenience.'

'You should have given us warning. The House of Hauteville takes pride in honouring the rules of courtesy and hospitality.'

Geoffrey smiled at the rebuke.

'I shall remember in future.'

The lady Fressenda settled herself more cosily in her blankets.

'Now . . . '

'First of all,' said Geoffrey, 'I would ask you to accept my sincere condolences upon the untimely death of my lord Tancred. The loss must be immeasurable.'

He was interrupted by a wave of a hand.

'The Lord has given and the Lord has taken away, and that is an end of it. It is my destiny to remain, and with that I must be content – for a while.'

The House of Hauteville also took pride, it seemed, in not showing emotion. Geoffrey apologised.

'I did not wish to cause distress. It was only that I too honoured my lord Tancred, and – '

'My lord!' The lady Fressenda leaned slightly forward.

Geoffrey stopped.

'My lord,' repeated Fressenda, 'I am an old woman with little time, and you are a young bishop in a hurry. Let us discuss what you came here to discuss.'

Geoffrey responded to her tone.

'In that case, my lady, may I ask you to dismiss the girls. What I have to say concerns only you.'

'And you.'

'Very well. And me. Now – will you?'

One curt nod was enough to send every girl in a flurry of straw and sandals to the door.

Without looking to see if she was being obeyed, the lady Fressenda beckoned to her stitching frame.

'I like to be occupied. I am sure you will understand. It takes my mind off aches and pains. At least my fingers do what I command them to do.'

Geoffrey pushed it closer.

'How is Sybil?'

Fressenda selected a needle.

'She is well.'

'And the child?'

'A bonny infant.' She looked up. 'Not unlike you.' The faintest of smiles appeared.

Geoffrey tried to follow her mood.

'I should hope so.'

Fressenda held out a needle and a length of wool.

'You sent the girls away.'

Geoffrey took them and began threading as if it were the most natural thing in the world. How many years was it since he had sat at his mother's feet and begged to do the same? Once more, his tongue stuck out of his mouth as he concentrated.

There was an awkward silence after Geoffrey returned the needle.

'Well?' said Geoffrey at last.

The lady Fressenda made the first insertion.

'Say what is in your mind, and I shall say what is in mine.'

'Why did she not wait?'

'She did. Longer than I should have done. Longer than we wanted her to.'

'I came as soon as I could.'

The lady Fressenda looked up sharply.

'You came here last.'

Geoffrey spread his hands.

'Montbrai is my home. Coutances is my charge.'

'And Sybil is your love – or so you say. Yet you came here last.'

'I have ties, responsibilities.'

'So did Sybil – Raoul.'

'Surely she must have known how much I wanted to come back and see him.'

Fressenda tugged at a stitch.

'I am sure she did. But it was not seeing the child that she doubted; it was marriage. She had to make provision.'

'Surely Ivo told you of our troubles on the road. Our return to Italy. The Council at Bayeux. Domfront. Alençon,'

'That was not relevant to her situation. All that mattered was that you were not here. And the child was.'

Geoffrey sighed. Fressenda dispensed with formalities.

'Geoffrey, if you lost a shepherd, would you wait for ever for him to come back, or would you find another to guard your sheep? And if you received a message which, being interpreted, said that he was not coming back, what would you do?'

'I am back now.'

The lady Fressenda sighed too.

'Sometimes it is worse to return late than not to return at all.'

Geoffrey tried another approach.

'Does she love this – this Torf?'

'That is something that Sybil must answer for herself – if you can get into Malbec to ask it. I can tell you, though, that she most definitely has something at Malbec, beside which love, as you put it, is totally irrelevant.'

She stopped stitching to emphasise her point.

'Status. Position. Security. Power.'

'Do not be so sure,' said Geoffrey. 'Have you not heard of the great conspiracy that is growing against the Duke? Torf is on the edge of it. He hopes to profit from it, like the scavenger he is, but he could well be crushed when it collapses.'

'*If* it collapses.'

My lady was better informed than Geoffrey had imagined.

They talked long into the dark hours. She amazed him with her command of affairs outside western Normandy, with her shrewdness, and with her common sense. She touched him with a kind offer:

'Would you like my lord Tancred's chessmen? He did so much enjoy playing with you. Roger does not play, and Humbert and Aubrey are too stupid for it.'

'I should be honoured,' said Geoffrey.

She impressed Geoffrey with her sense of realism.

'Humbert and Aubrey may go soon. One at least; they will draw lots to see who stays to guard the land. That will leave Roger. He will wait only until I die.'

She scandalised him with a sudden suggestion:

'Do you want Constance?'

Geoffrey was appalled.

'Constance?'

'None of Sybil's brains or character, I agree. But she has other qualities which she is only too willing to offer. I am a woman who has borne twelve children to a man who had five more by his first wife. I more than anyone understand a man's needs.'

Geoffrey spluttered. Fressenda reassured him.

'Constance would not be as demanding as Sybil. She will settle for bed and board without the altar.'

Geoffrey was still lost for an answer.

'Ah, well,' said my lady. 'Just an idea.'

Let Geoffrey think about it. She needed time to ascertain how he would react, how he would deal with the problem in front of him at Malbec. If he did not react at all, or if he tried and failed to solve it, then she had done right to leave the situation alone. The only thing that was important was the safety of Sybil and the child. If that were assured, she could die content.

If Torf joined the conspiracy, and it proved successful, then Geoffrey himself might be a loser too, and the situation was still best left alone. If Torf failed, or was punished, or lost his land – if only a little push was needed to tip the situation towards another solution, then perhaps she would have another talk to Geoffrey.

She laid down her needle and gazed into the fire. If men had to accomplish what they did in this life with only the puny weapons available to women, what on earth would they make of it?

*　　*　　*　　*　　*　　*

Sybil leaned down and wiped the soiled lips and chin. The worst seemed to be over. The crying had stopped too. Exhaustion probably.

She sat back and sighed. Beside Sybil Cecily coughed politely.

'If my lady would like to rest, I shall sit with him. You had no sleep last night.'

Sybil nodded wearily.

'But I shall stay down here. Wake me if anything happens.'

Cecily put more wood on the fire. She brought a heavy blanket from the solar and began to tuck it round Sybil's body. Sybil was so tired that she let Cecily pick up her arms as if they were dead weights and put them inside the blanket. Both Cecily and she caught sight of a dark bruise just below the elbow. They looked at each other, but neither said a word.

Cecily was a good soul; she was discreet and she was loyal. Of all the girls at Hauteville, she made the least fuss. Mother had allowed her to choose whom she wanted.

'I am not surprised,' said the lady Fressenda when she heard Sybil's decision. She frowned grimly at Cecily.

'Take proper care of the lady Sybil, or you will answer to me.'

Cecily gave her look for look.

'I know how to discharge my duty, my lady. All that is in my power the lady Sybil shall have.'

Very few girls answered like that to my lady Fressenda.

'You see, Mother? I knew I made the right choice.'

Now, as she listened to Cecily making crooning noises, Sybil wriggled into the blanket and sighed from head to toe. Even the sigh made her ache. And not only from bruises. Everybody at Malbec was tired from the effort of fighting the cold of the last week. They had had bad winters at Hauteville, God knows, but there was somehow warmth enough inside to keep the worst of it out, and it did not come entirely from logs.

It only added to the grim chill that had been steadily growing within her ever since – ever since the madness had begun to wear off.

After all those months at Hauteville, when her mind had been under constant siege – from doubt and longing, from Mother's advice and Roger's suggestions, from Torf's honeyed words and his physical presence – her release had been sudden and complete. Geoffrey's crucifix broke her down more effectively than his own words face to face; it seemed such a conclusive and apt gesture. She was furious at the futility of her prodigious effort. Consequently her surrender was as passionate and determined as has been her resistance.

It lasted barely a month. In that time she became aware of Torf's moods and whims, his love of power, and his conceit. The physical pleasure she experienced in his bed soon faded, as she came to realise that his flattery of her body was not to honour herself, but to provoke her to greater flattery of his. The more she recoiled, the more demanding he became; that was when the beating began.

It took her another month to realise that the more she cried and cringed, the more he bullied. If she stood up to him, he often relented and tried to turn the situation into a joke.

'Come now, Syb. We must not fall out. Look at the trouble I took to marry you.'

Only Father had called her 'Syb.' It somehow soiled the name to hear it on Torf's lips. The more she heard him talk, the more he stank of insincerity.

Thank God he was often absent, on errands of mystery all over western Normandy. Though these were blessed intervals of peace, it made the homecomings all the more to be dreaded. If his business had gone well – he liked boasting of how important his 'negotiations' were – she could expect a quiet time. If badly, she would need all her wits and all her spirit to avoid the bruises.

He had been particularly bad when Geoffrey had sent his two men back from Coutances. He had been unkind again when Raoul had first been sick.

All Sybil had now was Cecily. She had not been long enough at Malbec to build solid relationships with the women there. The ablest one, a scrawny creature called Mahaut, simpered too much at Torf for Sybil's liking. Mother was infirm, and could not travel to see her. Roger was taken up with Hauteville. Geoffrey was – Geoffrey was at Coutances, and might as well have lingered further in Rome or Apulia for all the help he could be. He was so near to her in person, and so far from being able to succour her in mind or spirit, that the distress it caused added to her tiredness. And Father – dearest Father – was dead. Perhaps as well; had he known, how he would have grieved for his treasure Syb.

*   *   *   *   *   *

'I wish he would stick to his precious cathedral.'

One of Geoffrey's knights threw down his gauntlets and pulled off his mail coif. Another scooped water from a new trough. He spat in loathing.

'God's teeth! It still tastes of the mortar. Thrown together. Have you ever seen a man in such a hurry?'

'If only he would give us credit for knowing our profession. Too many ideas for his own good. And ours.'

'No. It is that barking barrel beside him. He is the one who – '

'I shall bark again,' said Ivo, looming up from nowhere, 'and again – just so long as his Grace orders me to do so. He instructs me to tell you, my lords, that you have half an hour. Then we go again.'

'What about the horses? Does he want them ruined?'

Ivo walked away without arguing. They were not worried about the horses; they were smarting from being made to drill and practise like novices. They were annoyed at being dragged away from their half-built halls and their half-stocked enclosures. God alone knew what newly-appointed reeves, unused to the responsibility, were getting up to behind their backs.

It was only early March, and the morning edges were still trimmed and stiffened with frost. Far too early for any normal military training.

Geoffrey thought otherwise.

Easter was approaching fast, and the Duke would hold court at Bayeux. He would expect a show of support from all his vassals. Geoffrey was determined that his own contingent of knights should hold its own in the more fashionable company of the lords of the Evrecin and the Pays de Caux and the Roumois. He was going to wipe any sneer off Odo's face before it appeared.

Moreover, if William of Arques had been making progress with his great alliance of treason – and rumour was saying that he had – the Duke would want a clear idea of the resources that would be available to him. Geoffrey intended not only to present a contingent in good shape and ready for action; he had it in mind to offer a possible improvement in tactics. It took time, and he did not wish to present the idea until it was fully formed. It did not help that he seemed to have collected a dozen or so of the stupidest knights in Normandy – thick-headed young clods with horse-dung for brains, who could think of nothing but their precious honour. The simplest instructions went in one ear and straight out of the other.

Ivo had only to look at Geoffrey's face to know that his Grace was swearing in his head.

'They do have a point about the horses, my lord. You can not push them too far.'

'I know, I know. Just get them going again when they are rested.'

The mounts were barely adequate for training, never mind action, and the whole value of what he had in mind depended upon persistent practice with the horses that would be used in the fighting. He would have to see Walter Giffard soon. He had already sent Thierry to Roger of Montgomery at Bellême to confirm his rendezvous with both of them.

Still holding his drill mace, he put his hands on his hips and began his habitual pacing . . . Bayeux . . . Bellême . . . Goscelin at Coutances . . . the Montjoie quarries . . . the Lessay estates, not yet properly surveyed . . . Malbec . . . Ah, Malbec! Sybil! Barely time for a cursory reconnaissance, and that from a distance. He was determined to make no move in that direction until he was practically certain of obtaining profit from it. He could not bear the prospect of being outfaced by Torf on his own ground, and in front of Sybil.

One mercy was that he was left alone. He was discovering that one of the results of holding property at the end of all the world was that very few people were prepared to travel that far to satisfy their curiosity. Advantages had to be snatched wherever one stumbled over them.

'My lord! My lord!'

Geoffrey turned.

One of the boys from the new stables was running towards him as fast as his spindly legs and pigeon chest would permit. His excited treble cut the keen air.

'My lord!'

He stumbled to a halt in front of Geoffrey, so winded that he could get no words out.

Geoffrey waited testily.

'Come on, come on!'

Wheezing and gasping, the boy at last managed something intelligible. 'The Duke, my lord. Coming up the hill.'

*　　*　　*　　*　　*　　*

'You have been busy.'

From sheer habit, the Duke half turned to confirm it – 'Eh, Fitz?'

But Fitzosbern was not there. William checked himself, but Geoffrey had noticed the movement. William coughed.

'Fitz is at Breteuil – still building. As I hope you are.'

It was a neat sidestep and parry, as one would expect from a man used to sudden danger and swift reaction.

Ordering Fitzosbern to build a castle on his home ground at Breteuil was further proof of the Duke's trust in him and reliance on him. It was part of the Duke's plan for the frontier, and showed the energy with which he was pursuing it. Domfront and Alençon were now in Norman hands, and would be strengthened. Roger of Montgomery had married Mabel, and would doubtless improve the castle at Bellême over against the border with Maine and Blois. Further along Fitz was busy at Breteuil – things were going well. They needed to if the defences of the duchy were to be made proof against the conspiracy of William of Arques. To the west of Domfront there remained only the town and county of Mortain. If that could be adequately secured, the frontier was stiffened from the Eure and the Seine right round almost to Brittany. Geoffrey wondered what sort of man the Count of Mortain was. Loyal? Reliable? Likely to fall prey to the wiles of William of Arques and join the rebellion? And if he did, and was subsequently dispossessed . . . Mortain was not all that far from Montbrai and Coutances . . .

Geoffrey pulled himself together. Too many 'if's'. Take advantage of what was under his very nose – the Duke's company, and no Fitzosbern.

It was not easy, and not especially enjoyable either. Geoffrey saw a lot more of the Duke than he had before, but he did not get much nearer. William was not a likeable man. But what energy and resolve!

The Duke hummed a lot during his tour of inspection – a tuneless drone which could be trying for the nerves of his companions over a long period, but a good sign.

'If he hums, he is usually pleased,' said Roger of Montgomery at their last meeting.

'Or he is thinking,' said Walter Giffard. 'Then you never know what he is going to come out with.'

Geoffrey hoped fervently for the former, as he and the Duke picked their way between foundation trenches and barrows and piles of fresh earth. Seagulls whirled and swooped about their heads, prepared to risk life and limb for the

204

chance of fat pickings. A score of men moved about on deliberate errands of their own, seemingly totally unco-ordinated and purposeless. To the outsider, it was the chaos of large construction sites the world over.

William was prepared to get his hands dirty, and his feet, as he clambered and peered and asked questions, his restless eyes darting constantly to left and right. Individual workmen, heads bared and bowed in formal respect when he began to talk to them, looked up in surprise at the sharpness and knowledge in his questions, and forgot differences of rank in the interested talk that followed.

Goscelin as usual was suffering the tortures of the damned. The weather was not conducive, the workmen were of poor calibre, the shortage of equipment was pitiful; he was not entirely satisfied about the orientation of the original building begun by Bishop Robert so many years ago; the difficulties of clearing and preparing the site were almost insuperable.

His eyebrows soared.

'Half midden and half rubble pit, my lords.'

'Enough, I am sure, to deter many a lesser man, Master Goscelin,' said Geoffrey. 'But both the Duke and I think you have done wonders in the short time made available to you by the recent appalling weather. You appear to have triumphed over a host of adverse circumstances. Is that not so, your Grace?'

He looked meaningly at the Duke, who caught the drift.

'Indeed. I am most impressed. You have done very well.'

Goscelin almost simpered.

'Your Grace is too kind. You see us at our worst at present. Once the clearing and the digging is complete; once the calculations have been done; once we can get down to the stone . . . ' He almost growled the word 'stone' in his eager enthusiasm.

'I shall look forward to a second visit,' said the Duke.

Goscelin bowed obsequiously.

'Your Grace.'

As they left him, Geoffrey thanked the Duke.

William grunted.

'Least I could do. Keep up the good work – on the cathedral and on him.'

They both chuckled. Geoffrey had never seen the Duke in such a good humour.

William slapped a gatepost.

'The lady Matilda is with child.'

Ah – so that was it!

Geoffrey looked at William. For a brief moment, the tight, drawn look was gone, and he was what he ought to be – a lusty young warrior revelling in the fruitfulness of his marriage.

Geoffrey had hardly finished his congratulations when the old manner returned.

'We must hurry, hurry. Arques will not wait.'

He will wait even less now, thought Geoffrey, with an heir on the way, and a legitimate one.

'I expect to see you at Bayeux,' said the Duke.

'I shall be there, my lord, and so will my knights.'

William screwed up his eyes.

'Still training, are you?'

'Indeed I am, my lord. And I may have one or two new things to show you.'

He did not wish to commit himself further, and William understood.

'Good. Good.'

He turned to look back at the ant-hill of work that they had just visited.

'I must put Odo to work,' he remarked. 'I shall tell him what I have seen here.'

That should get him moving, thought Geoffrey.

William continued musing; almost unconsciously he was treating Geoffrey as if he were Fitzosbern.

'I must find something for Robert too.'

He brought himself up short.

'My brother Robert,' he explained awkwardly. 'Slightly younger than Odo.'

But rather less unpleasant, one hoped.

*　　*　　*　　*　　*　　*

After many enquiries all over Montbrai, Geoffrey found Mauger standing by their mother's grave. A profusion of Lenten lilies nodded in the breeze. One of the few things Mother had liked about her Norman home.

Mauger looked up.

'What are you doing here?'

Geoffrey genuflected and crossed himself.

'The same as you, I presume. It is the anniversary – or have you forgotten?'

Mauger stooped, plucked one bloom, and stuck the stalk into a tear in his jerkin.

'Who do you think plants more lilies here every year?'

Geoffrey was genuinely surprised.

'I am sorry; I did not know.'

Mauger grunted.

'One thing among many.'

'I said I was sorry. How was I to know? You never said.'

'One does not shout about one's deepest feelings.'

They began walking back towards the castle mound.

'Coutances – it goes well?' said Mauger.

'Well enough.'

They plodded in silence. Geoffrey acknowledged the delighted wave of Boso, brandishing his scythe so vigorously that he looked likely to do himself an even worse injury.

Mauger thrust his hands into his belt. Geoffrey had not come all this way solely to pray at Mother's grave – not with all the pressing business he must have at Coutances.

'Why else are you here?'

'To try and talk some sense into you.'

Mauger sighed.

'If that is to be your approach, you are wasting your breath.'

'You might try listening to what I am here to say. I should not have come for anybody else.'

Mauger beckoned to a carter to keep the gate open.

'Say it then and be done.'

Geoffrey threw a small coin to the carter's son, who beamed and saluted him. Mauger grunted in annoyance.

'Showing off our wealth, are we? Hauteville money?'

'Would it put a smile on your face if I went and asked him to give it back? Mauger, I have come here to do you a favour. I have had a visit from the Duke...'

More boys clustered round the carter's son and peered into his palm.

Geoffrey explained the latest situation about the rebellion, and the progress of the Duke's defence of the frontier.

'Avranches lies with Bishop Hugh, and Coutances with me. Domfront and Alençon are in the Duke's hands. Montgomery has Bellême, and Fitzosbern is building at Breteuil. The only gap is at Mortain.'

'Gap? The Count was well when last I heard.'

'But he is not building. It is just possible that the Duke will replace him. He seems satisfied with me at Coutances; it is a chance that he would consider my brother at Mortain.'

Mauger hawked and spat.

'Privy to the Duke's councils, are we? Close to the ear of his Grace? Sitting all the time at the very end of the world. Clever!'

Geoffrey flushed angrily, but kept his voice down as they passed a knot of women feeding lambs.

'I did not say it was certain,' he hissed. 'Only possible. You do have to use a little imagination, though I know that may come hard to you.'

207

'I prefer to call it fantasy,' said Mauger. 'It seems that it is I who must talk some sense into you. The Count of Mortain is, to the best of my knowledge, in good health and in good standing with the Duke. If he were likely to join the rebellion, I should certainly be the last to admit it to you. And if the rebellion succeeded, he would not hand it over to me. So either way there is no chance whatever of my becoming the lord of Mortain.'

'That is not the only territory,' said Geoffrey. 'I am not without funds now. I could perhaps purchase something for you.'

'With Hauteville money? Never. You may be content to take their charity; I am not.'

'But do you not see? It would bind you to the Duke. He would come to trust you, as he trusts me.'

Mauger stopped and turned.

'Brother, try to understand. Much as I may admire him, there is no point in being trusted by the Duke. I think he is a loser. I am sad and angry that you do not see that.'

'You are angry at only one thing – taking what you think is Hauteville money.'

'I will never be beholden to one of that family.'

'You foolish man! You say you want nothing to do with them, yet, if you follow this conspiracy, you will finish like them – gnawing bones round camp fires in caves. At the very best.'

'I will not take their money,' said Mauger doggedly.

'Then take some of mine,' said Geoffrey. 'I own half of Coutances, and many manors round about. I am lord now of fifteen knight's fees. I shall have rents and dues in my own right. Would you accept my money – your brother's money?'

'No.'

Geoffrey spread his hands.

'Holy Virgin! Why not?'

'You – a knight of Normandy – should not have to ask me that. I do not wish to be – to be provided for.'

'You provided for me. I had no choice but to accept.'

Mauger began walking again.

'Different matter. Different – entirely.'

*　　*　　*　　*　　*　　*

'Sir Walter drives a hard bargain.'

Ivo patted a rump or two.

'I think you have good value, my lord. Broken and fully trained. Blood from Spain as well as Brabant – some of the best stock on the market.'

'It had better be,' growled Geoffrey. 'It cost me enough. Now get them back and start training with the men as soon as you can.'

'They will grumble, my lord.'

'Let them grumble all they like, so long as they come. What are they training reeves for, except to leave them to carry on in their absence? Remind them that they are soon going to need all the practice they can get.'

Ivo narrowed his eyes.

'Arques?'

'Yes. He is not moving yet, but Anjou may be. And Sir Roger tells me that Godwin and his brood are back in England. You know what that means.'

'No crown for the Duke.'

'It begins to look like that. He can look for no support from the Confessor. Godwin and his sons are in nearly every earldom in the realm. Edward has already been forced to banish William of Jumièges from Canterbury. Some Saxon or other will take the primacy.'

'So the rebels here will strike?'

'If they do not strike, they will certainly be encouraged. If we are lucky, each will wait to see what happens when another moves. Which is why the Duke is anxious to make a good showing with the Council at Bayeux. It may deter the waverers.'

Like my lord Mauger, thought Ivo, but he kept his thoughts off his face.

'We must be there,' said Geoffrey, 'and we must be in good order.'

'I shall see to it, my lord.'

'When you leave, take my drill mace as a sign of my commission,' said Geoffrey. 'And tell them that neglect of training will render the offender answerable directly to me. Now – which way will you go?'

Ivo's answer reflected his own thoughts.

'Anjou could move at any time. The road through Alençon and Domfront could be easily raided and cut. I was thinking of going by way of Argentan and Falaise.'

Geoffrey nodded.

'All the same – '

'I know, my lord. I shall be careful. Good luck at Bayeux.'

He kissed the ring, and Geoffrey blessed him.

'A good man,' said Roger of Montgomery, as the cavalcade wound its way out of the bailey gate at Bellême.

'None better,' said Geoffrey. 'Taught me all I know about soldiering.'

They watched until Ivo and his men were out of sight.

To his surprise, Geoffrey felt a sudden lump in his throat . . . 'all I know about soldiering'. . . that, and so much more besides. Right now he was teaching him yet again about loyalty. Ivo was a rock. Could he, Geoffrey of Montbrai, show such loyalty to the Duke when the test came? Indeed, *should* he show such loyalty? Was Mauger right? Was he, Geoffrey, a fool? Was the Duke about to be swamped by the tide of the conspiracy of this William of Arques?

'Will he survive, Roger?'

'The Duke?' Roger laughed. 'Of course he will. He is head and shoulders above any of them. You know what it is like in Normandy – never rains but it pours. But the sun comes out again. We shall survive.'

Geoffrey felt sure enough of his new friendship to push it further.

'Those are emotional reasons. Give me some military ones.'

Roger put an arm round his shoulders and steered him back towards the castle.

'I shall do better than that; I shall give you some Fitzosbern reasons. Fitz says that the conspiracy will fail because all the ambitions of its members are – what was it? – "mutually in – incomp – "'

' – mutually incompatible,' said Geoffrey. 'All very well, assuming that the Duke is still alive when they start to fall out.'

'Fitz also said something about "interior lines". Half of it was beyond me, but so far as I can make it out, it means that they have to move around a lot and we do not.'

Geoffrey agreed. The Duke at least could strike outwards without warning, whereas any joint action by the rebels would take a long time and be very difficult to conceal.

'And there is something that even I can work out for myself,' continued Roger.

'Oh?'

'William of Arques can not start a rebellion without a base of operations; the last I heard, the garrison at Arques is still loyal to the Duke. The man can not get into his own castle.'

Roger clapped Geoffrey on the back.

'So you see? We have nothing to worry about at all!'

Geoffrey was forced to grin.

'Come for a ride before dinner,' said Roger. 'Mabel likes to go out about now. She would appreciate your company again before you go. She likes you.'

Geoffrey was not sure whether that was a lucky thing or not.

*   *   *   *   *   *

Chapter Fourteen

It was a day which shrieked for the outdoors.

Geoffrey fidgeted while Thorold's son, Canon Peter, the cathedral dean and chamberlain, solemnly went through tiresome lists of vestments, ornaments, altar furniture and decoration in his deliberate, finger-counting way. It was easy to see whose son he was. His head was beginning to develop an old man's wag, and he was already as bald as his father.

The work was necessary – Geoffrey knew that. Indeed, he was the one who had instituted it, and it had required all his energy to goad the dithering Peter into some semblance of urgency. That had been in the bleak, dark days of winter, when it was difficult to work outside. Now that the spring sunshine had come, Geoffrey itched to be in the open air; with perverse timing, Peter now chose to catch his bishop's former enthusiasm for indoor business.

'I suggest two full sets, my lord, for each season – that is to say, for each of Advent, Christmas, Epiphany, Lent . . . Then there are the great festivals . . .'

'Yes, yes, yes – I agree.'

Peter believed in dotting every 'i' and crossing every 't'.

'Vestments of the best quality are not easy to come by, my lord.'

Geoffrey sighed. Abandoned in this pagan wilderness, how was Peter to know what was best and what was not? How long was it since he had even seen a complete set of vestments?

'Then there must be chalices, crosses, altar linens. If I may be so bold, some embroideries ought to be from England – their women make the best – and if possible set with jewels. The best stones for this sort of work . . .'

Geoffrey knew that he ought not to complain. He was the one who had infused this interest and enthusiasm. It was a kind of compliment to himself that Peter and his brother Walter and his two sons, John and Richard, should now be bursting with ideas for the enrichment of their new cathedral. It was a tribute to the confidence he had been able to instil in them. Starved for so many years of the slightest shred of hope, they now flung themselves into plans and projects with the abandon of a hungry garrison gorging after a six-month siege.

The town was waking up too. Houses were showing signs of repair from one day to the next. Buildings were losing their lopsided look. Holes were being filled in, gates mended, piles of rubbish cleared. More and more labourers were becoming available for Goscelin's huge task of reinforcing some of the old foundations and digging new ones. Carpenters arrived from Avranches and St. Lô to begin construction of the carts and wagons to carry the granite blocks. Goscelin had managed to unearth a foreman with a capacity for improvisation that amounted to genius; there was no end to the man's resource. Geoffrey had no idea where he recruited the small army of ropemakers, tanners, wheelwrights, quarrymen, toolsmiths, loggers, cooks – just about every tradesman Geoffrey could think of, and many more he had not.

As well as inspiring it was frightening. Geoffrey knew that it was he who had in a sense unleashed this huge outpouring of energy, but he knew too that it depended entirely upon him for its continued momentum. He was amazed at the passion among his work force, and began to doubt his own ability to match it, or to continue to match it. More worrying still, even if the drive and energy were maintained, could he continue to supply the fuel for it in the shape of funds?

He thought when he first brought home the treasure of Robert Guiscard that he had enough and more for three cathedrals, but the demands were colossal, and endless. Already his own knights had cost a small fortune in equipment. They had all needed help in getting their holdings started after so many years of pillage by robber barons and wandering bands of sea pirates and deserting mercenaries. He had also supplied destriers, for which Sir Walter Giffard claimed, and rightly, high prices. By general consent, his mounts could not be bettered anywhere between Brittany and Vermandois.

Now the cathedral canons were so excited at the prospect of seeing their dreams fulfilled that they were losing all sense of proportion . . . 'the best linens, my lord, from England' . . . missals, bibles, crosses, copes, albs, illustrations, reliquaries . . . 'we must bring the relics of St. Lô – back to his proper resting place, my lord, and it must be a resting place of fitting grandeur' . . . one would think that they were re-designing Rome.

It was all very well for them; they did not have to pay for it.

Nor could Geoffrey bring himself to pour cold water on their almost child-like schemes, to point out that the cathedral was not even begun. There were a hundred problems to be overcome, a thousand demands to be met – and Goscelin was a perfectionist. If the canons had little idea of the cost of things, Goscelin was totally remote from all reality. To hear him wade through a list of all the items wanted for the coming weeks or months made Geoffrey's hair stand on end.

If he made a protest, Goscelin would pause in incredulous horror, lift his eyebrows in the great pointed arch that, already, every one of his workmen tried to mimic behind his back.

'Does my lord bishop want the best or does he not?'

Put like that, it deprived Geoffrey of any worthwhile reply. If he did show signs of fight, Goscelin usually managed to slip into the conversation some titbit of gossip he had heard about plans for a cathedral at Bayeux.

'My lord Odo is thinking of having it, your Grace.'

Geoffrey glared.

'In that case, we have it too.'

But Holy Virgin, where was the money going to come from?

Geoffrey got away at last. He snuffed the air, taking in great chestfuls, almost as if he could taste it. The weather for the first time since Christmas seemed safe; it had that kindness about it that induced confidence; it was not going to turn traitor and bite suddenly with a frost.

Peasants free from the tyranny of winter stretched their arms up to the sun like cats arching their backs before a fire, and began attacking tasks as if they expected solution and success. No more half-hearted poking with the ends of broken tools in frozen, dirt-cracked hands.

One or two of his villeins greeted him with a lift in their voice.

'Good day to your Grace.'

He returned their salute with a blessing. He knew they liked it.

The rhythm of the horse's progress helped to settle his mind; well-oiled reins nestled familiarly in his hand; leather and iron slapped and jingled. As he glanced to left and right, he saw purpose and enterprise and hope. He was feeling better already.

His horse was now familiar enough with the track to make its own way with barely a twitch on the reins. Geoffrey paused on his way down the hill to watch Ivo on the edge of the meadows below.

From his vantage point of height he could better assess the progress they were making. Ivo's voice boomed up to him.

'Once again, my lord – towards me when I drop the mace. Are you ready – now!'

From the far side, Geoffrey's knights began the advance.

'At the walk, my lords – the walk!'

Ivo rode in time with them, watching and correcting, cajoling and hectoring.

'Spacing, my lords . . . resting the weapons . . . points up . . . control, my lords . . . hands and knees . . . up, up . . . now the trot . . . steady, steady . . . now the canter . . . steady . . . only the canter, canter!'

It was too much for them. As the pace quickened, the formation broke. Men forgot Ivo's earlier commands; they wrestled with unfamiliar mounts of bounding spirit; one or two still seemed to regard it as a race.

Geoffrey sighed. Ivo had done wonders, but it still fell short of his conception. He waited while Ivo swore politely at the young knight who reined in noisily and sat waiting to be praised for winning.

Was he expecting too much from them?

Ivo joined him while they dismounted for a rest.

'I have my doubts, my lord,' he said, in answer to the question on Geoffrey's face. 'Youth, lack of experience, their precious honour – all are against them.'

'To say nothing of lack of brains,' grumbled Geoffrey. 'Their first action will curb them.'

Ivo said nothing. My lord Geoffrey's ideas were all very well, but they were only theory. My lord himself had yet seen little action.

'Remember, my lord, we are still testing this without noise. In an engagement – '

Geoffrey waved impatiently.

'Yes, yes, I know. You will not hear a thing. We could still try the trumpets.'

Ivo shook his head.

'Trumpets are still commands. If they can not learn those of the voice, how do you expect them to learn those of the horn? We do not have long enough.'

Geoffrey swore.

Why was he always so beset by lack of time? He would take his contingent of knights to the council at Bayeux, and he would not be able to demonstrate fully the ideas he had been trying to perfect. Should he try, and risk making a fool of himself and his men with a bad performance, or should he say nothing, and allow William's vassals to laugh at him for all his talk and lack of action? What would Odo say?

Ivo followed his thoughts.

'At least they look good, my lord.'

True. They sat well, they were fully equipped, and their mounts were the best on the market.

Geoffrey growled.

'If we have to use them against William of Arques, let us hope that the enemy take one look and run away.'

Ivo hawked and spat.

If William of Arques had hired sound Flemish mercenary infantry, or a batch of English housecarles arrived on loan from Godwin of Wessex, he did not think that they would run at the mere sight of my lord of Coutances' mounted vassals. Not yet.

Ivo diplomatically changed the subject.

'When will you get them to give hands?'

'Soon,' said Geoffrey. 'Before Easter. It has to be. The hall should be ready enough in a week or so.'

Geoffrey remembered his own consecration in a half-open nave at Rouen – a curious mixture of grandeur and improvisation, golden chalice and frayed rope-end. If he could possibly manage it, the ceremony at which his own knights were to swear feudal homage to him would be conducted in more uniform dignity. When he placed his hands round those of his new vassals and swore to receive and accept them as his men and to give them succour and protection, he was at least going to have a roof over his head.

After a winter of struggle and making do, Coutances badly needed a good, fat ceremony and a good, fat feast – something else for Canon Peter to count out on his fingers. Moreover, it had to be accomplished before he left for the Duke's Easter Council; when he arrived at Bayeux, it would be in the company of fully sworn knights who would be proof against the blandishments of Bishop Odo or anyone else.

Geoffrey pounded his fist on his thigh. Time, time . . .

*   *   *   *   *   *

'He behaved like a thief,' said Thierry, 'and a guilty thief at that.'

The new cook cuffed a boy who had stopped turning a spit, and came to sit down.

'What was he stealing?'

Thierry swallowed a huge mouthful.

'Time. He was so guilty at taking time off from here that he could not enjoy what he went to see.'

The cook snorted.

'Not surprised. There is nothing at Lessay.'

'That also made him miserable. But he rides without ceasing all round his properties, as if he expects them to run away when he is not there. He thumps his thigh and grinds his teeth if time comes up only to his elbow. He fusses and he frets; he swears if his plans do not turn into buildings overnight.' He grunted in surprise at his own recollection. 'Do you know what he wants now at Lessay?'

The cook shook his head in obliging wonder.

'A monastery,' said Thierry. 'I ask you.'

'Why?'

'Says it is too awful there for anything else. Something about "fighting the Devil in the wilderness" – beyond me. If I were the Devil, I should not be seen dead there. He says, "We must have a house, Thierry. Baldwin of Clair has Bec, Fitzosbern has two, Montgomery has three." '

The cook cut himself a chunk of end-of-winter bacon.

'Biting off more than he can chew.'

'Exactly what I say,' said Thierry. 'But always it is the same tune – "Thierry, we must hurry, hurry. We are so far behind." '

The cook sniffed the bacon, grimaced, and tossed it to the dog.

'You will never build anything at Lessay – mark my words.'

Thierry nodded.

'His Grace has too many irons in the fire at present, but he has a long memory. You wait and see.'

The cook grunted and wiped the fat off his fingers on his apron.

Thierry leaned forward and took an onion out of a sack.

'If you ask me, that was not the real reason for going.'

He waited for the cook to show the desired amount of interest.

'If you ask me,' repeated Thierry, 'it was to see Malbec. Where the lady Sybil lives. You remember I told you of the lady Sybil. Well, Malbec is only a few miles further on. It is not the first time he has prowled and watched from a distance.'

'Torturing himself.'

Thierry nodded.

'Guilty, sad, and angry all at once. He goes silent, but you can almost hear him thinking, he is working so hard.'

Thierry tossed the skin of the onion into the fire.

'It was worse this time.'

'Oh?'

'This Torf of Malbec has started to build – a mound. Barely bigger than a midden as yet, but it will grow. By the time my lord returns from Bayeux, it will be higher than three men, and swelling.'

'So she slips further away.'

Thierry burped.

'A house can be burned; a bailey and tower must be besieged.'

The cook went to a cupboard and rummaged for his hidden best biscuits.

'So it is this year or never?'

Thierry cut into his onion.

'It begins to look like that.'

*   *   *   *   *   *

Ivo waved the drill mace, and returned to the work in hand.

'Now, my lords, once again, at the walk . . . '

Ralph grinned, waved back, and began to climb the hill. Gravel from the river bed had been laid in the worst of the pot holes. Two men were clearing a ditch at the side. Two more were re-laying the top courses of a stone wall. From above came the confused murmur of a great number of busy people.

He had never been to Coutances before, but thanks to Ivo's cheery greeting he already felt at home. He looked forward to seeing his Grace again. All around him were signs of Lord Geoffrey's energy and inspiration. Ralph felt braced by what he saw, and sad by what it made him remember.

216

His homecoming to Gisors had been one shock after another . . .

Blackened beams sagging amid new, splinter-ridden uprights. Gaps among roofs as thatchers sweated all hours to make good. A cluster of sad earthen mounds beyond the bailey wall. Ralph had played games and gone fishing with every one of them. His father, ashen and weak, defiantly waving a bloodstained bandage over the stump – 'at least they let me keep the left.' His mother gazing vacantly past him and repeating the same phrases – 'if only Ralph would come home . . . Michael will get better, then all will be well.'

Biggest surprise of all – Aubrey had been a tower of strength. Everyone now depended on him. Only one flash of spite remained.

'. . . while you were off on your adventures.'

'You waved me goodbye longer than anyone else,' said Ralph.

After that, it was common sense and pulling together.

'Who?'

'William of Arques,' said Aubrey. 'Or at least knights from Ponthieu at his instigation. Since he left the Duke at Domfront, he and Count Enguerrand have been approaching most knights above the Seine and testing their loyalties. Father spoke for the Duke, so – last month – '

Aubrey shrugged and gestured.

'Do you think they will come again?'

'Why? They have made their point. We are in no position to influence the outcome.'

'I am,' said Ralph.

Aubrey, he noticed, made no effort to stop him. He was grateful for the help in rebuilding, but that was all. Father and his sisters came to the gate to see him off. Once again, it was Aubrey who waved the longest.

Ralph owed it to Bishop Geoffrey to return and serve, but his pleasure in following him was now taking second place to a darker desire – to join the Duke and be there when his Grace whipped the rebels. His stomach ached; whenever he was tense or excited, the wound in his stomach gave him trouble – almost as if the knife were still there.

He had nothing else now – only memories that would have to be buried deep, deep . . .

He saw Thierry waving and hurrying across the square.

'I wondered who it was tying his horse there, and then I recognised your walk. Come – his Grace will be pleased to see you. If we can get him to stand still for a moment.'

*   *   *   *   *   *

'Meet me in St. Lô; I shall wait there one day – no more.'

Ralph nodded.

'And if my lord Mauger refuses?'

'Then Devil take him. I have done everything I can. If he can come with me to the Duke – just come and see. That is all I ask. Tell him.'

'I will do my best, my lord.'

Before he left Coutances, Ralph had a word with Ivo.

'How do I approach this Mauger? What is he like?'

'Stubborn,' said Ivo. 'Argumentative. Like his brother. They are as bad as each other.'

'So what is the difference?'

Ivo grinned.

'Meet him, and you will find out. Take some trouble. My lord Mauger is worth saving.'

Geoffrey considered leaving at least half his contingent behind at Coutances. Ralph had brought news and gossip that the Duke of Anjou was showing signs of movement near the border. Would he strike at border knights in the west as William of Arques and Enguerrand of Ponthieu had struck in the east? Pinpricks, to be sure, but pinpricks had been known to goad many a beleaguered commander into rash action. Ralph had given a moving account of the misery he had found at Gisors. Geoffrey's heart went out to him; he remembered the stricken household when Ralph's brother Michael died.

However, he could not afford to be moved by sentiment; he had to make sound military appreciations. Hitherto nobody had ever bothered with Coutances; it was, as everyone knew, 'the end of all the world'. The Duke had not provided him with knights so that he could sit snug in his hall at the world's end while the rest of the duchy withstood a siege from the King and his allies. He had to place his knights where they would be most use to the Duke, and that meant Bayeux. All he would leave was one who had broken his ankle when it caught in the stirrup after a fall, and another who was prostrate with the flux. After all, who was to know how much progress he had made at Coutances since the beginning of winter? As far as anyone was aware, it was still a ruin.

Geoffrey sat at St. Lô and took his supper, well pleased with his planning.

'My lord!'

It was Ralph.

'What on earth are you doing here? I told you to – who is that?'

Geoffrey squinted into the shadows. Holy Virgin! It was Lambert's cousin from Montbrai.

'We met on the road, my lord,' said Ralph. 'When he told me his news, I came straight back with him.'

Mauger! What madness had he done?

'There has been a raid, my lord. Anjou.'

*　　*　　*　　*　　*　　*

Mauger met Geoffrey at the bailey gate. To Geoffrey's surprise, he bent and kissed the ring.

'He has been asking for you. I do not think there is much time.'

'I came as soon as I heard,' said Geoffrey. 'What happened to him?'

As they walked across the bailey, Geoffrey could see little sign of damage.

'I expect you heard from Arnulf – it was Anjou. He did not invest the castle – too much trouble. My guess is, we just happened to be lying at the very end of a long border sweep. He might even have stumbled over us by accident. He had no wish to be caught up in a siege so far inside Normandy with a long line of communication, so he started a few fires, maimed a few sheep, and left.'

'Seems a poor revenge for Domfront and Alençon.'

'He has to start somewhere. Perhaps he is just testing reaction.'

Like William of Arques and Enguerrand of Ponthieu. The timing was too close to be coincidence. This rebellion seemed to have planning at least behind it. Probe in the east and probe in the west. And the King sitting silent in the middle to keep everyone guessing. Impressive.

'Where were you?' said Geoffrey.

For once Mauger did not beat about the bush.

'Boar, if you must know.'

'How did Gori get involved?'

'Purest chance. He was out – by the big warren copse – said the weather was fine; wanted time to himself after being cooped up all winter. Took one of his books with him. In the excitement of the raid nobody thought of him. It never occurred to anyone that he could have been caught. Seems he ran into a party of them. They roughed him up and knocked him down – afraid of his tonsure, I expect. No weapons were used. But he was unconscious. Must have lain there for hours. Then the dew.'

They came to the gate at the foot of the mound steps. Mauger opened it for him.

'We only found out because Agatha came to me in tears and said she was worried.'

Geoffrey stared.

'Agatha?'

'Yes. Terrified, she was. Said she was afraid I would thump her if she had told me earlier. Then, when he did not come back . . . '

Geoffrey stopped half-way up the steps.

'Are you trying to tell me that, even now, at his age?'

Mauger stopped too.

'So it would appear. They had this rendezvous. Hence the business about the book and being alone – we now know who he wanted to be alone with.'

Geoffrey ran his hand through his hair, and resumed the ascent.

'God's Teeth! Does he never learn?'

Mauger followed him.

'The fever has grown steadily worse. We have tried everything, but – with his chest . . . '

'Did you beat Agatha?'

'No. I did worse. I told the stupid bitch that Gori's death would he her fault, for leaving him all that time.'

It was unlike Mauger – clear evidence of how upset he was.

'I have had him put in the solar.'

More evidence of how fond of him he was too.

They climbed the ladder. Bertha, in tears, popped a curtsey.

'Oh, Master Geoffrey!'

Gori's tired face creased in pleasure.

'Hallo, son.'

*   *   *   *   *   *

'Well?'

For several minutes they had been stumping in silence all round the meadow by the warren copse. A light drizzle blew into their faces. Boso, forewarned, hobbled out of sight behind a clump of bankside alders, and crossed himself when they passed.

Geoffrey had found the indoors quite insupportable. The closeness of the solar; the earnest discretion of everyone involved in moving the body – trying desperately to avoid causing them pain, and being conspicuous by their very effort; Bertha's wailings; the tears everywhere, and not only among women; Agatha hysterical with fear; so many people simply looking at them, as if they were waiting for something to happen. Geoffrey felt like a baited bear, with the crowd round him falling back but gazing raptly to catch the first signs of enraged reaction.

To his surprise, he found that Mauger's company was the only thing he could tolerate. Together they went round and round, kicking at tussocks of grass and breaking off innumerable twigs.

With a tremendous effort, Mauger put his hands in his belt.

'Did you – did he want to – ?'

'Yes,' said Geoffrey. 'I heard it. He – there was no fear.'

Mauger sighed.

'I am glad. Then God rest him.'

'You have still not answered my question,' said Geoffrey.

'Oh, that.'

'It may seem a trifle to you, but it is rather more important to me. Surely even you can see that.'

'Bit late now.'

'Why did you never say?'

'It was not right. I had a higher responsibility.'

Geoffrey tossed his head.

'Oh, Mauger, spare me.'

'That is precisely what I was doing. And sparing Father's soul too. I presume you find that to be of some value. And since we are talking of right and virtue, are you sure you should be telling me this?'

'Do not think you can get out of it so easily,' said Geoffrey. 'It was not part of his confession. He was most insistent about that. He had kept the secret, he said, until he felt that I should know. Just as well; I was not going to get it from you, obviously.'

'Not until I too felt you should know. It was difficult enough getting you to accept as it was. What would you have done had you known?'

Geoffrey grunted.

'You see?' said Mauger. 'Well, I decided that the safety of Father's immortal soul was more important than your precious pride.'

Geoffrey spread his hands.

'A sacrifice. That is all I am – a sacrifice.'

'You should feel flattered.'

'Flattered!'

'Yes. I was not up to it. Father thought you might be. I was beginning to hope that his confidence had been well placed – until now.'

Geoffrey snorted.

'Father wanted you here to keep the property going. I was the one who was expendable.'

'You are unfair to Father and unfair to yourself, but I am not going to swell your head any further by trying to prove it to you. Just for once try looking at it from Father's point of view.'

'Why should I? He was the one who killed a bishop – not me.'

'He was very young and wild – on his own admission. Probably drunk too, when it happened. Some senseless raid or other. He had no idea who the man was until afterwards.'

'So? Is that any reason for me to bear the burden of his guilt?'

Mauger screwed up his eyes.

'My God – are you that sunk in virtue? Is there nothing that bothers your conscience? Nothing that nags your mind? Nothing that you wish with all your heart had not happened?'

Geoffrey looked away.

'Ah!' said Mauger. 'I thought so. Well, be more charitable. Just think of the burden that Father carried all those years – the death of a prince of the Church at his own hands, albeit unwitting. What have you done? Disappointed the over-eager daughter of an upstart neighbour.'

'How dare you!'

'Be your age, Geoffrey. Why do you think Father went on all those pilgrimages? Compostela, Jerusalem, Monte Gargano. Are you going? . . . You see . . . When he left for the last time, he gave great thought to you. He knew from Gori the promise that you were showing. "Do not force the boy's learning," he said. "But if he does well, give some thought to it. At least I should have given back what I took away." '

'If this was such a dark secret, why did Gori tell you?'

'Because I became head of the family, and if anyone was going to get it for you, it was I, not Gori.'

'Thank you very much.'

'Go on all you like,' said Mauger. 'But I was not going to endanger Father's soul by telling you beforehand and having to put up with your righteous refusal.'

'How do you know I would have done?'

'Look at you now. I know you, Geoffrey. You would have fought me right to the end. As it was, you fought enough. But once I could get you to accept, I knew you would carry it on.'

Geoffrey opened his mouth to interrupt, but Mauger swept on.

'Oh, yes, you thought you were putting up a rearguard action, but I knew better. I told you – ` you do things right through.'

Geoffrey could have struck him.

Three more times they stumped and kicked and twig-snapped their way round the meadow.

'What are you going to do now?' said Mauger at last.

'Go to Bayeux – as soon as he is buried – and you are coming with me.'

'Why?'

'Oh, Mauger, for God's sake! What more inducement do you want? For all we know, Torf could have put him up to it.'

'Why?'

'Think, Mauger. Just think for a moment. He has somehow insinuated himself into Malbec; nobody knows exactly what happened to this mysterious kinsman who died so conveniently. He has been trying to terrorise his way into Coutances, until I put a stop to it. He has married his way into Hauteville, and is still trying to get all the brothers to go to Italy. Luckily, Roger is more than a match for him, so far. Now he tries to wheedle you into a rebellion, and, when that shows signs of slowing down, he persuades Anjou to pass this way – quite by chance of course – with any luck there might be a most unfortunate death. And the brave Torf will be on hand to clear up the mess and pick up the pieces.'

'You have Torf of Malbec on the brain,' said Mauger.

Geoffrey stopped pacing and looked at him.

'Then tell me this. Forget Torf. Tell me – what future do you have in a rebellion when one of the chief rebels attacks you before he attacks his enemy? Wake up, Mauger, before it is too late.'

Mauger rubbed his chin.

'Well, yes – I see what you mean.'

Geoffrey gestured to the meadow around them, to the track of discoloured and flattened grass that marked their restless pacing.

'Do you want to avenge Gori or not?'

Mauger looked at him sharply, then shook his head doubtfully.

'I do not have a string of well-equipped knights to offer.'

Geoffrey leaned forward.

'No. But you have a string of names. Places. Rendezvous. Timely information worth a score of fully-armed knights.'

Mauger lowered his head and sighed.

Geoffrey spoke quietly.

'Mauger, when I came down into this meadow this morning, there was only one person on all the earth whom I could have borne to have with me. You. Now I tell you there is one person whom above all others I wish to see with me at the Duke's Council at Bayeux.'

There was a long pause. Mauger kept his head down.

'I had to do my best for Father. If it had been you, would you not have done the same?'

*　　*　　*　　*　　*　　*

They reined in and looked across the flat, rich manors towards Bayeux.

Geoffrey's knights stopped a respectful distance behind.

'By the way,' said Mauger. 'I forgot to tell you. Torf suggested that I should marry one of the Hauteville girls – Muriella. Can you imagine! Family ties, he said – much stronger than feudal ones.'

223

Geoffrey grunted.

'That is nothing. The lady Fressenda offered me Constance. Perhaps that was Torf's idea too. Marry one sister; make widows of the other two; and there you are – somebody in the family is needed to run their fiefs. You have to hand it to him.'

'Bastard!'

Geoffrey suddenly chuckled.

'Do you realise that we could have become brothers-in-law?'

Mauger made a face.

'God's Bread! Bad enough having you for a brother!'

Roaring with laughter, they kicked their mounts forward towards Bayeux.

*   *   *   *   *   *

Chapter Fifteen

'Do you wish me to go over it again?'

Ivo put a foot in the stirrup.

'That will not be necessary, my lord.'

With a grunt he heaved himself into the saddle, coiled the reins round his gloved fist, and looked down at Geoffrey.

'Have no fear, my lord; everything will go as we planned.'

Geoffrey did not look entirely convinced.

'We must neglect nothing, nothing.'

Ivo took the liberty of smiling. Geoffrey would have tolerated it from nobody else at this time; nobody else knew how important this was to him.

'With your full force, my lord, and my lord Mauger, and the strength of Hauteville, how can he stand?'

'Roger is by no means certain yet.'

'He will be when you tell him of the treachery. The House of Hauteville is proud of its constancy. I am sure even my lord Mauger will allow that.'

'Grudgingly,' said Mauger, 'but I will allow it. If there is one thing that the Hautevilles abhor, it is disloyalty. Remarkable in a family of their standing,' he could not help adding.

Ivo smiled again.

'My guess is, my lord, that you will find the bird flown.'

'Maybe, maybe.'

Whether the bird had flown or not, Sybil's position gave cause for concern. If Torf had bolted, it was unlikely that he had taken Sybil with him. Flight would show that he was worried about his own skin, and he would thus be unlikely to worry about that of others. Far more dangerous if he had chosen to stay and fight it out, or even try and talk himself out of trouble; in that case they would have to find a way of getting Sybil and the child away from his clutches before he began to use them as pawns in the game.

That was where Roger of Hauteville was to play his part. Torf would accept a visit from his brother-in-law, especially the one who was closest to his wife. Roger should, with his resource, be able to arrange for Sybil to leave Malbec – some story about their Mother's illness, perhaps. Naturally she would take the child with her – a last glimpse of it for its grandmother?

Once the Hautevilles knew of Torf's treachery to the Duke, all the remaining brothers would ride to punish the man who had brought shame upon their sister.

It would not matter whether Torf could read the writ of confiscation and re-allocation that Geoffrey would bear with him; the seal would be familiar enough. Nearly a quarter of the page was taken up with the marks of the Duke and his family and senior vassals, to say nothing of the signatures of every bishop in Normandy – except Archbishop Mauger, who had taken flight and joined his rebel brother, William of Arques. The decrees that the Duke had issued from his council at Bayeux positively wilted under the weight of authentication that they bore; in such a trying time as this, William was determined that there should be no mistake about the force of his commands; there was to be no doubt and no uncertainty. And no excuse.

Fitzosbern and Giffard and Montgomery and a score of senior vassals bit their lips and fumbled with wayward pens and scratched away at dozens of spidery crosses, and fussy clerks hastened to scribble identification round them. Beside them, Bishop Hugh of Lisieux, the Duke's second cousin, and Bishop Hugh of Avranches, Bishop Yves de Bellême of Sées, William of Evreux, Geoffrey himself, and the young Odo of Bayeux raised their eyebrows and cast their signatures with flourishes of varying vanity, casualness, and relief.

Just as the Duke was taking no chances, neither was Geoffrey. For months he had prowled and pondered and schemed – circling the lands of Malbec and watching the mound growing; frowning before the fire beneath the fresh, sharp-chipped beams of his new hall; sitting up late with Roger of Hauteville; measuring the progress of his knights; weighing, estimating, calculating. Torf must be given no space for parry, for counter-attack, or for escape; no room for compromise or for wriggling; no scope for his wheedling tongue or his foxy wits. No matter how slow each step was to be, it had to be forward, and it had to be sure.

No longer was it a matter of a private war of vengeance conducted furtively outside the limits of the Truce of God; it was an official punitive expedition to deprive a proven traitor of his fief. Once Mauger had made public the names in his possession, many of the men so marked had not been slow to come forward with admissions of guilt in the hope of staving off the ducal wrath; they were only too happy to name Torf of Malbec not only as a traitor but as the fount and origin of the entire western conspiracy. Better to endure public scorn and ridicule as foolish dupes than to risk public disgrace – or worse – as fully-informed, clear-intentioned rebels.

Geoffrey now had behind him the full panoply of feudal law and ducal authority, enforceable by his own military power and his own episcopal jurisdiction. Torf of Malbec would be called upon to answer for his misdemeanours by his bishop, by his neighbour, by his new feudal successor, and by the executor of the Duke's decree of punishment.

Ivo was now sent on ahead to prepare a suitable encampment at Lessay, whence it would be a short, easy approach to Malbec, to invest it if need be. All due precautions were to be taken against surprise attack, and all due provisions were to be laid in; it was to be no weary, hungry, overridden, tag-and-tail detachment that rode up to the walls of Malbec to deliver the Duke's sentence of confiscation. Geoffrey and the rest of his knights would wait at St. Lô. Mauger would collect what force that he could and rendezvous with Geoffrey at Hauteville, where Roger and his remaining brothers would add their own resources once they were fully apprised of the extent of Torf's crimes and sentence. Thence, all to Ivo's new camp at Lessay, and the hammer was raised and poised.

Ivo might smile at his fussing, but there must be not the slightest crevice where this creature could hide or the smallest hole through which he could escape. Time and again Geoffrey paced anxiously over the ramparts of the plan in his mind; surely there could be no mistake now. Given only reasonable luck, they might be able also to enjoy the luxury of being able to 'slit the ferret's throat', as Robert Guiscard had so colourfully put it.

Mauger had his doubts.

'Have you ever killed yet? Deliberately killed? Not like a boar in a thicket, you know.'

'Half of Malbec will be yours; that involves you too.'

'Only in the confiscation,' said Mauger. 'He did not steal my woman. Nor did he try to have me murdered.' Though it would simplify things enormously if a stray knife were to find Torf's ribs in the confusion. Geoffrey might not have the stomach for it when it came to it.

Geoffrey was thinking beyond Torf. Once he was dispossessed, assuming he escaped with his neck, he could conceivably counter-attack. He would wait, naturally, for Geoffrey and Mauger and the Hautevilles to return to the Duke's host, and strike in spiteful retaliation at some undefended home. That meant that Sybil and the child could be in greater danger than before.

If Torf obliged everyone by getting himself killed, there was still the small matter of William of Arques' rebellion. If things went badly for the Duke – and Mauger's fears were not without foundation – then it still behoved Geoffrey to look to the safety of Sybil and the child.

It was with that thought in mind that he had stepped aside for private talk with Baldwin de Clair at the Duke's Council . . .

'Lanfranc? He is well, thank you. Sends his regards.' Baldwin grunted. 'He is costing me a fortune, I might tell you. You should see the library.'

'Do they not write all their own?' said Geoffrey.

'Never enough for Lanfranc,' said Baldwin. 'He keeps pestering me for more from Italy.'

'It all adds to Bec's reputation, surely?'

'Yes,' said Baldwin, wiping some beer off his lips, 'and to my expenses. I expected to pay a lot to repair the castle at Brionne, after the mess Guy left it in, but I did not reckon on a monastery as well.'

Geoffrey grinned.

'Serves you right for having a famous Prior.'

Baldwin looked glum.

'Mixed blessing. You should see the visitors. All have to be fed.'

Geoffrey had not met one of William's vassals at Bayeux who did not, sooner or later in the conversation, make some reference to crippling costs and enormous expenses. Times, it seemed, were changing; things were not, apparently, what they used to be. He had asked about Lanfranc only by way of politeness; if he did not get down to what he wanted to say, Baldwin could go on like this for ever.

When Geoffrey had finished explaining his problem, Baldwin looked surprised.

'Why ask me? One monastery is enough for me. I do not have a convent as well – thank God.'

'To whom should I refer then?'

Baldwin thought.

'This – lady of whom you speak. She would have the – what I mean is could she – '

'She is as well born as myself,' said Geoffrey, coming to his rescue. 'And there will be no difficulty in providing an agreeable offering to cover her keep and that of the child.'

'Ah.'

Baldwin looked a little awkward.

'You will forgive me for asking, I am sure.'

'Do not give it another thought.'

'In that case,' said Baldwin, 'you could do no better than the house at St. Amand in Rouen. My sister Agnes is there. If you like, I can have a word with Fitz about it.'

'Why Fitzosbern?'

Geoffrey could not yet bring himself to use the familiar diminutive form in front of a kinsman of the Duke.

'I thought you knew,' said Baldwin. 'His mother is the abbess.'

'The abbess!'

Baldwin's face tightened. He made a sudden excuse about other business and left him.

Geoffrey remembered the murders of 1040. He mentioned them to Roger of

Montgomery.

Roger nodded.

'Memories still run deep.'

'Long time,' said Geoffrey.

'You did not see your father killed in front of your eyes,' said Roger. 'Fitz and Baldwin did. Only boys, remember. Fitz's mother took refuge in St. Amand, and found she had a taste for the life. I have an idea that Baldwin's sister is the same. Baldwin is very fond of her, you know.'

To Geoffrey's bafflement, Roger also looked awkward, and he too soon left.

Geoffrey found Sir Walter Giffard, and told him of his talk with Roger.

'He suddenly closed right up.'

'Not surprised. It was one of his elder brothers who killed Fitz's father. I thought it was common knowledge.'

'Not to me.'

Walter Giffard grinned.

'I was forgetting. You come from the wild west. News never reaches you. Nothing ever happens out there.'

'It will, Walter. Wait and see. So how does Roger get himself into the Duke's confidence?'

'Because he is not like his brothers, and he has convinced the Duke. Took some time. I think marrying Mabel of Bellême helped; nobody else would touch her, not even for her castle.' Walter laughed. 'Now there is duty for you.'

Geoffrey pretended to shudder.

'You can say that again.'

'Take it from me,' said Walter, 'Roger of Montgomery is sound.'

It spoke well for Walter's sense of loyalty too; Geoffrey knew that the two were firm friends.

Walter sighed.

'And Fitz is still not convinced. Have you noticed that he talks very little to Roger?'

'He talks very little to anybody,' said Geoffrey.

'But he listens,' said Walter. 'He listens mightily. And what he hears he passes on to the Duke.'

'Is Fitz the only one who is close?'

'Really close? Yes, I would say so. At least I should have said so until recently. Now I think he has a rival – the lady Matilda. Have you seen them together?'

Geoffrey thought of the tall, striding William and the unbelievably short Matilda bouncing along beside him in full flush of joyous health. Her head barely came up to his chest. As she was so small, her pregnancy looked enormous. Were it not for their obvious contentment with each other, they would have been figures of fun. As it was, men smiled, but they smiled kindly. And they smiled carefully, behind the Duke's back.

'You know what I think?' said Walter Giffard in his direct way. 'I think he missed his mother. You never met the lady Arlette, did you? A great character. He depended heavily on her.'

A rare woman indeed, thought Geoffrey, to have a compliment such as that paid to her by a man like Walter Giffard.

'Never looked at a female,' continued Walter. 'Then Arlette dies. And behold! Within months he is married. Makes you think . . .'

Hauteville came into view.

Geoffrey flung out a gloved hand.

'There.'

He turned in the saddle, and his knights waved their acknowledgment. They had made a satisfactory showing at Bayeux, and had generally behaved themselves. Only one brawl, and that, mercifully, not with any of Odo's contingent . . .

Fitzosbern had complimented him on their appearance, and Giffard had gruffly admitted that their mounts were in good shape.

They talked war and tactics, and Geoffrey, without really intending to, found himself airing his ideas.

'Larger groups? You will never get the control,' said Giffard. 'Turn knights loose in the charge, and let God decide. It is the only way.'

'Surely,' said Geoffrey, 'if we can improve the drill and extend the practice.'

'They will never tolerate it,' said Giffard. 'Honour.'

'What about common sense?' said Geoffrey. 'There must be a better chance of winning if we can get more of them to reach the enemy line at the same time. You know – one solid punch at a particular spot.' He fidgeted in excitement as he developed his theme. 'And suppose we could use cavalry like a fist – which could be thrown and withdrawn quickly and at will.'

Giffard scoffed.

'Irrelevant. If you are fighting against cavalry, you will never have any order once you join battle. If you are fighting against infantry, it does not matter what formation you have; knights always fight better than footplods.'

'Have you seen English housecarles?'

'No,' said Giffard. 'Have you? But I have seen the best that Brittany and Flanders can offer. It matters not. You do not win from the soles of your feet; you win from the seat of your arse, in a saddle. There is only one way.'

Fitzosbern said little, as usual, but when the conversation broke up, he spoke to Geoffrey.

'Come and speak to the Duke. I think he might be interested in what you have to say.'

He was – very interested. They talked long into the dark hours. William did not mention England, but it was clear that it was on his mind. Geoffrey marvelled. This young Duke, beset as he was with rebels on two, maybe three sides – even more – Arques, Ponthieu, Artois, Anjou, and the King – had enough spirit, energy, and confidence in himself to listen to ideas that might have relevance only to a campaign of truly colossal dimensions at some time in the hazy, distant future.

At last he grunted.

'Well – one day, eh?'

He began humming, and lapsed into absent thought. Geoffrey thought he had forgotten all about him. Suddenly the Duke lifted his head.

'Right now it is a matter of marches and sieges. I have heard today that my garrison at Arques has gone over to the rebels. Fitz here will give orders to invest the castle at once. You too will return to take the place of this traitor Torf of Malbec. For both of us it will be drudgery and boredom. For both of us it will be a time of unease too: you must look constantly over your shoulder to see if Anjou will attack in force by way of Mortain or Alençon; I must be ready for a move from Ponthieu or from the King.'

'Do you really think they will march together as they plan?' said Geoffrey.

William looked at Fitzosbern. It was Fitz who spoke.

'His Grace has survived not by speculating but by being ready. See to it that you too are ready . . . '

They unsaddled in the wide stable yard at Hauteville. A small army of grooms, pages, squires, and servants dodged and jostled around one another on a hundred urgent missions. Geoffrey's new knights stamped their feet, stretched their backs, slapped their gauntlets on their thighs, and swaggered casually under the gaze of a score of hard-staring children. They gazed around at their lodging for the night, and took care to look mildly disapproving.

As they exchanged impressions, they held out their arms without looking at the deft hands which unbuckled belts, baldrics, and waist wallets; they bent over and swore as mail hauberks were tugged over their heads and caught in their hair. In leather jerkins that were covered with a million tiny ring indentations they walked stiffly to the privy pits at the back, where they stood and relieved themselves beside the stable midden, puckering their noses and making small puffing noises with their lips.

While everyone else sought warmth, company, rest, gossip, and food in

231

kitchen, buttery, barn, bakehouse, stable loft, forge, workshop, and storeroom, they made their way to the hall, where fresh napkins and wooden bowls of warm water were set out on rows of trestle tables against the wall. They slicked, rinsed, or washed according to individual taste, training, and inclination, ignoring giggles behind leather curtains at doorways.

Afterwards, while armful boys spread fresh dry straw and laid platters of cheese and bread on the re-set trestles, they lounged and sipped, stretching out bare feet to the blaze and wondering whether to indulge the luxury of clean hose. As the next resting-place would be Ivo's camp at Lessay, where facilities were going to be minimal, they decided that they could afford it; things could be dried much more easily here than dangling from mist-dripping lines in open camp.

They gazed at the remaining Hauteville brothers in expectant curiosity, as if they were waiting for each of them to turn into the giant Robert Guiscard, about whom stories grew taller every year. The youngest, Roger, with his uncharacteristic dark complexion and thoughtful manner, frankly baffled them. He asked no questions, made rare comments, and offered few explanations, yet it was clear that he missed nothing.

He and Lord Geoffrey had their heads together for most of the evening, so the knights had to content themselves with the food and drink, which was as good and as bad as they could have reasonably expected from a Cotentin knight's fee.

The lady Fressenda did not join them, which was a blessing; from what they heard of her continual rapping on the floor of the solar and her stream of demands; they counted their deprivation of her company as one of the few pieces of luck they had had since leaving the Council of Bayeux.

When they saw Geoffrey climbing the solar ladder, they felt almost sorry for him . . .

The lady Fressenda kissed the ring, waved Geoffrey to a stool, and cut short his polite inquiries after her health.

'Do not ask me how I feel; I feel terrible. Telling you about it will only make me feel worse. Now – when does Roger leave for Malbec? How many knights do you have? Where is your man Ivo making the approach camp?'

Geoffrey laughed.

'My lady, if you can ask me questions as sharp as that, my guess is that you know a lot of the answers already.'

Fressenda looked keenly at him as she pulled up a blanket to her chin. She liked this young man; he talked to her as an equal. If she could only be sure that he would . . . She pulled herself back to the conversation.

'I may be a crack-boned old spider, but there is nothing wrong with my web, and I still sit at the centre of it.'

'And Roger is a dutiful son,' said Geoffrey.

'The most dutiful one of all.'

There was a silence. Geoffrey read her mind.

'First, Sybil. Tomorrow, Roger will go to Malbec.'

Fressenda followed him intently.

'Alone?'

'Two body servants, no more. Not only must it behave like a mission of mercy; it must look like one too.'

'I am now at my last gasp – is that it?'

Geoffrey smiled.

'Something like that. You have asked to see Sybil and – '

The word stuck on Geoffrey's tongue.

'Raoul.' Fressenda put out a hand to touch his. 'Your son. A bonny infant, to be sure. Though – '

'Though what?' said Geoffrey, pouncing.

'Nothing. Only a child's ailments – sickness, a tender stomach.'

She wished she had not said anything about it. Sybil in fact was beside herself with worry. The child was finding it difficult to keep anything down. If Sybil took it into her head to decide that he was unfit to travel, that jaw of hers would set, and not even a full-scale war raging over her head would induce her to move him. Fressenda waved her hand impatiently.

'Pay no attention. Merely women's fussings. Her girl Cecily is in fact quite capable, if she gives herself a chance and uses the good sense that God gave her.'

Geoffrey looked as if he was going to ask more questions, so Fressenda forestalled him.

'And when Sybil and Raoul are safe under this roof?'

'We move.'

Fressenda gave him a wry look.

'Geoffrey, you can do better than that. I deserve it too. I am the one supposed to be dying, remember?'

Geoffrey grinned.

'I am sorry. We take our combined strength – Roger, Mauger, and myself – and we go to my manors at Lessay. From there we ride with all convenient speed to Malbec.'

Fressenda tightened her lips. So it was the end of the twisted road at last for the lord of Malbec. But only for the lord. Not for his family. Time to supply a new direction for them. She took a deep breath.

'What do you do with Torf?'

'We acquaint him with the terms of the Duke's writ of confiscation.'

'And your re-possession.'

'Mine and Mauger's.'

'What do you do with Torf?'

'Our writ covers expulsion from fief and exile.'

Fressenda leaned forward.

'What do you do with Torf?'

Geoffrey avoided her eye.

'The Duke specified no further punishment.'

'Did he have to?'

'He let Guy of Burgundy go into exile.'

'Geoffrey, look at me. You have a man in your troop called Ralph – is that not so?'

Geoffrey looked surprised.

'Yes. I do not see – '

Fressenda flapped her wrist.

'Listen, and follow me. Never mind how I know; I know. Old women like me exist by means of knowledge; the amount of food I can digest without pain these days would not keep a rat alive.'

Geoffrey suppressed a smile. The lady Fressenda was one of those prodigious old wonders who clung to life by a hair, ate hardly anything, had a pain for each muscle and each limb, and enjoyed about two hours' sleep a week.

'This Ralph,' continued my lady, 'went back to his home last winter, and found his father crippled, lucky to be alive. Others of his household were murdered.'

'Yes.'

'This Ralph now wants vengeance.'

Geoffrey began to see.

'I should imagine so, yes.'

'So much so that he is prepared to leave the service of the man he much admires –you.'

Geoffrey gasped. Was there no end to this woman's sources of military intelligence?

Fressenda nodded.

'I am sorry to be the one to tell you. He is devoted to you. But the fact remains that he will join the Duke the moment that an opportunity presents itself – solely in order to have a better chance of killing Count Enguerrand.'

'Enguerrand did it?'

'Ralph thinks so. Nobody else but the Count had the authority or the resources for a raid in such strength. The point is that Ralph is prepared to subordinate everything – even his loyalty to you – for revenge.'

Geoffrey spread his hands.

'What do you think I have been planning all this time?'

'Sybil's rescue.'

'Well?'

'Only Sybil's rescue. Every time I ask you about Torf's fate you sidestep.'

'How can I be sure at this stage?'

'Ralph is.'

'It was his father that was attacked, not mine.'

'He tried to murder you.'

Geoffrey rose, and began pacing.

'I can not predict my reactions. If I had had him at my mercy the next day after the ambush, maybe. Now . . .'

Fressenda fidgeted. This would not do. Geoffrey would never take his vengeance cold; the dish had to be re-heated to make it palatable. It would cause him pain, but only pain, it seemed, would make him react.

Perhaps she could prepare him for it in some way.

'You were at Alençon, I believe – at the siege.'

Geoffrey frowned.

'Yes.'

'You saw what the Duke did.'

'Yes.'

'You saw why he did it.'

'To capture the town, yes.'

'I mean the occasion of his decision.'

'The skins?'

'Yes. Dishonour to his mother and father.'

'Yes. He was almost off his head with rage.'

'Dishonour to a father,' repeated Fressenda. 'Just like Ralph.'

'Well? How does this affect me? Torf has not dishonoured my father.'

Fressenda folded her hands firmly in her lap.

'Geoffrey – Torf killed him.'

*   *   *   *   *   *

For two whole days Geoffrey paced. Without Ivo there, nobody dared come near him.

Mauger was all for moving at once.

'He was my father too.'

'No. We wait. We wait for news of Sybil. His throat will be just as warm.'

Mauger looked up from his knife blade.

235

'Only for you would I wait. I will not wait long once we are inside Malbec.'
Geoffrey stopped pacing.
'I should fight you for the privilege.'

*   *   *   *   *   *

Even Mauger did not speak to him during the ride to Lessay. He was still listening to the lady Fressenda . . .

'My son Drogo came home for the midsummer feast. He brought me the saddest possible news – William, the eldest, was dead. "William of the Iron Arm." ' She savoured the words with pride. 'Drogo also told me of this Torf. A scavenger, a talebearer, it seems. A turncoat who clung to the skirts of success whoever wore them. A man who hovered on the edge of camp fires, ready to slink away if it became too hot or too cold.'

'You professed yourself charmed by him,' said Geoffrey.

'So I was, for the same reason as my sons: he had a silver tongue, and he always had golden offers and jewelled prospects. It was he who brought to my sons the tale of your father and the treasure he carried. When they found out that it was the treasure of Duke Robert, in trust for young William, they wanted no part of it.'

Geoffrey's eyebrows went up a little.

The lady Fressenda shook her head.

'I am under no illusions about what my sons do,' she said. 'But I know too that they are loyal to their Duke, like their father before them. There is no honour in the country where they ply their trade, and there is little grace. Small wonder then that they preserve it in the country of their birth, and they look to you for grace at the time of their death.'

Geoffrey accepted the mild rebuke, while admiring yet again the resource of the Hautevilles; trust them to cultivate honour and grace in a country far enough away to be of no inconvenience to them in their present activities.

'There were plenty more treasures,' continued Fressenda, almost reading his thoughts. 'They sent Torf away. Drogo said they spent time looking for your father to warn him, but it seems they were too late. Your father and the treasure were never seen again. We must assume that Torf hired some men to do his killing for him; there is no shortage of brigands in Apulia.'

'Why did your son Robert not tell me this when I was there?'

'Why should he? He was not certain. It would have been pain to you. You are his spiritual father; why should he needlessly cause you misery about a father who died unshriven in some squalid ambush?'

Unshriven!

Fressenda saw the anguish on his face.

'I should not have told you myself if I had not thought it absolutely necessary.'

This woman constantly amazed him. As further light dawned, she returned him stare for stare.

'If you knew all this about Torf,' said Geoffrey, 'why did you let your daughter go to him?'

'By that time he had more than mere prospects; he had wealth, rank, position.'

Geoffrey began to understand.

'And with his character, you thought Sybil could manage him.'

Fressenda nodded.

'In time. She would come to full power with full realisation.'

'What about me?'

'Torf was there; you were not. My lord Tancred was dead. What else was I to do?'

'And now you have been proved wrong.'

Fressenda nodded again with complete readiness.

'Now I have been proved wrong.'

'So I am to take his place?'

'If that is what Sybil wants.'

You mean if that is what you want.

'Tell me,' said Geoffrey, 'since I am to be the – replacement, what makes you think that Sybil can manage me?'

Fressenda shrugged.

'I am . . .'

Geoffrey dug his spurs unnecessarily. The knights immediately behind him watched the gap open between his Grace and themselves, looked at each other, smiled, and continued at the same pace . . .

Blue and black and red marks – up and down her arms. Sybil had been unwilling to show them. Only her mother prevailed. Fressenda looked at Geoffrey . . .

Geoffrey swore mindlessly under his breath. This animal had to be put down. Sybil did not know what she was saying – too much stress and worry . . . 'It is all so easy for you; you just draw a sword and every problem is solved.'

'Sybil, he tried to have me killed. He killed my father. He has ill-treated you.'

'That was in the past.'

'What would you have me do?'

'Think of the future.'

'I am.'

'By dispossessing me?'

'No. Torf.'

237

'And I become the wife of an outlaw.'

'You have a roof here, and – '

Sybil tossed her head.

'I do not wish to become maiden aunt to the children of Aubrey or Humbert.'

Geoffrey swallowed.

'You have me.'

For the first time a tender look came into Sybil's blue eyes. She smiled, but shook her head.

'Dear Geoffrey. You do not see, do you?'

Geoffrey stood up and began to pace.

'No, I do not. Why is it that everything I do to remove a barrier between us serves only to put another in its place?'

'I have had my own household,' said Sybil. 'I do not want charity.'

'Who said anything about charity?'

'You said a roof.'

Geoffrey stopped, and turned. He licked his lips.

'There is always – marriage.'

Sybil smiled again.

'If I do not want a roof as charity, I certainly do not want marriage as charity either.'

Geoffrey ran his hand through his hair.

'I give up.'

Sybil put a hand to his cheek.

'My poor Geoffrey – I was once sure of you; I thought I was sure of Torf. How can I be sure of you now?'

But she would – when Torf was dead. And she was feeling better. And Raoul was well again . . .

At Lessay Ivo came out to meet them. He waited until the last of the knights and their servants had gone on ahead to his new camp. He patted his horse's neck, and murmured some friendly abuse to it.

'Well?' said Geoffrey.

Ivo sat back in the saddle.

'The bird has flown, my lord.'

*   *   *   *   *   *

238

Chapter Sixteen

Right through a sultry summer the storm clouds of the conspiracy against the Duke came and went; they lowered and threatened; they caused sweat and tension and shortness of temper – but they steadfastly refused to burst. Report and rumour jostled at the Duke's ear – a border raid here, a foray against a castle there; random wastings and trampling of crops; sudden incursion that turned out to be mere reconnaissance in force. The Duke had to cope with constant frustration and lack of decisive movement.

When would Count Enguerrand of Ponthieu come to the relief of his fellow-conspirator, William of Arques, now locked in his own castle by the sudden arrival of the Duke? Would the Count of Anjou invade again in the west by way of Alençon and Domfront and Mortain, or would he move north-east and effect a junction with the host of the King? Would King Henry sweep north from Paris with his united force, or would he split it and try to come at the Duke from two opposite directions? Or would he, as world-weary observers drily predicted, do nothing? Would he instead indulge in his favourite pastime of waiting for a cat to jump, and stand by while his two most awkward vassals in northern France, Anjou and Normandy, broke their weapons across each other's heads?

The Duke hummed to himself as he planned and calculated . . . Careful husbanding of resources; no wasting of men and energy chasing every false report. Vassals consulted at every opportunity; let them feel that they were partners, and they would not complain too much about exceeding their feudal commitment in time or distance. Shrewd purchases of swords and mail from the best smiths and forgemasters in Swabia and Lorraine.

Now he had someone to share his doubts and worries in the cold and dark of wakefulness after the nightmares. Matilda soothed and warmed and comforted; she listened and commented and encouraged; she knew also when to slap and sting and jolt the senses. Despite her swelling pregnancy, she went with him wherever possible, tolerating hardships with a good humour that sent her reputation soaring with the entire ducal court. She developed a cheerful camaraderie with her husband's chief vassals, waving aside their gallant compliments.

'Remember where I come from. When you have seen Flanders rain, you have seen everything.'

During the busy hours of daylight there was Fitzosbern almost constantly at his side – when he was not at Breteuil and Tillières chasing the engineers. Whatever the news – sudden, unexpected, ominous, baffling, disastrous – he met it with the same unruffled deliberation. A grunt, a slight raising of the eyebrows; if he was really moved, a slow rubbing of the back of his neck, with perhaps a hint of a wry smile. Before he had opened his mouth, he had put everything into a healthy perspective.

'There is a lot to be said, my lord, for being on one's own; there is nobody to let one down. Think of all the temptations they have to betray each other or to leave each other in the lurch. And think of the Guiscard.'

William did, often. If the plot against Normandy was worrying to a duke, the alliance against the Hautevilles in Italy was enough to make a king gape. Pope Leo, tried beyond endurance by the Normans in Apulia and Calabria, had resolved to rid the country of them once and for all. Rumour had it that he was in the process of building an alliance of all those princes and dukes in southern Italy who had cause to hate or fear the Normans – and there were many. He had also approached the King of France for assistance, and for good measure was negotiating for troops with the Emperor in Germany. As a final touch he was in contact with the Greek Emperor at Constantinople, with a view to recruiting an imperial army to cross the Adriatic and take the Normans in the rear; restoration of lost cities to Greek rule was a tantalising incentive.

Proof that his plans were more than the wistful dreams of a reforming priest had come with news that Drogo of Hauteville had been assassinated. The Count of Apulia, brother of the late William of the Iron Arm, was the second son of Hauteville to die in his adopted land. The manner and timing of his death – struck down outside the church where he had been attending a celebratory, if uncharacteristic, mass – suggested that there was a brain behind it with both military and clerical leanings, and Pope Leo had been a soldier before he had been a pontiff.

The Normans had responded by electing the third son, Humphrey of Hauteville, as their commander, and he in turn had the towering Robert, the Guiscard, at his shoulder, or rather over it. Behind them stood a veritable cohort of brothers – the stolid Serlo, Geoffrey, Mauger, another William, and young Tancred, recently arrived.

If the Hautevilles were undismayed by the awesome forces being arrayed before them – a king, two emperors, and a pope – what need had the Duke of Normandy to be concerned by the same king (who could not be in two places at once), a count or two, and some disaffected border barons? At least the men around him that were left – the Fitzosberns and the Giffards and the Montgomerys and the Clairs – were the loyal ones.

'Ha!'

William clapped his hands and issued his orders.

If troops were to be kept on demesne, at least they were to be kept in constant readiness. Ducal messengers maintained regular contact with mercenary captains in Lorraine and Brabant and Hainault. Sulky peasants bent over their haymaking cursed with the knowledge that bigger portions of it than usual were already promised to swell the stores of fodder in border fortresses. The fortresses themselves – Mortain, Domfront, Alençon, Bellême, Breteuil, Tillières, right round to the line of the River Epte – seethed with sweating sappers and rang with the swung iron of freshly-forged tools.

In the two bishoprics of the west, Avranches and Coutances, the lords of the diocese were urged to give their prime energy to the building of town walls, even at the expense of work on the cathedrals.

For once Geoffrey and Goscelin were in total agreement, if for different reasons.

Geoffrey paced and swore.

'He demands the impossible! The cathedral, the town, castles at Malbec and Lessay – and now walls. To say nothing of bridges, mills, a market. As for the aqueduct . . . And the cost. The cost!'

Ivo waved everyone out of his way until he had calmed down.

On the other side of the square, Goscelin munched a mournful pasty which Thierry had brought out to the site for him.

'He wants a mere nailer of planks, not an artist. Walls, Thierry, I ask you! I am a designer, not a carpenter. Even if I were, I can not be in several places at once. If this sort of thing continues, I shall soon see no option but to resign.'

It was not the first time that Goscelin had dropped dark hints like this. Thierry, like most people round him, took them merely as signs of pressure rather than dire threats. It was Goscelin's way of saying that not enough attention was being paid to his artistic temperament. Thierry, like Geoffrey, had learned the remedy.

'You must appreciate that my lord Geoffrey is under great strain at the present time, and looks for help to his most trusted advisers. A word or two of advice from yourself would, I am sure, be most welcome. He depends a lot on you.'

Goscelin's eyebrows began at once to lose their triangular anguish.

'Do you think so?'

'Sure of it,' said Thierry, with his mouth full of pasty. He kicked a few blobs of half-set lime mortar with his toe. 'He was saying to me only the other day, "Thierry," he was saying, "I should wager that Goz could help us here." '

Goscelin's eyebrows rose in delicate arches again.

'He calls me "Goz"?'

'All the time. He said, "Goz knows everybody; there must be someone who could help." '

Goscelin hoisted his crane-like shoulders in a huge shrug.

'He had only to ask. God knows, I am a very reasonable man.'

There was a pause, as Goscelin wiped his tongue across his teeth to get rid of the crumbs.

'Would you like another?' said Thierry. 'Assuming of course that you have time. I know that you work without pause.'

Goscelin pondered deeply, and cast a glance over his shoulder. The foreman was looking in his direction.

'Perhaps if you were to bring me two – to eat later, you understand.' He gestured over his shoulder. 'There are so many demands upon me.'

Thierry nodded solemnly and stood up to go.

'Though I say so myself, it is a good thing that you have in me a friend who appreciates.'

Goscelin's brow grew another dozen wrinkles as he beamed beatifically.

Thierry paused.

'Oh. About that name. Was there anyone you had in mind?'

'Ranulf of Dreux,' said Goscelin. 'A distant cousin. Dreadfully temperamental. And little artistic sensibility. But sound.'

'I am sure my lord Geoffrey will be most grateful.'

'Difficult,' called Goscelin after him. 'But sound.'

'Well?' said Geoffrey five minutes later.

Thierry grinned in triumph.

'He gave me a name.'

'Where?'

'Dreux.'

Geoffrey nodded in approval.

'Good. Not far from Paris, though. You will have to be careful.'

'How long do we spend?'

The answer was wrenched out of Geoffrey like a diseased tooth.

'As long as it takes. You can keep up the search as well.'

Thierry wanted to make absolutely sure.

'But find Ranulf first.'

Geoffrey swore.

'If that is his damned name, yes. Find him first. And hurry.'

For weeks it had been a song with only one verse – 'Find Torf of Malbec. Talk. Ask. Drink with them. Somebody must know something.'

The Duke's orders – 'Build, build. And listen for news of Anjou' – must have become very pressing indeed, to cut across this obsession.

Now it was 'find Ranulf of Dreux'.

Thierry sighed. Things had been much less complicated in the old days at Montbrai.

*   *   *   *   *   *

242

Every sound was still in the tiny wooden chapel save for the steady rustle of straw and the noise of the iron ferrule on the end of the stick. Geoffrey, in a new chasuble for the feast of St. Lawrence, stood with the Host in his hand, willing her to reach the altar steps.

Sybil, Constance, and Muriella clasped their hands in silent prayer until their knuckles showed white. On either side of Geoffrey and slightly below him, Aubrey and Humbert and Roger waited, their faces ashen, their eyes fixed on the figure in the aisle.

Slowly, with no rhythm save that of purpose, the floor-bound feet shuffled closer. The ferrule of the stick, each time it moved, sought out a secure place to plant itself as if it had an eye in the end.

At the back, every woman of the household shed tears into the shadows. Scullions and smiths, who had so often sworn as they heaved on the sling, tried to swallow lumps, and made private promises to themselves that they would never complain at it again.

As she made her endless way to the altar rail, the lady Fressenda was binding afresh the entire domain – family, servants, labourers, tenants, every man, woman, and child – in bonds of shared grief, loyalty, discipline, and pride.

'Today,' she said, 'is the anniversary of the death of Drogo. I shall receive the Host this day, if you will say Mass, and I shall walk to receive it in precedence before my family. Will you do me this honour?'

Geoffrey bowed.

'I assure you, my lady, that the honour will be all mine.'

It had been Geoffrey's sad duty to bring from a ducal council the news of Drogo's death, nearly a year after the event. It was the least he could do to say the requiem for his soul.

When the lady Fressenda reached the steps, Roger put out a hand. She tried to swing her arm out of the way. Roger leaned down to her ear.

'Mother, God has given you the strength to get here. He has given us the wit to see that you kneel and rise with dignity before the world.'

Fressenda nodded. Aubrey and Humbert took her elbows, Roger took her stick, and Geoffrey administered the Body of the Lord. A great sigh went up from the congregation, who crossed themselves to the last child.

All three brothers took the Host, then Constance and Muriella. Sybil knelt a short distance apart, her face white and drawn, the skin stretched tight across her broad brow. As her brothers and sisters received, she watched out of the corner of her eye, like a rabbit bewitched by the relentless sliding approach of the snake. When Geoffrey at last stood before her, and their eyes met, she suddenly stood up, turned, and ran. Remembering herself, she stopped momentarily at the door, genuflected, and was gone.

When Geoffrey at last found her, she was at her mother's frame, stitching as if her life depended upon it.

'Why? Why did you do it?'

Sybil fumbled with a new thread.

'I am a shocking needlewoman. Always have been.'

'Why?' repeated Geoffrey.

Sybil frowned in concentration.

'You of all people ask me that?'

Geoffrey swallowed.

'If we were married – '

Sybil flashed a direct glance at him, her blue eyes blazing.

'But we are not. Only I – to someone else.'

'Which of the two is it that bothers you? The first never did before.'

'Geoffrey, it is impossible. It is – it is flaunting it under God's nose.'

'I see. So if we do it in a corner of a field where only your washing women can see and God can not, that is all right.'

After such a long separation and after so many trials, their lovemaking, when at last it happened, had taken them by surprise, and had been so violent and passionate that Sybil trembled merely to recall it.

She looked down at the needle.

'You can tie me in knots with your reasoning and your cleverness. Normally I can argue back, and I should enjoy it. But now I am too full – so full that I am losing control. I have always prided myself that I had a mind that could sort out these things. I used to pour scorn on the heads of my sisters for being mindless. Now look at me.' She raised her eyes to him. 'Oh, my darling, do you not see? My body agrees with you. My heart agrees with you. Half my mind agrees with you.'

'Well then.'

'But God does not. At least I assume that it is God who is causing the trouble. Surely the Devil would not be keeping me from your arms. The Devil is the only person I can think of who would fully approve of what we did.'

Geoffrey took her hands.

'My love, you are torturing yourself unfairly. You have had so much to bear; you must be given time.'

Sybil shook her head miserably.

'I see no way in which time can help. The minute you hear news of Torf's whereabouts, you will be gone to catch him.'

'Do you blame me?'

'No. In your position, I should have wanted to do the same. But think of me. I

244

may soon wave you off on a mission to kill my husband. My husband. The longer we leave it – to give me "time" – the more we shall sin. And how do I relieve the burden on my soul? By confessing to you? And when I am shriven, if shriven I really can be, what do I do? Receive the sacrament from you?'

Sybil took her hands away from Geoffrey, then, on impulse, put them back on top of his. She looked down at them.

'Should I receive the Host from these hands, Geoffrey? Think where they were last night, and where I want them to be again. I tell you, it is impossible.'

Geoffrey heaved a huge sigh.

'What will you do then?'

Sybil heaved an even bigger one.

'Do what you suggested. Go to St. Amand.'

Geoffrey stared.

'When I first mentioned it, you flatly refused.'

Sybil nodded.

'I know.'

' "Charity," you said.'

'I know.'

'And I said it was not my charity this time, but God's, and you still refused.'

'I know, I know. And I know there could be danger if Anjou invades. I did not mind that. I did not want to be provided for.'

'And now?'

Sybil's face puckered in pain.

'Now it is a different danger, a much greater one. This time I am providing for myself.' She waved her hands in the air. 'Do not ask me to explain further, my love. I can not. I know that I must do something, and this is the only thing I can think of that will not send me mad. At least not at the moment.'

Something Lanfranc had said returned to Geoffrey's mind – 'I simply drew up a list of last resorts to save my sanity, and adopted the one which seemed the least unpromising.'

He tried to reassure himself.

'It is as I said: you need time. I think it is a good idea. I shall make the arrangements with Fitzosbern and the lady Emma as soon as possible. What about your mother?'

Sybil sniffed, like one who has been crying.

'Mother understands, and she has Constance and Muriella. The boys too. They will stay with her for a while – after Drogo. Serlo stayed after William died.'

She took a deep breath, as if a great weight had been lifted.

'You must not stop visiting just because I have gone. You know you are very welcome here.' She smiled mischievously, if slightly falsely. 'Constance thinks you are very nice.'

Geoffrey turned away and jumped to his feet.

'Sybil, please!'

It was as much guilt as pain. While he had schemed to get her away from Malbec, he had spent many hours here with Roger, and afterwards at table with the family. He could still recall the scent of Constance as she leaned over him.

'More wine, my lord? I can not talk like Sybil, but I can – serve just as well.'

She lowered her dark lashes as she concentrated on pouring, conscious of the silence between them. The slight glow of sweat across her nose and cheeks beat like rams on the door of his resistance.

Did Sybil know of her mother's outrageous suggestion?

He stopped pacing, and turned round.

'When will you go?'

'As soon as Raoul is better.'

*   *   *   *   *   *

'I hope you were careful.'

Ralph smiled. His Grace was fussing again.

'No danger, my lord. I am from the east. Now, if I had been Thierry, they would have spotted the accent at once.'

'Or the appetite,' growled Ivo.

Geoffrey silenced him with an impatient gesture.

'How will they come?'

'As you guessed, my lord. Straight up from the Mortain gap. Vire. Then to St. Lô, and come upon Bayeux and Caen from the west.'

Geoffrey nodded. Gather up waverers on the way. Take the Duke in the rear, and cut him off from the Cotentin – possibly the Bessin too – all at one stroke. Then if Ponthieu attacked from the north-east, and the King came up from Paris through the Vexin, William would have to give up the siege of Arques, or risk losing his capital at Rouen. Quite well thought out.

'It depends on timing,' said Ivo, reading his mind.

'True,' said Geoffrey. 'Meantime, the Duke depends on us stopping the Count of Anjou.'

'Hm!' said Ivo.

Not head on. Geoffrey could hear him thinking it. The combined strength of Montbrai, Coutances, and Hauteville. Bishop Hugh's knights from Avranches.

Geoffrey pointed to the door of the tent and finished his counting out loud.

'There are six contingents just in from Saint-Sauveur and Carentan.'

'Seven,' corrected Ivo. 'And I should not give you thanks for any of them. At least a score of those men were sworn to Torf's conspiracy.'

'It cuts both ways,' said Ralph. 'Many of Anjou's force are from Maine, so they had to change overlords less than two years ago. Who is to say that they will not do it again?'

'The Bretons are not up to much either,' said Ivo, craftily changing his ground. 'Too full of talk, most of it about their pay.'

Ralph and Ivo exchanged glances. Geoffrey fully understood the message that passed between them.

Loyalty in this sort of war – in almost any sort of war these days – was the child of two inconstant parents: success, and a long pocket.

Geoffrey scratched a cheek.

He had not asked for this command. Somehow it had grown up round him. He and Mauger had first brought news of the western conspiracy. Then had come the removal of its source, Torf of Malbec, which had brought about a union of Montbrai and Hauteville forces. Those knights who had speedily confessed their complicity in the incipient rebellion were instructed by the Duke to prove their new-found loyalty by serving under Geoffrey's orders. It was the only way; he did not have the opportunity or the resources to punish them.

During the long wait in the hot, heavy days of summer, William could not be everywhere. Montgomery was committed to border guard at Bellême. Domfront and Alençon and Mortain had their garrison commanders tied to the spot. Walter Giffard had been detailed to take over the day-to-day running of the siege at Arques, and was, by all accounts, fuming at the boredom of it. The Duke had two mobile reserves at Evreux and Rouen, awaiting any move on the frontier. Most of the remaining vassals were on their own fiefs, in constant readiness.

Fitzosbern, the Duke's voice, put it with customary frankness.

'There is nobody else. You have the Cotentin, Isigny, St. Lô, all the Avranchin, and the Duke has hired some swordsmen from Brittany. You will have to do the best you can.' A ghost of a smile came and went. 'Chance for you to try those ideas of yours.'

Some chance!

Geoffrey looked again at Ralph.

'Do we know how he got into Mortain so easily?'

'Bribery, or treachery, or both,' said Ralph. 'Seems they tried Alençon and Domfront, but the castellans snapped their fingers.'

'New fortifications,' said Ivo.

'Yes. But the Count of Mortain has been negligent. Weaknesses in the towers. Even more weaknesses in the pocket.' Ralph coughed slightly. 'And there was someone in Anjou's camp who said he knew the Count and could – er – approach him.'

Geoffrey and his brother shot to their feet.

'Torf!'

Ralph nodded.

'That, I believe, is his name. Very persuasive man. He says moreover that he knows how to prise several knights away from their service to you, men who were sworn to the rebellion in the first place.'

'What did I say?' said Ivo. 'A score of them at least are no good.'

Neither Geoffrey nor Mauger was listening. They were both pacing and swearing in feverish unison.

In the end Ivo had to bellow.

'My lords. My lords! You will win this by thought, not by rage. Any fool can get angry!'

For a moment all three stood glaring at each other. At last Geoffrey nodded, and motioned for them to sit down.

'So,' he said. 'Leaving out all those whose loyalty we now know to be unsound, what do we have?'

Ivo told him.

'We have only two advantages then,' said Geoffrey. 'Knowledge of the ground, and possibly surprise.'

Ralph agreed.

'They are expecting little resistance. To hear Torf, you would think it is going to be a triumphal progress.'

'Torf all over. Is Anjou falling for this?'

'Yes, I think so. Partly because he wants to. Partly because he knows nothing about you. If you will forgive me, my lord, there is something to be said in this instance for being a relative newcomer.'

Ralph was beginning to feel familiar enough to indulge in Ivo's habit of honesty.

Ivo commented on the thought already in Geoffrey's mind.

'Surprise means speed – and that means leaving out the Bretons as well.'

Geoffrey thought fiercely.

It would depend then on one short, sharp, blow. The concentrated power of impact. He had trained his own knights to attempt this; could he get the others to fall in with the idea? If they agreed, could they carry it out? Look how many tedious hours it had taken at Coutances, and Ivo was still far from satisfied.

Ivo cleared his throat.

'Do you still think your idea is a good one, my lord?'

248

Geoffrey looked up.

'Yes. I do.'

He had answered his own question to himself. There was only one way to find out, and there was only way to convince the Duke that it would work.

*   *   *   *   *   *

Ralph tied the last knot.

'The good Lord has given you time to muse on your mistakes. Use it.'

He stood up, left the three Angevin scouts tied like fowl for market, and went to report to Geoffrey under the last trees at the top of the valley slope.

In response to the question on Geoffrey's face he nodded.

'Safe. Not very talkative, but they can not tell us much at this stage that we can not see for ourselves.'

He gestured down the hill.

One third of the Angevin knights were across the river to the northern bank. A handful of infantry surrounded them in loose order. Helmets were hung from saddle horns. Coifs were back. It was yet another leaden day of oppressive heat. Eyes were shaded to try and see where the scouts had penetrated. The line of trees on the upper slopes of the valley showed nothing.

Others turned in the saddle to watch drovers goading tired oxen into the water. Wagon wheels swung and creaked. A detachment of swordsmen made it worse by climbing up for a dry ride. A few younger knights splashed past noisily on either flank. Jeers and commands and swearwords floated up the hill.

On the southern side a larger formation of knights congregated round what was clearly the Count of Anjou's travelling headquarters. Pennons hung limp from standards in the windless air.

On the north side, towards the hill, meadows and a huge fallow field stretched for nearly two hundred paces. Geoffrey focussed his eyes on the grass beneath the horses. There were no tell-tale pale patches of rushes. No hooves were disappearing into waterlogged turf. Ralph had collected his information thoroughly. There were not many wide places in this cursed bocage where knights could be safely deployed on firm ground, but Ralph seemed to have found one, and on the Mortain-Vire road. What a good man to have. For how much longer? Devil take his cursed revenge. Why was it always the good ones that left?

Geoffrey looked to his left and his right. His own men of Coutances were closest. Then the Hautevilles. Beyond them on either side the rest waited in tense silence. Ivo sat bolt upright a little to the rear, ready to give the word of command. With any luck, they would at least start together.

How many more men did he allow to cross the river? How long would it take him to reach the bank at the controlled pace that he planned? How many more of the enemy would be able to cross the river to meet the sudden threat?

He had to destroy as many as possible at the first onslaught, but he also had to be completely sure of success. Half a success, and the remainder of the enemy would be across and around them as their sword arms hung limp with fatigue. Too early a success over too few of the enemy, and the rest would come to crush them at will.

What would happen then if Anjou fulfilled his plans and cut off one third of Normandy? If Torf were to return to Malbec? If Sybil were to be snatched from Hauteville or St. Amand? And Raoul . . .

Geoffrey's eyes became needle-points of concentration.

He became conscious of Mauger's voice beside him.

'I should put on your gloves. You are getting like me.'

Geoffrey looked down. He had been rubbing his hands. Holy Virgin!

He lifted his mace. His battle mace. A rustle and jingle stirred along the line.

'Steady, steady.' Ivo, rock-like, still held them back.

The mace dropped.

'At the walk – forward!'

The command carried down to the river. Men looked up and gasped. Where there had been a line of benign green trees, there had now appeared a line of coifed and helmeted, faceless knights, a looming arc of iron.

'Christ and Mary!'

Some stared in immobile disbelief. Others crossed themselves. Drovers paused with their whips in mid-air.

'*Diex aie*!'

The war-cry stung them into frantic activity.

As soon as Geoffrey's men saw the enemy reacting, they instinctively hastened.

'Steady, steady!'

It was hopeless. Within fifty paces, Geoffrey's mood went through disquiet, alarm, exasperation, despair, and fury.

'*Diex aie*!'

As the cry was taken up, not only did separate detachments forge ahead; individual knights saw it as their path to glory and success to be in front even of their own group. The dispersal was completed as more men on the flanks swung wider to give themselves, as they thought, more room. The intoxication and the pumping of excitement was too strong for all of them.

Or nearly all. Ivo performed a miracle by keeping the men of Coutances and Hauteville to the walk. Geoffrey came within a hair of ordering them to charge; if there was to be confusion, they might as well kill as many Angevins as possible in the course of it. Then he realised what Ivo was trying to achieve.

On impulse he spurred his destrier forward so that he was riding a few strides in front of his men. Ivo came in as close as he could behind. He roared over the din of the fragmenting charge.

'The first man to dig his heels will feel my spear up his arse!'

Geoffrey held out his mace to his side as a further check. Unbelievably, his line held. The pace was restrained. The gap opened further between them and the yelling and thundering to their front.

The first hotheads crashed into the enemy, flinging spears almost blind before wheeling off to one flank or the other. Some were so excited that they allowed their momentum to carry them right into the river. With water up to their spurs, and furious hands grabbing at their ankles, some were unhorsed before they could draw sword or mace. They disappeared in a flurry of foam and blood.

Behind them, on the bank, the initial impact had spent itself. One or two spears had found their mark, and wretches in leather jerkins were screaming on the grass, clawing at shafts that had almost come out through their backs. Two destriers had been knocked right over, and struggled with broken limbs, flailing with frantic hooves and kicking unhorsed riders insensible.

The attackers turned, drew swords, and renewed the assault. The Angevin survivors, bareheaded, cursing, half winded by the shock, swung round to meet them, vowing vengeance for the dastardly surprise. All formation had been lost on both sides, and the engagement speedily degenerated into a *mêlée* of individual combats – the very thing that Geoffrey had been trying to avoid.

It was every man for himself. No hope of control, much less recall. No knight could afford to lift his head to catch the drift of an order; no knight dared to glance over his shoulder for an instant to see where Geoffrey's standard was.

On the southern bank, the Count of Anjou was bawling orders to get some of his remaining men into the water and across the river. Prudently he decided not to commit all of them; it was a long way back to Le Mans.

As the reinforcements spurred their way forward into the current, the drovers in the middle panicked. With the chaos in front of them, and the roaring and splashing behind them, they tried to turn their wagons to go back, and presented sudden sidelong obstacles. Terrified animals both in and out of the yoke lumbered aimlessly. Infuriated men found themselves hacking at the necks of oxen; others ran full tilt into the huge solid wheels. One was thrown right over a wagon and drowned in a yard of water, trampled by a score of feet. In rage at the barrier, knights wasted valuable energy trying to kill the drovers responsible.

Inevitably, some broke through, and threshed their way towards the northern bank.

Geoffrey gripped the reins convulsively. God bless Ivo!

251

He raised his mace.

'Coutances, ready!'

Beside him, he heard Mauger roar, 'Montbrai!'

Aubrey, the eldest Hauteville present, drew his sword.

'For honour and for Hauteville!'

Urgent elbows, dripping flanks, flared nostrils were surging out of the water and towards the *mêlée*.

Geoffrey dropped the mace.

'Now! *Diex aie!*'

The Angevins did not even see them until it was too late. Geoffrey's charge took them on the flank and shattered them. Many barely saw the blow that felled them. The rest, totally unnerved by the shock, backed, tumbled, or wheeled into the water again.

The impetus carried the men of Montbrai, Coutances, and Hauteville into the thick of the original fight, where their freshness and strength swept aside the tiring parries of the enemy.

The remaining foot soldiers began the flight. Some jumped into the river. Others thought it was quicker to run. It was seeing them flee that decided the knights who remained in the saddle. They broke off and forced their terrified mounts into the chaos of bodies, blood-flecked mud, and wreckage.

'Let them go! Stay back! Enough!' yelled Ivo and Geoffrey. Mauger personally restrained one or two by seizing their bridles.

This time most of them obeyed, if only from exhaustion. Moreover, they had no wish to provoke the last of Angevin strength, as yet untried on the far bank.

They paused, arms aching and chests heaving, watching their late enemy reach the southern side, where a second battle nearly developed, as roars of recrimination and jeers of cowardice and treachery echoed right through the Angevins and Manceaux who jostled there.

The Hauteville brothers exchanged silent handshakes. Mauger looked enormously pleased with himself.

'That for Anjou!' he roared, making a vulgar gesture in the Count's direction. He turned to Geoffrey. 'He will not come again. We have burned his fingers. And the Manceaux will not go through that for him again.'

'My compliments, my lord,' said Ivo.

Geoffrey wiped his face.

'What for? It was a mess, and you know it.'

'Yet you saved it.'

'Only thanks to you.' Geoffrey grunted. 'So much for my marvellous ideas.'

'Nothing wrong with ideas, my lord. You simply have to get men to learn them first.'

Geoffrey threw out a hand towards the river.

'You saw just how well we did that.'

It was nervous reaction. Lord Geoffrey was a worrier and a perfectionist. No doubt shaken too by the closeness of their brush with failure and death. When he had a few more years' campaign experience, he would learn to be grateful for success, no matter by what agency it had come.

'Nevertheless, my lord, I am glad that you were here.'

'I agree,' said Roger of Hauteville, pale but excited.

Geoffrey grunted.

'I can not think why.'

Ivo had seen lord Geoffrey like this before.

'Never mind your precious ideas, my lord. Three things won us this battle.'

'Oh?'

Ivo slid back his mail coif.

'Timing, choice of ground, and God. And you have a connection with all three. Let us leave it at that.'

*　　*　　*　　*　　*　　*

Chapter Seventeen

'I shall go nevertheless.'

'Then you are a fool.'

Sybil shrugged. A year ago, she might have said, 'I thought you reserved that sort of abuse for Constance and Muriella.'

'So I did, up to now,' her mother would have said, and they would have plunged into a much-relished, parry-and-thrust family argument.

Now, Fressenda was wondering why she bothered. There was no fight left in Sybil. No energy. No looking forward. Worst, no reaction. The lady Fressenda was scoring hits against the air.

Everything she had said since Geoffrey's departure . . . she was not sure whether Sybil had even been listening properly.

'Do you not see, you silly girl? He is the saviour of western Normandy; the Duke will most definitely reward him further. He sits high in the Duke's esteem, and he will one day sit high in the Duke's Council.'

When that failed, Fressenda tried the immediate future.

'Rest assured, Torf will be found and punished.'

Sybil said nothing, but her eyes spoke.

'You have arranged it, then, Mother?'

'It is only a matter of time. Both Geoffrey and his brother want vengeance, and the Duke wishes to execute a traitor.'

Sybil's eyes carried the same accusation.

Fressenda spread her hands.

'All I did was to tell him about Torf and his father. Was that a crime? Did he not deserve to know?'

Sybil sighed, as if the mere act of opening her mouth were too much trouble. She put out her hand absently, and began to rock the empty cradle. The polished wood still smelt of baby.

There had been a time, years ago, when it always smelt of baby. Eleven Hauteville children had lain there, including Sybil herself.

The lady Fressenda stitched in tight-lipped silence for a while. When she could stand it no longer, she laid down her needle.

'That life is not for you, Sybil. I have seen you now with two separate men. You have not the calling.'

With Papia it had been otherwise. If ever there was a born nun, it was her eldest daughter. When she had finally announced her wish, and asked lord Tancred for a presentation gift to the convent, everyone at Hauteville was surprised only that she had not said it earlier. There was something about Papia. None of the stable lads had ever tried to get a hand up her skirt. Everyone somehow knew.

Sybil was different. The trouble was that she was also different from Constance and Muriella. There were times when the lady Fressenda was not sure whether she had begun to understand her youngest daughter. There were great depths to her, just as there were great depths to her youngest son, Roger. Of all her children, she felt closest to these two, and at the same time furthest away. She knew that they loved her deeply, probably more devotedly than the others did, and this space that now and then opened between her and them caused her much pain. Yet alongside the pain went frustration, almost annoyance; their unfathomed minds meant that she could not anticipate and control them as she did the others. It was a standing challenge to her will to power, yet its very existence caused her to respect her two youngest children above the rest.

Sybil made a faint grimace of resignation.

Her mother resumed her stitching, but so fiercely that she pricked herself with the needle. She muttered curses under her breath that she would have never have uttered in my lord Tancred's presence when he was alive.

'Devil take it, girl! Anyone would think you were the first woman to lose a child.'

Sybil flashed a sharp glance, but said nothing. Fressenda continued the prodding.

'I had one born dead, and I miscarried three times.'

Another flash from the blue eyes. The Hauteville eyes. At least it was a reaction.

'You can not mourn for ever,' said Fressenda.

'I can where I am going.'

'Then you are a – !'

Holy Mother, this was getting nowhere.

Fressenda laid down her needle.

'Sybil . . . Sybil. Surely you would want another. I saw you with Raoul; I know you would love it.'

Sybil barely looked at her.

'And who shall be the father? Torf or Geoffrey? How would you like your – new grandson? As an outlaw or as a bastard?'

Fressenda shook her head in annoyance.

'Geoffrey will rid you of Torf and will – '

' – will provide for me. Yes, I know.'

'He will marry you, if you will let him.'

'You mean if his conscience will let him. Or if he can spare time from his precious cathedral.'

'From what you said about your last meeting, I received the impression that it was *your* conscience that was causing the trouble.'

Sybil sighed again.

'Oh, Sybil, give him a chance; give him time. He has so many burdens to carry at the present.'

'Time?'

Yes, time. That was all she needed. If she could get him to the pitch whereat he would contemplate killing, it should not be too difficult to get him to contemplate matrimony. Sybil was the problem, not Geoffrey.

'Time?' repeated Sybil. 'Time to go to Italy and raise more money from my brothers for his bishop's hall and his cathedral? Time to say masses for the Duke's Council? Time to scour France for my husband, so that he can wreak the vengeance that he considers his due? Time to make Malbec his own? Malbec – the property that is mine by right of marriage.'

Fressenda began to get cross.

'Self-pity. All self-pity. You do not mean half of it. It is the child.'

Sybil's face began to crumble.

'Self-pity? No lover. No husband. No status. No home. No child. No future. No peace. Self-pity?'

Fressenda leaned forward.

'Yes! Most definitely it is self-pity.' She held out her hands. 'Look at these. They are almost the only parts of me that work properly. I have lost my husband. I have lost two sons, dead in a foreign land. Even as we speak, I may have lost two more.'

'Stepsons,' corrected Sybil, rising to the bait of an argument without realising it.

'Sons!' shouted her mother. 'Because I made them mine. Just as I made Lord Tancred mine. Just as I made you mine, and Roger, and all the others. Because I fought. Because I did not sit down and weep. A cornered stranger in a household of males – a grieving husband and five stricken sons. Hostile servants who did nothing but reminisce about a saintly lady and make unwelcome comparisons . . . Just as I made Hauteville mine.'

Sybil wiped away a tear with the ball of her thumb.

'And what do I do? Fight the wrath of God and make Him give me back my son? Connive at the murder of my husband at the hands of my lover? Cohabit meanwhile with a prince of the Church and produce more bastards? Do I then defy the Holy Father and marry this prince? And when I go to burn, do I fight the Devil and make Hell mine?'

*　　*　　*　　*　　*　　*

Geoffrey stumped noisily through the puddles. He could barely make out the rider's shape against the blackness.

'God's Bread! Where have you been?'

The rain lashed his face as he looked up.

'Everywhere, my lord. Absolutely everywhere.'

Thierry's voice came foggily through the downpour.

Ivo bent to look at the horse's legs, and felt its flanks.

'He has treated it well, my lord. Long, but not hard. It is to his credit.'

Geoffrey shook the rain off his eyelashes.

'Go and get into some dry clothes. Then come and see me. And do not waste time gossiping.'

Thierry scattered more rain from his travelling cloak as he dismounted.

'I shall not gossip, my lord,' he puffed, 'but not a morsel of hot food has passed my – '

'Devil take your stomach; if it were not so big it would not get so empty. Do as I say. Ivo will take your horse. Now hasten.'

Thierry looked at Ivo. He had expected grumpiness, perhaps bad temper, but that was usually a sign of my lord's concern. He was hurt by the savagery in the voice.

Ivo bent to peer at a saddle girth.

'What is this, Thierry?'

'What?'

Thierry bent down beside him. Ivo whispered in his ear.

'The child is dead. Bad stomach.' He nodded in Geoffrey's direction. 'He has been like this for months.'

'Ah.'

Thierry looked furtively over his shoulder, and turned back to Ivo.

'All the same, we have been on the road since dawn.'

Ivo pretended to point, and said loudly, 'Get that seen to when you have made your report.' Then in another whisper he said, 'I will have some food brought in. You can eat while you are talking.'

Geoffrey turned away, towards the bar of light that marked the half-open door of the hall. If anyone else had left it open like that, he would have sworn at them and probably had them beaten. After the sweating and cursing of the long summer, it had begun to rain early in September, and it had not stopped. They could count on one hand, it seemed, the number of dry days until Christmas. January had been no different, except that it was much colder. The great western sea sent its clouds to whip them endlessly with wind and water. Everything dripped and shivered. Logs hissed and spat. Clothes continually steamed on inside lines. Floor rushes smelt far worse; dogs took one look at the weather and relieved themselves indoors when they were not being watched.

'What about me?'

The voice came out of the darkness behind Thierry's horse.

Geoffrey stopped, swung round, and squinted into the murk.

'Who are you?'

'Ranulf of Dreux – master engineer.'

Geoffrey scowled.

'I know what you are; I hired you.'

'Your man made me an offer, my lord. I have not yet accepted.'

'You are here.'

'In the face of exceeding difficulty, may I say. If the problems of the work you contemplate match the hardships of the journey, my lord, I am not at all sure . . .'

Oh, God, not another one. Recommended by Goscelin – I should have known.

Geoffrey resumed his trudge back to the hall. He called over his shoulder.

'See to him, Ivo . . .'

'Well, what then?'

Thierry stifled a burp, and wrenched his eyes away from the new fittings of the hall. Always there was something new. Probably concentrating on indoor work; Goz could not be expected to accomplish much outside in this weather.

'Where was I?' Thierry caught sight of the look on Geoffrey's face, and frowned fiercely. 'Ah. Yes. Yes. Dreux. It seems I had missed Ranulf by only a week. I went through Paris, to pick up the news, as you said.'

In answer to Geoffrey's look of concern, he held up a hand.

'I was careful, as you told me. Pretended to have a stutter. W - w - w - would you like a sample?'

Thierry pulled the most painful faces. Ivo and Ralph guffawed. The servants at the back of the hall nudged each other and sniggered.

Thierry took advantage of the respite to snatch another pasty.

'Had them all falling about laughing. Thought I was half-idiot. They talked about me as if I were not there. You would be surprised at what I heard.'

Geoffrey glared.

'Well?'

'I can tell you, for instance, why the King did not move against the Duke during the summer.'

'Oh?'

Thierry had rarely enjoyed himself so much. All eyes were upon him.

'Had big plans. Italy. Join the Pope and snatch the lands of the Hautevilles.

Crossing the Alps and taking on the Guiscard – can you imagine? Bewitched, he was. Rome . . . Empire . . .' He tugged at a bit of gristle between his teeth. 'Funny how they all get fascinated with Italy. Now if you ask me – '

Ivo nudged him sharply.

'What? Yes, well, as I say, he thought about Italy a long time. Collected a lot of troops too. His own men and mercenaries. I have an idea I saw that creature Fulk there, with his crew.'

Geoffrey looked at Ivo. With a scheme like that – and no doubt vast promises of enough loot to dazzle his imagination, it was small wonder that King Henry was not pursuing the Normandy campaign with suitable vigour. It also gave him a splendid excuse to carry on with his favourite policy – of waiting to see. Enguerrand of Ponthieu had not moved. Neither had the north-eastern vassals of the Duke. The Count of Anjou had burned his fingers in the west. There was no decision at Arques – Count William was sitting behind his stone walls – hungrily, no doubt, but still sitting – and defying an irate Sir Walter Giffard to do his worst. There was no question of the Duke attacking royal territory, of carrying the fight to the King; the Duke would not bear arms against his feudal overlord unless pressed to the point of fighting for survival.

It suited the King down the ground – dream, boast, accept the Pope's money, and wait for someone else to take a decision.

'Hoping for his enemies to cancel each other out,' said Ivo, finishing it for him.

Geoffrey turned back to Thierry.

'What happened?'

Thierry brushed some crumbs away.

'The feudal levy went back at the end of their term, and the mercenaries mutinied. Boredom, mostly. He had to send them away. Would have torn the place apart.'

'Including Fulk?' said Ivo, who was thinking of scores worth settling.

'Far as I know,' said Thierry.

There was a lull. Thierry looked nervously from Ivo to Geoffrey and back again, trying to chew as silently as possible.

Geoffrey rubbed his cheek with a fingertip.

Desperately, Thierry jumped into the yawning gap in the conversation.

'Ranulf,' he said. 'Shall I tell you how I found Ranulf?'

'Yes,' said Geoffrey with ominous quietness.

Thierry swallowed an enormous mouthful.

'As I said, I missed him at Dreux. Heard he had gone north. I followed the gossip. Seems people remember him. An awful misery. If there is a black side to look upon, Ranulf will find it. All dumps and humps. Make a good cleric – sorry, my lord. Slipped out.'

'Get on with it.'

'You will never guess where I found him.'

He paused, and looked again at his listeners. Geoffrey's face was clouding darker and darker. Ralph grimaced a warning.

'Arques!' Thierry burst out, more loudly than necessary. 'Yes, Arques,' he repeated, regaining control. 'He had gone to work for Sir Walter Giffard. Siege engines. Yes.'

'How did you persuade him to come away?'

'Your money, my lord, and – though I say so myself – my own persuasive powers. I get on with these temperamental people. Look at Goz.'

'More likely he fell out with Sir Walter,' observed Ivo.

Thierry turned on him in amazement.

'How did you know that?'

'Because I know Sir Walter,' said Ivo. 'He has been fretting in front of those stone walls at Arques for months, and getting nowhere. Along comes some misery-laden outsider – and a commoner to boot – and tells him he is making a mess of it. Worse still if Sir Walter knows the commoner is right. He kicked him out – yes?'

Thierry nodded reluctantly.

'Yes, as a matter of fact he did.'

'So he came back with you because he had nothing better to do.'

Thierry looked crestfallen.

'My lord's money did help. And I did tell him good things about Coutances.'

Before the lull turned into another oppressive silence, Thierry jumped in yet again. He cleared his throat.

'I – er – stopped at Montbrai on the way, and saw my lord Mauger.'

He licked his lips. Ivo lowered his head and waited for the inevitable. Poor Thierry had been trying to stave it off ever since he had started.

'Where is he?' said Geoffrey at last. 'What news have you?'

Thierry looked for moral support to Ivo, but saw only the top his head. Ralph had disappeared.

Thierry swallowed. This was going to be worse than his recent painful interview with my lord Mauger.

'Well – this is hearsay, you understand, my lord. Only hearsay . . .'

Geoffrey lifted one of his elbows off his knees and poked the fire. He pushed scraps of moss and bark towards the embers with the end of his stick. Taking careful aim, he flicked Thierry's apple core neatly into the heart of the flames.

So Torf had moved up in the world. In the King's counsels now. Maybe the Count of Anjou had been thankful to get rid of him. His advice had not been much good to the Count's invasion.

Geoffrey shook his head. The man's resilience was unbelievable. Picking up the message between Thierry's gossip, it appeared that Torf had talked himself into the position of resident expert on Norman loyalties at the King's court. Giving advice on who could be bribed and who could be scared; who needed coercion and who needed to be eliminated. Now Henry had sent him to Enguerrand's base in Ponthieu, and from there he was going round the vassals of the north-east, to try and bring about some sort of joint action. Waverers would be cajoled with fine words; hawks would be baited with promises of much loot.

'A serpent's tongue on horseback,' was Ivo's comment.

It decided the next move, at least.

'I shall send Ralph north to listen. When Enguerrand moves on Arques, we shall be there,' said Geoffrey. No doubt brother Mauger would resolve to do the same. Ralph too, though for different reasons.

It was obviously on his mind from day to day. Revenge for a wronged father. Ralph wept when he spoke of it.

'He was cheerful. He was trying to be cheerful. He waved his stump in the air like – like a defiant battle standard. A man who had harmed nobody.'

Geoffrey toyed with more embers.

Perhaps the pursuit of Torf would offer some balm to his own pain. He had held the child only twice. He felt again the anguish from the sight of his pinched little face, and the ever-present dried vomit round the pouting bud of the lips.

Sybil had gone. Neither he nor the greatest efforts of the lady Fressenda had prevailed against her sleep-walking resolve. Her brothers would take her, naturally.

Roger kissed his mother on her cheek by way of farewell.

'Would you have expected a daughter of yours to be other than steadfast in her decision?' he asked.

Aubrey and Roger had escorted her to Rouen, to the house of St. Amand. The lady Emma, Fitzosbern's mother, had been very kind, they said. Humbert stayed behind with the lady Fressenda, and neither could think of anything to say to the other for a fortnight.

Geoffrey sighed and looked glum. Perhaps in the spring, when she had had time to reflect in different surroundings . . . Though only God in His Wisdom knew when he was going to be free to visit her.

Goscelin was already behind his own plans, thanks to the diabolical weather. That did not prevent him, however, from presenting Geoffrey with terrifying lists of 'necessary' expenses. Nothing was right – the timber, the mortar, the stone, the ropes. He talked about new quarries much further away, and went into a maze of detail about quality and style of granite. To Geoffrey stone had always been stone. It meant more carts, longer journeys, higher wage costs. It was never-ending. The new manors were beginning to show signs of solvency, but they needed time to develop. His new knights were working hard at home when their military training permitted, but it was not enough. He had plans for a market in Coutances, but it would take years to show a regular profit.

Canon Peter, the chamberlain, was anxious to obtain furnishings for the episcopal offices, cloth for new habits. Everyone was infected with the new disease of spending. Goscelin's foreman had faced him one morning with a demand for silver chasing on his wand of office – said he had heard it was common practice. The gall of the man!

Some day, and not too distantly, Geoffrey knew he would have to go to Italy again. Better hurry up, before the Guiscard was swamped by this huge alliance of the Pope's. Would there be any Hautevilles left to beg from by the time he arrived?

Geoffrey tossed the stick into the fire. First things first. As if in response to his movement, he heard a sound at the door. He looked up.

'Your man Ivo said you would see me, my lord.'

'Ah! Come in. Approach, approach. Sit down. Ranulf, yes? You have fed well? ... Now, about these walls ...'

*　　*　　*　　*　　*　　*

The lady Fressenda flopped into the chair, leaned back, and shut her eyes. She was breathing hard, and her chest pounded, but she felt pleased with herself.

It had been worth it if only to see the consternation on their faces. When she appeared in the doorway of the kitchen, Alice had screamed in shock; two more girls dropped bowls and contents where they stood, rooted to the spot in disbelief.

When she clapped her hands and waved her stick, everyone ran to obey as if the Devil were after them. Never, in nearly forty years, had she enjoyed such speed and co-operation when she went through the remains of the winter stores and made her plans for the new, thrusting year.

'Saints and angels, what have you been up to these last few months?'

'Oh, my lady!'

Gaping and trembling, they were deprived of the power of reasoned speech. No tricks, no hasty whisperings, no furtive clatters, no excuses – just silent awe as if they were witnessing a re-incarnation.

There had been wisps of warning, of course, ever since the famous mass for

Master Drogo, and the drama in the aisle . . .

'I saw her with these eyes – on her own – standing.'

'She had reached the hearth from the foot of the ladder – and there was no one else there. She must have done it by herself.'

'She is eating more. I have to take things to her. She says it is for the dogs.'

'Something happened in chapel that day. I swear it was a miracle.'

'Have you noticed she spends more time down in the hall these days?'

'There is something on her mind. You can tell.'

'The lady Sybil, silly.'

'No – more than that. She looks into the distance. She does not notice things as she used to. Alice dropped her needles the other day, and she never said a word.'

The lady Fressenda waited for her breath to come back. Alice and Hawise hovered in the background, craning to see whether she was going to sprout wings and take off. She waved them away.

'Stop goggling and get my broth. I am not a ghost.' They hesitated. 'At any rate not yet!' she added. They bolted.

Fressenda hitched up a blanket and made herself comfortable. She was fully aware of the sensation she had caused, and had enjoyed every minute of it.

Perhaps they were right; perhaps it was a tiny miracle. It had been a gradual miracle, for all that. When she had fought her way down the aisle on Drogo's saint's day, she had no plan beyond getting to the altar rail. It was only a few days afterwards, when she had recovered from the strain, that it occurred to her that if she could do it once, she could do it again.

Furtively, when nobody was there, she took to trying a few steps. Slow, and painful, yes, but steps undeniably. Unaided too, except for the stick. Next day, she tried again, and managed some more.

It became a regular task which she set herself. Accustomed to the loneliness of authority, she accepted readily the equal loneliness of the challenge. Natural cunning also told her that this was best kept secret until it could be employed to advantage. She once fell, and explained the accident by lying that one of the girls had let her slip and had run away.

'Do not punish her; she was only afraid.'

It made Alice even more frightened of her.

If she were honest with herself, she admitted that it had been partly forced on her by circumstances. Sybil had gone, so there was one less steadying hand at her elbow. With the child dead, there was no need to sit for hours watching and ministering. She got fidgety; she could not sit at the stitching frame all day. As her infirmity had increased, her neglect of household detail had grown in proportion; some of the servants were getting away with murder. The more she learned to move, the more she could regain her grip. They would not obey an invalid for ever. She found too that the physical effort eased the pain of loss and softened the blow of Sybil's departure.

Muriella was also gone – married, at last, to a long-suffering, and desperate, widowed knight of Isigny.

Young Tancred had long since left to join his brothers in Apulia. Aubrey was itching to go. That left only Roger and Humbert. Humbert was duller than Serlo – if that were possible – and Roger, she suspected, was waiting at Hauteville only out of love and duty towards herself.

She did not know which was worse – to sit and watch Roger wait for her to die; or to make Roger go, and face life at Hauteville opposite Humbert as the sole occupier, with Constance wailing in the background at being left on the shelf. All she would have to look forward to was another solemn-faced, toe-twiddling messenger – 'It is my sad duty, my lady, to bring you the most tragic news from Apulia . . .

From what she had heard of this tremendous alliance of the Pope's against her son – Henry the King, Henry the Emperor, the Greek Emperor, dozens of Italian counts and princes – it could not be long now.

She looked up at a small sound. Nobody was there. A bowl of broth steamed at her elbow.

She sat up and began to sip.

She had tried to make Sybil fight. Was she about to give up herself?

*   *   *   *   *   *

Geoffrey met Ralph in the stable yard. He was so anxious that he elbowed the boy out of the way and grasped the bridle himself. A strong westerly wind blew his thick black hair forward over his ears and brow.

'Well?'

'It is as you suspected, my lord,' said Ralph. He dismounted and handed the reins to the boy, who, after a frightened glance, eased the bridle out of Geoffrey's hand. 'The Duke anticipates a move from Ponthieu some time in the summer.'

Geoffrey waved an impatient hand.

'I could have heard that from any message from Fitzosbern. I sent you to find out for yourself.'

'Patience, my lord,' said Ralph, pulling down his jerkin and taking off his gloves. He was developing Ivo's habit of ease and assurance with his master without any loss of respect or courtesy. Geoffrey valued it, and in a quieter moment would have felt proud of it; it was a sign of Ralph's confidence in him. Now he merely waited and glared.

Ralph gestured towards the hall.

'Away from the ears, perhaps?'

Geoffrey grunted.

'Privacy? In my hall? You must be joking. It is full of petitioners. Come to the training field. All the knights are on their own demesnes at the moment.'

They waded through a meadow by the River Soulles, where the thick grass swayed and flattened in the wind; great surging bars of lighter green billowed continually from one side to the other.

Ralph gestured to his right.

'The hay should be good this year, especially after all that rain.'

Geoffrey grunted.

'Need some sun. Plenty of sun. Talk to me as we walk.'

'I did as you requested, my lord. I went to see for myself. As far as the frontier at Eu. The Duke gave me free passage at the castle there. I fed very well too. Ponthieu is bustling. I really think that Enguerrand is going to move soon. Or at any rate as soon as the hay is in.'

Geoffrey grunted again.

If Enguerrand was typical of border counts, he would not be able to keep sufficient discipline over his troops to prevent them wasting senselessly and indiscriminately, hayricks and all. So he would have to bring a lot of his own fodder with him in the baggage train.

'What about the King?'

'Alas, my lord, I did not have time to go to Paris as well, but the Duke's best intelligence is that Henry plans to move at the same time.'

'So the great Italian adventure is over?' said Geoffrey as they reached the training field. They picked their way through the hoof-ridden mud in the gateway.

Ralph smirked.

'The Pope's money is drying up. Henry now feels that there is more loot, and more easily available, in Normandy. But he will wait for Enguerrand to come down south first towards Arques.'

'Typical,' sneered Geoffrey.

'He plans to wait for the Duke to attack Enguerrand by way of shielding his besieging force at Arques, and then he will take the Duke in the rear.'

'Sounds clever, I know. But it still means that he waits for someone else to make the first move.'

Arques was vital. If neither Enguerrand nor the King made any serious attempt to raise the siege of Arques, not only would Count William, and his wife – Enguerrand's sister – and the whole garrison starve; the vassals of north-eastern

Normandy, faced with a triumphant Duke, would think again about joining the conspiracy. It could turn the whole tide of affairs. Sir Walter Giffard's family lands were between Enguerrand and Arques; he would fight like a demon to save them from the wasting parties. Probably why the Duke had chosen him in the first place.

He heard a polite cough slightly behind him.

'If my lord will slow down just a little. I have been in the saddle for three days.'

'What? Oh.'

Geoffrey allowed Ralph to catch up, and they resumed together.

'There is news from England too.'

'England?'

'Yes. Earl Godwin is dead.'

'Godwin!'

'Yes. Choked to death on a piece of bread. Quite a story. It seems – '

Geoffrey waved away the gossip.

'Are you sure of this? Does the Duke know?'

Ralph nodded.

'Got it from a ship fresh out of England – Dieppe. Near Arques.'

'Mmm.'

Did that bring the crown nearer the Duke's grasp, or put it further away? Godwin had been the leader of the Saxon interest, for all that he was half Danish himself. When he and his sons had returned from exile, it had meant the expulsion of Archbishop Robert of Jumièges from Canterbury. Many Normans, afraid of Saxon reaction, had left England with him. What would happen now? Would King Edward recall his old Norman friends, or would he still be in the clutches of Godwin's arrogant brood of sons? Sweyn was dead, and good riddance, but Harold was, by all accounts, of great promise. Would he succeed to his father's earldom of Wessex? What of the others? Tostig, the unstable one, had married a half-sister of Count Baldwin of Flanders. Since the lady Matilda was Count Baldwin's daughter, that made Tostig some kind of uncle by marriage to the Duke – father-in-law's half-brother-in-law, to be precise. Holy Virgin! Whose side would Tostig be on if it came to a clash?

'What are the other brothers called?'

'After Harold?' Ralph produced a handful of fingers, and began to count them off. 'Tostig. A charmer, but unreliable, I hear. Prone to jealousy. Then there is Gyrth. Leofwine. I know nothing about them. And the youngest of course is here. Wulfnoth.'

'What outlandish names!'

Wulfnoth, a mere boy, was at the Duke's court, a hostage – a pledge for the good behaviour of Godwin. King Edward's idea, presumably. What would happen to the boy now?

'I should think the Duke will hang on to him even tighter,' said Ralph, who was catching Ivo's habit of following his thoughts. 'If Harold should come out as the leader of a new Saxon interest against Normandy, the Duke will need that guarantee for his own succession.'

'Mmm.'

'Could the Duke not go to England again, and get a proper statement from King Edward?'

'How can he?' said Geoffrey testily. 'With things as they are. Use your sense, man.'

'Sorry, my lord.'

They continued wading through the swaying grass.

'I have a favour to ask, my lord,' said Ralph suddenly.

Geoffrey looked up.

'Oh?'

Ralph came straight to the point.

'When we move against Enguerrand, may I ride with the knights? May I be excused from scouting?'

Geoffrey looked at the intent, travel-stained face, then looked away. Ralph was not properly trained for knightly combat, nor did he have a proper mount for it. Both of them knew that. Both knew that the risks were therefore that much higher. Geoffrey had come to rely upon this young man; he liked his approach; no fuss. Be honest – he liked him too.

Geoffrey knew what was driving him. He knew that Ralph would ask to leave his service altogether if he did not see a chance to fulfil his desire. Fressenda had told him that. Besides, he had earned his chance. He had a right to it – risks and all. Geoffrey grimaced; he too was being driven by a similar devil.

'So be it.'

'Thank you, my lord.'

When Ralph had gone, Geoffrey continued by himself, round and round . . .

To that young man, revenge was as much a cold fact as next winter. It was coming, and it was to be lived for, and it was certain – nothing else.

Would he, my lord Bishop of Coutances, face Torf with the same resolve when the time came? In passion he suspected he could be capable of anything. But in cold blood. Deliberately. Perhaps it would be better if it came in action, in heat . . .

He shrugged. Mauger would be there too. God's Teeth, between the two of them, they should be able to see the creature into the Fire which his diseased soul so greedily deserved.

If he concentrated upon his anger, at least it might help to bandage the wounds of his grief, if only for a while. He remembered the many times Mauger used to tease him when he was small. Twisting his wrist with both his hands in different directions, so that the skin burned; crushing nettles into the soft underside of his forearm; dropping sand down the neck of his jerkin. He discovered that by striking out in rage he forgot his pain.

Right now he felt he could strike out at anybody, friend or foe, if he thought for one minute it would ease the pain.

*   *   *   *   *   *

Chapter Eighteen

Sybil sighed.

'Maybe, maybe, maybe. Perhaps if Raoul had lived.'

Geoffrey spread his hands.

'We could have had some more.'

'Could have had', noted Sybil. Not 'could have'. Significant.

Geoffrey looked over his shoulder. The lady Emma, abbess of St. Amand, stood by the window, letting the warm summer sun stream over her face. If she was trying to overhear, she betrayed no sign of it.

Nevertheless, he kept his voice down.

'It is no vulgar liaison that I seek. I am prepared to kill to secure you in grace and peace.'

'No, Geoffrey. You are prepared to kill to secure *yourself* in grace and peace, to honour the memory of your father. I am still not sure that marriage will bring you that which you say you seek. I certainly do not think that it will bring it to me.'

Geoffrey resisted the urge to get up and start pacing.

'You talk as if you were the only one in the world with a conscience.'

'I am the only one in the world with *my* conscience,' said Sybil. 'I can not speak for anyone else.'

'You had no such scruples when – when we first began.'

Sybil smiled briefly but fondly at the recollection.

'That was a whole century ago. Things change.'

'I have not.'

Sybil put a hand on one of his.

'But you have, my love.'

'I do not see it.'

'You are different. Think of the mitre that you wear. Think of the pain that it first caused you. Are you struggling now to shed it?'

'That is not fair,' said Geoffrey. 'You are playing with clever arguments. Trying to trap me.'

'It is what you used to do with me.'

'I am a prince of the Church. It is because I am such that I can make you such a good offer. Wife of a prince! How many women will rank above you? Think of it.'

'Geoffrey, it can not be done.'

'It is being done all the time. *Popes* have had wives before now. The Duke's chaplain, Father Arnulf, has a wife, and a daughter, right under the Duke's nose.

The Duke himself defied a ban of Pope Leo to marry the lady Matilda.'

Sybil sat back in stubborn silence, her jaw tight.

Geoffrey glanced over his shoulder again. The lady Emma had her back to them. Her shadow threw a great long bar of darkness across the sun-blazed wooden floor, all the way to Sybil's stool.

'Take my case,' persisted Geoffrey. 'When Mauger bought me the mitre, I freely own I was appalled. But when I found out how common the practice was, I was forced to change my mind.'

Sybil smiled.

'Oh, my darling, you will have to do better than that.'

'It is true,' said Geoffrey stoutly. 'And look at the bishops on our own doorstep. Hugh of Lisieux has a wife. Bishop Yves of Sées has had one for years. God's Bread – even Odo keeps a woman at Bayeux, at his age. Little puppy.'

'And Pope Leo,' said Sybil. 'Does he? And Hildebrand? And Abbot Hugh of Cluny? Do they? Does Lanfranc?'

Geoffrey said nothing.

'Now tell me,' persisted Sybil. 'Which of all these men do you talk of? Which do you admire? Which do you respect? Which are adornments to their Church?'

Geoffrey sighed. Sybil held his hand again.

'I admire the same ones, my love. And I want you to be among them.'

Geoffrey shook off her hand almost roughly.

'You are not doing this all for me, any more than I am doing it all for you.'

Sybil sat up stiffly.

'Very well then. If thus you will have it. I do not know why I am doing it. I know only that I can not do what you ask.'

Geoffrey stood up.

'So be it.'

Sybil's face puckered in grief.

'And I love you.'

As Geoffrey left the room, he did not speak to the lady Emma. If he opened the gate to words, he would open the gate to tears.

Damn Mauger, and damn him – 'I know you, Geoffrey; you do things right through.'

*   *   *   *   *   *

'*Ite, missa est.*'

One or two knees cracked audibly as older vassals puffed to their feet. The congregation stood in respectful silence as the Duke and his lady left the chapel. Matilda's second pregnancy was just beginning to show. Early morning sunlight flooded the nave from a small square window behind the altar left open in the recent hot weather. It caught Matilda's shoulders; she positively glowed with health.

Geoffrey felt well pleased. In the absence of Archbishop Mauger – deserted to join the rebellion of his brother, Count William of Arques – the Duke had ordered those bishops present to take turns each morning with early Mass. Bishop Yves of Sées and Hugh of Avranches were seasoned practitioners, and wasted not a moment of valuable Council time with long-drawn-out liturgy. The Duke's recent creations, however – Hugh of Lisieux, Odo of Bayeux, and Geoffrey – were anxious to outdo one another. Hugh and Odo both lingered over pompous detail and solemn ceremonial till the Duke, normally a patient man before the altar, began to fidget. Only Geoffrey had the wit to keep a sense of proportion.

'Congratulations,' said Roger of Montgomery afterwards, while they waited in the hall. 'I heard him humming as he walked up the aisle. First time in six days he has done that.'

'You should have heard what he said to brother Odo,' said Walter Giffard, with a smirk. 'Told him not to fill his tiny head with pomp and incense.'

Geoffrey smiled.

'I should have liked to be there.'

Giffard laughed.

'A wonder it is that his mitre does not fall over his ears. With a head like that, his mother must have dropped him without knowing.'

Sir Walter Giffard was in a most cheerful frame of mind. After the recent months of nail-biting frustration before the walls of Arques, any excuse to get away was welcome. It was a joy to him to be again in the company of his peers, to exchange gossip, feel good strong boards under his feet, eat decently-cooked food. He drew strength from his own kind. It was small payment indeed – enduring early Masses from spotty-faced brothers of the Duke.

Good cheer verily seemed to be present on all sides. The Duke told everyone – several times – what they could already see for themselves, namely, that the lady Matilda was again with child. His firstborn, Robert, was brought forward to crawl and bawl in public for loyally admiring eyes. Roger of Montgomery was plagued with ribald jokes about his greater feat in bringing about a similar condition in his wife, the lady Mabel – whose reputation for spite and hooded malice left the average viper well in the shade. He endured the sallies with his customary quiet patience. Bishop Odo, flushed with the success of his newly-begun cathedral, enjoyed numerous cheap jibes at the expense of the pile of granite rubble at Coutances; Geoffrey in return was gratified with his own stroke of guile – he lured away several of Odo's masons with higher wages.

Sir Walter Giffard had received happy news from his home at Longueville-sur-Scie; seven of his prize mares had been delivered of healthy foals. The others were progressing most satisfactorily. The money he had paid for the Spanish stallions looked like proving a wise investment. Three of the Duke's vassals had already shown interest.

The summer sun gave its warm blessing to everyone's backs. The hay was pouring in sweet and fast. Stores were up. Crops were coming along nicely. Every afternoon, when the business of the Council was over, the Duke hunted, with great success. Never stopped humming, they said. Pulling Fitzosbern's leg. Both of them romping like boys.

Count Enguerrand of Ponthieu was on the move; it could not be long now. But what of him? What of the startled rabbits in north-east Normandy and Artois and Beauvais and Vermandois, who had been scared or driven or lured into revolt and conspiracy along with him? Bewitched, it was said, by some honey-tongued renegade from the Cotentin. Let them come – King and all. If the Guiscard could do it, the Duke could do it.

Since the second week in July, men had talked of nothing else. The news had flown on wings of fever and fire all the way from Apulia.

A mighty victory – a battle of epic proportions. Civitate. Where? Civitate. Near the shrine of the Archangel Michael at Monte Gargano. As close as that, what else could you expect the Archangel to do but to help? The Hautevilles have made the shrine rich enough.

But you do not know the half of it. The army of his Holiness is destroyed. Cavalry put to flight – all the Italians running like chickens before the Friday chopper. What do you expect? I have always wondered what happened to Roman prowess; it certainly was not handed down to the Italians. What about the Pope's infantry? Swabian giants – the pick of Germany – each and every one six feet tall – professionals. Cut down to a man. The Guiscard was in the thick of it – lance, sword, bare hands. Off his horse three times, but back in the saddle at once. Must have killed dozens. Cut off their heads, they say, just to bring those Swabians down to size. Sir Humphrey of Hauteville was there too. Richard of Aversa. Pah! It was the Guiscard who did it. Taller even than the Swabians. What a voice! What an eye! God's Teeth – what would I not have given to be there.

Where is the King of France now, eh? Shivering by the Seine? Where is the Emperor? Hiding in some Bavarian forest? Where is that decadent despot of Constantinople? Cowering among his pink-skinned eunuchs in his golden, perfumed palace?

That is not the end of it. They have taken his Holiness prisoner. Get away! Gospel. I tell you, the Hautevilles are dictating terms – to the *Pope*.

The stories grew as they flew. Minstrels followed swiftly, and closely, behind, composing their heroic couplets in the saddle, pocketing the proceeds of the new sensation round every camp fire and in every feudal hall from Lombardy to Brabant, from Marseilles to Maine, from the mountains of Savoy to the plain of Paris. Overnight, it seemed, a new hero had arisen to take his place alongside those of the past. Suddenly, the world of knights – and especially Normandy – had a new Roland. Except for the uncomfortable fact that the victory had been won not on behalf of the Holy Father, but against him. The Hautevilles themselves, it appeared, had the grace to shuffle a little shamefacedly about that; Count Humphrey tried to make up for it by making a great show of leading his Holiness's bridle with his own hand whenever they appeared together in public – conducting him from one place of security to another.

William sat up late and often with his close advisers, shaking and sifting the stories and rumours and gossip to get at the truth; shaking and sifting them again to extract the lessons.

How had the Norman forces been deployed? Had Richard of Aversa not been foolish to pursue the Italians right off the field and leave Count Humphrey's flank in the centre exposed? If the Papal army had had a competent overall commander, would they have performed better? How much advantage had been gained by the Normans striking the first blows? Had they not run the risk of tiring themselves by their repeated attacks against the immobile Swabian centre? How effective was the German double-handed sword against mailed Norman knights? What had made the Swabians so difficult to overcome – their numbers, their concentration, their weapons, or their professionalism? What exactly had been the Guiscard's contribution – in tactical rather than personal terms? Was it the shock of his attack? The position of it? Or the timing of it? Was it Richard of Aversa's final onslaught in the enemy's rear that sealed the Swabians' fate? Was it sheer luck that he had returned from the pursuit, or good generalship? How much thinking and discipline was really behind it, and how much good fortune and chance incident? And how much the Hand of God?

Fitzosbern looked at Sir Walter Giffard and read his thoughts: it was diffi-cult to see how God could have chosen to intervene against His own Bishop of Rome, against the Vicar of His own Son. Neither thought it a good idea to upset the pious conclusions of the Duke by voicing misgivings in public.

'Any ideas?' said Roger of Montgomery to Geoffrey afterwards.

Geoffrey shook his head and grinned.

'It is as much as I can do to speak His Word from the altar steps. I have no intention of attempting an interpretation of His Mind.'

Roger laughed.

'Very diplomatic.'

Geoffrey was gratified at being called in to the Duke's Council on two separate occasions; he was not going to jeopardise this favour by speaking out of turn. He found the Duke listening attentively to his account of the battle at Sourdeval against the Count of Anjou, and was flattered by the number of questions asked about the deployment of his knights at the ford.

'This idea of yours,' said the Duke, in his harsh, slightly over-loud voice. 'Concentrated impact. Did it work?'

Geoffrey hesitated.

The temptation was huge. For the last three days they had done little but ponder the glory of the Guiscard's victory, marvel at the power of his personal achievement, drool over the massive loot available in the ruins of a Papal army. Every man on the Duke's Council was envious. Minstrels were already singing the battle into a legend. Honour ... glory ... booty ... what more could a man wish? Geoffrey himself had been given great credit for his victory against Anjou; all he had to do was to claim that his 'master plan' had been a complete success, and he would be given even more. And nobody to gainsay him.

From behind his seat came a familiar sound – Ivo hacking at his cough. Not quite nobody.

Geoffrey took a deep breath. God bless Ivo!

'Only partly, my lord. The first charge was fragmented.'

'Why?'

'Lack of training, lack of discipline, and the ground.'

'You said the ground was good.'

'So it was, my lord. Well chosen by my scouts. Firm and open. But it sloped perhaps overmuch. It allowed too much scope for hotheads to get in front.'

'Would they not have done so anyway?' said Giffard, sticking out his chin. He was rarely impressed by new ideas from young men.

'Probably, Sir Walter, but not to the same extent. I freely admit that I was far from satisfied. But my dissatisfaction lay with the operation of the idea, not with the idea itself. I maintain that, with more training and more discipline, it can be done. There must be more corporate intent; individuals must not be thinking constantly of personal honour and success.'

Giffard bristled.

'Would you take away a knight's honour?'

'No, Sir Walter,' said Geoffrey, meeting him head-on. 'I would give him the chance of more – but through command and control. Through professionalism. What was the strength of those Swabians at Civitate? Concentration, unity of purpose, professionalism.'

'They lost,' said Giffard.

'Only at the end of a long day,' said Geoffrey. 'And only when they were attacked suddenly, and from more than one side. Just as my own men were successful when we were able to use a second wave. It was not the numbers so much as the concentration, the joint impact.'

Geoffrey pounded a fist into his other palm.

'Now just imagine – if we could do that, not with a few score knights, but with several hundred. We should be unstoppable.'

Giffard laughed.

'Ridiculous. You might as well try to keep a landslide together.'

The talk shifted. They spoke of King Henry's present intentions, of the state of his invasion preparations. Of the great debate between the Pope – from his unwelcome position of captivity – and the Patriarch of Constantinople, of their rivals claims of sovereignty.

'Waste of time – theology,' muttered Sir Walter Giffard before he dozed off. 'We are men of this world, not the next.'

They discussed the health of King Edward of England, the recent death of Earl Godwin, the even more recent elevation of his son Harold to the Earldom of Wessex. A new man, Stigand, had been created Archbishop of Canterbury to usurp the place of the exiled Norman, Robert of Jumièges. Uncanonically elected, he was in line for a bull of excommunication from his beleaguered Holiness, who still found time and energy to hurl anathemas from his prison sickbed in Benevento.

The Duke took little part, but was content to let the discussion run on. Not for the first time, Geoffrey noted that William could on occasion be a very good listener.

'And thinker,' said Roger of Montgomery. 'Did you notice his eyes?'

'Restless, you mean?'

'Yes,' said Roger. 'That is when he is watching and listening. But they go still sometimes. That is when he is thinking. He looks as if he is continuing to listen, but he is not; he is thinking.'

Geoffrey grinned.

'You are now going to tell me what he is thinking about, I suppose.'

Roger ignored the thrust in his deliberate, unoffended way.

'Yes, I am. You made him think, with all that talk of hundreds of mailed knights attacking at the same instant.'

'You think so?'

'I know so. And I can tell you why.' He jerked a thumb over his shoulder towards the hall of Rouen castle, where debate and discussion still rumbled.

'They are talking in there about two-handed Swabian swords; the Duke is thinking about two-handed Saxon battle-axes.'

*   *   *   *   *   *

'I want look-outs at every turn of every track. The rest report to the camp; they can help with extra digging. Tell them to cut stakes on the way for the palisade.'

Fulk the Angevin pulled off his gloves and tucked them into his belt.

'My men are trained professional infantry, Sir Walter. They are not scouts and sappers.'

Sir Walter Giffard flushed.

'Your – hirelings are engaged to obey orders.'

'Exactly. The Duke's, not yours. We are an extra shield for the Duke against the King's invasion, not an extra fatigue party for your run-down siege camp.'

Sir Walter tugged unnecessarily at his horse's reins.

'The Duke has no need for infantry at the present; the real fighting is being done by those best fitted to do it – the knights.'

Fulk spat.

'Commanders always need infantry – in the end.'

Giffard smiled in triumph.

'Yes. When it is all over. To dig holes. Meantime, you obey me, because I carry the Duke's commission to hold the lines before Arques. If the King breaks through my force and gets supplies to the castle, it will not be my money that the Duke stops; it will be yours. Now get your men moving.'

Sir Walter dug spurs and cantered back to the siege camp. For an hour he prowled restlessly, while a late sun dispersed the autumn morning mists. He barked orders and swore at every underling in sight, and it was not his usual gruff temper.

He leaned on a gate and bit the side of his thumb.

What was going on in the Scie Valley? Had they reached Longueville? What of his precious horses? He had begged the Duke to let him go with the attacking force.

'My home, sire. The land of my fathers.'

The Duke kissed baby Robert and handed him back to his nurse.

'Precisely why I say no. In an ambush we must have surprise, we must have concerted action, and we must have timing. You could ruin it by rushing to do the natural thing. It is for your own good.'

As the Duke embraced the lady Matilda, Fitzosbern edged up beside him.

'Do not fear for your horses, Walter. Remember, I have a bid in for six of them.'

The Duke whispered to Matilda.

276

'I swear he is more worried about his horses than he is about his family.'

She smiled, and kissed him.

'All the same, look to it. And be careful.'

The Duke swung himself into the big wooden saddle.

'Count Enguerrand will barely see us strike him. The King will not even know that we have left Rouen.' He turned to Sir Walter. 'There is no other man I could safely leave to do what I leave you to do.'

Sir Walter Giffard could think of nothing to say.

Fitzosbern smiled to himself. The Duke was learning.

So the Duke had galloped off in the early hours to catch Enguerrand in the valley of the River Scie, shortly before Enguerrand began his confident last march down the valley towards the relief of Arques and the destruction of Sir Walter Giffard and his besieging force. Enguerrand was so delighted with his plan of coming at Arques from the west instead of from the east, from Ponthieu, that he became careless.

The Duke's ambush took him completely by surprise. Charged by feudal cavalry from both sides, his force splintered at the first onset. Unfortunately, the attackers also fragmented before impact.

It became yet another gigantic brawl of separate skirmishes, random clashes, even a few single combats. Just like Val-ès-Dunes. Geoffrey swore. His long training sessions barely held his own Coutances contingent together; they were disturbed by proximity to the other groups, each swearing slaughter and revenge, each eager for the Duke's favour, each remembering the Guiscard at Civitate, each with an eye, or rather an ear, to the next minstrel's camp-fire song.

Ralph was an offender too. He saw Enguerrand hovering on the edge of the *mêlée*, and urged his horse around the fighting towards him. Long before he could get near, Enguerrand had realised that the adventure was over. He turned, and, with a handful of knights, began the flight.

Ralph lost sight of him in a tangle of brushwood. Thierry appeared on his left hand, and three of my lord's knights of Coutances. Ralph pointed up the Scie Valley from where the attack had come.

'Up there! He flies. Enguerrand. Follow me.'

With his lighter horse, he was soon in the lead. The others, smelling reward from his Grace, or perhaps from the Duke himself, spurred to follow.

Half an hour later, Ralph reined in.

'Well?' said Thierry, puffing beside him. 'Where is he?'

The look on Ralph's face was answer enough.

'Then I suggest we return,' said Thierry. 'We have broken formation as it is, and we have deserted the field with nothing to show for it. God knows what Ivo will say.'

Ralph turned his horse back towards the scene of battle, his face wet with tears of mortification and shame. To have had him so close, and on the run. And he, Ralph of Gisors, a scout, used to following a single man over hard ground – never mind a cluster of galloping horses in panic flight over forest and downland – had lost him. The image of his father came again before his brimming eyes – waving his bloody stump of a wrist in the air. Ralph cried aloud.

'I have failed you – failed you!'

'What did you say?' said Thierry . . .

The Duke reorganised his force at the village of St. Aubin. Casualties had been very light, tactical success complete. Count Enguerrand's invasion column no longer existed as a coherent military unit. The Duke was jubilant; the northern wing of the conspiracy against him had been shattered. With any luck the southern wing would lose the will to attack the victor single-handed.

'Enguerrand has escaped,' reported Fitzosbern.

The Duke shrugged.

'No matter; he will not trouble us again.'

It saved William the problem of deciding what to do with him. He had no jurisdiction over the Count of Ponthieu beyond a very loose, unformalised overlordship. Ponthieu was not part of Normandy. If he had executed Enguerrand, there would have been bad feeling between the two lands for a long time. Better a chastened neighbour than an heir swearing revenge. More embarrassing, his sister Adelaide was married to the man. It could have been very awkward indeed.

'Ha!'

William slapped his thigh.

'Now to Arques. Tell Giffard his precious horses are safe. Come!'

His men cheered as he cantered past. William saluted them with a great wave. He was positively bursting with pleasure. It may not have been an engagement to set beside Civitate; he was no Guiscard – not yet. But it was a start . . .

Half way to Arques they had a shock. For a sickening moment the Duke thought that he himself had ridden into an ambush. It turned out to be the mercenaries, with that blackguard Fulk at their head. They burst like startled game out of the brush.

William reined in furiously.

'Splendour of God! What are you doing here?'

'Completing the work left undone by the cavalry, my lord duke.'

William, shaken at the sudden surprise, and annoyed at his insolence, went red in the face.

'Watch your words, Angevin. I have still to pay you.'

Fulk bowed elaborately.

'As is only right and proper, my lord duke. When you see what I have to show you, what has been achieved by effort over and above the call of duty, I fancy that you will contemplate offering a bonus.'

'Explain yourself.'

Fulk turned and waved to a group of his men.

'Bring on the dancing bear, lads.'

The grinning mercenaries came forward, clustered round a bound and hooded prisoner. At a word from Fulk, they fell back, wrenched off his hood, and pushed him on to the ground at the hooves of the Duke's horse.

A bloodstained Count Enguerrand of Ponthieu spat grass and glared at one and all.

Fulk favoured him with a kick or two in the ribs.

'He ran straight into us. Saved us all a great deal of trouble, do you not think so, my lord?'

William glared down at Fulk.

'Why have you deserted your post?'

Fulk dusted his hands.

'I used my initiative, my lord.'

'Your orders were to guard against any move by the King to relieve the castle of Arques.'

'And so we did, my lord, to the point of total inactivity on the part of the enemy. But you surely would not have wished your crack troops to lose their – cutting edge in the unmanly work of digging trenches and humping timber.' He shrugged. 'So – I decided to seek a little action. After all – ' he smiled devilishly ' – I did feel that we needed to do something to earn our pay.' He winded Enguerrand with another kick. 'And so, it turns out, we have. What more fitting contribution could we have made?' He paused so as to give maximum effect to his jibe. 'Succeeding where your knights had failed.'

William's face went blotchy. His voice dropped to a sinister level.

'You disobeyed orders.'

Fulk was about to bow again, but William kicked his horse forward, and jostled him out of the way.

'Bring him to Arques,' he called out over his shoulder. 'And without further harm. See if you can obey that order . . . '

Sir Walter Giffard offered no excuses, and the Duke piled no blame upon him. The truth was all too obvious.

'They broke through where the Angevins should have been. You can see for yourself.'

279

The Duke nodded, his jaw tense.

'How much damage?'

'Not much,' said Giffard. 'But I lost five good men trying to plug the gap – and failing. They got men and supplies into the castle.'

'How much?'

'Hard to say. Perhaps a score – who knows? Some cartloads of food. I fancy they would have got more, but the news arrived about Enguerrand, and the King thought better of it.'

'How far has he gone?'

'Henry? Only a few miles, but he is still moving south. He is out on a limb now, and it is late October.' Giffard sneered. 'Our sovereign lord is no Guiscard.'

William fumed.

'And Arques is full for the winter.'

He could barely sit still for his anger.

'Where is the Angevin?'

For an hour no man dared go near the Duke's tent. Senior vassals stood in furtive clusters at a safe distance, still able to hear the two raised voices inside. For a while Fulk was giving as good as he got, but as time passed his replies became fewer and fewer, and the Duke's tone dropped.

Roger of Montgomery leaned towards Geoffrey.

'When he is whispering, watch out!'

The flap of the tent was flung back, and the Duke stalked towards his horse. Caught at a standstill, everyone tried to make it look as if they were walking somewhere.

William mounted, called to his squires and personal staff, and was gone.

Shortly afterwards, Fulk appeared. His fleshy face was suffused with blood, his eyes pointed with cruel purpose.

'Aimery!'

Ralph's old comrade appeared breathlessly.

'Get the captive,' said Fulk. 'I want six of you, and I want a block.'

Aimery frowned.

'A block?'

'You heard,' said Fulk, not even looking at him.

Aimery swallowed.

'You mean – like Alençon?'

'A block, Aimery. Bring it with you. And tell no one.'

'Where?'

'In front of the main gate of the castle of Arques . . .'

'Christ and Mary, what a bastard!'

'Why did Giffard not stop him?'

'No time. We had no idea what he was going to do until he called for Enguerrand's sister to be brought up on to the walls. Sir Walter was just about to go and see if his horses were all safe. By the time someone had found him and told him, Fulk had started chopping.'

'The Duke had given orders – safe keeping, he said.'

'What did Fulk care? The Duke had disgraced him in public.'

'Do you think Fulk worked all this out?'

' 'Course he did. I tell you, he is evil, that man. To stand there, counting all the pieces. Looking up at the walls after each one – nose, ears, hands, feet . . . '

The soldier crossed himself.

'Knew what he was doing though, eh? After Alençon.'

The soldier spat.

'He did not care about Alençon, or Arques. He was simply getting his own back. That poor devil Enguerrand was convenient, that was all.'

'It worked. They threw open the gates – thought the Duke had ordered it.'

The soldier shook his head in wonder.

'Do you know what he said when the Duke arrived?'

'No.'

'He flung Enguerrand's privates on the ground in front of him. "Behold!" he said. "The keys to the castle of Arques. Now what about our pay?" '

Ralph turned over and shut his eyes with little hope.

Enguerrand's screams would live in his sleep for a long time. God help his wretched sister; she must have been demented up there.

Ralph thought of his father's severed hand and Enguerrand's dripping sword; he thought of Fulk's dagger in his own stomach . . . and yet . . . He felt almost grateful to Fulk – if that was revenge, he wanted no part of it. Father, he was sure, would understand.

*　　*　　*　　*　　*　　*

Chapter Nineteen

'For God's sake, girl!'

Alice sniffled for the hundredth time.

'I cad dot helb it, m'lady.'

Alice firmly believed that if she gave ample evidence of her distress everyone would feel sorry for her. Repeated efforts in this direction, and repeated failure, in no way diminished her optimism, or her persistence.

Alice and Hawise had been sniffing and sneezing for nearly a week. The lady Fressenda noticed that it was usually mild weather that seemed to bring on these bouts, rarely a cold spell. It was no help towards soothing her mood. Bitter weather gave her something to fight; this never-get-started winter only added to her frustration. Not a decent frost since before Christmas, and it was now the last week of February.

A whole winter of rain and Humbert.

Exactly three paces in from the door he would clap his hands.

'Ah! A good fire, to be sure!'

If Humbert said that once more she would go mad. She now dreaded his return from his rounds.

'Ah! A good fire!'

That would be followed by a series of grunts as he pulled off his boots and leggings and called for something to eat.

'Did you have a good day, Mother?'

He slurped noisily.

It was as much as she could do sometimes to refrain from leaning across the hearth and using one of her sticks to tip his soup into his lap.

As if that were not bad enough, there was still no word from Roger.

'No news is good news, Mother.'

If Humbert had said *that* once, he had said it fifty times.

'No news is good news.'

It was nothing of the kind. It was agony. Roger was the last and the sweetest fruit of her womb (save only Sybil), and right now he could be lying with face upturned in some nameless boundary ditch, or writhing crippled amid a pile of bodies, begging death to release him before the scavengers reached him.

Roger, as usual, had made up his mind with no fuss, and with no consultation with anybody.

'The King is on the march again, Mother. It must be the mild weather that has brought him out early. The Duke needs every man, and he needs them quickly.'

Fressenda made some feeble resistance.

'What about Italy?'

'Italy can wait.' Roger looked at her. 'It has waited until now.'

'You think there are rewards to be had in Normandy?'

'Geoffrey de Montbrai has done well out of it. His brother has hopes. Why not an Hauteville? We are just as loyal. We proved that against the Count of Anjou. I want to be there when the Duke celebrates his victory against the King.'

'And if he does not?'

Roger deliberately missed the point.

'Then there will be plenty of time for Italy.'

Roger squeezed her hand.

'Mother! Anjou suffered a bloody nose, and I was there. Enguerrand of Ponthieu was destroyed, and I was there. The castle of Arques is taken, and the Count of Arques is in exile, along with his brother – our late, unlamented Archbishop. Now – if the King is sent packing, the Duke's triumph will be complete. Nobody can unseat him then. It will be like Robert's triumph at Civitate. And I want to be there. Think of the rewards – all those rebels' estates.'

Fressenda tried again.

'Robert defeated a Pope. An alliance of emperors.'

Roger smiled.

'I shall settle for a mere king for the time being.'

It was useless to try further. He was more steadfast than Sybil.

So now she waited. Just as she had waited for my lord Tancred to recover or to die. Just as she had waited for news of Robert from Apulia, as he and Humphrey and the others braced themselves to face that terrifying alliance of the Holy Father and two emperors. Robert! The eldest of her body, the lion of her brood of adventurers, with his glittering eyes and his booming laugh. She could feel his strong hands as he picked her up bodily and pretended to throw her into the pond, while Sybil and Roger cried in infant alarm. 'No! No!'

'Did you have a good day, Mother?'

A good day – with Constance wailing from her self-imposed exile on the shelf, and Alice and Hawise dabbing wet noses over everything. A wonderful day!

This would never do.

The lady Fressenda looked down at her hands, for once idle. The cost of embroidery was to have Alice and the sniffs at her side. Too high.

Fressenda was proud of her hands. No matter how hard a woman tried to hold back the tide of the years with ointments and potions, how much she veiled her face, how much she wrapped her falling figure in wide gowns, it was her hands which usually gave her away. Fressenda's hands were those of a woman twenty-five years her junior.

The only thing about them now which distressed her was the colour. The time was when they were a rich, healthy brown. So were her arms, her neck. Now they were a dank white, like the underside of a dead fish. All those hours, days, weeks on end in summer, had she spent out of doors on a hundred tasks of supervision – as she had said to Sybil, making Hauteville hers. As often as not there was a little file of infants at her heels – barefoot, half-naked, brown as berries.

'Like a line of ducklings,' my lord Tancred used to say.

She grimaced in distaste as Humbert slurped again.

It was time to try and get out more. There was no ice or frost underfoot. She had been practising all the winter, managing more steps almost every day. As she progressed, it became increasingly more difficult to maintain the secret, but she gradually ceased to care.

Slowly the servants allowed themselves to 'notice' it. One day Alice plucked up the courage to refer to it.

'My lady is a miracle to us all.'

To her amazement, my lady did not box her ears. From then on, her improvement became public property, a shared pride. The moment she saw that it was yet another way to bind them all together, to keep her central position, she began to turn her furtive struggles into an open part of daily household routine.

One of the haywards, after laying a kitchen garden hedge in January, made her another stick. She found it easier to get about with two. Her hands had always been powerful. Now her arms grew stronger too. If she could get out of doors, the fresh air could do nothing but good. Away from smoke, away from Humbert's feet, away from Constance's long face.

As the days went by, she found each effort less fatiguing. The time spent flopped and panting in a chair became shorter and shorter. It did seem as if the girls, for once, were right; God was arranging, it appeared, some sort of miracle.

God did not send miracles for no purpose . . .

Robert had only got where he was because he seized opportunities. However he had won at Civitate, she was sure it was because he had jumped upon every chance that had presented itself – miracle or no miracle.

Roger would return to Hauteville or he would die under the Duke's standard. If he returned, he would either stay or he would in time follow the others to Italy. Whichever he decided, he would wait dutifully for her to die before embarking upon any adventures. Yet now she had never felt less like dying.

She could not hold him back, when she had never stood in the way of the others. Nor could she contemplate the pain of seeing him go.

If, God forbid, he should not return, life held very little for her at Hauteville

. . . Aubrey, furious at having missed the victory of Civitate, had rushed off to Apulia to join in the spoils. Sybil languished in a convent to which she was not suited, because she did not know a good opportunity when she saw one, and Constance really would die an old maid if someone did not put some eligible, and pliable, men in her path. If only she could lay her hands on some funds for a marriage settlement . . .

The lady Fressenda stood at the open door of the hall and looked out at the sky. She snuffed the air and breathed freedom . . .

An outrageous idea was taking shape . . .

* * * * * *

'I am impressed, Geoffrey. I make no bones about it; I am impressed.'

Mauger sat back and undid his belt. He watched while a servant poured more wine. Fresh straw smelled sweet beneath his boots. Three days of unseasonal warm sun in early March had enabled Geoffrey to have his hall thoroughly aired and cleaned. Peter the Chamberlain rushing everywhere with flying skirts. Doors wide open, endless buckets of water, a fury of sweeping and scrubbing and polishing. Small pots of dried petals and herbs refilled and replaced in every alcove and cranny. The last of the noisome hanging hams and the bundles of sprouting onions removed from beams. Cracks between winter-warped planks refilled, sills and steps re-aligned, hinges greased.

It was a pleasure to relax here and eat one's fill.

Geoffrey felt comfortable but by no means satisfied. It would be a long time before his hall attained the grace and smoothness that he had so envied at the house of Lanfranc's father in Pavia. No fashionable glassware, no expensive German silver, no table basking in the glow of generations of elbow grease.

Still, he was proud of what he had been able to show his brother – both in the hall and outside in the town – and he was gratified by the genuineness of his compliment.

Mauger cleared his throat and rubbed his hands.

Geoffrey read the signs.

The relief was past.

They had embraced, and that was that. Mauger gave him a playful punch on the cheek.

The excitement was over.

'We caught them at Mortemer – totally unprepared. Confusion, disgrace. The King's own brother in flight.'

'And Henry?'

Geoffrey slapped his thigh.

'The King is on the run. Never even tried to press on when he heard the news of Mortemer. Turned round and went straight back to Paris.'

Mauger drove a fist into his other palm.

'What a victory! Nobody will dare challenge him now. Anjou, Ponthieu, Arques, the King – he has done for them all. What a man!'

In his delight Mauger slapped the table.

Geoffrey could not resist a reminder.

'What became of your advice to go against him?'

Mauger shrugged hugely.

'A man can make a mistake. I tell you, I would rather own a mistake that puts me on the winning side than own one that puts me with the losers.'

Geoffrey smiled drily.

'Especially when the rewards are handed out. Have you seen yours yet?'

'I have been to Saint-Sever,' said Mauger. 'But not yet to Sourdeval. I expect to give hands for them at Easter. Time enough for that. Now – ' Mauger laughed in sheer pleasure and good spirits, and punched him once more on the chest ' – show me this town of yours. This town at the end of all the world.'

The proud procession was also complete.

The town square, the hall and its surrounding buildings, the new houses; crosses, conduits, paving, troughs; the human anthill on the cathedral site, the forest of ropes and wooden ramps and survey poles; the endless procession of carts and swearing drovers along the line of the new walls; the anguished sensibilities of Goscelin and the surly gloom of Ranulf.

Mauger was newly arrived from his post of frontier guard over against Anjou.

'The Count will not try again. Not after Mortemer. Nobody will tangle with the Duke now. I can go back to Montbrai. I can go and see my new estates.'

Mauger walked beside Geoffrey and listened and stared and was, as he freely admitted, 'impressed'.

It was his turn to tease Geoffrey.

'Are you glad I bought it now?'

Geoffrey grinned and sidestepped.

'You should see what I now have. I once thought Coutances was the end of all the world. Do you know what the Duke has given me now? Jersey and Guernsey.'

Mauger looked blank.

'Where are they?'

Geoffrey flung an arm out towards the west.

'Out there – halfway to nowhere.'

Mauger gaped.

'You mean – islands – out there?'

Geoffrey nodded.

'Yes. They say it is pure paganism. Turf hovels and charms to Odin. God's Bread!'

Mauger laughed. Geoffrey pretended to be cross.

'You just wait. Wait and see what else the Duke finds for you. Some cluster of peat bogs and heathen shrines up in the Cotentin – you see.'

'It is Mortain that I covet. The Duke has dispossessed the castellan, after his poor showing against Anjou. Well . . . '

Geoffrey shook his head.

'Do not count on anything. Look at what I got.' As they walked across the town square, Geoffrey said, 'You never can tell with that man. Do you know what he did after Mortemer? Instead of celebrating? He went round with a long face. And do you know why? Because he had just heard news that King Edward had sent one his bishops – Aldred, I believe – to Germany to search for the Atheling.'

'What is an atheling?'

'Not "what". "Who." "Atheling" is the English word for "prince". The Atheling is the last survivor of the royal family. Edward has no issue. This Atheling is his nearest relative. Nobody knows where he is, and they have sent Bishop Aldred to look for him. You know what that means?'

'No crown for the Bastard.'

'It is beginning to look like that. I smell the work of Godwin's family. No sooner is Harold installed in the earldom of Wessex than Aldred is packed off to look for a Saxon heir. At any rate, that was all William could think about.'

Geoffrey wagged his head in amazement.

'That man had just defeated an alliance so large that it could have swept him away like a leaf in a gale, and all he could think about was getting a crown – a crown, mark you – in a foreign country five times the size of Normandy. Any other man would have fallen on his knees and thanked his Maker. He was swearing and thinking years ahead to the moon.'

'Ah!'

The high spirits were bound to dry up sooner or later, and the leaden weight of hate and revenge began to pull once more at their mind, dragging them down.

The relief was past; Mauger was pleased almost to tears to see Geoffrey safe again after Mortemer. The excitement, the intoxication of victory, the pride in new possession, for all that it was beyond the end of the world; the glow in achievement, the unalloyed pleasure of sharing it with a brother – all were fading.

Mauger had rubbed his hands.

It was time to see to that leaden weight.

'Did you get any news?'

'He has gone south,' said Geoffrey. 'Rumour only.'

'How do you know?'

'My scout, Ralph, has been scouring the Vexin.'

'Dangerous, on his own. Do you trust him?'

'Yes. He has a companion now. A man called Aimery. They have worked together before.'

Mauger frowned in the effort of recall.

'Did he not once belong to the troop of Fulk the Angevin?'

'Yes. They both did.'

Mauger stared.

'And you trust them?'

'I do now. Ralph will carry the scar of Fulk's knife to his grave.'

'And this – Aimery?'

'Sickened by Fulk's work before Arques. After Alençon it was too much. He left.'

'So be it – I accept that they are trustworthy. How can you be sure of their information? Are they not saying this simply in order to please?'

Geoffrey shook his head.

'Looking for Torf is not so difficult as you may think. Or rather finding him is not difficult. The trick is to look in the right place.'

Mauger looked annoyed.

'Do not talk in riddles.'

Geoffrey smiled.

'There can not be many men like Torf of Malbec – you agree? He has a knack of getting himself remembered.'

'So?'

'So – we keep asking questions until we find someone who has recently met him. And we follow.'

Ralph had put it more earthily.

'There is no secret, my lord. I am a scout, used to trailing. You track an animal by its droppings. A serpent like Torf leaves a double spoor – the sweet smell of honeyed promises and the rancid stink of betrayal. We shall soon have news, I assure you.'

'It could be a long trail,' said Geoffrey to him. 'Are you willing to follow it to the end?'

Ralph shrugged.

'You gave me a chance to follow my trail to the end, my lord. It is the least I can do to repay the favour.'

He made no reference to the doubtful rewards that awaited Geoffrey when

288

the quest was over.

Mauger also thought of the moment when Geoffrey and Torf of Malbec would come face to face. His brother had talked with popes and gambled with the Guiscard and sat on the Duke's Council; he had fought at sieges and ambushes; he had looked death in the face at the point of Fulk's knife; he had commanded in the open field; he had given absolution to maimed and gibbering cripples before Alençon. Was that enough to forge and temper the steel for a deliberate thrust of retribution?

He had seen Geoffrey sitting at Mother's knee, copying Latin under Gori's proud eye, saying Mass in the chapel at Montbrai, mooning after that sister of the Hautevilles. Had God, Faith, and Charity taken too big a hand in his education?

Mauger had just followed Geoffrey around his town – seen him arguing with Ranulf beside the first courses of the walls; saying sweet words to Goscelin in the mud of a foundation ditch and furtively dispatching Thierry to get some hot pies for his workmen; wading up to his thighs to examine timbers in a bridge; hectoring and bullying a set of reluctant reeves for being lax with plough team maintenance. Was this the way to create the will of an avenging angel of the Lord?

Would Geoffrey's blood lie cold enough to see that Torf's ran hot?

*   *   *   *   *   *

Sybil kept them waiting. The lady Emma entertained them with conversation until she arrived.

'Hailstorms in May. And after such a mild winter. One simply does not know what to make of the weather these days. I trust your journey has not been too uncomfortable, my lady.'

'We came in easy stages,' said the lady Fressenda. 'I have not travelled for a long time.'

'In safety too, I sincerely hope?'

'No safer hands than those of a prince of the Holy Church.'

Geoffrey smiled.

'I think the knights helped.'

The lady Emma rose.

'I think I hear Sybil now. I shall leave you. Refreshment will be ready whensoever you choose to call for it. My lady. My lord.'

She insisted on kneeling to kiss Geoffrey's ring – Thorold's great ruby set in gold.

'Mother!'

Sybil burst into the room in a flurry of skirts and eagerness, and nearly bumped into the lady abbess. She apologised, and tried to compose her demeanour into something more reverent. Under my lady's eye, she came forward and kissed the ring.

As soon as the door was closed behind her, Sybil flung herself into her mother's arms.

'I am so sorry for being late. The laundry. I now work in the laundry. The old nun in charge died a short while ago. It really is in a most dreadful mess, though I should not be saying so. And before that there was singing practice – oh, we do so much singing. They say I have the head for it.' She laughed. 'Must be the big jaw. But Mother! You! It is a miracle.'

The words tumbled thick and fast. Glowing eyes, pure delight at seeing a beloved parent. A squeeze of the hand for Geoffrey. And questions, questions.

And explanations . . .

Geoffrey could not remember when he had last seen Sybil so happy, and said so. He did not know whether to be pleased or sorry at the sight.

Sybil turned to him in surprise.

'The two people I love most in the world? Why should I not be? And so suddenly. Tell me, how is Roger? He's the third. Has he returned? I knew he was safe after Mortemer. Sir William has visited since the battle.'

So Fitz, besides being a dutiful friend, was also a dutiful son.

Family news, servant gossip, word from Apulia . . . Geoffrey waited with increasing discomfort for the silence to fall. When it did, it did not last long. The lady Fressenda, brisk and businesslike, came to the point at once.

'I shall now tell you why we are here . . .'

Sybil listened with widening eyes.

'Why, Mother? To what end?'

'The journey itself is the purpose. What is there for me at Hauteville?'

'You might die on the road.'

'I might have died on my way to the altar rail for Drogo's Mass, but I did not. I should not have minded if I had; I had a purpose. I have a purpose now.'

'Just for a journey?'

'Do not be stupid. I do not know what will happen. I walked to the rail for Drogo's soul, and this miracle has happened with my legs. I shall go to Apulia to see my other sons. What is the point of waiting in Normandy to hear news of their death? Who knows what will happen when I get there?'

'Practising a few steps in the hall at Hauteville is one thing – '

'I reached here from the Cotentin,' interrupted her mother.

'But it is so far,' persisted Sybil.

'You silly girl, I am not going to walk all the way.'

'Never mind your legs; what about your general health? Journeys like that are fearsome undertakings.'

'There is nothing wrong with me. I am not ill – only old. So the sooner I start the better.'

'And if you die the minute you arrive?'

'Then I shall ask Robert and Humphrey to bury me near the shrine of St. Michael the Archangel at Monte Gargano. Your father always longed to go there. Geoffrey's father used to talk to him about it. Did you know that, Geoffrey?'

'No, I did not. I was too young to understand when Father went away for the last time, and I am afraid my brother did not talk much about you.'

'I knew your mother too. We shall have much to talk about on the road.'

Sybil stared at her mother, then at Geoffrey.

'You are going – together?'

'Yes,' said Fressenda. 'That will save you the trouble of worrying about my safety. I am taking Constance too. Poor girl – we must find a husband for her somehow. Robert can find her a dowry.'

Sybil looked horrified.

'Mother! Robert's soldiers? Where is your sense of dignity?'

'It is not my sense of dignity that is relevant; it is Constance's. She will be only too grateful for almost anything. But do not worry. Robert will find someone suitable, rest assured. His own sister? Some rich Italian count, perhaps, anxious to be an ally of the victor of Civitate. I shall be there too, remember.'

It was only as she said it that the lady Fressenda realised just how much she was looking forward to it. What had begun as an outrageous notion, a mischievous escapade, had become an absorbing purpose, and had now emerged as an all-consuming prospect of unimaginable interest and enjoyability. She could not wait to get there. Once again, she found herself growing more respect and affection for my lord Tancred. It would have been only too easy for him to do what his friend, Sir Nigel of Montbrai, had done, and go careering off to adventures and pilgrimages – Monte Gargano, Compostela, Jerusalem. But he had not; he had stayed to keep guard over his brood of children and his wife; in later years, because he had remained poor, he was forced to break up the household that he had so lovingly built; he had watched, uncomplaining, while one son after another had gone to seek the fortune he had so often coveted, in the land he had so often dreamed about. The pain of separation, the envy of success, the agony of bereavement. He had never said a word.

'What does Roger say about all this?' asked Sybil. 'Surely he tried to talk some sense into you.'

'He said, "Mother, I never thought it would be *you* leaving *me* behind."'

Sybil blinked.

'Is that all?'

'Yes. Roger understands. And so, I am sure, will you, when you have had time to think about it.'

'Why is he not going with you?'

'Roger's plans are Roger's business. I do not intrude there. You must ask him that yourself.' Fressenda looked down at her hands. 'However, we shall be a goodly company – myself, Constance, Geoffrey – and you.'

Sybil sat up straight.

'It took you a long time to get to the point. Not like you, Mother.'

Fressenda was ready for her.

'Do not flatter yourself, my girl. We have not arranged all this solely for your benefit. Be assured that I shall go to Apulia with or without you. Whatever remains of my life has its purpose there.'

Sybil rose to a familiar bait.

'And whatever remains of my life has its purpose here.'

Fressenda flapped a wrist.

'Rubbish. Your life has barely started.'

'I am still the mistress of it. That is what you have always told me.'

'I told you to do something with it, to meet the world, to – '

'Yes, I know, to fight, to rule. Mother, I keep telling you, I am not a fighter like you.'

Fressenda spread her hands.

'But you are, you silly girl. Look at you. In charge of the laundry, and you have barely arrived. Singing. Before long you will be leading the choir. You can not help yourself. You are an Hauteville. You will never be content with rehearsing chants and washing dirty napkins.'

Sybil looked at Geoffrey.

'Tell her, Geoffrey. Tell her why I can not go.'

Geoffrey and Fressenda exchanged glances.

'I may be silly, Mother,' said Sybil, 'but I am not stupid. A prince of the Church is not going all the way to Italy as a bodyguard to an old woman from western Normandy. He is going to seek and find, and probably execute, a man who he considers has done him a wrong.'

'A great wrong,' said Geoffrey.

'You see?' said Sybil. 'And he wants this man's wife to accompany him on the journey so that, when this man is safely into his sinner's grave, she can plunge into an even greater sin by going through a form of illegal marriage with his executioner. Remember, they will be passing through all kinds of holy houses on the way to Italy; there is bound to be an obliging abbot or bishop known to him.

292

A bribe here, a dispensation there . . .'

'That is enough,' said Fressenda. 'I always said that you were the most stubborn of all.'

'I wonder where I get it from?' said Sybil.

*   *   *   *   *   *

Mauger waited until Geoffrey had crossed himself and stood up.

Geoffrey turned to him and indicated the grave.

'Summer flowers too.'

'Every season that permits,' said Mauger. 'I have had them put on Gori's as well.'

'I saw.'

'Why did you come?' asked Mauger. 'It is not the anniversary.'

Geoffrey shrugged. It was hard to put into words. He was about to go to Italy. The lady Fressenda was to accompany him. She had known Mother. Mother came from Italy. It was no more logical than that.

The two brothers started to walk back to the foot of the mound.

'You really are taking the old woman?'

'Yes. I have left her at St. Amand for a week or two – to rest and say goodbye to Sybil.'

'You mean to get her to change her mind?' Geoffrey shook his head.

'I do not think she will succeed. But time enough for that. When I return . . .'

'When *we* return,' corrected Mauger.

A group of men who had been straining at a broken wagon paused to rest their backs. They caught sight of Geoffrey, beamed all over the faces, and waved vigorously. Geoffrey waved back.

'It was my father too,' said Mauger.

'So be it. I can not stop you. I thought you would be occupied with your new estates.'

'I have given hands for them and installed new reeves. It looks as if they have been neglected for years; a few more months more or less. I can be spared – for this. If you can leave your precious cathedral –'

'I can – for this.'

'Then so can I. What amazes me is that you are willing to tolerate the lady Fressenda with you.'

'She wants to go. I can not stop her either.'

'Do you have to act as escort? How do you know we shall finish in Italy? How do you know that Torf will run there?'

We shall finish in Italy because I must ask the Guiscard for yet more money, but if I say that now, I shall get a lecture on grovelling.

293

'If we catch him first, then we go on to Italy for my lady. I should also like to see where Father died. If Torf runs to Italy, it will simplify matters.'

'Sister Constance too, I hear,' said Mauger innocently. 'Are we merely acting as – escort to her?'

'That remark is in poor taste,' said Geoffrey.

Mauger kicked at a molehill.

'This fever for Italy. It is an Hauteville disease. Even their women suffer from it.'

'That family can do nothing right in your eyes, can it? I wonder – something the lady Fressenda said to me – it is not jealousy, is it?'

'That remark is also in poor taste.'

Poor taste, maybe, but near the mark. Sir Tancred had stayed to raise his sons. Sir Nigel had spent much of his life away on adventures. Mauger had had only half a father, Geoffrey barely any at all. Mauger had had to be master of the house at seventeen, and father to his baby brother. Had he resented it? Had he longed for what Sir Tancred had provided for his household?

'I shall leave Ivo behind,' said Geoffrey.

Mauger laughed.

'Have you told him?'

'Not yet.'

'I thought not.'

'Ivo is not getting any younger. His cough is much worse, and his ankle troubles him. One of these days it will let him down, and he will have a serious fall. I am worried about him.'

Mauger nodded.

'I see. And you are going to tell him all this?'

'Yes. I have Ralph, and Thierry. And Ralph's man Aimery. I shall take six of my own knights. As many servants. My crozier too will act as a shield. Roger will send men from Hauteville.'

Mauger laughed again. Geoffrey flushed.

'What is so funny?'

'I was thinking: if you can not stop me coming with you, and you can not stop the lady Fressenda, what makes you think you can stop Ivo?'

*   *   *   *   *   *

294

Chapter Twenty

'Paris?' said Geoffrey in amazement.

'Why not?' said the lady Fressenda. 'Torf was with the King when last we heard of him.'

'My lady, surely you have not forgotten that the King is smarting from what the Duke did to his army at Mortemer.'

'The campaign is over. They have made their peace. And surely *you* have not forgotten that it was the King's brother who was defeated at Mortemer. The Duke did not have to raise arms against his feudal overlord after all.'

Geoffrey looked doubtful.

'All the same – '

'All the same,' persisted the lady Fressenda, 'it would be sensible for you to travel as a bishop rather than as a knight. A lady and her daughter on a pilgrimage for the soul of her husband and dead sons, guarded by a prince of the Holy Church. What harm would we be to anybody?'

If it were possible to produce a smile with barbs on it, the lady Fressenda did so.

Geoffrey hesitated.

'You said it would be easier for me to travel by water as far as possible,' said my lady.

'I meant the Loire,' said Geoffrey.

'Loire or Seine – what does it matter? Surely we are more likely to pick up news in the King's lands than in those of the Count of Blois?'

Ivo cleared his throat.

'My lady could well be right, my lord.'

'You – be silent!' snapped Geoffrey.

Ivo and my lady exchanged confident smiles. . .

They had appreciated each other from the first. Fressenda realised that Ivo was the best way into Geoffrey's head.

'Give me an hour with any group of serving girls in any holy house or tavern within twenty miles of Paris, and I shall bring you news of every man who travelled the main roads in the last month.'

'I shall see what I can do, my lady,' said Ivo. 'But he does not like being managed.'

'I know . . .'

Geoffrey paced for a while, and came to a halt in front of Ivo.

'Very well. Up the Seine it is. But we still overlook nothing. Ralph and Aimery will check as far north as Noyon – just to make sure that he has not doubled back. They will then cross to Rheims, and come down the main road to join us at Paris. We shall wait there, then at Corbeil, Melun, and Sens. We shall follow the Yonne to Auxerre.'

He turned to Fressenda.

'My lady must not forget that one can gather gossip around camp fires as easily as in a convent guest chamber or a tavern.'

He swung back to Ivo.

'And do you send two of Roger's men back to Bellême.'

Ivo frowned.

'Bellême?'

'If you want plans altered, you must inform your allies of the fact. They must tell Sir Roger of Montgomery of our proposed change of route. They will then go on to say the same to Sir William Fitzosbern and Sir Walter Giffard. If the creature tries to get back into Normandy, they will hear sooner or later, and they will then know where to send the news.'

'Suppose he goes back to the Cotentin?'

'True ... Then they go on to Hauteville and tell Roger as well. After that, they rejoin us on the Seine. We shall be going in easy stages because of my lady.'

'What do you wish me to do, my lord?' said Ivo.

'You and Thierry,' said Geoffrey, 'will swing west, out to Orleans. Take the Roman road down to Bourges, double back, and pick us up at Auxerre.'

'A long detour,' observed Ivo.

'Indeed,' said Geoffrey. 'I intend to leave no hole for this rat to escape.'

'Ah!'

Geoffrey glared.

'You wanted to come.'

*   *   *   *   *   *

Constance edged her horse up besides Mauger's.

'Is it not a delight to ride on an afternoon such as this?'

'Certainly better than a boat,' admitted Mauger.

'You dislike boats?'

'Yes.'

Mauger, from force of habit, scanned the borders of the road ahead. Beside them on one side the Seine sauntered through summer-soaked furrows of ripening grain. Lazy boys dozed, and allowed sheep to wander over boundary banks. On the edge of a village common a self-satisfied magpie perched on the back of a piebald cow. At the fringe of the forest two men were stripping a newly-felled trunk to replace a rotted gatepost.

Constance prattled on.

'I too do not like boats. I was so glad when you decided to ride for a change.'

'We are not all old women,' said Mauger gruffly.

'I do so agree. It is not often understood that we young women can ride, though, sadly, we do not get as many chances as we would wish.'

Mauger looked at her briefly, and turned away again.

'You ride well,' he said.

Constance laughed.

'With twelve brothers, what would you expect? We learned to ride, or we stayed at home and missed all the fun.'

'Yes.'

'It is a pity that you did not visit us more in time past.'

'Busy,' said Mauger. 'Lot to do. I was master, remember. At a very young age.'

'Indeed?'

'Seventeen.'

Constance gaped.

'Seventeen! Truly a heavy burden for one so young. So little time for – for anything but duty and work.'

Mauger shrugged.

Constance pretended to gaze at the weather.

'When shall we reach Sens?'

'Two hours, if all goes well. Geoffrey and my lady will be ahead of us.'

'Did you hear any news when we stopped?'

Mauger grunted.

'No. Only that the Duke has appointed a new archbishop of Rouen, and I already knew that. Told them so.'

Mauger did not have a gift for small talk, and was amply demonstrating it for the second time that day.

Constance guided her mount round a pothole.

'Nevertheless, I have enjoyed the longer journey. I trust you have not found my company tiresome?'

*   *   *   *   *   *

'A cah- cah- cah- cousin of mine,' said Thierry. 'His real name is – '

He grimaced agonisingly, but no further words would come.

'His name is Torf,' said Ivo.

'Exactly,' continued Thierry. 'But he may well be travelling under another name, because he is on a per- per- per – '

'Pilgrimage,' said Ivo.

' – and he does not wish to draw undue attention to his h-h-h-h-holy purpose. Like the humble publican in the parable, as I am sure you rer- rer- remember. By

297

such a device he hopes to obtain that much more Divine Grace when he comes to his journey's end.'

The men round the fire shook their heads.

'He did not wait for me,' said Thierry, 'and I too wer- wer- wish to - and I wish to . . .'

More hideous faces.

One or two of the soldiers nudged each other and sniggered.

'He tells stories!' said Thierry suddenly, as if something had suddenly become unblocked. 'A charmer! Promise you the earth.'

Ivo looked at the stubble-strewn cheeks in the firelight. Amusement, scorn, contempt – not a flicker of recall.

As they laid out blankets under a wagon, Ivo growled into Thierry's ear.

'Pilgrimage! Your stories get taller every day. Where do you get them all from?'

'It breaks the monotony,' said Thierry. 'It is tiresome work stammering all day. You try.'

Ivo pulled the blanket up his chin.

'No thank you. Bad enough listening to you.'

'How long do we continue with this?' said Thierry.

'Until we get to Bourges,' said Ivo. 'Exactly as Master Geoffrey said. And all the way to Auxerre.'

Thierry uttered a blasphemy with his mouth full of cheese and stale bread.

Ivo jabbed him in the ribs.

'Just suppose he slipped through our hands – and it turned out to have been because of one question we had not asked. Just one. Would you like to be the one to face Master Geoffrey with that? . . . Eh?'

*   *   *   *   *   *

Aimery gave out a monumental sigh, and looked sidelong at Ralph.

Ralph took no notice.

'I think your brother has done wonders,' said Aimery.

No reply.

'You would hardly know that there had been a raid.'

'Mm.'

'You do not think his Grace will mind, do you? A detour like that?'

Ralph grunted.

'Who is going to tell him?'

'Oh, not I, not I,' said Aimery. 'You know me – silent as the grave.'

Another half-mile. They should be back on course for Noyon soon.

Aimery sighed again. God's Breath! As if it were not bad enough sleeping in one monastery after another, every day on the road was yet more penance of silence.

Still, he must have been upset about his mother. And his father a broken man if ever I saw one. Looks as if he had aged all of a sudden. Odd to see someone using the left hand so much – looks sort of lop-sided. His brother had a good grip on things though. Hospitable too. Came and waved us off.

'Do you think it was Torf that your brother saw?' said Aimery.

'Possible,' said Ralph. 'We need to confirm it.'

They reached the road, and, to Aimery's surprise, turned right instead of left. Aimery pointed.

'Noyon is that way.'

Ralph spoke over shoulder, pointing ahead of him.

'And Aubrey said that Torf went that way. Come. We have had some luck; let us not abandon a warm trail.'

'I hope you know what you are doing,' grumbled Aimery.

'We hear; we check; we confirm – then we report,' said Ralph.

'And if we lose him? Or if it is a false trail?'

'Then we turn about and follow orders,' said Ralph. 'Do we have to say more – and you silent as the grave?'

Aimery thought of Geoffrey's dark face in anger, and looked at the set shoulders of the young man in front of him.

'You do not give a curse, do you?'

'I give a curse about using my common sense; that is why my lord employs me. Come.'

More miles and more silence.

Aimery coughed.

'I liked your sister. The tall one.'

*   *   *   *   *   *

Mauger eased his back and flexed his shoulders.

'Praise God for a good road – for once.'

'This one will take us through Autun,' said Ivo, 'and all the way to Châlons.'

'Best road I have ridden on.'

'The Romans knew their job,' said Ivo.

'I have seen some sights,' admitted Mauger.

'Wait till you see Italy.'

Mauger nodded.

'It seems that is where he is going.'

'If I had had to wager,' said Ivo, 'that is what I should have said from the start.'

'You do not think he will turn off to Provence or Spain?'

'No. He will return to his first haunts, to the scene of his first successes. Besides – ' Ivo gestured vaguely.

'Besides what?'

'There is something about Italy,' said Ivo.

Mauger laughed scornfully.

'Surely you have not caught the Hauteville fever.'

He looked over his shoulder at the small cavalcade behind them. Heat tremors distorted the sight of the shaded wagons. Horses placed their hooves in a sleep-walking fashion. Barely a sound reached them through the heavy air.

'No,' said Ivo. 'I am too old for that.'

'The lady Fressenda is not, it seems.'

'She has half an army of sons there; it is blood that pulls her, not Rome.'

'And what is pulling you, Ivo?'

It was certainly not Rome. You could keep all your temples and fountains and colonnades, all your cardinals and basilicas and incense. A sharp frosty morning and a good canter were preferable every time.

Sir Nigel had been bewitched by it. He had gone at first for absolution, but stayed for adventure, and been overtaken by love. A triple bond. When he had brought his bride home in triumph, it was hoped that he would settle at last, that he was at peace. No – he soon was off again, pulled by the remaining two bonds – excitement, and conscience. Perhaps if he, Ivo, had been with him on that last trip, he would have been able to protect him from treachery; he might also have been able to extricate him from the ties that still held him. If he had slit that creature Torf's throat eighteen years ago, just think how much trouble they would all have been saved.

Ivo jutted his stubbled jaw. He had failed with the father; he was not going to fail with the son. Master Geoffrey would not suffer the ambush or the knife in the back. There would be no more sweet, tempting schemes and devious promises. It would be finished once and for all, and there would be no lingering ties afterward – no twinges of conscience, no yearnings for what might have been. Master Geoffrey's destiny lay in the north, where a great future awaited him. Nothing was going to hold him in Italy.

'What is pulling you, Ivo?'

Ivo scratched his whiskers.

'We are all chasing a kind of Torf, my lord. It is lucky that all these quarries are walking around inside the same man.'

*   *   *   *   *   *

Abbot Hugh of Cluny had a very good memory. Nor had his hospitality declined.

'Four years almost to the month. I am glad to find you well. Even more glad to see the mitre rather than the helm.'

Geoffrey ignored the compliment.

'We go to see the Count of Apulia. To raise more funds for my cathedral church.'

Abbot Hugh inclined his head in the direction of Fressenda.

'My lady will find her sons in good fortune,' he said. 'And therefore, we trust, in a position to be generous.'

Geoffrey looked puzzled.

'Did you not know?' said Hugh. 'His Holiness, before he died, confirmed the brothers Hauteville in all their disputed fiefs.'

Probably the only way he could get out of their clutches, thought Mauger, but he spoke with studied piety.

'So he died in Rome as he would doubtless have wished?'

'In the Lateran Palace,' said Hugh. 'In April. We still await news of his successor.'

Another reformer? Were there more where Leo had come from? If there were not, it would not be for want of looking on the part of sub-deacon Hildebrand. Or would Emperor Henry descend upon Rome and impose his will? Or again would the corrupt nobles of the Eternal City seize the initiative and elevate one of their own number? Would there be more fulminations from the Papal Chair against clerical marriage, or would an official blind eye be turned again in Rome, just as it had been turned everywhere else in Christendom? Would Geoffrey be able to return to Normandy with the way ahead open and inviting – enough to settle Sybil's fears? Or would he be pursued by further blistering condemnations of formalised fornication, uttered by the new incumbent, but no doubt put into his mouth by that fearsome little penpusher, Hildebrand?

Geoffrey renewed the conversation with an effort.

'Your man Goscelin is working well.' He grimaced. 'Though I can not speak so well for his temperament.'

Hugh betrayed the slightest of smiles.

'I said he was good; I did not say he was easy.'

'He is an angel of joy compared with my brother's engineer,' said Mauger.

'How long do you plan to rest here?' asked Hugh politely.

Not long, thought Mauger. Please God and Geoffrey, not long. They were supposed to be pilgrims already; too much time in this prayer palace and they would finish as saints. It was unnerving.

'The season is advancing,' said the lady Fressenda. 'We must reach the passes before the weather closes in.'

Fressenda could not remember when she had enjoyed a summer like it. The journey had become a new way of life. Normandy was in another world as distant as childhood and just as irrecoverable. As she closed her eyes that night, it occurred to her with a jolt that it could be like the journey of the soul between the two worlds of earth and Heaven. She felt no fear whatsoever – only curiosity and impatience, and tremendous excitement. No doubts either. Total certainty.

*　　*　　*　　*　　*　　*

'Well?'

Ivo caressed the nose of his horse, flung his gloves into a corner, and sat down on a bale of straw.

'Tomorrow – early. The Little St. Bernard. Wagons as far as they can go, but we prepare litters here – ready for immediate use. Lord Geoffrey says he wants – '
Everyone chanted in unison.

' – "no avoidable delay".'

Thierry cursed.

'Those two! They are as bad as each other.'

'Do you think she will survive it?' asked Aimery.

Ivo grunted, and reached out for a leather flask.

'After what I have seen this summer, I should think she will laugh all the way. If the wagons break down, she will not need the litter; she will get out and walk!'

'It will provide a spare one for my lady Constance,' said Ralph. 'She can make eyes at him through the curtains.'

Aimery sniggered.

'Did you ever see anyone so desperate?'

'Talk about doing it the hard way – said Thierry ' – kneeling up in a litter between two mules on an Alpine pass.'

Everybody chuckled.

Ivo swallowed the cheap wine, made a face, and tossed the flask to Ralph.

'I should not worry about her,' he said. 'You will all have enough to do before the snows fall down around your heads. Two of us have to go back up the river and round the Great St. Bernard, and he wants the other two to scout right down as far as Avignon.'

'But we know he is going to Italy,' complained Thierry. 'Five separate stall-holders said so in Lyons; they can not all be wrong.'

'No. But they can all be deceived,' said Ivo. He gestured towards the hall. 'There is no arguing with him. Double checks. No gaps. I tell you – two of us must ride as far as Avignon, then come back and cross the Mont Cenis. Any volunteers?'

'Where do we meet again?' asked Aimery.

302

'The Mont Cenis pair go through Turin. The Great St. Bernard pair meet Lord Geoffrey at Aosta. Then we all make for Pavia and wait there.'

'Lanfranc's house?' said Ralph.

'No. We call there regularly to inquire, that is all. We can not eat the old man out of house and home.'

Ivo tapped a wallet on his belt.

'We have been amply supplied for expenses.' He grinned at Thierry. 'Even for your appetite.'

*   *   *   *   *   *

'It is my greatest regret that I probably shall not look upon him any more.'

The old man's hair had gone completely white.

'You must not talk like that,' said Geoffrey. 'He will come again, I am sure. There is always the matter of pleading the case of the Duke's marriage in Rome. He would, I know, seize any opportunity to visit you.'

The old man sighed.

'There is little likelihood of a papal court being convened for the Duke's case so long as there is no pope to convene it. We are no nearer an election.'

Geoffrey revelled in the firelight, in the reflected polish of the table, the shadows and gleams thrown upon the wall by the glassware. Two serving girls, all dark eyebrows and blooming skin, moved about the room on errands of silent mystery.

'Has Hildebrand not been able to arrange anything?'

Lanfranc's father beckoned for more wine.

'Hildebrand may be influential in the Holy See, but he is not all-powerful – thank God.'

Geoffrey looked up sharply with a question in his eyes.

'Many of us are all for reform, God knows,' said the old man, lowering his voice. 'But there must be some sense of proportion. If Hildebrand and his party get their way, the Church will be reformed out of existence. Do you know the story of the virtuous abbot?'

'Yes,' said Geoffrey. 'Expelled all his monks for sin, and had no monastery left.'

'And went to Hell for the sin of pride. I tell you, this "reform" has become an obsession, a disease that is worse than the ills it seeks to cure. The patient has hitherto survived the fever, but is in great danger of dying from the treatment. Have you heard the latest madness?'

'We are recently arrived,' Geoffrey reminded him.

Lanfranc's father leaned forward.

'In July of this year, they went to the ultimate lunacy. A cardinal of our Holy

Catholic Church went in solemn process to the Church of the Holy Wisdom in Constaninople and laid upon the altar a bull of excommunication against the Patriarch of that city – the Patriarch!'

'How can he issue a bull,' said Geoffrey, 'when there is no Pope to authenticate it?'

'Exactly. The document, I gather, is a piece of spurious scholarship that would disgrace the stupidest novice; and it has been delivered with no authority whatsoever. Cardinal Humbert has not only made a fool of himself; he has made a laughing-stock of the Church of Rome throughout the entire Greek Empire. Now – do you know who in Rome is the closest friend of this idiot Humbert? Hildebrand.' The old man sat back. 'That is what your reformers are doing for us. No imagination, no sense of moderation, no common sense.'

Geoffrey smiled.

'Perhaps it needs your son to come to Rome to knock their heads together.'

A different look came over the old man's face.

'I do not know what my son – "needs" to do, Geoffrey. But I know that he has it in him to be a great man. I shall not be there, but you will. I ask you to remember my words. He may not excommunicate kings or try to shatter churches – frankly I would rather he did not – but he will do great things and he will be held in the highest regard. He will be like –' he clenched his fist ' – like a rock!'

Geoffrey swallowed a lump.

'I promise you that I shall remember. And when that time comes, I shall tell him of your faith and of your pride.'

'In that case, I shall die content.'

Lanfranc's father relaxed his manner.

'See to it that you too pursue your own destiny.' His eyes twinkled. 'In both directions. I am in favour of moderate reform, and I expect you to use the spoon that has been put in your hands to give the pot a stir. But I am also in favour of moderate human weakness, and I am moreover Italian.' He punched Geoffrey playfully on the arm. 'Prise her out of that nunnery. From what you (and your mother) say about her, I do not think she will get to Heaven on a couple of psalms and a pile of dirty washing.'

*　　*　　*　　*　　*　　*

Geoffrey came in, sat down, and kicked a fallen log towards the blaze.

'No sign of letting up. We can wait a day if you wish.'

The lady Fressenda looked down at her hands. My lord Tancred's gold ring glowed richly against tanned skin. She knew from what her girls said that her face was the same colour. She had spent more time out of doors in the last few months than she had spent in the hottest summers at Hauteville, when the line of chicklings skipped behind her billowing skirts. Her appetite had never been better. Her pains were now merely a burden instead of a cross. She had enjoyed herself enormously.

Constance had not quite lost the martyr's air. Mauger was now conspicuously avoiding them. Was that shame, hypocrisy, or reluctance? For the last week or so, he not known what to do with himself in their presence. From the way Geoffrey's men smirked between themselves, it seemed that something had been going on. No matter: it had silenced Constance's wailings and eased the journey. Robert would sort everything out when they at last arrived. If it turned out that the silly girl had slipped up, she could do a lot worse than Mauger.

The lady Fressenda had been moving Heaven and earth for a union between the House of Hauteville and the House of Montbrai; what was so wrong with a double one? Geoffrey was rising fast; he would certainly take Mauger with him, if only part of the way. It would simply mean that Constance would miss the Italian count that Robert might have arranged for her, and would have to go all the way back to Normandy. Serve her right for being careless.

'I have sent word ahead to Robert,' said Geoffrey. 'He will make ready to receive you. I am sure you will have royal treatment. Last time I was here he was living in some ancient king's marble palace.'

Fressenda smiled to herself.

Geoffrey was if anything more anxious than herself to reach journey's end. Torf's trail had led with increasing clarity towards Apulia. Fressenda was not in the least surprised. Like so many adventurers seeking to re-kindle their luck, he was returning to the scene of his first successes. Men who lived by their wits were charmers and optimists all, ever trustful of the source of their good fortune. If Apulia had looked kindly upon him once, it would do so again.

Even now, at this stage of the chase, Fressenda found in herself a lingering glimmer of admiration for Torf of Malbec; like all charming men, it would never cross his mind that his charm would not continue to work – given of course that it was exercised in the right quarter. His resilience and his confidence were truly remarkable.

However, between them, they should be able to put an end to his serpent's spells once and for all. Geoffrey would return to Normandy with no more ties to hold him to the south. Rival removed; father avenged and his soul provided for; fortune, fame, and love awaiting him in the north.

She had had to be careful not to spin another web to hold him when she spoke of his mother. His questions had been most insistent – out on the road, away from straining ears.

'You must realise, Geoffrey, that we met only a few times, and then not for very long.'

'But you must have talked.'

'She spoke only vaguely about – about that. Sir Nigel rescued her from some danger, and they fell in love. He took her home with him. You know this, I am sure.'

'Did she speak of her family? Was there some princely blood? Was she a hostage of war?'

Fressenda frowned fiercely.

'That – may have been possible. Please – it was a long time ago. I am now an old woman . . . I can tell you this, though; there was something of the truly high-born lady about her. And she was beautiful, Geoffrey. Beautiful.'

Geoffrey smiled at the recollection.

'Yes. Yes, she was.'

Fressenda allowed a tender look to come upon her face.

'I am sure you loved her very much.'

Knowledge was power; it always had been. Using it to produce necessary action was legitimate; but inflicting it to cause pain was an abuse of power.

What good would it do for Geoffrey to know any more? Did Fressenda know herself? Not really. She had only glued together a possible part of the truth from a myriad of broken pieces of reminiscence. Who was to say whether the pattern she had rearranged bore any resemblance to what had really happened?

Helena of Montbrai was indeed a lonely woman, a foreigner from the land of the sun, neglected and chilled in a remote castle swept by wind and rain for half the year. Worse, an intelligent woman, who fretted helpless before the universal assumption that no female was expected to have any intellectual pretensions whatever. Small wonder that she doted on a bright younger son who showed scholarly promise, and tolerated a tipsy libertine monk who could construe two ancient languages and converse in three modern ones. Less wonder that, when presented with the opportunity of converse with a woman of similar age and rank, she should fall upon her and pour out her troubles and desires, her hopes and aspirations.

What if the memories took on a slightly rosy glow? What did it matter if the reminiscences often sounded more like excerpts from a *chanson de geste*? Of what significance if the lady Helena had been rescued by her brave Nigel in Emilia on one occasion, and snatched from the jaws of death in Spoleto on another?

During the short stays that Sir Nigel permitted himself on his own demesne, he enjoyed many a late pot with his neighbour, Sir Tancred of Hauteville. My lord Tancred, like his sons, was in the habit of passing on to my lady whatever news he heard. Many disjointed pieces of Sir Nigel's communings, garbled by alcohol and nostalgia, and by Tancred's random memory, reached my lady

Fressenda's ears in the end.

Fitting Sir Nigel's version of the past with that of his wife's provided many an intriguing hour of speculation and supposition to while away the boredom of dark-bound winter.

Sir Nigel's account carried references to the ransacked palace of a Greek princess, a terrified and bedraggled household of refugee servants, corrupt private tutors to a Moorish harem, Saracen slave-traders in an auction in Amalfi.

No doubt both Sir Nigel and the lady Helena were culling from the harvest of their motley past only the choicest fruits, and were making discreet shifts of status and ownership and responsibility to suit their present situation. It did not detract from their virtues; indeed the very weakness it displayed added to the sum of their humanity.

The truth – whatever it was – no longer mattered. It would never be used – never by Fressenda, and there was nobody else now to use it – to bind Geoffrey in any way.

'Do you mind if we travel today? It is raining quite hard.'

The lady Fressenda adjusted the clasp at her shoulder.

'Geoffrey, I have travelled through drought in Burgundy, through frost and storm on an Alpine pass, through flood in Lombardy; I have survived a skirmish with Saracen pirates near Lucca, and a week of the flux at Gaeta. Now tell me – why should I suddenly quail at a little rain near journey's end?'

Geoffrey gestured awkwardly.

'What will you do?' he asked.

Fressenda looked surprised.

'Do? Why, go. That is what you wish, is it not?'

'No. I mean when you arrive. We have been on the road now for many weeks. On a journey as long as this, the road itself becomes a sort of purpose.'

'I agree. And I have enjoyed every minute of it.'

Geoffrey tossed his head impatiently. He knew he was not expressing himself clearly.

'I know. But this evening we shall be with Robert. With all your other sons. What then?'

Fressenda looked surprised.

'What do you mean – "what then?" ?'

'What will you do?'

Fressenda laughed.

'When we arrive, I shall tell that to Robert. He will laugh too.'

Geoffrey looked blank.

'Why?'

'Geoffrey, if you had said to Robert, as he was about to ride to the field at Civitate, "What are you going to do?", do you know what he would have said?'

Geoffrey made a wry face.

'No. What?'

'He would have said, "Live, or die." That is precisely what I am going to do when I reach my sons. I am going to live, or I am going to die, and I have no way of knowing which. You could try asking God, I suppose; He has played some considerable part in getting me here. He probably has something in mind.'

Geoffrey smiled.

'Yes, He probably has. I expect He will tell us when He is good and ready.'

*   *   *   *   *   *

My lady Fressenda of Hauteville arrived like an empress.

The evening sun shone on a glittering cavalcade – God having seen fit to play yet a further part by stopping the downpour of the morning. Geoffrey's knights paraded in gleaming mail and their best spurs, their destriers under rich trappings and nodding plumes. Jewelled pommels of swords and daggers glittered and leather shone. Men-at-arms from Montbrai and Hauteville marched in freshly-oiled jerkins, leading their lighter ponies, brushed and groomed until they gleamed.

My lord Mauger of Montbrai, on his best horse, forgot his awkwardness, and grinned with total gratification at Constance, who rode at his side; she in turn gave herself up to the occasion, smiled at him with genuine grace, and waved excitedly to absolutely everybody.

'Leave my lady to me,' said Ivo to Geoffrey. He, and Thierry, Ralph, and Aimery, carried the lady Fressenda in an open litter; from its four corners brightly-hued kerchiefs fluttered in a gentle breeze.

'I trust that you will not regret this decision of yours,' said my lady to Ivo, when they were half-way there.

Ivo, for once freshly-shaven, grinned through his sweat.

'You may be a weight, my lady, but you are not a burden. Not one of us has witnessed an achievement that is the like of yours. How else would you have us pay our tribute to you?'

As they came closer to the palace that Robert of Hauteville had prepared for his mother, the banners and the pennants and the tents and the pavilions clustered thicker and richer; the Hautevilles had ransacked their vast stores of loot from old campaigns, and their more recent masses of plunder from the Papal camp at Civitate.

On either side of the lady Fressenda's litter rode three of her sons: on the left Geoffrey, Serlo, and the newly-arrived Aubrey; on the right were the second

William, Mauger, and young Tancred. Count Humphrey was away in Rome, still trying to secure a favourable outcome to the Papal election. Thus there was nobody to dispute pride of place at the head of the column to the eldest of my lady's womb, to the giant Robert, Robert the Guiscard, the hero of Civitate. Towering over all in his huge saddle, his blue eyes fairly glittering like sparks on an anvil, his face flushed permanently with pride, his whole countenance challenged the world to produce a better spectacle.

A few paces to the rear, my lord Geoffrey de Montbrai – himself tall, handsome, striking – in full episcopal robes and mitre, was totally eclipsed, and was content to be so. Those arriving, those receiving, those watching, those clapping in sheer wonder and delight – all agreed that it was my lady's day.

As they neared the throne he had prepared for his mother, Robert stopped the parade. Dismounting, he strode up to the litter and ordered it to be placed on the ground.

Reaching inside, he embraced his mother, took her bodily into his arms, and began to carry her the last of the way. The cheering redoubled.

Marble paving covered the ultimate twenty or thirty paces. As they reached it, my lady spoke in Robert's ear.

'Put me down.'

Robert paused in surprise.

'Put me down,' repeated his mother. 'It was walking unaided that started me on this journey; I shall finish it in the same way.' She waved her hand. 'Someone get me my sticks.'

Silence fell as if God had waved a wand. All eyes were on the tense, determined figure in black – my lady liked jewellery, but frowned on frivolous colours. 'For flirts and jesters,' she always said.

Everyone craned and prayed as the two sticks tap-tapped their way up the marble avenue to the polished throne. Seven Hauteville brothers crept like cats at her heels and elbows, dry-mouthed and wet-palmed, praying as they had never prayed before battle.

When at last she reached journey's end, and a dozen hands lowered her on to her empress's throne, the noise that burst out was deafening.

Robert came round to stand before her, his brothers on either side of him. They saluted formally. Then Robert knelt before her, kissed the hem of her robe, and asked for her blessing. The other six followed.

Robert stood up, stepped back a few paces, and raised his head. A colossal grin spread across his burnished face.

'Welcome to Apulia, Mother.'

He waved all round him at the forest of hands and spears and fluttering pennants. The din almost drowned his booming laugh.

He put his hands on his hips, cocked his head sideways, and looked out of the corner of his eye.

'What do you think of your boys now, eh? Eh?'

He beckoned to a small group of his men.

'I should like to present to you an unexpected guest, who will make this family reunion complete.'

The group came forward, escorting someone between them. Robert gestured to Geoffrey to approach.

'Ah, my bishop. I do not believe that you two have met before. May I now introduce you to each other . . .'

*　　*　　*　　*　　*　　*

Chapter Twenty-One

Geoffrey did not know how he got through the rest of the day.

'Patience, patience,' said the Guiscard. 'He will keep.'

'You have had him with you for days, running loose,' said Geoffrey, scandalised.

'Naturally. If I had given him any idea of what I intended to do, he would have hatched a conspiracy against me by this time. God knows there are plenty of men willing to listen to such a scheme. Much better to have him here thinking me a fool than to have him running around wild proving me one.'

'Under your very roof, was there not a greater danger?'

Robert looked surprised.

'Of violence? No – that is not the way of such people. No, it was safe so long as he thought I was deceived. When a charming man thinks his charm is working, his guard begins to slip.'

'He has charmed many people,' said Geoffrey.

Robert smiled, producing great creases in his broad, tanned face.

'Since our victory at Civitate, we have been swamped with new arrivals, trying to charm their way into a share of the spoils. They are easily discerned, and at a great distance.'

He lowered his head, and gave Geoffrey his one-eyed, sly glance.

'They do not call me the Guiscard for nothing.'

Geoffrey found himself caught in the spirit of Robert's breezy confidence, and was forced to smile.

'What is your secret then?'

'No magic secret. Just thinking clearly, seeing the truth. Your Torf of Malbec bases his tricks upon contempt for his dupes; I base mine upon respect for their capacities. That is all.'

He placed a great paw of a hand upon Geoffrey's shoulder.

'Do not disturb yourself. He is well watched tonight. He will do no harm and he will go nowhere, and his bonds will be invisible to him. He is under my roof, and so are you. He will keep until tomorrow.' He gestured towards the uproar of celebration behind them. 'Today is my Mother's day.'

*   *   *   *   *   *

'What is it, Ivo? I am very tired.'

Ivo made a gesture of deference.

'I should not intrude upon my lady's tiredness unless it were important.'

'Say it, Ivo. Say it.'

Ivo waited for the Italian girls that Robert had provided to stop staring and

311

retire. He looked around the chamber – mosaics, silks, gleaming cushions – luxury straight out of eastern legend.

'Fit for an empress, my lady.'

My lady Fressenda waved an impatient hand.

'Ivo, I have had flattery and spoiling today enough to turn the head of ten saints. Come to the point, and speedily, or I shall have you thrown out.'

Ivo smiled easily, as with a good friend.

'Very well. It concerns my lord Geoffrey. We each have reasons for wanting him to return to Normandy without leaving anything of himself behind.'

'No guilt.'

'Exactly. My lady is as usual ahead of me.'

'I can not stop Geoffrey.'

'Neither can I,' said Ivo. 'But we are all under the roof of your son. Sir Robert will dictate tomorrow's proceedings. Even my lord Geoffrey will have to accept his authority.'

'Well?'

Ivo cleared his throat.

'My lady – at the risk of being accused again of flattery – only one person here has any sway over Sir Robert.'

*　　*　　*　　*　　*　　*

'Mother, you are up so early!'

The lady Fressenda waved to the small cloud of girls who enveloped her with a veil of fluttering hands and waving silks. Unheard-of toilet luxuries were scattered over every ledge and surface. Perfumes and flower scents filled the air.

'I never get the time to ask for anything; it is there before I can think of it.'

'Are you not tired?' asked Constance.

'Surprisingly, no. And I must look my best.'

Constance looked shocked.

'You are surely not coming?'

Fressenda gave her a surprised glance.

'Of course. I have good reason to. More than you.'

Constance lowered her voice.

'Do these girls speak French?'

'Not enough to worry about. What is it?'

Constance took a deep breath. Fressenda knew at once that some kind of revelation was coming.

'Mother, I have a very good reason for coming. He once wronged me.'

Fressenda stared.

'You?'

Constance rushed on.

'Long ago, you understand. Before Sybil. He deceived me. With his sweet words and his promises.'

Fressenda narrowed her eyes.

'Are you sure that you were not the one making the offers?'

Constance crossed her hands piously across her bosom.

'No, Mother! On Father's grave I swear.'

'You showed little sympathy for Sybil,' observed Fressenda.

Constance blushed, and lowered her head.

'I – I was jealous. I felt cheated.'

'It took you long enough to admit it,' said her mother. 'Why now?'

Constance kept her head down.

'Confession is always good for the soul, however late.'

The lady Fressenda smiled drily.

'You mean that if you are going to enjoy his punishment with a clear conscience, you need to establish first that you have suffered injury at his hands. Well, rest easy, my dear; your mother hears you and duly acknowledges your just motives. And you know that your secret will remain with me.'

Rare for Constance to show such discernment. Was she beginning to grow some sense at last?

Constance helped to fasten a cloak round her mother's shoulders.

'Tell me, Mother, what do you think of Mauger?'

Fressenda looked blank.

'Mauger? Your brother?'

'No. My lord Mauger of Montbrai. Is he not a knight of honour? We never became acquainted with him in the past as we should have done.'

'I have no doubt, my dear, that you have taken many steps to remedy that omission during the course of the journey. If, however, you are asking me what I think of him as a possible husband, I can only say that you have left it a little late to mention it. You could have suggested it before we started, and saved us all a great deal of trouble.'

The lady Fressenda spared her daughter the further embarrassment of reminding her that it had never crossed my lord Mauger's mind either.

* * * * * *

Advent came in with a heavy storm.

Sybil lay in bed and listened to the howling of wind and the creaking of timbers. No matter how secure the house, a storm at night was a frightening thing, and a reminder of the wrath of the Almighty.

Moreover, the house at St. Amand was not in the best of repair. The abbess, my lady Emma, had often mentioned it to her son. Sir William Fitzosbern had taken note of it.

'I shall see what I can do, Mother.'

He then went off to fortify his castles at Breteuil or Tillières, or to accompany the Duke on a progress through the Evrecin or the Roumois, or to sit at his Grace's Council table at the new town of Caen – a growing favourite with him. Despite the Duke's recent victories – the conspirators dispersed into exile; a new archbishop, Maurilius, in Rouen; the King nursing his wounded pride in Paris; the Count of Anjou venting his spleen instead on Maine or Brittany; the new Count of Ponthieu accepting him as overlord – there were still plenty of problems left.

'I shall see what I can do, Mother.'

He meant well.

The wind had dropped by the morning. Sybil found it a struggle to get up. Although the storm had abated, the sense of foreboding would not leave her. She felt intensely depressed, almost physically dragged down.

She looked so low that the lady abbess asked after her health. Sybil tried to explain, but it was difficult because she had no clear idea herself, and she could not put into words the fierce longings and grievings and misgivings about Geoffrey, and Raoul, and her mother. Torf too, for that matter. After a whole lifetime with such a huge family before whom she had so few secrets, she could not remember feeling so completely alone. How often had she yearned for privacy at Hauteville, just an hour or two with her own thoughts and emotions! A chance simply to be herself. Now she would give a king's ransom to be enveloped with brothers and sisters again. And yet, and yet – at the very moment that she felt that, she knew also that it was not the answer.

The lady abbess found her a puzzle, and, to tell the truth, a slight embarrassment.

'Surely it is merely – that is, we women know that – there are times when – after all, you are in charge of the – if you need to go to the infirmary . . .'

She tailed off. Sybil kindly came to her rescue.

'Yes, you are probably right. Reverend Mother. Do not worry; I can cope with it.'

It was easier to leave it at that.

*   *   *   *   *   *

'Am I not to be allowed to speak in my own defence?'

Torf of Malbec raised his voice so as to carry to the very corners of the hall. Men-at-arms lounging against the doors lifted their heads.

'Is this – ' said Torf, raising his arms in wide entreaty to the world ' – is this the famed justice of the Guiscard?'

Robert of Hauteville stood up, and remained still until he had commanded the full attention of all present.

'You – Torf of Malbec – are in my hall and in my court. You stand accused. In such a situation, you are under my protection until such time as you are found innocent and leave my presence, or until such time as you are found guilty and possibly quit this earthly life. Since you are alone and have no man to swear on your behalf, there is all the more reason why you should speak for yourself.'

Torf took a breath in preparation to begin, but was stopped by the Guiscard.

'However – I must warn you of the danger. If you were not to speak, our deliberations could lead to your acquittal or to your condemnation – you agree?'

Torf nodded, wondering where the argument was going.

'By the same token,' said Robert, 'if you do speak, your own words could lead to either of the same two results. You accept the condition?'

Torf almost sneered in his confidence.

'I accept.'

'So be it.'

Robert waved agreement, and sat down.

Torf walked to the centre of the hall, turned, and looked at the assembled principals before him.

In the centre of the table, Sir Robert of Hauteville. On his right, his mother, the lady Fressenda. On his left, his sister, the lady Constance. To the right of my lady mother, my lord Geoffrey de Montbrai, Bishop of Coutances, and his brother, Sir Mauger de Montbrai. On either side of them, the remaining six sons of my lady – Geoffrey, Serlo, the second William, Mauger, Aubrey, and young Tancred. At a side table sat Ivo, one of the accusers, and behind him stood Ralph, Thierry, and Aimery. Beside Ivo sat a noble guest of Sir Robert's – Sir Richard of Carel, Count of Aversa, another of the heroes of the Battle of Civitate, come to visit his comrade in arms. All round the hall stood small groups of Sir Robert's men, mailed and armed. One or two select servants, their ears fairly flapping, were allowed in to serve simple refreshments. Outside the doors, more men-at-arms kept away the crowd of gapers.

Torf turned himself in a full circle, trying to take in his whole audience with his eyes.

Seeing him alone like that, with such space around him, Geoffrey was surprised at how unimpressive he looked. He was shorter than one would have imagined, and certainly older. Father had been killed by this creature in 1035, nearly twenty years ago. That put Torf at least into his forties, but he looked more – well, almost more wizened. He had a domish head, only half covered with scrubby hair that had tinges of grey at the edges. His eyes lacked lustre, and there were dark patches beneath his cheekbones. Beard shadow covered his face almost up to the eyes. Nor was there was anything physically impressive about the body or the stance.

Holy Virgin! What had Sybil ever seen in him? What had anybody seen in him?

Then he began to speak.

Geoffrey had been prepared for pleading, for whining, for hectoring, for declamation, for challenge, bombast, defiance, remorse, abject servility – anything but what he heard. It was so measured, so gentle in tone, so logical, so absolutely reasonable, that he had to pinch himself to remember where he was and whom he was listening to.

A tiny fragment of memory recalled how often the word 'honey' had crept into the conversation of people who tried to explain the effect that Torf's speech had had on them. They could rarely quote actual words, much less whole sentences; they had been reduced to feeble attempts to convey the general drift of what he said – what glowing promises, what exciting prospects, what intoxicating ideas; yet how ordinary everything sounded, how sensible, how possible, how easily attainable. One had only to reach out a hand. One and all they testified to how pleasurable his voice was simply to listen to; they admitted having been taken in with one breath, and in the next they confessed their amazement afterwards that they had allowed it to happen.

Everything Torf said was moreover true . . . He had been the comrade-in-arms of the gallant Nigel of Montbrai, and had been with him right to the death; he had come all the way from Apulia to see the young Sir Mauger of Montbrai, in order to bring the sad tidings of his father's death; he had inherited property to the west of Hauteville and had come initially to the household of Sir Tancred only to pay his respects to a worthy neighbour; he had been welcomed by both the master and the mistress of the household; largely upon their invitation, he had continued to visit, and had paid court to their youngest daughter, according to the strictest terms of etiquette. He had been willing to accept the most modest of dowries from the bride's father, and had thus married into one of the most noble houses of western Normandy, notwithstanding that the young lady in question was the mother of his rival's bastard; he had taken the infant into his house and had raised him as if he were his own son.

Despite his overtures of friendship to his neighbour, Sir Mauger of Montbrai, that neighbour had rejected him, and had gone on to bear false witness against him to the Duke. The Duke and his Council, misled by this treachery, had persecuted him, Torf, and punished him without allowing him recourse to the statement of his case before his peers. He had had no choice but precipitate flight, having first made sure that his wife and son were in safe hands with her family. He had taken temporary refuge with the Count of Anjou, and was on his way back into Normandy – what other reason could he have had to put himself in this danger but to show his true loyalty and seek to make his peace with the Duke? – when he had been set upon by his ex-rival and ex-neighbour, whose obsessive desire for mindless revenge over some nameless offence had forced him into a second flight for his very life.

Thereafter, he had had no choice but to seek the justice of his supreme overlord, the King, in the hope that His Majesty could bring about a much-desired reconciliation between himself and his Duke, who in turn would bring about a resumption of friendly relations between himself and his family and his neighbours. What else could he have done? What else could any man have done? His family would not grant him a hearing; his neighbours would not grant him a hearing; nor would his feudal overlord; where could he have turned but to the King?

Corruption and avarice had turned the mind of His Majesty in the end, just as bitter jealousy had twisted the mind of his rival, Geoffrey of Montbrai – who, hypocrite that he was, was trying to possess both mitre and mistress – and obsessive hate and prejudice had warped the brain of Sir Mauger of Montbrai. Hence he, Torf of Malbec, who had sought nothing but peaceful enjoyment of his fief, his wife, and his household, had been forced to leave Normandy as a fugitive of injustice. Where else should he have gone but to Apulia, where he had first made his fortune with Sir Nigel of Montbrai and his brave comrades-in-arms, the brothers Hauteville? There he could rebuild the fortunes of his life that had been so unfairly shattered by greed, hate, and jealousy. There he hoped to find again the simple virtues of loyalty, companionship, and mutual trust; to face once more the challenges of the simple soldier of fortune; to meet the future with something like the same courage and optimism that was constantly shown by the present master of the situation – Sir Robert of Hauteville. His only regret, apart from all that had happened, was that he had been too late to share the tests and perils of battle, when Sir Robert had shown that his Normans were a match for any army that marched into Italy, be it sent even by his Holiness.

It was a staggering performance. Geoffrey felt drained of any power of argument, any will to reply, if only in simple denial. He looked at the others; everyone sat in fascinated, stone-like silence. The only noise in the hall apart from Torf's voice was the occasional hiss from the fire. The servants had long since sat down, and watched, open-mouthed, one with a pot half-spilling into his lap.

Now Torf had stopped talking about the past; he was painting a picture of the future; he was talking to one man – the master of the house . . .

Sir Robert was master of this house, master of this present situation, master of the fate of all under this roof. The initiative lay completely with Robert the Guiscard, whose actions would not be clouded by outmoded sentiment or misguided by juvenile obsessions. If Sir Robert would permit the observation, and allow the presumption, the two of them had this much in common – namely that both he, Torf of Malbec, and he, Sir Robert, had got where they were only by the exercise of shrewdness and capacity for resource; both had seized every opportunity that a good God had placed in their path. Both looked the world in the face, and accepted the world for what it was. It surely was no coincidence that they were both of roughly the same age; they had seen far more of the world than the young men of Montbrai. Lack of years was not of course the fault of these young men; as God was witness, he, Torf of Malbec, bore them no real ill will, but anyone surely would allow a man to defend himself against unprovoked and unfair attack. The brothers Montbrai were trying to deprive him of his wife, his fief – nay, even his life. Holy Writ itself allowed a man to fight against injustice such as this.

But enough of this pleading; Sir Robert understood the situation with total clarity. His sense of realism had always been a cause for admiration among his contemporaries. If only he knew how much he was discussed and admired throughout Normandy. It was indeed only because he set such little store by this adulation that he was ignorant of the enormous potential of his position in the duchy . . .

There was a stir in the hall. One or two of the brothers glanced at each other.

Torf, after a suitable pause, leaned forward and continued. He was a great leaner forward; many of his listeners testified to his trick of intentness, whether talking or listening. He was able to convey the impression that, for the duration of the conversation, the other person was the most important living creature in the entire earth and firmament. He focused his intent now upon the table in front of him, in the centre of which sat Robert of Hauteville, expressionless and totally still.

Could he, a fellow Norman, take the liberty of reminding Sir Robert of what a pleasant land Normandy was? Green? Mild? Fruitful? Free from blinding dust and drenching winter rains and scorching summer sun. Peopled by men who all spoke French – not Italian, Greek, and Arabic. And had he, Sir Robert, stopped to consider recently the extent of the resources of the House of Hauteville? The family home, the new rewards that his brother Roger would be receiving from the Duke, the lands at Malbec that he, Torf, a loyal brother-in-law, would be only too willing to place at his disposal for the further advancement of the family fortunes? The knight's fee at Isigny into which his sister Muriella had married? Moreover, if there was any justice, he, Torf, had suffered so much at the hands of the brothers Montbrai that the only equitable solution would be for their lands to become forfeit. Put all these estates together, and the House of Hauteville would have a power base in the west that would be unrivalled from Valognes to Avranches. The Duke had never succeeded yet in making his rule effective west of Bayeux; his sale of a bishop's mitre to a penniless, callow second son of a poor knight was evidence of how desperate he was.

Indeed, the Duke had survived in the east only by a combination of luck and bad management among mistrustful allies. In 1047 the Duke had looked likely to go down before his enemies, and was rescued only by the timely intervention of the King. Barely had he expelled Guy of Burgundy from the castle of Brionne when he found himself in the coils of yet another attempt to wrest the ducal throne – this time from William of Arques. The Duke could take no credit for winning the castle of Arques – Sir Robert could ask anyone – and had survived at Mortemer because he was fighting only half an army and a vacillating King.

William's fortunes had changed as rapidly as a weather vane swung in a storm, and he foolishly attributed it to his own ability. In reality it was luck, and the caprice of God. Such tenuous luck could not survive against a determined, resourceful leader with half the magic of the Guiscard.

Moreover, it was also an undeniable fact that the Duke had incurred the wrath of his late lamented Holiness, in that his marriage was incestuous, being within the prescribed degrees of family relationship. How could God continue to look with favour upon a ruler thus reviled and condemned by His Vicar on earth?

Whereas it was also an undeniable fact that the Holy See would very soon have to turn to Sir Robert of Hauteville as its only possible protector in a violent land. The Emperor of Germany had let Rome down; nor was there any reliance to be placed in the Emperor at Constantinople, especially now that his Patriarch had been declared anathema by one of Rome's cardinals. If ever a prince had been singled out by Fate and by God to be the shield and sword of the Bishop of Rome, it was the Guiscard. Therefore, as naturally as night followed day, who better to punish a Norman sinner at Rouen – and a bastard at that – than a Norman hero and protector of the Church in Italy?

The King of France would be happy to have a legitimate vassal of such proven honour and reputation instead of the bastard adventurer he was now burdened with. Between them they could squeeze the nuisance of Anjou out of existence and establish proper and lasting peace throughout the whole of northern France. Brittany was cowed. Ponthieu already accepted the overlordship of Normandy.

Flanders would soon come into line; the sister of Count Baldwin was married to Earl Tostig of England. If Tostig could be bribed with suitable promises, his help could be obtained in all sorts of adventures stemming from the assurance of the crown by King Edward. It would not be too difficult to find out where the Atheling was living, or to waylay him on his journey to England. Even to befriend him, to gain his confidence. Thereafter his disposal would be at Sir Robert's whim. A sudden seizure, a rapid decline, a lingering illness – all common occurrences. It was a regular subterfuge, accepted by all. The Duke's own uncle, the late Duke Richard III, had departed this life in mysterious circumstances. Did anyone seriously believe that Earl Godwin had died as a result of choking on a piece of bread? Of course not – but everyone accepted the convention of publicly believing it. It was common practice of statecraft. Whatever the method, the result would be the same; there would then be no heir, and King Edward would be forced to honour his original promise.

In case my lord Robert was thinking that he, Torf, was trying to deceive him into neglecting his fortunes in Apulia, could he take the liberty of pointing out that it was Sir Robert's very strength in Italy that could be of material assistance to success in Normandy, and it would be success in Normandy that would be further reflected in Italy. For, faced with news of such prowess and territorial expansion in Normandy, allies would flock to the Guiscard's standard in the south. With the blessing of the Pope, and perhaps a judicious marriage of his sister, the lady Constance, to a neighbouring prince – a union that, one could be sure, would be welcome to my lady herself – and an army of proven superiority after Civitate, there would be nothing to stop Norman domination of the whole country.

'And it can all start here, my lord. With one step. The vision is not mine; a man such as yourself can encompass it at a glance. All I have done is to take the liberty of daring to look at it in your company.'

Mauger felt a shiver . . . Montbrai, Hauteville, Malbec, the Cotentin, Normandy, Anjou, Ponthieu, Flanders, England, Italy, crowns and sceptres and fortunes and lordships – a veritable empire . . . strewn before the glittering blue eyes of the most ruthless and most successful opportunist in Christendom. All that stood in his way, at the outset, was a lonely young bishop of a bastard duke and a poor bachelor knight of the Cotentin.

'It can all start here, my lord – with one step.'

Suddenly it all looked so possible – a diabolical picture woven by a master spellbinder, that cunningly threaded the weft of dreams in and out of the warp of shrewd practicality, to produce a glowing tapestry of future glory and blinding power.

Torf had finished speaking.

In the terrible silence, Mauger's mouth went dry . . .

My God! He will do it. How could we possibly stand against all that? What could we offer in its place? Geoffrey is not a bishop; he is a pawn – I am a pawn – both to be swept aside in a master game of high stakes far beyond our puny selves. We are done for.

Mauger's hand strayed under the table towards his knife.

Sir Robert of Hauteville stood up and came round to stand in the centre of the hall. His head was lowered, as if in deep thought.

He turned to face the table and looked at Geoffrey. He bowed slightly.

'If my lord bishop will accept my apologies in advance. Reasons of state, you understand.'

Mauger gripped the handle of his dagger.

The Guiscard beckoned to two of his largest men-at-arms. They came forward. Robert indicated.

'See that his Grace does not rise from his seat until I give you leave. With courtesy, mind!'

At a gesture from Robert, two more soldiers stationed themselves behind Mauger.

Mauger looked desperately at his brother. There was a scraping noise from nearby, as Ivo began to push back his chair.

Geoffrey felt only a great sadness – to have come this far! And Father still unavenged.

Robert turned back to Torf of Malbec. He draped an arm over Torf's shoulders, and turned him right round in a circle, so that they looked together at everyone present. A huge grin creased the Guiscard's face.

A murmur of mystery ran through the assembly. Torf began to preen himself.

Without any warning, Robert punched him in the stomach with his free hand. As he doubled up, Robert loosed a second tremendous blow, which knocked him to the floor.

'How dare you strike our Sybil!'

Robert turned to speak to his mother.

'On the arms too, you say?'

'And on the back,' said my lady.

Robert seized a spear from one of his men, broke it across his knee, and grasped the splintered haft. He rained blows upon the cowering body beneath him.

Torf screamed.

Robert continued.

'Did – you – not know – that such blows – hurt? Especially – if you are – a woman?'

He flung away the remains of the handle, and dragged Torf to his feet. Grasping him by folds of his jerkin, he pulled him close, and very deliberately spat in his face. Then he pushed him back again, as if he were repulsive to the touch, and felled him once more with another rock-like blow to the face.

He looked round at Mauger and Ivo.

'We have paid the debt of Hauteville. Now take him outside and pay the debt of Montbrai. We shall not interfere.'

He bowed to Geoffrey.

'I regret, my lord, that we can not allow a prince of the Holy Church to participate in this matter. I am sure that my lord Mauger and Master Ivo will be content to shoulder the burden of the executioner's duty.'

'Too true,' growled Mauger, as Ivo tied Torf's hands behind his back none too gently. Ralph, Thierry, and Aimery stood by as escort.

Torf screamed denials and entreaties. Sir Robert winced.

'Take him outside; the sooner you silence that tongue the better.'

Geoffrey struggled to stand, but was held down by Robert's obedient soldiers.

'Let me at him,' he shouted. 'The wrong was greatest to me.'

'It was *my* father too, Geoffrey,' said Mauger, 'and I am the elder. It is my place.'

Geoffrey hesitated. Sybil was in everyone's mind, but could not be voiced. Instead Geoffrey said, 'He did not try to have you killed.'

'He did me,' said Ivo. 'I faced the knife too, my lord. I shall strike for you.'

He clapped a ham-like hand over the gibbering mouth, and began to drag the body towards the door.

'Then let me fight him!' roared Geoffrey. 'Not as a bishop – as a knight. I have that honour, and I have that right.'

'You may have the right, my lord,' said Robert, 'but, with respect, you do not at the moment have the power.'

'He is not worth a duel, my lord,' said Ivo. 'One does not enter the lists against vermin; one puts them down.'

'I command it,' said Geoffrey desperately. 'As your bishop.'

Robert allowed himself a smile.

'You can not have it both ways, my lord. And it is precisely because you are a bishop – and above all *my* bishop – that I am unable to accede to your understandable wishes.'

'Why not?' said Geoffrey, still struggling and red-faced.

'Not for you, my lord; for myself. You have our cathedral, our spiritual

322

welfare, in your safe keeping. I must protect my investment. Do you think I would endanger the immortal souls of my entire family for the sake of some petty duel with a – with a serpent like this? It would be just like God to punish me for my stupidity by allowing you to be killed, and serve me right. Besides, we should only kill him afterwards, so what is the point?'

Still squealing and wriggling, like a pig before the autumn fire, Torf of Malbec was dragged to the door and outside.

His voice gradually faded as Ivo and Mauger and the others took him to a discreet distance. The silence created by his caressing voice was now matched by the silence of his imminent fate. Geoffrey recalled something in a story that Gori had once told him about a ring of king's councillors turned into a circle of stones.

There was one agonised scream.

The sigh in the hall was unmistakably one of relief.

After a short interval Ivo appeared at the door.

'My lord. He is calling for a priest. What do we do?'

Geoffrey flung off the hands of the soldiers.

'We give him one.'

As he started towards the door, Robert stood before him.

'We give him a priest, my lord. Not another knight. Your knife, if you please.' He held out his hand.

After glaring, Geoffrey handed it over, and strode past him. Robert followed, but paused to gesture to his chief sergeant.

'Keep everyone in here.'

A tangle of spears at once blocked the doorway behind him.

Geoffrey stepped into a steady drizzle. More of Sir Robert's men held back the pressing crowd. About thirty paces away stood a clump of men beside some stunted bushes.

Mauger turned as he approached. His face was a mask of chagrin.

'I missed the heart. Now look what we have.'

Ralph, Thierry, Aimery and Ivo stood back. Torf lay in a huddle on the rain-darkened ground, clutching his wound. Blood ran with rain through his fingers and over the backs of his hands.

'You must hear my confession, Father. Bless me, Father, for I have sinned. You must – it is your holy duty.'

Geoffrey stood over him, fighting almost physical nausea of revulsion.

Those poor blinded cripples at Alençon was one thing; this obscene mess of a rotted soul was another.

'A sinner at the gates of Heaven, my lord. Not the righteous, but the sinners to repentance.'

Damn him and damn him!

Hugh of Cluny spoke in his ear.

'You are not there to like it, only to provide it. You are the vessel of God's Grace; would you – could you – knowingly block the holy unending stream of God's Love?'

'My lord, my lord – you must give me absolution. You must. It is the right of every sinner. Your father at least did not die unshriven.'

Mauger whirled round.

'What did he say?'

Geoffrey snapped into action.

'I will hear him. Retire, all of you. Go!'

'Only out of earshot, my lord,' said Robert. 'There we will wait. Be about your business.'

Geoffrey knelt beside the tortured, restless body. It was hard to tell whether it was rain or sweat on the darkened cheeks. The thinning hair was plastered across the veined scalp. There was a lot of swallowing and licking of the lips.

'Bless me, Father, for I have sinned . . .'

It was a sickening chronicle.

When at last Torf stopped, Geoffrey looked down at him.

'You must hurry; there may not be much time.'

Torf swallowed again.

'Time, my lord?'

'For absolution, you scum. What about Father? Father!'

It was as much as Geoffrey could do to refrain from grasping his clothes.

Instead Torf clutched Geoffrey's robe.

'There will be absolution, will there not? For every sinner?'

'For every sinner who makes a full confession. Now say it, damn you!'

So at last the treachery came out . . .

'But I had a debt of honour to pay, my lord. You must understand. Like you, a murdered father, long ago. A holy man, with an infant son, left defenceless in the world.'

Geoffrey stared.

'Oh, yes, my lord. They did not tell you that, did they? Now, my lord – there is – little time – your pardon, God's pardon.'

Geoffrey gritted his teeth and raised Torf with an arm round his shoulder.

'You are sure that is all?'

Torf coughed.

'Please hurry, my lord.'

'Repentance must be complete. Every sin recalled and admitted. Full penitence. Resolve not to sin again.'

'Again?'

'Is that all?' insisted Geoffrey.

'Start your prayers,' hissed Torf.

Geoffrey bullied his mind into reverence.

'By virtue of the power vested in me as a prince of the Holy Church – '

'Only one more.'

'Ego te absolvo – '

'A sick infant hastened to his grave, that is all.'

Geoffrey stared in horror and disbelief.

'Say it, Father, say it – "in the name of the Father" – say it!'

Geoffrey felt sick with shock.

'Raoul! Poison!'

'No matter. You have heard me. *"Ego te absolvo"* – you said it. You have lost and I have won.'

The effort brought on another fit of coughing.

Geoffrey's hands closed round Torf's throat.

'Animal! Demon! I revoke it! To the fire! God's curse upon you!'

He was aware of hurrying footsteps. Daggers rasped from sheaths. Torf convulsed beneath his hands as Robert pulled him away. By the time he was on his feet, the body was still; Mauger, Ivo, Thierry, and Ralph were all wiping blades on clumps of grass. Silent drizzle floated like a shroud.

Geoffrey was overcome with a fit of trembling. Ivo came to put an arm round his shoulders. Mauger came to support him on the other side.

'Take him inside,' said Robert. 'Get something hot into him. Leave this dog to us.'

When Geoffrey had gone, Robert looked down at the twisted body.

'I hope he has gone to Hell,' he said.

'Why?' said Aimery.

Robert glanced sidelong.

'Because I would not have wished him on God. Would you?'

✻   ✻   ✻   ✻   ✻   ✻

Sunlight streamed through the open eastern window and flooded the nave of the chapel.

The sisters in the choir responded as if they had seen a miracle. Sybil had been at St. Amand long enough to understand that many services became a duty, but that every so often one occurred which was different. Without warning, the slightest chance happening could lift it into a new realm far beyond mere observance and discipline – into spontaneous delight. One knew even as it was happening that the moment would not last long; one must hold on to it as tightly as possible while it ran its course; one must live it as fiercely as the body and mind would allow. It gave a faint glimmer of the near-blinding hope that the saints claimed in their visions.

Sybil had no idea whence had come this pleasure; for all she knew, it could as well have a physical as a spiritual genesis. Relief after the storm? The purge taken in the early morning at the infirmary? Clean clothes? The joyful, stabbing rays of an Advent sun? A chance insight into the meaning of a prayer? An unexpected harmony?

What did it matter? She was singing, and her heart was light. High notes rang inside her broad forehead. God was certainly pleased about something.

*　*　*　*　*　*

Chapter Twenty-Two

'It is time I got married.'

The sun had made one of its rare winter appearances. Travelling cloaks were dry and wrapped in saddle-packs. A monastery meal was still fresh under the belt. Everyone had long since said anything that was new. A man jogged along and followed his own thoughts. Every so often they rose to the surface. After eating they tended to optimism.

'I think I shall marry,' said Mauger.

If Ivo heard him he gave no sign. He continued his gentle, non-stop abuse of the animals. It was one of the noises of the trail, like the whining of wind in bare trees, or the crunch of stones beneath hooves. Nobody took any notice of him either.

Ralph and Aimery were scouting ahead. Behind them came lord Geoffrey's knights, who loathed Italy to a man, and who opened their mouths only to swear about it. Having established themselves and begun to build around Coutances, they could not wait to get back; Italy was a tiresome diversion, undertaken only under severe pressure and dark hints of deprivation from lord Geoffrey.

'They would not see it that way if they were landless second sons,' remarked Ralph to Aimery.

'Then why are you going back?' asked Aimery.

Ralph grinned.

'Different.'

He had turned down an offer from the Guiscard, but characteristically said nothing about it.

In the centre was the pack train, with the precious treasure, in the very heart of which lay the venerable relics and crucifix that Sir Robert had given them. Behind again came lord Mauger's men, now much better mounted, thanks again to Sir Robert's generosity. However, though the horse was stronger, the saddle was just as unyielding, and foot soldiers did not have the knack of long riding. They cursed in the mindless repetitive way of all soldiers the world over.

'For two straws I would sell the accursed animal and march on full meals for a month.'

Nobody did.

In the months since leaving Normandy, the whole company had come to know one another through and through – the way a man curled the reins over his hand, another's habit of resting a hand on his thigh, lines on the back of a neck, a gesture, a sniff, a trick of clearing the throat. On hot days, one did not have to look to see who was riding alongside; one could often tell by the distinctive odour.

Thoughts were old, opinions stale, prejudices boring. Most secrets had long since come out round endless philosophic camp fires, in the candlelit fug of a bleary tavern, or in a fit of unwonted fervour and fear following a monastic mass in the dark before a dawn departure.

'Travelling is a bit like being in a monastery,' observed Thierry, in one of his more replete moods. 'You are shut away with the same people day and night. The only difference is one is indoors and the other is outdoors. Perhaps that is why the brothers understand us so well.'

However, Thierry was not talking now; he was already beginning to feel hungry again, and he rarely spoke on an empty stomach except to draw attention to it.

My lord Geoffrey had hardly put two sentences together since they had left Apulia. He roused them early and he drove them far each day.

'Restless like a beetle,' grumbled someone. 'And he has nothing to worry about now; she is not going to run away.'

My lady Fressenda said substantially the same thing. So did Sir Robert.

'Stay with us; enjoy the winter. We keep good house.'

'I thank you for the invitation, but I must not lose time.'

'Our cathedral will not disappear,' said Robert, teasing him.

'Nor will Sybil,' added the lady Fressenda.

Geoffrey fidgeted.

'The sooner I am back the better. There are many things . . .'

Robert spread his hands.

'You can not cross the passes before the spring.'

'True. But I can wait in Pavia, and be ready to move as soon as the snows run.'

'Lanfranc's father?'

'Yes.'

'He sounds an impressive man, judging by what you say. I should like to meet him.'

'The son is even more impressive.'

'Another reason for your anxiety to return?'

'You could say that.'

'From what I hear,' said Robert, with his sly glance, 'he will not approve of your plans any more than his Holiness approved of the Duke's marriage.'

'Lanfranc acted only as the Pope's messenger,' said Geoffrey.

'You want his support rather badly?'

'I should value his respect,' said Geoffrey carefully.

Robert clapped him on the shoulder.

'If we spent our lives waiting for signs of approval before we did anything, even from those we respect, we should get very little done, my friend. Look at me.'

He beamed, positively glowing with confidence.

Geoffrey made a noise.

'Nevertheless . . .'

Robert shrugged massively.

'Very well, very well. So be it, so be it. Ask what you will for the journey, and it shall be yours.'

To his surprise, Constance made a point of speaking to him and giving him a parting present.

'I never thanked you properly for bringing us safe to Apulia,' she said. 'Please take this scarf.'

For once there were no fluttering eyelashes or double meanings. She looked him straight in the eye.

'I owe you much.'

Geoffrey thanked her, and ran his fingers over the expensive material.

'Silk! A rare luxury. Are you sure that – '

Constance tossed her head.

'One of many – in a collection given to me by my lord Richard. A bargain in a Greek market at Bari, he said.'

'The Count of Aversa?'

Constance blushed.

'Soon to be Prince of Capua. He has great plans.'

When Geoffrey told the tale, Ivo grunted.

'She was not thanking you, my lord; she was apologising – if you will permit me to say so. And she was apologising to the wrong brother.'

My lady Fressenda was more direct than her daughter.

'Tell Sybil to fight, to seize the world – as I did.'

'And marry?'

'Most definitely. Let her leave scruples to the theologians; that is their business. Women have enough trouble surviving in this world without bothering about fine points of dogma.'

She looked at Geoffrey.

'Besides, from my observations since arriving in this country, it is the Hildebrands of this world who are the rarities. Marriage among the clergy seems to be the norm here rather than the exception. So why not you? God did not make you half a man, and He is the one who has seen fit to place a mitre on your head.'

'That still troubles me sometimes,' admitted Geoffrey.

'Then do not let it. You are not made of the stuff of saints, Geoffrey. And I do not mean that as a criticism. You are still a good bishop. Moreover, you are a man on earth, and you are a man *of* earth, doing man's work. You are entitled to a man's rewards, for which you are prepared to make a man's vows. God and His angels! What do they want? You with a concubine like so many of them? Coming straight from the arms of a mistress to hear confessions about fornication?'

'It is a familiar enough compromise,' said Geoffrey. 'We only point the way; we do not necessarily travel along it. A signpost is helpful only because it is still and unchanging.'

Fressenda shook her head.

'It is not your way, Geoffrey, and it is not the Hauteville way. My lord Tancred could have taken that path. His first wife, the lady Muriella, died, leaving him five sons. He could have lived the rest of his life as an honoured, grieving widower, peopled the countryside with his bastards by way of consolation, and nobody would have thought any the less of him. Instead, he chose to live within the bounds of matrimony; he believed that liberties entailed duties as well. He took me. And look what my boys have achieved – all twelve of them,' she added pointedly.

Geoffrey smiled. She could not resist the boast.

His last view of her was on the marble steps of Robert's Greek palace, surrounded by eight of her sons; Humphrey was back from Rome. A slender but firm figure in black, amid broad, beaming men in the prime of life, whose every gesture about her betokened admiration and respect.

'I wonder if they will think the same when they have had her here for six months,' murmured Ivo.

Her last thoughts were of Sybil and Roger, her two youngest.

'Muriella is married and secure. Constance will shortly get what she came for, by the look of this Count Richard. She will be happy to make her own bed, and happier still to lie in it. I am where I want to be – I too have made my own bed. So it is up to you to see to Sybil. I am relying upon you. If she gets stubborn, tell her to behave or I shall come all the way back again and put her across my knee. Better still, put her across your own knee.'

She pressed into his hand a small silver cross, beautifully engraved.

'From Monte Gargano – blessed by the holy Archangel. See that Roger gets it.'

For the first and only time, Geoffrey noticed something akin to a tear in the corner of her eye. The moment did not last. She conjured up a smile.

'Constance will not have the courage to say this, so it is up to me. Tell Mauger how sorry I am. But a prince! Poor Constance – she really could not help herself. And it does happen to fit Robert's plans . . . '

'A wife – that is what I need.'

Ivo wagged his head. The Hauteville hussy had snatched away the cup but had left him with the taste. Eight weeks out of Apulia, and he was still thinking about it. Lord Geoffrey had driven them through southern Lombardy, round the Alps on the shelf above the sea, and into Provence in an attempt to steal a march on the winter weather. As they rode towards the Rhone and set their teeth into the wicked Mistral, there was little time or scope for thought, much less comment. It was in a rare respite from the bitter wind that my lord Mauger came out with it for the hundredth time.

He could be forgiven for it. Ivo, alone of the company, knew what a long struggle Master Mauger had had: at first to hold the fort – literally – while his father was away; later, when he was dead, struggling for mere survival; later still, working to make good the long neglect of Sir Nigel and his many adventures. All the while to make life secure for his mother, the lady Helena, and his young brother, Master Geoffrey. It had not made him exciting or interesting like his father, but he had remained constant and loyal. A lot of the natural light of a young man had been blotted out of him by the cloud of his worries.

'On, on, on – you long-eared, misbegotten, stubborn, three-legged . . . '

Odd how unfair life was. Sir Nigel went off on forays and expeditions, often for many, many months, with scarcely a thought for what he left behind – or so it seemed. When at last he returned, it was difficult to remain annoyed with him for long; he had such 'good' campaigns and journeys, he had so many stories to tell, so many gifts to bring back. Only a close, trusted companion saw a different man round a feeble fire in the creeping evening frost, under a soaking blanket beneath a storm-lit wagon, before a fight against odds. It was then that his love came out. Then too that his cross slipped into view. Somehow he must shift the burden of guilt, perform some monumental atonement, so that no looming retribution lingered to threaten his loved ones. Whatever he did was not enough; there always remained one further prodigy of penitence that would cleanse the soul once and for all.

'Just one more, Ivo. This really is the last. And this time you will stay behind – to help Mauger, and to watch over Master Geoffrey. Explain to the lady Helena for me if I do not return.'

Damn the man! Was it penitence? Or was it that he could never resist a jaunt? He was wrong – of course he was wrong. He was irresponsible, selfish if you like. But what a companion! What a swordsman! What an adventurer! Life was never dull when Sir Nigel was there.

331

Only for the poor people left behind to cope – like Master Mauger at seventeen. He was the one who stayed, and struggled, and coped; and he was the one who was dull. People shook their heads and smiled when they talked of Sir Nigel – even those he had left behind. Like Lambert, who would rest his hammer in order to reminisce; and Boso, who would lean on his upturned scythe and finger the blade fondly as if caressing a sword; and Gaimar, who barely knew him, but who still stirred his pot with glowing, faraway eyes. They did not do that when they talked of my lord Mauger. No. Life was unfair; there was no doubt about that. My lord Mauger deserved a wife. It was only to be hoped that life would relent sufficiently to provide him with a good one . . .

The ambush was a surprise as well as a shock.

Saracens? As far up the Rhone as this? And at this time of the year?

'Infidels do not respect season, convention, place or person,' said Geoffrey. 'Damn them and damn them!'

'Rather like the Hautevilles.' Mauger could not resist it. After Constance, who could blame him?

Surprise and shock, but no real danger. Geoffrey's column was too well armed and too well disciplined. After only a few minutes, three Saracens lay dead, and two wounded. The remainder galloped off on their light horses.

'Stay where you are!' bawled Ivo. 'We do not follow. Get their horses instead.'

He had heard stories of such temptations; apparently it was a common infidel trick. The deception by Fulk the Angevin came also freshly to mind. It was quite likely that Fulk had learned such subterfuges from Arabs or Turks; he was evil enough to have consorted with the Devil himself.

The only casualty was Aimery. He had been struck with one of their curved swords, unhorsed, and later trampled.

Ralph gnawed fingers.

'Well?'

Ivo grimaced.

'We ought to get him to shelter and care.'

'Stupid. How can he travel like that?'

Ivo made allowances for the worry, and did not take offence.

'How far is it to Cluny, my lord?'

'Two days,' said Geoffrey. 'Now, it will be more like three or four.'

Ralph cursed and swore.

'Very well,' shouted Geoffrey. 'We camp here for two days, and then move. It is the best compromise I can think of. It will also give us time to make a litter. See to it; he is your friend.'

Geoffrey was just as furious at the delay as Ralph was upset at the injury to

Aimery. For a moment they stood glaring at each other.

'Here,' said Thierry. 'I will come and help you.'

Round the fire that night, Geoffrey paced and muttered.

Ivo cleaned and polished his sword.

'You have made your decision, my lord. If you want my opinion, it is a good one.'

'I did not ask you for it.'

'You saved Ralph's life,' continued Ivo imperturbably, 'by getting him to Cluny alive. It gained you a man's loyalty. Why risk losing it by riding his friend into an avoidable grave?'

'You were all for leaving him, as I recall,' said Geoffrey.

'I was wrong. Ralph lived. Now Aimery can live. Do you want this devil of yours to kill him, and give you another cross to carry?'

Geoffrey stopped pacing, and came and sat down.

'How did you know?'

'My lord, you wear it like a boil on the neck for all to see. I do not mean the lady Sybil,' he went on, before Geoffrey had a chance to interrupt. 'I mean Torf. My guess is that he said something to you.'

Geoffrey sighed, and nodded.

Ivo spat.

'I thought as much. The peddler of poison leaves one of his barbs in the flesh even of his executioner. Christ and Mary, Master Geoffrey, when are you going to free yourself of this man?'

Geoffrey scraped together remains of fallen, half-burnt logs, and replaced them deliberately in the fire.

'I suppose, strictly speaking, it was not part of his confession . . . '

Thank God – it was coming at last.

'If you must know, Torf said that Father had killed his father.'

'Well?'

'The bishop. Torf's father was the bishop murdered by my father.'

Ivo grunted, and spat into the hissing flames.

'Is that all?'

'All?'

Ivo held up his blade and looked along it.

'My lord, Torf was always a liar. In that situation, he would have said anything.'

'How did he know? Where did he get the idea?'

'From your father, of course.'

'Did he talk to you about it?'

'I was your father's companion,' said Ivo, 'not his confessor. Nor am I a charming man. I do not drag things out of people. Perhaps – '

Ivo stopped himself.

'Perhaps what?' said Geoffrey.

'Nothing, my lord.'

Had Sir Nigel been granted a few moments before death to relieve his soul, as Torf had? There was nothing to be gained by torturing lord Geoffrey with the idea.

'But supposing it is true,' persisted Geoffrey.

'True or false, it is no matter. Torf either avenged a father with just cause or he did not. If he did, he has done it, and that is an end of it. If he had no just cause, then his soul is in Hell, where it belongs, and it was not you who put it there.'

Geoffrey rubbed a cheek with a fingertip.

'Mmm.'

'My lord,' said Ivo, 'you will find, as you listen to more and more confessions, that there is a certain type of villain who will always claim just cause, no matter how the truth is abused. It is not penitence; it is cowardice; it is the rot of fear. That is why I have more regard for a swine like Fulk; he at least made no bones about his villainy; he did not care what anybody thought, including God. He is not afraid; Torf, ultimately, was. He would do anything to stay the hand of retribution.'

'I pray you are right.'

'Take it from me, my lord, you have justly avenged a wronged father, and you have justly avenged a great wrong to yourself – and to me.'

And to a son!

Ivo returned his sword to the scabbard with a great slap.

'I saw your father darken his whole life with a sin he had committed in ignorance, and for which he paid several times over. Do you wish to darken yours – and ours – for the same reason? Is it for this that you wear the mitre? How long must penitence – or excuses for penitence – endure? Is this God of ours a shepherd or a hound? Is life a gift or a sentence?'

Thierry was ordered to take Aimery's place up ahead with Ralph. He was glad to get away from my lord Mauger's endless musings about his future.

'I think I shall seek a wife further east; I know the Cotentin too well. Fresh blood – that is what we need. The Beaumonts, Warennes, Tosnys, Clairs – a better class of family. there ought to be a suitable girl among them somewhere. With Saint-Sever and Sourdeval added to Montbrai, and Mortain to come, in all probability . . . Sir Mauger de Montbrai, Count of Mortain . . .' If ; Mauger had not been wearing his gloves, he would have rubbed his hands. 'Sounds good . . .'

After two days with Ralph, Thierry was going mad with frustration.

'He never speaks. He simply does not speak. The only words he utters come at the end of the day, when he rushes back to ask how Aimery is. As for bad temper . . . '

Ivo took Thierry's place. Ralph did not swear at him.

Thierry had never thought that he would be glad to see again the Abbey of Cluny.

'At least a change of prison.'

Geoffrey asked if he could buy some books for Coutances. Abbot Hugh provided one or two.

'Have you none of the ancients?' asked Geoffrey. Lanfranc had shown him impressive libraries in Italy.

'None, either for you or for ourselves,' said Hugh. 'I am surprised you ask.'

'I am not familiar with many,' admitted Geoffrey, 'but I am informed that they numbered among them men of great ability and insight.'

Gori had always said so, and told many stories.

'Possibly,' said Hugh, 'but all in error.'

'Error? All?'

'Of course. Why else did God send us the Light if the world had not been in total darkness? Of what guidance is the learning of darkness? How can it compare with writing compiled in the Light of the Truth?'

'I should like to see Lanfranc argue with that man,' said Ivo later to Geoffrey.

'You would not understand a word,' said Geoffrey.

'I know. But I should enjoy seeing the sparks fly. That abbot is too confident for his own good or anybody else's.'

Aimery died the next day.

Abbot Hugh undertook the funeral arrangements. Ralph asked, as a special favour, if Geoffrey would say a Mass for Aimery's soul.

As he stood at the altar in the massive abbey church of Cluny, Geoffrey could not help but recall the last requiem mass he had said.

Not in a soaring nave, but in a booming underground cavern, with a glistening roof and streaming walls. The floor was wet and slippery; the lady Fressenda had to be supported at each elbow by one of her sons.

She fought to be freed.

'I walked to the altar for Drogo in Normandy; I shall walk to the altar for Drogo and William in the shrine of the Archangel.'

Robert stood before her.

'Mother, have some sense. These public performances must have gone to your head. It is as much as *we* can do to stand. God may expect you to perform prodigies, but not miracles. If you argue, I shall pick you up and carry you there. And we may both fall. I say dignity before pride.'

So the Mass was said –for my lord Tancred of Hauteville, for Count William of the Iron Arm, for Count Drogo, for Sir Nigel of Montbrai, and for Ralph's brother, Michael, namesake of the Archangel himself – in a heady atmosphere of stale incense and hundreds of guttering candle flames that waved and hissed in the incessant drops from the roof. As Geoffrey faced the congregation and raised the Host, he caught his breath at the sight of dozens of rapt faces, underlit by the candles, the glow of their skin leaping at him out of the darkness behind and around them, the silence broken only by the eternal drip, drip, drip. On either side loomed the yawning mouths of black alcoves hiding, deep in their throats, long-neglected altars; shadowed, crumbled offerings of grateful past centuries lurked against their walls like half-glimpsed diseased teeth.

It did not seem to bother the Guiscard that much of the wealth that decorated the altar and the reliquary of the Archangel had been looted from pilgrims on their way to the shrine for the express purpose of making their own offerings.

'Pah! God gets it in the end. Besides, I do it with so much more style . . .'

'Ite, missa est.'

Outside the abbey church, they waited for the monks to file past to their ghostly duties.

Ralph thanked him.

Geoffrey shrugged.

'The least I could do.'

Ralph offered some coins.

'Would you ask my lord abbot to have some more said after we have gone? I am happy to pay.'

Geoffrey looked at the pale, tight face. It reminded him of the distraught young man he had seen with a drawn knife between them, or the stricken boy in the death chamber at Gisors.

'That will not be necessary. Aimery was in my service, not yours. I have already seen to it.'

Ralph's face relaxed very slightly.

'I thank you, my lord. All the same . . . the more masses the better. And I want one said again for my brother.' He held out his hand with the coins in the palm. 'For my friend and for my brother. I should feel more at peace myself, as you yourself did at Monte Gargano.'

Geoffrey took the money.

'I shall see that my lord abbot gets it. Thank you.' He swallowed. 'I am – I am sorry about Aimery.'

Ralph's eyes twitched.

'My sister will grieve; she liked him.'

Geoffrey tried to make things easier.

'Whom do you want to go ahead with you on the trail? Name anyone.'

Ralph had already turned away, and was making off in the slightly swaggering stride that had become his own.

'Whoever you like, my lord,' he said over his shoulder. 'A man is a man.'

But not a partner . . .

Spring in Burgundy! Mauger snuffed the air. He could barely sit still in the saddle. The rains, the fogs, the ice and snow, the piercing wind, bitter mornings and bone-chilling evenings – they were all behind them. Ahead – soft slopes, gentle rivers, burgeoning summer. Nevers, Bourges, Orleans . . . they were practically home. He was anxious to begin his search for someone suitable.

The still formality of Abbot Hugh's farewell on a blooming morning contrasted vividly with the bear-like embraces and playfulness of the Guiscard's goodbyes just after a chilling, soaking Christmas . . .

'I must thank you for many things,' said Geoffrey.

Robert waved hugely.

'It is I who am in your debt, my bishop. For good company, for good sport, for good riddance – of some tiresome vermin – above all, for the gift of my mother. Oh – and for my sister,' he added with a mischievous chuckle. 'Nearly slipped my mind.'

He looked back along the column to make sure that they were not overheard.

'If you ask me, I think your brother is probably well out of it. I have no idea whether Count Richard will thank me after a year or two. He will think it is some dastardly plot of mine.'

Geoffrey grinned.

'Is it?'

Robert gave him his famous sidelong glance.

'My lord, what a leading question! Ha!'

Geoffrey indicated the laden donkeys.

'This is generosity indeed. Far more than I should have dared to ask.'

Robert lifted his massive shoulders in a mountainous shrug.

'What are treasures but potential gifts? I should never get our cathedral by sitting on my gold and silver here, should I? Now you are in my debt all over again; I am doubly sure of Coutances now.'

'Trebly so,' said Geoffrey, 'after the memorial to my father.'

'It is no more than you will do for Father and William and Drogo at Coutances. And us, when the time comes.'

Geoffrey reached inside one of his saddlebags, and pulled out a large leather wallet.

'In that case, I offer this not as payment, or as thanks, simply as a mark of esteem and respect.'

'What is it?'

'My lord Tancred's chessmen. I brought them in case I had to play you again.'

Robert laughed.

'That was not necessary, thanks to the generosity of his Holiness after Civitate.'

Robert touched the wallet.

'May I see them?'

'Of course.'

Geoffrey laid the package on a tree stump and unwrapped it. Robert's face lit up with recognition. He took out two or three pieces and stood them up. Tears ran down his brown cheeks. He took a pawn in his hand and caressed it with a large, square-nailed thumb.

'Father was a dreadful player.'

Very carefully he began to replace them. The last piece to go back was a bishop.

Robert gently tied the parcel and returned it to the wallet. He handed it back to Geoffrey.

'They were a gift from my mother to you, and were a sign of her regard. I endorse her decision, and see no reason to reverse it. Besides, my father belongs in Normandy, and so do these. But I thank you for the compliment.'

Geoffrey bowed slightly.

'I thank you for a greater one.'

Robert bowed in return.

'What will you do now?' asked Geoffrey, as he re-fastened his saddlebag.

Robert laughed uproariously.

'Do? Survive, of course. If that gets boring, I shall give the pot a stir and see what tempting morsels come to the surface.'

'Like another alliance of Pope and Emperor.'

Robert snapped his fingers.

'Pah! We have no Pope yet – or we had none when Humphrey left Rome. So who knows what we shall get – a corrupt Roman nobleman, a puppet of the Germans, or a burning reformer, another Hildebrand? As for the Emperor, it is a long time since Henry showed his face in Italy. When the cat is away . . .'

There was another gust of laughter.

'I tell you what: if the new Pope does not agree to your marriage, I shall lay siege to Rome until they elect one who will. How about that?'

Geoffrey had never met anyone of such superb self-confidence. No wonder the Duke in distant Normandy drew inspiration from news of this man's exploits. Geoffrey too felt that he could approach any future task or problem totally untroubled by any thought of failure.

'And mind!' said Robert. 'I may still find time to come and see this cathedral of ours. Big, remember! Style! And class – plenty of class.'

He knelt to kiss the episcopal ring. He had offered another – larger, richer. Geoffrey had thought it a trifle vulgar. He declined.

'You know the story of this ring,' he said, touching Thorold's ruby. 'It never leaves my hand.' He pointed to his mother`s garnet. 'Neither does this.'

'I understand. Just an idea.'

Robert got to his feet.

'And now, a safe journey to you, my bishop. My love to Sybil, and take good care of her. My love too to baby Roger; I expect we shall see him here one day. Oh – and dear old Humbert. Nearly forgot. Funny – I always think of Humbert as old . . . '

'Just smell that!'

Thierry screwed up his nose and took another deep, ecstatic breath.

'I never thought the day would come when I should say that about a Norman midden. Home!'

They had swung north-west from Orleans to avoid Paris, and had crossed the border at Bellême.

It was in the hall of Sir Roger of Montgomery, in a corner away from my lady Mabel's gimlet eyes, that Ralph sprang his surprise.

Geoffrey was dumbfounded. And hurt.

'Leave? Why?'

Ralph looked awkward.

'I – I am not good at explaining, my lord.'

'Aimery.'

Ralph's eyes twitched.

'I can not work with the man you gave me.'

'I can easily find others,' said Geoffrey. 'Name anyone you like.'

Ralph shook his head.

'I know now that I shall never become a knight. I have found my calling.'

'You are a very good scout,' said Geoffrey. 'I am happy to keep you in that capacity. I repeat – '

Ralph held up a hand.

'Please, my lord. I am trying to explain . . . I am solitary, silent. It suits me. In my sort of work, one does not look for others to work with as one would cast about for a lost shoe. One wakes up one day, and there he is, has been there all the time. Sometimes, one does not even realise until he is gone . . . '

Ralph looked desperately to left and right.

'When – when Michael died, I tried to stay and help; I really did. But the bung was fast in the barrel; nothing could get out. I was impossible to live with. It was not all Aubrey's fault by any means. Mother's tears and Father's silent suffering made it worse. The ache eased only when I was alone, out of doors, away . . . Some men ease the pain with drinking or whoring, even with prayer, they say. I have tried all three, but it is no good. They are like a bandage to cushion the cut; take it away, and the cut is still there.'

Geoffrey sat in silence. He had never heard Ralph put so many words together at one time.

'I was rude to Aimery at first, just as I was rude to everybody. Only he took no offence. That was why I liked working with him; he did not argue; it was so peaceful. It was only when he was wounded . . . Michael is back in my dreams . . . my lord, the bung is in the barrel again.'

'Is there friction between you and anybody in particular?' asked Geoffrey.

Ralph shook his head vigorously.

'Nothing. My lord, it is not because I have not been content in your service. Look at me: what I now am I owe to you. Just as I owed life itself to my home and my mother and father. But I could not stay there. I beg you to understand . . .'

'Let him go,' said Ivo, when Geoffrey told him. 'If he does not go in broad daylight with your blessing, he will slink away in the night without it. Which do you want?'

'I want him to come back,' said Geoffrey. 'So I must send him away.'

And come back soon. Ivo was not getting any younger. The limp was more pronounced. The cough was harsher. He was beginning to make old man's noises . . .

'I think I shall come with you to the next Council,' said Mauger.

'If you are invited,' warned Geoffrey.

'Oh, not to sit with them,' said Mauger. 'Not yet. Just to be there, in case.'

In case Mortain, by the merest chance, should slip from the Duke's table of rewards for his loyal followers. How convenient for Mauger to be there to hold out his hands to catch it, and to be able to give hands for it straight away.

What was it that Sir Roger was fond of saying: 'Favours do not get thrown long distances.'

'A man in my position,' said Mauger, 'in search of a wife, needs to be well endowed . . . What are you laughing for?'

*　　*　　*　　*　　*　　*

They sat with bowed shoulders at opposite ends of a fallen tree-trunk. Midsummer sun warmed the back of their necks as they looked down at folded hands.

The gardener almost brushed Geoffrey as he stumped past.

'I am afraid that Felix is very grumpy,' said Sybil. 'I have been getting him to plant vegetables that he does not agree with.'

'Ah!'

The remark was barely a ripple in the flat pool of silence that surrounded them.

*   *   *   *   *   *

Chapter Twenty-Three

Goscelin's eyebrows soared into arches of disdain.

'Might I ask where your Grace – gleaned such – individual ideas?'

He made it sound like an accusation.

'Italy, of course. Where you yourself trained. It takes the breath away – Roman, Greek, Moorish. It is like being in the midst of some great stream. It – it immerses you. Surely you have sometimes felt that.'

'If I may say so, my lord, there is a difference between being immersed in a stream and being drowned in it. The trained mind – selects.'

Geoffrey knew his man well enough not to take offence. He returned to the attack.

'Sir Robert has very definite views,' he said. 'And he is paying.'

It was the nearest Geoffrey came to seeing Goscelin laughing. That is, a sort of trembling shook his angular frame, like a badly-built siege tower in an earthquake. He pretended to wipe away a tear.

'The Hautevilles! Oh, my lord – really!' After this lapse of self-indulgence, he retrieved his Olympian calm. 'My lord, it is my invariable experience that the one who pays for a work of art is the last person fit to pass comment on its artistic merit, or on the manner of its production. The very fact that they possess the wealth to commission it means that they have been worshipping Mammon rather than God; Art, to them, is merely something that they can afford to make them feel good. What can they possibly know?'

Geoffrey was not going to admit defeat as easily as that.

'Sir Robert is a remarkable man,' he said. 'He lives in a Greek palace. All around him are splendid examples of the best art from three worlds – Roman, Greek, Arab.'

'I am not talking of appreciation, my lord, but of imagination, of desire. Not what they are content to use, but what they think they wish to create. Men who come into sudden riches, as Sir Robert has, tend towards ostentation and vulgarity rather than innovation and purity.'

Geoffrey would have admitted to catching some of Sir Robert's taste for magnificence, but would have bridled at the charge of vulgarity.

'You are not the only expert, you know,' he said.

Goscelin drew himself up.

'It may interest you to know, my lord, that during your absence I was consulted by master-masons from Avranches, Rouen, and Jumièges, all three of which are far more advanced in their construction than I am in the cathedral church of Our Lady at Coutances.'

He waited to let his next remark have full effect.

'And from Bayeux.'

'What! I hope you did not tell him anything. Bishop Odo can do his copying elsewhere.'

Goscelin preened himself.

'My lord, it will be the most sincere form of flattery. Your cathedral will become the talk of Normandy, I promise you – the exemplar, the inspiration.' He paused. 'So long as it is free from Italian – extravagances.'

'Goscelin, what is so wrong with statues and carvings? They are all over Italy. What about all the Roman sculpture too? Italian ideas are spreading – Provence, Burgundy. You should see the wonder on people's faces when they look at them.'

'I would not know, my lord; I am not an – image-chipper.'

'I want my cathedral to be a wondrous place,' said Geoffrey.

'True wondrousness, my lord, comes from what people feel, not from what they see. My cathedral will have such grace, such proportion, such harmony that a man will feel the ineffable, sense the unfathomable.' He drove his fist into his palm. 'My lord, you want it to be a monument; I want it to be a prayer.'

'A simple man must see before he feels, before he begins to understand,' said Geoffrey. 'I want it to be a hand reaching out to him from God.'

Ivo's jaw dropped. As they walked round the site, he could not forbear to remark:.

'I have never heard you speak like that, my lord.'

'No,' said Geoffrey, and came near to wry smile. 'No.'

He looked at the growing walls. There was no question now; a great building was beginning to rise out of the ground. It was the first time he had seen it as bigger than the men working on it. They had ceased to tramp over it; they were now toiling in it; God willing, they would one day be labouring beneath it.

The walls rose like hopes – more reliably than other walls of motte and rampart.

*　　*　　*　　*　　*　　*

At first, after such a long separation, they had talked politely like a couple of ambassadors waiting in an ante-room.

'I hear we have a new pope.'

'Yes. A German bishop – of Eichstadt. His Holiness "Victor II" now.'

'So he will be another puppet of the Emperor,' said Geoffrey.

'Hildebrand petitioned the Emperor for him,' said Sybil. 'We get news here too.'

'So who will pull the strings behind the Papal throne?'

Will the new man forbid us to marry or not? Or so Sybil read the look on

343

Geoffrey's face.

Sybil walked into the garden, and held open the gate behind her.

'Did you know that Earl Siward had died?'

'And Tostig gets Northumbria?'

'The Godwins now hold two of the great earldoms – half of England.'

'And Stigand is still Archbishop of Canterbury. No hope for Robert of Jumièges.'

'Pope Victor has excommunicated Stigand.'

'So did Pope Leo. It made no difference.'

Geoffrey followed her.

'It still makes no difference.'

Sybil turned and looked at him.

'Would you face excommunication for me?'

Geoffrey tossed his head.

'Sybil, we have been through this before. Besides, Stigand was uncanonically elected; my appointment has been confirmed by a Church Council. Being married has nothing to do with it. They can not excommunicate every married priest.'

Sybil sat down on the end of a fallen trunk.

'If Raoul had lived, I might have faced the fire for you – and him.'

Geoffrey sat down too, at a gentle distance.

'Your mother thinks it is a good idea; so does Robert. I have their blessing.'

Sybil flashed a glance at him; the Hauteville eyes blazed.

'They are not me. And their – blessing will avail nothing. After Raoul. There! There was the judgment of God.'

Geoffrey felt tears start at the back of his eyes. How could he tell her that it was not the wrath of God, but the spite of a devil?

Sybil looked down at her hands.

'I have had time to think while you were away, Geoffrey.'

'So have I. And I tell you – '

'Geoffrey, please. Your thinking has been all looking forward – to arrival and marriage. You have been in movement, and you have looked forward to stillness. I, by contrast, have been in stillness these many months; for me the future you would have is fraught with disturbance. To you it is an end; for me it would be a beginning.'

'Well, of course, it would be that too,' said Geoffrey.

'No, listen, please, my love. I do not wish to say this, but I owe you the truth, and I know it may hurt. I – I am not sure, now, that I have the calling for marriage.'

Geoffrey stared.

'But – '

'Yes, yes, I know what you are going to say.'

Lines appeared in her broad forehead as she frowned in concentration.

'We made love, and – I was happy. I admit that Torf even excited me, but I know now that it was flattery.'

Geoffrey burst out.

'What about when I came back from Apulia for the first time? Do not tell me that was merely response to flattery.'

Sybil considered carefully.

'No. That is true. That was a violent craving, quickly assuaged. A madness. Understandable after a long separation. Like a hermit after a long fast.' She twined her fingers in her agitation. 'I have felt passion on rare occasions, I admit, but I am not conscious of desire as a regular part of my life. I do not seem to be made that way. When I think of Constance – '

Geoffrey stood up and began pacing.

'This is guilt – all guilt. You have had far too long to think about it. Far too much stillness, if you ask me. If Raoul had lived – '

Holy Virgin! He was doing it himself now.

*　　*　　*　　*　　*　　*

'You have done wonders, Ranulf – wonders.'

Ranulf grunted. 'In the face of exceeding difficulty, may I say, my lord. Fighting the constant bias in favour of the cathedral. If you will permit me to say so, Goscelin enjoys far too privileged a position. This town will live and die as much by its walls and its market as by its cathedral – whenever that extraordinary edifice should show signs of nearing completion.'

'Goscelin is your cousin,' Geoffrey reminded him.

Ranulf looked pained.

'Has your Grace no relatives?'

'Very well, very well, I take your point. I will talk to Goscelin. Now – about the new wagons.'

Ranulf had indeed done wonders; it had not been flattery on Geoffrey's part. Well, not entirely.

Besides the wall, he had completed repairs to the bridge across the River Soulles. At St. Lô, he had begun a completely new bridge over the Vire, and laid the foundations for a mill. Despite his bitter complaints against his cousin Goscelin, they had in fact worked together in the matter of transporting the huge quantities of stone needed, though brawls broke out now and then between rival gangs of labourers, usually at weekends when an extra mug of drink was doled out.

*　　*　　*　　*　　*　　*

345

Outside the town, Geoffrey's knights were working hard on their fees – only too glad to hang up their mail for a while and prod their reeves into the sort of activity into which Geoffrey had been goading them for the last six months.

Thierry, who had an ear for gossip, provided the titbit that men were already beginning to complain.

'About what?'

'Efficiency, my lord. They say they are being driven too hard. Oppression. That is what they call it. Not like that in the good old days, they say.'

Geoffrey threw up his hands to Heaven and stormed out of the hall.

Thierry looked at Ivo; they grinned at each other.

'Where has he gone now?'

'Probably to clamber over fallen masonry underneath the aqueduct and to talk about "degrees of incline" with Ranulf. If only those grumblers of yours could see him, they would know that he drives himself hardest of all.'

Thierry pulled a huge piece of cheese out of his jerkin.

'Is he driving himself towards something or away from something?'

'Your guess is as good as mine. I should not like to be the one to ask him though . . .'

On the edge of the town square, before turning away towards the aqueduct, Geoffrey stood back and surveyed the rising cathedral. Some day soon, he would travel to the new fiefs in the Channel Islands, despite his horror of the sea. To come at Coutances from offshore – that would be quite new.

Wherever he found himself during the day, he liked to turn about and view it from a fresh angle – 'just to see how it appears from here,' he would say to the question on Ivo's face.

'He looks at it every time he can,' said Ivo.

Thierry swallowed his last mouthful.

'Like a father gazing into the cradle. Immortality, I suppose.'

'Something like that . . .'

*　　*　　*　　*　　*　　*

Geoffrey was pacing.

'I always thought you longed for me. I did for you.'

'I longed for your soul, your heart, your mind, your spirit; I longed for the honesty of your constant search. I thought it answered the quest in me. You are searching still, and that means wearing the mitre. Believe me, Geoffrey, I understand. I respect it. But I can not be part of it. Not fully.'

Geoffrey stopped and turned.

'Even if what you say is right about the mitre – and I am not saying it is

– why can a man not love his woman and love his God at the same time?'

'It is not a question of love; it is a question of commitment. If you are not committed to me fully, ultimately you would not respect me fully, and I could not bear that. And I should hate myself for causing this torture in you. Nor would you want this conflict – not really.'

Geoffrey started pacing again.

'It is what I said – guilt. Guilt and scruples and damned dogma.'

Sybil stayed still.

'No, my love. I honestly do not think so. Though I might have thought so once. Perhaps when I ran from you at the altar rail in Hauteville. Now I have had time to work it out more clearly. It is not a question of dogma, or virtue, or scruples, or guilt. It is not vain morals or fear of the fire, although the fear is still sometimes there. It is a matter simply of room.'

Geoffrey paused and stared.

'Room?'

'Yes, a matter of room. I think I understand Hildebrand now; a priest does not have room – not to fight the sort of fight that Hildebrand has in mind. There must be no ties – family, legal, social – nothing. People say he is a madman, but his is the will; he knows exactly what he wants, and he will move many men from his path towards getting it, because their will is not as strong as his. Like my brother Robert. He would laugh to hear it, but they are both unstoppable in their different ways.'

'You can not make men chaste by a Papal bull,' said Geoffrey.

'One does not have to. It is not a question of fleeting moments of passion; it is a question of binding commitment. Hildebrand is not concerned with moral lapses, but with the life of devotion *between* the lapses. And he does not want devotion in another direction. Think too of the loyalty demanded of you by the Duke. There are two causes; could you serve a third to the uttermost?'

'Why not?'

Mauger's remark came back to him: 'I know you, Geoffrey; you do things right through.' Sybil was being just as annoying. Why?

Geoffrey ran his hand through his dark hair. He had always hated the clerical tonsure.

'Very well! I shall give it up. Perhaps Hugh of Cluny was right after all.'

Sybil raised her head.

'Give it up? The mitre?'

'Yes.'

'And Coutances?'

'The cathedral, yes. I still have property there. And the Islands. And Malbec.

Others too.'

Sybil smiled and shook her head.

'Impossible, my darling.'

'Why? That is all we wanted when we started out.'

'Turn our back on six years of life? Pretend they never happened?'

'They have brought us little happiness.'

'Neither would the future, on those terms.'

'I do not see why not.'

Sybil leaned towards him, and beckoned him to come and sit down again.

'My darling, no matter what you may say, you like being a bishop. I like being here at St. Amand. Think how much bigger the world has become for you – for me too, it may surprise you to know. Now suppose we both give up all that, hurry away to Malbec or to these islands of yours, and become the household of Montbrai the Younger. Poor relations. Lonely vassals in the back of beyond. I with a string of pregnancies, and you with a crushing burden of worries and debts – unable to do more than keep the wolf from the door.'

'Hundreds of knights and their ladies do the same. Look at your mother.'

'Yes,' said Sybil, pouncing. 'But they know nothing else. For Mother it was a challenge, not a refuge. Think of us in the long darkness of winter – with nothing for company but our memories. I should become like your mother, pining for something that could never be. You? You would bore people with your stories of a brief, great past, or you would be forced to live through your children – like my father. Or, worse, you would desert me to go off on adventures, like your own father. We should become mere reflections of the regrets of our parents. Is that what you want? Repetition? A wasted, sterile generation that goes nowhere? A talent buried in a forlorn sigh before a remote hearth?'

Geoffrey looked down at her hands closed over his.

'Devil take the mitre!' he muttered. 'You are wrong, you know. I hate it sometimes.'

'No, my love. You do not hate it; you hate only what being a bishop entails. Just as I like being at St. Amand, but my heart breaks at what relentlessly follows.'

Geoffrey swallowed.

'The thought of seeing you – our life together – it kept me going, all those months on the road . . . '

* * * * * *

'I think we need to be realistic, my lord.'

Geoffrey liked Canon John. He was young, but he was intelligent and imaginative. More so than his father, Canon Peter. Curiously, he reminded Geoffrey

348

of Peter's grandfather, Thorold – something to do with the way he held his head. Perhaps the premature baldness too. It seemed to run in the family. Thorold's other son, Canon Walter, was as shiny as a pebble in the bed of a brook.

'We must not hope for completion in the foreseeable future, no matter how well the work progresses. If your Grace will permit me to say, I fear that none of us foresaw the complexity of the task before us.'

John spoke plainly, like Ivo, without fear or flattery.

'Or the standards to be set by Goscelin,' added Geoffrey, with a wry smile.

John caught the spirit of his remark.

'If the length and the agony of the labour are anything to go by, your Grace, the offspring, when it finally appears, should be something quite prodigious.'

'Let us hope that we shall all be here to witness it.'

'More seriously, my lord, I recommend therefore that you proceed with all speed with the wooden chapel.'

'Are you going to tell Ranulf, or must it be me?' asked Geoffrey.

John continued imperturbably.

'Once you have strengthened the doors and the locks, we can at least think of safety for the relics and the treasure.'

'I shall consecrate the temporary reliquary and the new altar there next month,' said Geoffrey, steeling himself for the uncomfortable interview with the overworked and gloomy Ranulf.

John nodded.

'I agree. The sooner we add Almighty God to the iron of the locks as guardians of the treasure, the quieter we can sleep at nights.' He smiled again. 'After four months, my father says he can not get used to having a giant silver crucifix under his bed.'

'Now,' said Geoffrey, 'have you fixed a date for the homage of the new canons?'

'Indeed I have, my lord. Word has gone out. And the new vestments are nearly complete. Altar cloths are here already.'

John was efficient too. Geoffrey liked a servant who kept pace with him.

'Oh, and the matter of Canon Thorold's tomb, my lord. I have at last prevailed upon Goscelin to mark out a spot for his final resting-place. If your Grace will be good enough to follow me.'

Geoffrey recalled Thorold's passionate plea: 'Would you have denied us every consolation?'

A similar consolation was about to be denied to the Bishop of Coutances, or so it seemed.

*　　*　　*　　*　　*　　*

'Suppose you returned to Malbec,' suggested Geoffrey. 'I could endow you.'

'It is not all yours,' said Sybil.

Geoffrey made a dismissive gesture.

'Mauger will let me have his half. He has high hopes of Mortain. He would do it for me.'

'And for me – an Hauteville? After Constance?'

'I am sure he would,' persisted Geoffrey.

Sybil shook her head.

'Whether Mauger would or would not matters nothing. Everybody would know what I was.'

'You would have everything you need.'

'Except status.'

'A legal vassal.'

'For how long, if something should happen to you? And how comfortably, when you were away on your many travels? No, Geoffrey. It will not do.'

'I do not see why.'

'Because you look at it from your own point of view. You see nothing untoward in a liaison because it does not conflict with being a bishop. Even Hildebrand has not yet tried to get rid of all concubines. Only wives. You can not see that a liaison conflicts with my sense of survival. For me, survival depends upon status. At Malbec, as kept woman or as vassal in my own right, I should have no real status, because everyone would know what it depended upon.'

'Is status that important to you? In preference to all else?'

Sybil tossed her head.

'The people who say that a certain thing is not that important are never the ones in serious danger of losing it.'

'I can not follow you,' said Geoffrey. 'You reject marriage, yet you say you love me. I offer an arrangement which will achieve the same ends without the difficulties you mentioned, and you reject that too.'

'Because it will achieve the same ends only for you, Geoffrey. Not for me. Can you not see? Instead of becoming a partner whom you may live to resent, I should all the sooner become a scandal and a liability, whom you would plan to dispose of when the burden became too great. It would not bring you closer; it would drive you further away. I do not want such a thing. I was not brought up to it.'

'What does that mean?'

The bright blue eyes looked steadily into his.

'It means, Geoffrey, that it is also a question of upbringing. Father had strong views on marriage. I take no credit for it. It is just the way we are. Father, Mother, Muriella. Even Constance, for all her waywardness, wanted marriage in the end.'

'Yes – in the end. Not first. Try asking Mauger.'

Sybil set her jaw. The high colour was beginning to return to her cheeks.

'Nevertheless – it is status. Status. In this life it is everything – it is what sets our rank at birth; it is what sustains and protects us in a hostile world; it is what shows our path in life. Why else do you think God has ordained all these roles for us? There is a scheme for all; everyone fits somewhere. Leave our place, and we risk falling into limbo, and serve us right. God must know. How else can we have order in a chaotic world? It is only Divine Common Sense, if you like.'

'You can argue just like your mother. She said you were like her; she was right . . . '

*   *   *   *   *   *

'Did you have a good trip, my lord?' asked Canon Peter, the cathedral chamberlain.

Geoffrey strode past with thunder across his face. Immediately behind him, Ivo made an expressive gesture to convey vomiting. Peter wisely kept out of his Grace's way.

It was the next day before his Grace could face solid food. Or before he was approachable.

'It is terrible! Unspeakable! Scarcely a Christian building visible on either of the two main islands. As for the others, a pagan midden, each and every one. Clumsy charms and rotting animals hanging from every nail and every branch. Holy Virgin! Where does one start?'

Somewhat unwisely, Canon Peter opened his mouth to answer.

'And do not tell me,' said Geoffrey.

Builders, toolmakers, carpenters, smiths, draught animals – dear God! It was everything. And the cost! Few expenses need be grudged on the cathedral; after all, it was Robert's money. But the Montbrai habit of thrift died hard in other places. And they would need priests . . . Bishop Hugh of Avranches! What about his school? And Lanfranc. He would have some ideas. Come to think of it –

'Start a school!' he burst out. 'Why not? A school.'

Canon Peter stood patiently while the familiar tide of ideas swept over his head. As it subsided, he coughed politely.

'In your absence, my lord, there have come two communications.'

'Oh?'

'Yes, my lord. First, an official pronouncement of his Grace, the Archbishop Maurilius of Rouen.'

Peter paused.

Geoffrey looked up.

351

'Go on, go on.'

Peter made a despairing little gesture.

'Alas, my lord. It was an official condemnation of clerical marriage. The first in the duchy. I presume the Duke is in agreement, otherwise . . .'

He wilted under Geoffrey's stare.

'What is the second?'

Peter grasped the straw.

'The second, my lord, is a summons to attend the Duke's Council.'

Geoffrey swore.

'Another? Where?'

'Lisieux, my lord. It concerns – '

'Too far. Much too far. At this time of the year. There is no threatened invasion. Anjou is quiet. The King sleeps. No bad news has come from Brittany. How does he expect us to "build!", as he keeps on telling us?'

'I am sure I do not know, my lord.'

'Send Canon John to me.' Geoffrey paced impatiently until he arrived.

'Did you have a fruitful voyage, my lord?'

'Not you as well. If you must know, I suffered the pains of the damned.'

But the first glimpse on the return journey – haze or not – seeing a hill like that from the sea – imagining what it would look like when the tower was complete. Yes, it had been worth it . . .

*　*　*　*　*　*

Sybil nodded.

'Yes, I know, people talk about the Hauteville fever, the Hauteville drive – call it what you will. I never wanted to go away, like the boys. But I did have a lust for I knew not what. Why had God given me a mind that thought the things I did? Life had to be more than what Constance saw – gossip and giggle and grope under the blankets before sleep, and dream of babies and fine clothes. Nor did I have the strength to cope with the sort of life that Mother had accepted.'

'You have all her energy, and more,' said Geoffrey. 'Look at you now – the laundry, the choir, the garden.'

'Please, my love, let me finish . . . Then I fell in love with you. You, I thought, answered all these cravings, and more. But the mitre came between us, and your travels took you away, never mind for what reason. God took Raoul from us . . . Now look at me here. I have privacy, for which I always yearned. I have security. I have purpose. I have scope for this tiresome mind of mine. Who knows? Perhaps Mother was right; perhaps I do have her capacity for rule – only not in the way she imagined. I would confess it only to you, but the thought of being an abbess does not appal me. I would relish the challenge.'

'You could have just such a challenge beside me,' said Geoffrey.

Sybil shook her head.

'Here there is no risk of losing it. Marriage now makes me food for the Devil. Mistress at Malbec makes me an object of gossip and scorn. Widow at Hauteville would make me an object of pity, dependent upon Humbert's charity; worse, dependent upon his company. Can you imagine?'

Sybil mimicked Humbert's hunched posture, smacked her lips, and rubbed her hands.

'Did you have a good day, Sybil?'

Geoffrey was forced to smile.

Sybil put her hand once more over Geoffrey's.

'Oh, my darling, everything would hang on such a slender thread. To leave all this certainty for such a frail chance – however beautiful that chance may seem. To be haunted by the near-certainty of seeing that beautiful thing dashed into pieces – and then to burn. It is too much. The very thought of it is almost worse than the fire itself.'

* * * * * *

'You called, my lord?'

Thierry furtively licked a crumb from his lower lip.

'Preparations,' said Geoffrey. 'We shall attend the Duke's Christmas Council at Rouen.'

'All that way, my lord? In Advent? In this weather?'

Geoffrey sneered. 'You left some crumbs behind.'

Thierry put up a hand to his lips, and looked at what he had wiped off.

'It was a vegetable pie, my lord.'

'Get out. Find Ivo.'

Advent made Geoffrey as bad-tempered as it made Thierry mournful. Neither of them took easily to deprivation of food.

Geoffrey paced while he waited.

Mauger would want to go as well – just in case. He fretted whenever Geoffrey decided to absent himself, for fear they missed anything. On two occasions he had gone by himself, though what Giffard and Montgomery and Fitz and the rest had thought of him, Geoffrey could not imagine.

Would Lanfranc be there? And Archbishop Maurilius? It was time to get to know him better, especially after his pronouncement on clerical marriage. Was this Maurilius made of the stuff of Hildebrand? Or was he merely a well-meaning ex-monk scattering decrees and prohibitions as a means of pleasing God and the Holy See? Was it all smoke, or did Hildebrandine fire lurk at the heart?

The lady Matilda would probably be pregnant again.

When Ivo limped in from a training session, they spent a long time in preparations both for the journey and for supervision in his Grace's absence. As Ivo picked up his sword belt and spurs and turned to go, Geoffrey cleared his throat.

'There was one other thing, Ivo.'

Ivo coughed, hawked, and spat into the fire.

'Yes, my lord?'

It was one of the most embarrassing statements Geoffrey had ever had to deliver, and he did not make a good job of it. Ivo listened in total silence and complete stillness, which only made it worse.

'Is that all, my lord?' he said, when Geoffrey had finished.

Geoffrey nodded.

'I am only concerned for your welfare, Ivo.'

Ivo then did something that he had never done before: he sat down without being invited.

'Master Geoffrey, I put you on your first destrier. I put your first weapon in your hand. Everything you know about military training you learned from me. I have saved your skin more than once, as we both know. Yes, and you have saved mine too. Sir Nigel, your father, gave me that charge many years ago. It has not always been easy; neither, frankly, have you. But it is a charge that I have been happy and proud to fulfil. After my little maid died, it has been the only charge to fulfil.'

A savage winter, and near famine, had carried off Ivo's wife and daughter. He was drunk for a month. Sir Nigel had kept him supplied until the worst of the pain had gone.

Ivo leaned forward.

'So long as I continue to fulfil that charge, my lord, I shall remain. Let us have none of this "concern for my welfare".'

Ivo turned and drew his sword out of its scabbard.

'See that blade? Forged and folded on the banks of the Rhine. I can beat you with it, Geoffrey de Montbrai, any time you like. And I can hold off any of your enemies. So long as I do not put you in danger with any weakness on my part, just so long will I ride at your side. When the time comes, I shall know, and then I shall stop. I shall not need you to tell me.'

Ivo stood up and collected his gear.

'Now, my lord, I shall go and see that your orders are carried out, as I have always done. And I shall make sure that your pack horse carries a spare mace.

Stick to the mace, my lord. It is a bishop's weapon anyway. Convenient really, when you think about it.'

'What did he want?' asked Thierry outside. 'Was he giving orders?'

'No,' growled Ivo. 'I was.'

Thierry stared after him.

*　　*　　*　　*　　*　　*

'It is not a beginning or an end, Geoffrey; it is a continuation. I still feel great love for you, and I shall always pray that no harm comes to you.'

Geoffrey heaved a mountainous sigh.

'I am still not sure that I understand – not completely.'

'That is only because you are not me. I am completely sure. That is why God's Will is often seen as a mystery; it may not seem sensible to others, but it is the simplest thing in the world to ourselves. Mother warned me to steer clear of theology, and I have. It comes down in the end to seeing the sense in something. Once you do, you know it is right; theologians talk about God's Will, but it is exactly the same thing really.'

'I see. So you become a nun and I become a monk.'

Sybil smiled. 'No, my love. No mitre will snuff out desire for you. Neither will my passing. You will have other women, Geoffrey, and you will enjoy them. Perhaps you will love them too. I suspect they will enjoy you, and love you. Loving you is easy – but then I am biased.'

'Hm!'

'But we shall remain friends, because we respect each other. You will visit, I know, and I shall look forward to it. I shall hear about you too from other quarters. You know about the lady Emma; her son visits often. And did you know that the sister of Sir Baldwin de Clair is also here, and a second cousin of Sir Walter Giffard? You see, I shall hear all the gossip. So behave yourself!'

For the first time, she laughed – that broad, full-jawed laugh that he had always cherished.

'Has it occurred to you that I shall probably see more of you in the next six years than I have in the last six? If we had married, you would not have bothered; you would have got used to me.'

*　　*　　*　　*　　*　　*

It takes a lot to dig you out of Coutances these days,' said Roger of Montgomery, clapping Geoffrey on the shoulder.

'What do you have there?' asked Walter Giffard. 'A gold mine?'

'I should need it, to buy some of your horses, Walter,' replied Geoffrey.

Roaring with laughter, they edged their way into the Council hall, where

355

the usual groups had their heads together in drink and gossip.

'Any news of Aldred? Has he found the Atheling yet?'

'Yes. In a monastery in Magdeburg.'

'I heard he was a guest at the court of Bavaria.'

'My brother has just come back from Cologne. Take it from me, the Atheling is in Flanders. Only a day's sailing from England. So much for the Bastard's crown.'

'Then your brother must be deaf. The Atheling is in Hungary.'

'Hungary? Where the devil is that?'

'Talking of Saxon princes, have you seen that young hostage?'

'The Wessex boy?'

'Yes. Harold's brother. Some outlandish name – slipped my mind. The Bastard has brought him here. They say he is quite fond of him.'

'What game is he playing?'

'Your guess is as good as mine. But I tell you this: Atheling or no Atheling, hostage or no hostage, the Bastard has not forgotten the crown for one minute. It may not be consuming his mind, but it is gently nibbling at the edge all the time. You wait and see.'

'Madness.'

'Maybe. But then who would have wagered on his getting this far?'

His Grace the lord Bishop of Bayeux was dressed as grandly as an emperor. The spots had gone, but the pout had not. The tiny head looked just as ridiculous atop the huge padded shoulders of the episcopal robes.

'Ah, my lord Bishop of Coutances! Our perpetual voice crying in the western wilderness. A rare pleasure to see you honouring my brother's summons.'

Geoffrey could have killed him. Instead, he bowed, and deliberately thickened his western accent.

'I trust that your Grace is managing to overcome his labour problems in Bayeux. So difficult to obtain reliable workmen these days – especially those of suitable skill. Like you, we poor men of the west must seek them where we can.'

It was Odo's turn to look murderous.

While they listened to the Duke in formal session, Geoffrey found his mind tugging away to a piece of gossip he had heard about Odo.

'Fathered a bastard. At his age. Brazen about it too. But then, that is ducal privilege for you.'

Geoffrey could see the pitiful little grave at Hauteville, under the drooping, faded flowers of late summer.

'The Truce of God,' said the Duke. 'I am here to warn you that henceforth, it will be enforced to the letter. Infringements will be met with confiscations.'

That made Mauger prick up his ears. Land on offer!

After tedious business concerning charters and writs and ducal justice, there was a general discussion about military matters. Geoffrey found that his opinion was heard with respect and attention.

'I still think, my lord, that there is potential in the idea of massed, simultaneous impact. We have the manpower, the equipment, the resources; all we lack is the time and the organisation for the training. Surely Val-ès-Dunes and Mortemer, and a host of other smaller engagements, should have shown us that knightly honour and bravery are not enough.'

'We won,' said someone.

'We left too much to chance,' said Geoffrey. 'If we are to be true professionals, we must prepare far more. I see no sense in widening our margin of risk simply for the sake of "honour".' He glanced in the Duke's direction. 'Especially if one needs to plan any really big project . . . '

Lanfranc as usual stood out among the black-robed abbots and priors.

'I am glad you did not,' he said.

Geoffrey grunted.

'I can not think why.'

Lanfranc grimaced.

'Perhaps God was speaking to you through Sybil,' he said.

'Then God should make Himself clearer,' said Geoffrey. 'Why could He not just appear and tell me?'

'He did – once,' said Lanfranc. 'He told everybody – and we still did not listen.'

*　　*　　*　　*　　*　　*

'That puppy! I can still not believe it.'

Mauger could not get it off his mind. Every two or three miles it came out again.

'Mortain! A border fortress. A frontier county. God's Teeth! He is only sixteen.'

'Ducal privilege for you,' said Geoffrey. 'His brother got Bayeux when he was thirteen.'

Mauger gestured in wide appeal to the world.

'What has he done to deserve it? I ask you, what has he done?'

'Been born into the right family, that is what he has done.'

Mauger almost spluttered in frustration and disbelief.

'Robert has more spots than Odo did.'

'It is the blood under the spots that counts, my lord,' said Ivo.

'Now you know how I feel about Odo,' said Geoffrey.

357

'I could have thumped him.'

'Try thinking instead of thumping.'

Mauger looked across at his brother.

'What do you mean?'

'We can return by way of Mortain – yes?'

'Yes, but I do not see – '

'They are still building there to strengthen the castle?'

'Yes.'

'And you need some labour for your motte at Saint-Sever.'

The light began to dawn. A huge smile began to spread across Mauger's face.

'Like the masons you stole from Odo.'

Mauger slapped his thigh.

'What a splendid idea! I feel better already.' He looked at Geoffrey again. 'What are you going to do about Odo?'

Geoffrey had Maurilius to thank for that.

The new Archbishop of Rouen was not a likeable or a particularly impressive man at first meeting, and Geoffrey was already on edge because of the Archbishop's recent decree against clerical marriage. Their conversation had not strayed from the cold and formal – not until Geoffrey discovered that Maurilius also had conceived a strong dislike for Odo. From then on, their relations improved markedly.

Maurilius asked detailed questions about the state of the buildings at Coutances.

'I suppose you know that Odo is building too.'

'Not as fast as he was,' said Geoffrey, grinning smugly. 'I stole some of his masons.'

'With his family resources, he can get more. However,' said Maurilius, before Geoffrey could curse, 'I think I can suggest a way of stealing something of a march on our young, unpleasant colleague.'

Geoffrey was liking Maurilius more and more.

'From what you say,' said the Archbishop, 'it would appear that your nave is now above ground.'

'Yes. Just. Chancel and transepts are still at foundation level.'

Maurilius waved aside the objection.

'A nave is enough.'

'Enough? What for?'

'A consecration.'

Geoffrey blinked.

'Are you serious?'

'Absolutely. I must travel to the west sooner or later, and I ought to visit every diocese. I should think that a formal consecration by the metropolitan of the duchy would suit the occasion admirably. Can you hasten the work on the nave?'

'I shall ensure that they work on nothing else,' said Geoffrey.

'Good. The Duke, I am sure, will be attracted by the idea. He is always looking for ways of displaying his power and authority in the west. Between the three of us, I should think we could arrange an extremely distinguished gathering – enough to make our – junior colleague from Bayeux sick with envy. Does the idea appeal to you?'

Geoffrey grinned broadly.

'It is the best New Year's project I could ever have thought of.'

'Good. I leave it in your hands then . . .'

What a prospect! Every tenant-in-chief in Normandy; all six bishops; every abbot and prior; border counts and castellans; perhaps, if Maurilius had any influence, other prelates from Anjou, Paris, Champagne, Flanders, Burgundy – even Rome! If that did not get the Guiscard out of Apulia, nothing would. It would be something to talk about round winter hearths for years to come. Colossal expense, to be sure, but worth every half-clipped silver penny just to see the look on Odo's face . . .

*　　*　　*　　*　　*　　*

They looked a rabble. They sprawled across the road without formation or discipline. Filthy, unkempt, probably leaderless too. Hungry weapons were already drawn. Landless outlaws? Unpaid mercenaries far from home? Fugitives from the King's justice? What did it matter?

Ivo spat.

'Carrion!'

Thierry stowed the remains of his pie into his jerkin.

'Do we bother to negotiate, my lord?'

Mauger looked at Geoffrey.

Geoffrey flung back his bishop's hood and reached for his mace.

'There is only one language that this scum will understand.'

Ivo adjusted the chinstrap of his helmet. His whiskers rasped.

'Give us the word, my lord.'

'Are you ready?'

'And willing, my lord. Ha!'

Out came Ivo's Rhenish blade. He kissed it familiarly as if it were a daughter's forehead.

Geoffrey raised his battle mace.

'Then – for God and Coutances – forward!'

Mauger drew his sword.

'Montbrai!'

Ivo and Thierry came in close beside them. Hoofbeats swelled and thundered.

'Diex aie! Diex a-a-a-i-i-i-e-e-e-e!'

*   *   *   *   *   *

THE END

Acknowledgements

I am lucky, once again, to have at my disposal the combined talents of Mark Webb of Paragon Publishing, Stephen Goodwin of sgssdesign.co.uk, Yvonne Reed, sworn enemy of typos and scourge of printing gremlins, and, as always, my son Stephen. For their interest, industry, and support I have many reasons to be grateful.

Also by Berwick Coates

The Perjured Crown
ISBN: 9781787920316

Teach to learn, learn to teach
ISBN: 9781782229506

Deus Le Volt
ISBN: 9781782228936

National Service - Earning the Pips:
Reflections on Officer Selection - 1947-1963
ISBN: 9781782228530

The Trojan Brotherhood
ISBN: 9781782227915

Roses Round The Door: The Great Cottage Dream
ISBN: 9781782227175

On Teaching
ISBN: 9781782226192

Still on Record: The Return of the Archivist
ISBN: 9781782225966

Nearly off the Record - The Archives of an Archivist
ISBN: 9781782224631

Past Hysteric
ISBN: 9781782221906

The Perfect Christmas Present
ISBN: 9781908341303

All titles also available in the Kindle Store

The Perfect Christmas Present

Berwick Coates

'To be a knight, you would have to go to knight school.'

Past Hysteric

BERWICK COATES

NEARLY OFF THE RECORD

The Archives of an Archivist

Berwick Coates

STILL ON RECORD

The Return of the Archivist

Berwick Coates

On Teaching

by Berwick Coates

ROSES ROUND THE DOOR

Berwick Coates

DEUS LE VOLT

1095
A city in the grip of crusade fever.
Innkeeper Albert asks; minstrel Bertrand asks why

Berwick Coates

Author of The Last Conquest and The Last Viking

BERWICK COATES

THE TROJAN BROTHERHOOD

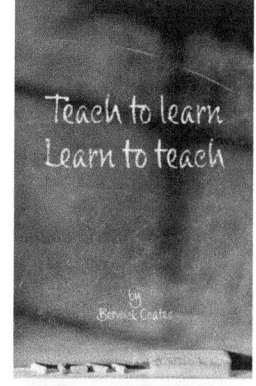

Teach to learn
Learn to teach

by
Berwick Coates

THE PERJURED CROWN

Berwick Coates

Author of The Last Conquest and The Last Viking

THE LAST CONQUEST 1066

TWO ARMIES, TWO GREAT LEADERS,
ONE BATTLE FOR A KINGDOM

BERWICK COATES

THE LAST VIKING 1066

THE BATTLE OF STAMFORD BRIDGE.
A WAR FOR ENGLAND'S CROWN

BERWICK COATES